Little Caesar
The Silver Eagle
W. R. BURNETT

Introduction by Matthew Sorrento

Stark House Press • Eureka California

LITTLE CAESAR / THE SILVER EAGLE

Published by Stark House Press
1315 H Street
Eureka, CA 95501, USA
griffinskye3@sbcglobal.net
www.starkhousepress.com

LITTLE CAESAR
Published by Lincoln Mac Veagh/Dial Press, Inc., New York, and copyright © 1929 by Dial Press, Inc. Copyright renewed July 31, 1956 by William Riley Burnett.

THE SILVER EAGLE
Published by Lincoln Mac Veagh/Dial Press, Inc., New York, and copyright © 1931 by Dial Press, Inc. Copyright renewed January 9, 1959, by W. R. Burnett.

Reprinted by permission of the Estate of W. R. Burnett. All rights reserved under International and Pan-American Copyright Conventions.

"Points of No Return" copyright © 2023 by Matthew Sorrento

ISBN: 979-8-88601-030-5

Book design by Mark Shepard, shepgraphics.com
Proofreading by Bill Kelly

PUBLISHER'S NOTE
This is a work of fiction. Names, characters, places and incidents are either the products of the author's imagination or used fictionally, and any resemblance to actual persons, living or dead, events or locales, is entirely coincidental. Without limiting the rights under copyright reserved above, no part of this publication may be reproduced, stored, or introduced into a retrieval system or transmitted in any form or by any means (electronic, mechanical, photocopying, recording or otherwise) without the prior written permission of both the copyright owner and the above publisher of the book.

First Stark House Press Edition: June 2023

7
Points of No Return:
W. R. Burnett's *Little Caesar* (1929)
and *The Silver Eagle* (1931)
By Matthew Sorrento

15
Little Caesar
By W. R. Burnett

141
The Silver Eagle
By W. R. Burnett

304
W. R. Burnett
Bibliography

LITTLE CAESAR

Rico is a small, pale man, but he has guts, endurance and a steely single-mindedness. When Vettori sends the gang out to rob a local nightclub, Rico shoots a cop who pulls a gun on him. They get away, but Vettori is shocked. He had told Rico, no gunplay. That's when Rico realizes that Vettori has gone soft. He's too old to control the gang anymore. So Rico takes over. With the faithful Otero at his side, the rest of them quickly shift their allegiances. Now the world is Rico's. It's *his* gang, and he's calling all the shots. But there is always a weak link, someone who's ready to spill when the bulls get tough. And sooner or later the nightclub killing is bound to catch up with him.

THE SILVER EAGLE

Harworth comes from the school of hard knocks. He knows what it's like to be poor, and rejected. So when he takes his horserace winnings and invests them instead of turning them over again at the faro table, all of a sudden he finds himself well-to-do and in a new class. He decides to act the part as well, and sports a monocle and a walking stick. But Harworth isn't fooling the rich folks he falls in with, nor the gangsters who want to help him with his investments. To Helen and Louise, Harworth is an intriguing bit of rough trade. To Canovi and Molina, he represents a mark who can easily front for their crooked dealings. But where does Harworth himself fit in? To whose world does he really belong?

Points of No Return: W. R. Burnett's *Little Caesar* (1929) and *The Silver Eagle* (1931)

By Matthew Sorrento

The opening of Mervyn LeRoy's *Little Caesar* (1930) doesn't depict imagery of 1920s-era gangland. Instead, under the Warner Bros. logo appears a copy of W. R. Burnett's source novel. While reminding the public of the best seller on which the film is based, the graphic mirrors the book's fascinating and complex legacy. The shot choice was unique for the time, especially for a movie centered on a gangster. While Hollywood had begun using graphics under opening credits, not even Warner's own 1930 adaptation of *Moby Dick* presented book imagery (opting, instead, for a still of a ship). On one hand, the opening of LeRoy's film introduces the groundbreaking crime thriller as a literary production, and likely, asserts it to be one. Previous films featuring gangsters, like *Regeneration* (1915) and *The Racket* (1927), used black title cards, while Warner's *Doorway to Hell* (1930) begins with a news copy graphic to tie this gangster-themed film to the newspaper drama, like the 1928 Broadway hit *The Front Page* (to be released as a film after *Little Caesar,* in 1931).

Burnett's book, in its prominent display—which, notably, doesn't include the author's name on the cover, though he's credited in the first title card—also highlights the historical legacy it borrows: of course, Julius Caesar. In this regard, the imagery suggests highbrow connections to this underworld tale, should any viewers become appalled by the content, which was a major concern for films under the watch of the Hay's Code. (The novel's first edition, similarly, stresses in a front matter note that the "characters and events in this book are entirely imaginary.") Additionally, the framing of the book, as if on a high shelf, implies that viewers should approach it cautiously, or in the case of the young or "morally questionable," just stay away. In this way, the shot recalls the "school scare film," a trend appearing in the late 1930s under control of the Production Code Administration censorship board, with *Tell Your Children* (later known as *Reefer Madness*, 1936) and the short *Birth of a Baby* (1938). Though overall, by directing viewers to *Little Caesar's* source material, the studio aimed for commercial appeal while underscoring that the novel, which LeRoy and producers Hal B. Wallis and Darryl F. Zanuck acquired for its suspense,[1] offered a compelling perspective for the screen, and one that would prove influential to this day.

In *Little Caesar*, Burnett restricted nearly the entire book to the point of view of Cesare "Rico" Bandello, a unique approach with so many crime stories involving the police on the hunt. In the novel, Burnett established the gangster-centered narrative so integral to the 1930s genre. *Scarface*, the 1930 Armitage Trail novel and the 1932 film adaptation (directed by Howard Hawks, and shooting script completed by Ben Hecht during the release of LeRoy's film, after Burnett had contributed to the adaptation) and *The Public Enemy* (William Wellman, 1932, also from Warner's, which went into production around the time of *Little Caesar*'s release) both followed suit, by making a gangster central to the plot and the title directly referring to him. Burnett's *Little Caesar* and its film adaptation also laid the groundwork for the criminal-centered noir novels of the 1930s and films of the 1940s, both offering a flavor of torn-from-the-headlines sensationalism. The author directly influenced James M. Cain's alignment to criminal psychology in *The Postman Always Ring Twice* (1934), later novels, and, in turn, Cain's influence on the film noir works of Billy Wilder, Tay Garnett, and others.

The portly look of *Little Caesar* star Edward G. Robinson, his character's brazen attitude, and the Chicago gangland setting immediately brought associations to Al Capone, the low-level hood who arrived to Chicago to take control of organized crime. The screen version introduces Rico in the rural Midwest, where he knocks off gas stations, to place him in the US frontier and, briefly, tap into the Western's considerable fanbase (the Academy Award for Outstanding Production that year went to the epic frontier yarn, RKO's *Cimarron*). Burnett, however, places this origin of the character much later in his novel, in a brief mention, and introduces Rico *in medias res* to immerse

---

[1] Peary, Gerald, "*Little Caesar* Takes Over the Screen," in *Little Caesar*, edited by Gerald Peary, Madison, WI: U of Wisconsin Press, 1983: 10.

readers in the Chicago setting, a platform for suspense and fatalism. At a gang meeting, Rico has already integrated himself as a key underling to Sam Vettori, and—in a note of tragic foreshadowing—suspects a weak link among the gang. This milieu will make Rico into a modern Macbeth, led on a path of—in Burnett's words [2]—his own over-impulsive action. With Rico helping to plan a nightclub robbery in this scene, the novel commits to action and suspense until the tragedy of this antihero looms near the end.

This "preparation" scene, one that leads right into the execution of a robbery and its aftermath, presents the economy of Burnett's style. It's one that avoids excessive description, like the flowery style of the novel at the time that Burnett despised,[3] to focus on dialogue and action. The swift drive of the author's prose reflects the story's pace, which mirrors Rico's empowerment. And in the tradition of classical tragedy, the style signals his fate. If Rico shows no fear in committing the opening robbery, predestination looms once he commits an error that both motivates and dooms him.

While suspenseful throughout, the novel assesses the grandeur that encouraged such deviance. The gang's opening robbery transpires like a gathering storm against the carefree roaring '20s, as readers, especially after the market crash of '29, could see Rico as a bleak fantasy hero, according to Robert Warshow in his cornerstone 1948 essay, "The Gangster as Tragic Hero." While the New Year's festivities promise hope and even greater rewards for the better-haves, their dreams are shattered by unlikely empowerment of a "little man" surrogate. With the gang working under a strict plan and set of rules, when a weaker member (Joe, operating as an inside man) panics, it signals a latent weakness in the central hood on the rise.

Rico's origins are far from the magnitude of Chicago, if not that remote. Rico hails from Youngstown, Ohio, at that time an area whose industrialization brought an influx of immigrant laborers.[4] If a boomtown, Youngstown had its share of strife and discord, becoming a center of white supremacist activity in the early 20th century, with a local sect of the KKK preaching toxic ideas against non-whites and Catholics, specifically targeting the Italian and Irish population,

2 Mate, Ken, and Pat McGilligan, "W.R. Burnett: The Outsider," in *Backstory: Interviews with Screenwriters of Hollywood's Golden Age*, edited by Pat McGilligan, Berkeley, CA: U of California Press, 57. 3 Ibid.

3 Ibid.

4 Blue, Frederick J., Jenkins, William D., Lawson, William H., and Joan M. Reedy, *Mahoning Memories: A History of Youngstown and Mahoning County*, Virginia Beach, VA: The Donning Company, 1995: 80–82.

according to historian William D. Jenkins. This context shapes Rico as a product of his new land, one that drew immigrants who then migrated to bigger prospects in local cities, for better or worse. Rico wants notoriety, not so much money: early in his novel, the text notes that he loves three things: himself, his hair, and his gun, the second and third asserting his prominence and power, respectively. He's also not directly interested in women, though one comes as a prize later, leading the way for the platinum trophy molls of the 1930s gangster yarns. Rico contrasts with Trail's *Scarface* (a novel that Burnett didn't think much of[5]), whose first criminal act, in the opening pages, is for a woman. Unlike Edward G. Robinson's role that recalls Capone, Rico in Burnett appears small and pale, his power all from attitude and drive.

Burnett's supporting cast may be calculated, with minor characters reflecting syndicate roles well known by the late 1920s.[6] The side man role, Otero, would resound in later gangland tales, while LeRoy's film used Joe for his ties to dance and desire for family life, as a weakening to Rico (and conflict with Rico's repressed sexuality, appearing in the screen version only, as a perversion). But really, Burnett's gang serves as an embodiment of an unfettered capitalist machine going too far for success. In response to his own initial fatal flaw, Rico goes after underlings to assert power, a move that fuels similar actions to come, in more devastating ways. The progression shows Rico's effectiveness burning too bright and eventually combusting, according to Warshow. The novel's famous closing line, "Mother of God, is this the end of Rico?" confirms Rico's sense of spiritual damnation and guilt but also a swift end to his quest for grandeur. If the "little" of the title was meant to connect with the "little men" wanting more at the time,[7] it also signals his little chance from the start.

■ ■ ■

Burnett had worked in fiction long before this breakthrough debut novel in 1929. His interests in literary naturalism inspired his previous writing, consisting of several unpublished novels and stories. While depicting how setting shapes character, especially for a loner who wants something better, *Little Caesar* also shows Burnett's use of voice and speech rhythms borrowed from Mark Twain. And yet Burnett's

---

5 Mate and McGilligan, 60.

6 McCarty, John, *Hollywood Gangland,* New York, NY: St. Martins, 1993, 64-65.

7 Kaminsky, Stuart, "*Little Caesar* and Its Role in the Gangster Film Genre," in *The Gangster Film Reader*, edited by Alain Silver and James Ursini, New York, NY: Limelight, 2007/1974, 49.

novel, overall, relies on a more melodramatic treatment of plot, putting action before character.

Burnett had left his hometown of Springfield, Ohio in his late 20s to work as a statistician in Chicago, to immerse himself in the city and engage with the underclass (as would crime writer David Goodis years later). Here Burnett mixed with a North Side payoff man, putting himself in harm's way at times (even being followed at one point). The budding author was present outside the carnage of the Saint Valentine's Day Massacre, though he couldn't bear to go in and look.[8] These experiences shaped his debut, and its success allowed him to explore other stories closer aligned to naturalism.

Meanwhile, *Little Caesar* attracted Hollywood producers looking for more crime and melodrama-inclined screenwriters, which Burnett became. After contributing to the script for Warner's *The Finger Points* (1931), about a journalist bought by the mob, Burnett wrote the screen story for *The Beast of the City* (for MGM, released in 1932), a gangster tale with a strong police presence (if turning vigilante[9]). Both projects showed the versatility that he would later bring to the screen; Burnett, in fact, thought *Beast* to be "one of the best crime pictures" at the end of his life.[10] While he wrote scripts to finance the writing of his novels, this productivity for the pictures led him to be commended for his treatment of suspense and action: an Oscar nomination for the script of *Wake Island* (John Farrow, 1942), and Writer's Guild nomination for co-adapting Paul Brickhill's novel *The Great Escape* for the screen in 1963.

Burnett's follow-up novels showed varied productivity. He used two popular traditions: the boxing novel in *Iron Man*, and the Western in *Saint Johnson* (both 1930), a retelling of the story of Wyatt Earp. In the following year, he made a departure with *The Silver Eagle*. The project offered Burnett a chance to move towards drama in the naturalist tradition, while critiquing small business ownership in Prohibition-era Chicago. Frank Harworth (born Frank Keogh, whose chosen name hides his Irish-Catholic roots) owns a group of nightclubs and restaurants. Coming from poverty, Frank profited from chance winnings at the Kentucky Derby, from which he began to invest wisely. Like Rico Bandello, Harworth's determination prevents him from touching drink. And if both are outsiders, Harworth has entered the legitimate world

---

8 Mate and McGilligan, 57.

9 Though the police presence had already appeared in the 1931 MGM gangster-focused film *The Secret Six*.

10 Mate and McGilligan, 62.

of business. Approaching an upper class based on old money, Harworth desires entry, though the crowd pegs him for a non-member immediately. Some of this clique even have financial pressures, which shows how secure the class is for them, and nearly impenetrable to a self-made man like Harworth. He meets them by easing the collections method for one man, whose name Harworth recognizes from society columns. Friends in this group come relatively easy for him, though finding a gal from the group proves trickier. Dating a series of them suggests that he lacks the certain quality that comes from being raised in their ranks. With one noting that he "ought to be shoveling coal with them shoulders of his, but here he is all dressed up like a chorus man," Harworth struggles to hide his working-class roots. The monocle he wears, intended to show seriousness and focus, really serves as a shield from hiding embarrassment. While the women respect his financial power, they find the eyepiece to be another strange distraction.

Stylistically, Burnett picks up from the last act of *Little Caesar*, after Rico becomes a fugitive in "little burgs" in Illinois and then, Ohio, back near his hometown. Here, the 1929 novel slows the pacing to underscore Rico's inability to disappear back into the crowd from which he had emerged. Rico navigates through his connections in smaller towns and their distrust of him. The events in *The Silver Eagle* similarly build a character study of Harworth, in a dialogue-based style nearly akin to the 1929 novel's prose. While continuing his attention to the voice of the locals, the author invokes F. Scott Fitzgerald's interest in social climbing, as noted by Cullen Gallagher.[11]

Burnett cleverly introduces Sam Michaelson, before Harworth, in the opening scene. With Michaelson a mob-connected employee of Harworth's, Burnett invokes his earlier crime tale to gather steam for a different treatment. Harworth attempts to rise in social class while navigating the influence of organized crime in small business ownership. (The opening quote from Francis Bacon guides the reader in understanding Harworth, though his experience offers a fresh perspective on the quest for power.) Noting the draw of such figures, Harworth attempts to exploit them while keeping their control at bay, which, naturally, proves futile. He comes to a point of no return when accepting a deal that cements his personal connection to them (Burnett's personal experience with politics, though his father's work and Burnett's own on Ohio Governor James Cox's failed presidential bid, proved

---

11 Gallagher, Cullen, "Pretty Big Once: W. R. Burnett's Cynical Americana," *Los Angeles Review of Books*, August 12, 2022, https://lareviewofbooks.org/article/pretty-big-once-w-r-burnetts-cynical-americana/, accessed February 23, 2023.

helpful[12]). Soon Harworth must deal with gangsters on the North Side as well as his immediate connections in the South, as the control of organized crime tightens its grip. Even while eyeing the gangland tradition, Burnett produced a complex social novel that, like James M. Cain's Depression-era *Mildred Pierce* (1941, according to writer Jon Raymond[13]), stems from earlier crime-centered works by its author.

And while not one of the several Burnett titles to make it to the screen, *The Silver Eagle* would have been a fine property for a pre-Code film on industry, crime, and corruption. But Hollywood wasn't ready for a character study focusing on such material. Perhaps 1970s producers were, though by then Burnett, at the end of his career, was largely ignored by the industry. Thanks to the fine work of Stark House Press to return *The Silver Eagle* to readers, we see in this companion novel to *Little Caesar* an author expanding the parameters of crime fiction, a category that he hardly found limiting, and one to which he certainly wasn't limited.

—March 2023

Matthew Sorrento teaches film history and genre cinema at Rutgers University-Camden and Temple University. He is the editor of *Film International* and *Retreats from Oblivion: The Journal of NoirCon*. Sorrento's latest book is *David Fincher's Zodiac: Cinema of Investigation and (Mis)Interpretation* (co-edited with David Ryan, FDU Press, 2023), and he has contributed to *The Los Angeles Review of Books, Senses of Cinema, Film & History, Middle West Review, The Journal of the Fantastic in the Arts,* and *Critical Studies in Television*.

---

12 Smith, Cecil, "W.R. Burnett," *The Los Angeles Times,* September 19, 1954, https://www.latimes.com/archives/wr-burnett-1954-8588, accessed March 12, 2023.

13 Raymond, Jon, "Of Time and Place: An Interview with Writer Jon Raymond on *Meek's Cutoff* and HBO's *Mildred Pierce*," *Bright Lights Film Journal,* April 30, 2011, https://brightlightsfilm.com/of-time-and-place-an-interview-with-writer-jon-raymond-on-meeks-cutoff-and-hbos-mildred-pierce/#.ZB4SHHbMLIU, accessed January 27, 2023.

Little Caesar
W. R. BURNETT

To Marjorie

The first law of every being, is to preserve itself and live. You sow hemlock, and expect to see ears of corn ripen.
Machiavelli

PART I

I

Sam Vettori sat staring down into Halsted Street. He was a big man, fat as a hog, with a dark oily complexion, kinky black hair and a fat aquiline face. In repose he had an air of lethargic good-nature, due entirely to his bulk; for in reality he was sullen, bad-tempered and cunning. From time to time he dragged out a huge gold watch and looked at it with raised eyebrows and pursed lips.

Near him at a round table sat Otero, called The Greek, Tony Passa, and Sam Vettori's lieutenant, Rico, playing stud for small stakes. Under the green-shaded lamp Otero's dark face looked livid and cavernous. He sat immobile and said nothing, win or lose. Tony, robust and rosy, scarcely twenty years old, watched each turn of the cards intently, shouting with joy when his luck was good, cursing when it was bad, more out of excitement than interest in the stakes. Rico sat with his hat tilted over his eyes, his pale thin face slightly drawn, his fingers tapping. Rico always played to win.

Vettori, puffing, pulled himself to his feet and began to walk up and down.

"Where you suppose he is?" he asked the ceiling. "I told him eight o'clock. It is half-past."

"Joe never knows what time it is," said Tony.

"Joe's no good," said Rico without taking his eyes off the cards, "he's soft."

"Well," said Vettori, stopping to watch the game out of boredom, "maybe so. But we can't do without him, Rico. I tell you, Rico, he can go anywhere. A front is what he's got. Swell hotels? What does it mean to that boy? He says to the clerk, I would like please a suite. A suite! You see, Rico. We can't do without him."

Rico tapped on the table, flushing slightly.

"All right, Sam," he said, "someday he'll turn yellow. Hear what I say. He's not right. What's all this dancing? A man don't dance for money."

Sam laughed.

"Oh, Rico! You don't know Joe."

Tony stared at Rico.

"Rico," he said, "Joe's right. I know what I'm saying. All that dancing is a front. He's smart. Have they ever got him once?"

Rico slammed down his cards. He hated Joe and he knew that Tony and Vettori knew it.

"All right," he said, "hear what I say. He'll turn yellow someday. A man don't take money for dancing."

"I win," said Otero.

Rico pushed the money toward him and got to his feet.

"Well, if he don't show up in ten minutes I'll take the air," said Rico.

"You stay where you are," said Vettori, his face hardening.

Tony watched the two of them intently. Otero counted his money. One day Vettori said to Rico, "Rico, you are getting too big for us." Tony remembered the look he had seen in Rico's eyes. Lately they had all been talking about it. Rico was getting too big for them. Scabby, the informer, said: "Tony, mark what I say. It's Rico or Sam. One or the other."

"I'll stay ten minutes," said Rico.

Vettori sat down by the window and stared into Halsted Street.

"Two-fifty," said Otero.

"I'll match you for it," said Tony.

"No," said Otero.

Joe Massara opened the door and came in.

"Well," said Vettori, "you call this eight o'clock?"

Joe got out of a big ulster. He was in evening clothes. His black hair was sleek and parted in the middle. He was vain of his resemblance to the late Mr. Rudolph Valentino.

"Sorry," said Joe, "the bridge was up. Well, what's the dirt?"

"Draw up a chair," said Vettori, "all of you."

They grouped themselves around the table under the green-shaded lamp. Joe put his hands on the table so they could see his well-manicured nails and the diamond ring the dancer, Olga Stassoff, had given him.

"Now," said Vettori, "I'll do the talking. I know what I got to say and you birds keep quiet till I'm through...."

"How long will it take?" asked Joe, smiling.

"Shut up and listen," said Rico.

"All right, all right," said Vettori, patting them both, "no bad blood. Now: ever hear of the Casa Alvarado?"

"Sure," said Joe, "it's an up and up place. One of Francis Wood's joints. I nearly got an engagement there once."

Rico spread out his hands.

"See? They know him. He won't do."

"No, they never seen me. It was all done through an agent."

"All right," said Vettori, "that's the place."

Joe looked startled. Rico smiled and taking off his hat began to comb his hair with a little ivory pocket comb.

"It'd be tough," said Joe, "what's in it?"

"Plenty," said Vettori. "They only bank once or twice a week. They're careless, get that; because they've never been tapped. It's easy."

Joe took out a gold cigarette case which he handled with ostentation. "Well? I'm listening."

Vettori refused a cigarette and pulled out a stogie. Downstairs a jazz band began to play and a saxophone sent vibrations along the floor.

"Nine o'clock," said Otero.

Vettori lit his stogie.

"They got a safe," he said, "that a baby could crack. Too easy to talk about. But that's on the side. What we're after is the cashier. The place is lousy with jack. I got the lowdown from Scabby. Well, what do you say, Joe?"

"Yeah," Rico cut in, "take it or leave it. We ain't begging you."

Vettori's face hardened but he said nothing.

"If you say it's good," said Joe, "it's good with me."

"All right, all right," said Vettori. "Now, you Tony; we want a big car. Get that. A big, fast car. Get one when I tell you. Steve's got the plates all ready. Yeah?"

"I'm on, Sam."

Tony pulled out a cigarette and lit it with a flourish, but his hands shook a little.

"Rico and Otero," said Vettori, looking at each in turn, "will handle the rods. Yeah?"

Rico said nothing. But Otero smiled, showing his stained teeth, and said:

"That's us, eh, Rico?"

"Well," Vettori went on, "I guess we got that over. Now, Joe, I want you on the inside. Dress yourself up like you are, see, and fix it so you'll get there at midnight. All the whistles'll be tooting and everybody'll be drunk and won't know nothing. See? Now you get there at midnight and go to the cigar counter for change. At twelve-five the fun'll begin. We'll set our watches by telephone, because I don't want you here that night. All right. Rico and Otero come in quick, maybe Tony, too, if you can get a good safe place to park. That's up to Rico. He's bossing the job."

Rico looked at Joe.

"Now, they'll stick you up if everything's O. K. If not, give them the high sign and they'll beat it. We ain't taking no chances, because one night don't make much difference, only New Year's Eve's a good night, see? All right. You play like you don't know them, got it? But while they're working, you got your eyes open, see? And if something happens, you got a rod, but don't use it. We got to watch that."

Vettori shifted his stogie and shook his finger sideways at Rico. "That's your trouble, Rico. The Big Boy can't fix murder. He can fix anything but murder. Get that. You're too quick with the lead. If that guy over at the pool room'd died we wouldn't none of us be sitting here right now...."

Otero broke in vehemently, surprising them. "But he had to! He had to! Rico does what is right."

"All right," said Vettori, "but take it easy. Now, Joe, you got your hands up, but you watch. If nothing happens nobody knows the difference. But if something does happen you pull the rod and help the boys get out. All right. Here's the dope. Get what's in the cash register first. Get that because that's easy. If things go right, tackle the safe; it'll probably be open. Another thing: no frisking in the lobby. That's too dangerous and takes too long. Let the yaps keep their money. All right."

Vettori took a map from his pocket and spread it out on the table. The men crowded round him.

"You go straight in," said Vettori, marking the route with a pencil, "on the right is the checkroom; watch the girls behind the counter, Joe. On the left is the cigar counter and the cashier's desk. At the end of the lobby is a big door; the real joint's beyond that. If things go right, nobody in the place'll know it's been stuck up, except maybe some yaps in the lobby. Get the idea? With all them horns tooting and all that damn noise, see? All right. On the right of the lobby is a door and that goes into the manager's office. The box is in there. The manager's a goddam bohunk and there ain't an ounce of fight in him. See? Scabby give me the lowdown."

Vettori rolled up his map, put it in his pocket, then looked at his watch. "Well," he said, "got it all?"

Joe turned his diamond ring round on his finger and looked at the table.

"What's the word, Joe?" said Rico.

"It's a tough one, Rico. What's the guarantee?"

"Guarantee, hell!" cried Rico. "Why, a blind guy could do your stand."

"Well, I ain't doing no time for fifty bucks," said Joe.

Vettori laughed.

"I'll give you a couple hundred now," he said.

Joe nodded.

"All right. I'm in. Never mind the couple hundred."

They all got to their feet. Below them the jazz band was still playing and the saxophone was still sending vibrations along the floor.

"What'll you have, boys," said Vettori, "want some drinks sent up?"

"Not me," said Tony, "I'm going over and see my woman."
Otero clapped his hands.
"He's got a woman."
Rico hit Otero on the back.
"The Greek's got a woman too," said Rico.
Otero with his hands cupped made a series of curves in the air. Joe was patronizing; Olga Stassoff, the dancer, was his woman.
"A beauty is she, Otero?"
"Sí, señor."
"Well," said Vettori, "want any drinks sent up?"
"Sure," said Joe, "send me up a snort. I guess Rico'll take milk."
Rico didn't drink.
"All right about Rico," said Vettori in a good humor, "he's a smart boy."
Tony went out followed by Vettori.
"I think I go see my woman," said Otero.
Joe laughed. Rico said:
"Goodbye, Otero. Give Seal Skin a rub for me."
When Otero had gone, Joe said:
"Has old Seal Skin got The Greek hooked yet?"
"Well," said Rico, "he spends a lot of jack on her. She ain't much to look at and she's pretty old, but what's the difference?"
Joe never could figure Rico out. Women didn't seem to interest him.
Rico went over to the window and stood looking out at the electric sign on a level with his eyes.

CLUB
P
A
L
E
R
M
O
DANCING

Rico and Joe felt queer alone together. They were silent. Joe took out his gold cigarette case and lit a cigarette. Snow began to fall past the window.
"Look," said Rico, "it's snowing."
"Yeah," said Joe, looking up mechanically, "snowing hard."

II

Vettori was sitting in his little office on the main floor. On the other side of the wall the jazz band was playing, but he paid no attention. The noise of the jazz band was the same to him as the ticking of a clock to an ordinary person. He felt very pleasant and comfortable over his bottle of wine and his plate of spaghetti. Things were right!

He congratulated himself on his subordinates. Each man a specialist. Yes, yes! That was the way to do. None of this hit or miss stuff for Sam Vettori. Rico the best gunman in Little Italy; a swelled head, all right, but he can be handled, and there you are! Otero so crazy about Rico he "don't know nothing." Follow Rico any place; do anything Rico tells him. And handy with a rod. Well, well. Not bad for a Mexican. As a rule foreigners were not right with Sam Vettori, but in general he had an open mind, and Otero was the goods. And look at Joe Massara, there was a man for you! A swell Italian who could pass anywhere. One winter in Florida, so they say, Joe passed himself off as a count and hooked a rich widow for plenty. Yes, yes! That was Joe for you. As an inside man you couldn't beat him. And Tony! He could drive a car sixty miles an hour straight up the Tribune Tower. Only one thing, sometimes Tony was undependable. Used to be a choir boy at St. Dominick's and that stuff. But he had outgrown that, maybe; anyway he was dead scared of Rico and that would shut his mouth.

Vettori leaned back, wiped his mouth with the back of his hand and unbuttoned his vest. Spaghetti and wine, what is better!

The band stopped playing. Bat Carillo, the bouncer, put his head in the door.

"Couple of hard guys looking for trouble, boss," he said.

Vettori looked up.

"Yeah? Know them?"

"Never seen them before."

Vettori heaved himself to his feet and walked with Carillo to the swinging doors which separated the back rooms and kitchen from the club proper. He pushed the door open about a foot and peered in. Carillo pointed.

Vettori laughed and closed the door.

"Some of them dumb Irish," he said; "let 'em alone unless they get bad and start something, then bounce 'em."

"O. K., boss," said Carillo.

Waiters passed Vettori in the corridor, sweat dropping from their faces, steam rising from the dishes on the slanted trays. Vettori rubbed his hands.

"Business is good. Well, well! We won't none of us die in the poor house."

When he got back to his office he found Scabby, the informer, waiting for him. Scabby was dark and undersized with a heavy, sullen, blotched face. Passing as a police informer, he was in reality a member of the Vettori gang. He played a dangerous game as he informed on other gangs. His life wasn't worth a cent and he was jumpy and quick with a gun.

"Well, well, Giovanni," said Vettori, "what's the news?"

"Everything's jake," said Scabby, taking off his hat and revealing a shining bald head.

Vettori called a waiter.

"Some spaghetti for this man here," he said, "and a bottle of wine."

"That's the ticket," said Scabby without smiling; he never smiled; his face was melancholy and lined, and sagged like a hound's. "The boys on?"

"All set," said Vettori. "It looks easy."

Scabby nodded.

"It ought to be. But no gunplay, get that, Sam. The Big Boy'd raise hell if he knew what was up."

Vettori's face hardened.

"I heard that once, Scabby. That's enough. This is too good to pass up."

"All right," said Scabby, "I've had my say. But things ain't what they used to be, Sam. It's getting dangerous. They've even got the Big Boy scared. It's the damn newspapers. They play that crime stuff off the boards. Big headlines, see? That's the trouble."

They sat silent. Vettori, absorbed, puffed on his stogie. Finally he said:

"Listen, Scabby, you ain't heard nothing, see? I got to keep these boys on their toes. Especially Joe. Don't spill nothing about the Big Boy."

Scabby shook his head vigorously. Vettori took out his billfold and handed Scabby a fifty.

"That's part of your split, Scabby. Keep your eyes open, that's all."

Scabby pocketed the money. The waiter came in bringing the spaghetti and the wine. Carillo put his head in the door.

"Reilley, the dick's, up front."

Vettori nodded.

"He's O. K. If he sticks around, send him back in about half an hour."

"Sure," said Scabby, "I'll be out of here in less than that."

III

Otero lay looking out the window at the electric sign across the street.

CLUB
P
A
L
E
R
M
O
DANCING

Snow was falling past the windows. Otero lay smoking a big twenty-five cent cigar and singing softly to himself. He always sang when he was with Seal Skin.

"Some snow," said Otero.

"Yeah, some snow," said Seal Skin, who was sitting with her feet on the window sill, smoking one of Otero's cigars.

"Heavy like cotton," said Otero.

"Yeah," said Seal Skin.

"Where I used to be it never snowed."

"Didn't it?"

"No, it never snowed."

Seal Skin blew out a cloud of smoke.

"How come you ever left Mexico, Ramón?"

"Well, I don't know." Otero scratched his head. "I just left."

"Was they after you?"

"No, I just left."

Otero got up and put his arms around Seal Skin.

"Some girl," he said.

Seal Skin gave him a push.

"Wait'll I finish this."

"Sure, sure," said Otero, smiling and patting her on the shoulder.

"Look," said Seal Skin, "you're a good guy, Ramón. But dumb. How come you hang after Rico?"

"Rico is a great man."

Seal Skin laughed out loud.

"Yeah? Great, but careless. He'll never die of old age."

Otero didn't understand.

"What you say?"

"They'll fill him full of lead. He's too cocky."

Otero shook his head.

"No, they'll never get Rico."

"They get 'em all."

"No," said Otero, "they'll never get Rico. Once I say to him, 'Look, you must be careful.' But he say, 'Not me, they'll never get Rico.'"

Seal Skin opened the window and flung her cigar down into the street. A gust of cold air rushed into the overheated room.

"Listen," she said, "that's bunk. Rico's no different from anybody else. You stick with Rico long enough and you'll have a swell funeral. Why don't you get into the beer racket? That's safe."

"I go with Rico," said Otero. "What do I care? I have no people. Once I had a brother but they shot him."

"The cops?"

"No, the rurales. He was with Villa."

"Who the hell's Villa?"

"Villa was a great man, like Rico."

Seal Skin got up and took a drink from a bottle on the bureau. Then she said:

"Let's hit the hay, Ramón."

"Sure, sure," said Otero.

IV

It was nearly two o'clock when Tony left his woman. A lake wind was blowing hard and the snow fell heavily past the street lights. Tony muffled himself in his overcoat and pulled his cap low. He felt tired and disgusted.

At the corner near his home, he turned into Sicily Pete's restaurant. Three Italians were playing cards at a table in the back. Up front a mechanical piano ground out The Rosary.

"Hello, Tony, how's the boy?" said Pete.

"Not so good," said Tony.

"You ain't looking any too good, Tony," said Pete.

Tony ran his hands over his face and stared at his image in the mirror behind the counter. Pale; circles under his eyes.

"Well, I guess I'll live," said Tony.

Pete smacked the counter with both hands.

"Love of God! Sure you'll live. You be O. K. tomorrow morning. I know, Tony, my boy. Don't forget I was a young fellow once. I know. I know."

"Sure you know," said Tony, sarcastic.

"Sure I do. You think I don't know about that little redhead. Hot stuff, Tony, my boy. Only don't be a fool. Save some for tomorrow night."

Pete laughed shaking all over and smacked the counter with his hands.

"What the hell's wrong with you, Pete?" cried one of the card players.

"Never you mind. All right, Tony, what'll you have?"

Tony couldn't decide. Pete went to wait on one of the card players. The mechanical piano finished "The Rosary" on a discord. Tony went over and put a nickel in the slot.

"I got a combination to go and two Javas," cried Pete.

The mechanical piano began to play "O Sole Mio."

"I'll take a combination," said Tony, "and a cup of Java."

"O. K.," said Pete; "I got two combinations, one to go and three on the Java."

"How's business, Pete?" asked Tony.

"Oh, what you call so-so. Not good, not bad. I never get rich here."

"Why don't you put in a line of bottled goods?" said Tony, smiling.

Pete raised both hands over his head and brought them down hard on the counter.

"None of that for Sicily Pete. Oh no. Pete's too smart for that. If the bulls don't get you, why, some of them gangsters do. I know. One say, you buy from me; the other say, no, you buy from me. All the same. No matter who you buy from, bango!"

Pete brought Tony his combination and his coffee and stood at the counter with him while he ate it.

"Tony," said Pete, putting his head on one side, "you know you look like your old man. Other day when you was in here I say to the missus, look, ain't he just like his old man? Well, well. That is good. A boy should look like his old man. That is a good sign."

"Knew the old man pretty well, didn't you, Pete?" said Tony, finishing his coffee.

"Yes, pretty well. When he was a young fellow he was like you. Full of pep and always after the girls. But I don't know, your mama she got hold of him, then he wasn't like he used to be. He wasn't like the same fellow. Pretty soon he died."

Tony laughed.

"Hard on the old lady, ain't you?"

"Love of God, no," said Pete, an expression of acute misery on his face, "you don't get me, Tony. I mean he got to be a good fellow, like me. Work, work, that's all he knew. Well, work is a good thing. It keeps you out of trouble, but I don't know …"

Pete wiped the sweat from his forehead and meditated. Tony flipped him a fifty-cent piece. The mechanical piano stopped on a prolonged, slurred discord.

"Well, I guess I'll hit for home," said Tony, "so long, Pete."

"Good night, Tony," said Pete, with one of his blandest smiles, "come in again."

The wind struck Tony in the face as he left the restaurant. The streets were white and silent. Tony walked home slowly, tired and disgusted.

As he entered the flat he saw a dim light in the front room. He tried to sneak into his bedroom, but his mother heard him. She rose from her chair, a monstrous silhouette against the dim front room light.

"A fine time for you to come in, Antonio," she said. "Have you been out again with them good-for-nothing loafers?"

"Yes," said Tony, in a bad temper.

"So ...!" said his mother, "you don't even lie anymore. Well, well! You are doing fine. Pretty soon you won't come home at all, you bum."

"You said a mouthful," said Tony.

"Sure, you won't listen to your mother. Someday you'll remember what I told you. You loaf with crooks and bums long enough, you'll see what will happen."

"All right," said Tony, going into his room and banging the door behind him.

His mother stood in the middle of the room for a minute, then she put out the light and sat in the dark, crying.

V

The little blonde check-girl helped Joe take off his big ulster, her hand lingering on his arm. He handed her a quarter.

"Don't go on a bat with that two-bits," he said.

"No sir," said the check-girl.

She watched him walk across the long dance floor, pick his way among the crowded tables, bowing from time to time to one he had jostled, and disappear through the employees' door at the back. Then she put checks on his coat and hat and hung them up.

"God, what a hot-looking man," she said; "I don't see how that little hunky got him."

Olga Stassoff was just putting the finishing touches to her make-up. Joe came in softly and stood watching her. She began to sing.

"If you're singing for me," said Joe, "you can stop any time."

Olga turned around.

"Well, what are you doing here? Broke?"

"Shut up," said Joe.

Then he turned and walked out of the room. Olga jumped to her feet and ran after him. She caught him near the employees' door. He pushed her away.

"Ain't that a fine way to say hello to a guy!" he said. "Why, you must think you got me roped and hog-tied."

"I was just kidding, Joe," said Olga, "honest I didn't mean it. I was just kidding."

"Well, get this," said Joe, "I'm goddam sick of that line. What do you take me for? That goes big with some of your swell boyfriends who've got ugly wives and ain't any too particular, but me! I don't take that kind of talk from nobody."

Olga put her arms around him, but he pushed her away.

"Listen, Joe," she said, "I got good news for you, so get out of your fighting clothes and come to earth. Can't you take a little kidding?"

Joe took out his gold cigarette case and selected a cigarette. He always smoked the best, when Olga had plenty of money, and he usually carried three or four different brands. With a flourish he put away his case, then, very preoccupied, he placed the selected cigarette on the back of his left hand and, with a slight tap of his right hand, flipped it into his mouth. Olga laughed.

"Now," said Joe, "spill the good news."

DeVoss, the manager, came through the swinging doors.

"Have you told him yet, Olga?" he asked.

Joe gave the manager a most ingratiating smile.

"What's the big talk, Mr. DeVoss? Am I missing something?"

"You sure are," said DeVoss. "The Stranskys broke their contract and I'm putting you on in their place."

Joe leapt into the air and executed a twinkle. Olga burst out laughing.

"Well," said Joe, "how much?"

"One hundred to start, Joe, then we'll see."

"Well," said Joe, "I can't buy no limousines with that, but I'll take it."

Joe and DeVoss shook hands.

"Now," said the manager, "there's a girl out here who's just dying to dance with you, Joe."

Joe shook his head.

"No, I don't like that stuff. They always think they got to hand you something. What the hell! I don't want no dame handing me nothing."

Olga put her hand over her mouth.

"Don't worry about that, Joe," said DeVoss, "she already asked me about that and I told her you'd be insulted so she gave me a ten." DeVoss took a crumpled bill out of his pocket and handed it to Joe. "There, now get this. She's an up and up girl and she means lots of business to this place. Her old man's got a couple of million bucks and she's the real thing. All right, Joe?"

"Sure, sure," said Joe, "always willing to oblige."

DeVoss went through the swinging doors and stood waiting for Joe on the other side. Olga took Joe by the arm.

"Listen," she said, "none of your funny business now. Just do your stuff and leave it at that. I'm on to these society women. I know what they want."

Joe leapt into the air and executed another twinkle.

"Alley up!" he cried, "don't you trust me, baby?"

Olga put her hands on her hips and began to laugh. How could you be sore at a guy like that?

VI

Rico was standing in front of his mirror, combing his hair with a little ivory pocket comb. Rico was vain of his hair. It was black and lustrous, combed straight back from his low forehead and arranged in three symmetrical waves.

Rico was a simple man. He loved but three things: himself, his hair and his gun. He took excellent care of all three.

PART II

I

"Hear me," said Rico, his face twitching, "he's turned yellow. He's turned yellow. What the hell you expect from a choir boy!"

Otero said nothing but sat with his chair tipped back against the wall smoking a cigarette, his eyes closed. Sam Vettori stood in the middle of the room and stared at his watch.

"Keep your shirt on, Rico," said Vettori, "you're on edge."

"Sure, Rico," said Otero.

Carillo came in without knocking. Vettori put away his watch.

"Well!"

"O. K., boss," said Carillo, "Tony's in the alley."

Vettori took out his watch again.

"Rico, it's eleven thirty-five. What do you say?"

"Let's get going."

Otero got slowly to his feet, stamped out his cigarette, and, taking the riot gun from the table in front of him, slipped it under his overcoat. Rico examined his big automatic.

Carillo went out, softly closing the door. Otero walked over and patted Rico on the shoulder.

"O. K. now, eh, Rico?"

Rico smiled. Vettori's face was covered with sweat and he pulled out a big white silk handkerchief to mop it.

"Rico," he said, "from now on you boss the job. Only, get this: for the love of God, no gunwork. That's all. I ain't ripe for the rope."

Rico said nothing. Otero shrugged.

Vettori, still mopping his face, opened a window and a gust of cold air rushed in.

Rico took out his little ivory pocket comb and mechanically combed his hair. Then he put on his hat and tilted it over his eyes.

"Well," he said to Otero, "let's go."

Otero followed Rico out. Vettori called:

"Make it clean, Rico. Make it clean."

They went down the back stairs. Carillo was waiting at the foot of the stairs and held the alley door open for them. The alleyway was dark and Otero stumbled.

"Caramba!"

"Watch that gun," said Rico.

Tony was sitting at the wheel of a big, open Cadillac. He tossed his cigarette away and said: "Well, here we are."

Rico said nothing, but got into the front seat with Tony. Otero got into the back seat. Carillo stood looking at them for a moment, then closed the door. Tony stepped on the starter.

"All right," said Rico, "let's go, but take it easy. We got lots of time."

They took it easy. Tony drove along as leisurely as though they were going to a New Year's party. Rico leaned back and smoked, watching all the passing cars. Otero, who had removed the riot gun and had it on the seat beside him, was sitting bolt upright, his hands on his knees. He could never get used to riding in an automobile. Rico turned and saw the gun.

"Put that rod on the floor," he said.

Otero obeyed.

It had got colder. The snow was no longer falling and a chilly wind was blowing up in gusts from the lake. The streets were nearly deserted. Over west a whistle began to blow, discordant and shrill.

"Well," said Tony, nodding in the direction of the whistle, "it won't be long now."

But Rico leaned over and hissed in his ear. "Police car!"

A big Packard with a hooded machine-gun in the back seat passed them. There were two plainclothes men in the front and two in the back.

"What'll I do?" asked Tony.

One of the men leaned out and stared back at them.

"Jesus," said Tony, "he's looking at us."

"Keep your shirt on," said Rico, putting his hand on Tony's arm.

Otero took a cigarette from his pack and rolled it between his palms. The police car slowed up. Rico's fingers closed on Tony's arm.

"Here's an alley," said Rico, "duck!"

Tony took the turn on two wheels, just missing a parked car. Otero was thrown from one end of his seat to the other, losing his cigarette. The Cadillac's exhaust roared in the narrow alleyway. There was nothing but darkness ahead of them.

"It's a blind," said Tony.

"No," said Rico, "I know this place like a book. Turn to your right at the end."

Rico leaned out and stared back. Then he laughed.

"Ain't that like the damn dummies! Nothing in sight."

They came back to Michigan Boulevard by a wide detour. Here the wind blew fiercely, raising little whirlwinds of snow. Now there were whistles blowing in all parts of town. Rico looked at his wristwatch.

"Five of twelve. All right, Tony. Step on it."

"What time, Rico?" asked Otero.

Rico told him.

"Fine, fine," said Otero, "eh, Rico?"

Half a block down the street they saw the huge electric sign of the Casa Alvarado. The street was deserted except for the parked cars. They drove along slowly now.

Rico leaned out.

"That's a break," he said, pointing to a parking place where they couldn't be hemmed in. "Listen, Tony, this ain't going to be no cinch, so you better give us a lift."

Tony pretended to be preoccupied with parking.

"Get me?"

Tony was pale and his lips were twitching.

"That ain't my stand, Rico," he said.

Rico looked at him. Tony sat silent for a moment, then, pulling at the visor of his cap, said: "But you're the boss, Rico."

"O. K.," said Rico, smiling. "Now, Otero, get this. I go first. You follow me with the big rod. I stick up the cashier. Tony swings the sacks. Got it?" Rico took three small neatly-folded canvas sacks out of his pocket and handed them to Tony. "Otero, you watch the door. If you see anybody coming in, let 'em come in, then back 'em up against the wall. If things go right, I'll tap the box. Got it?"

Rico looked at his watch. It was three minutes past twelve.

"Let's go," he said.

Otero got out lazily, hiding the riot gun under his coat. Rico got out, followed by Tony.

"Got your rod, Tony?" asked Rico.

Tony nodded.

"All right, keep it in your pocket. Maybe you won't need it right away. If anybody gets funny, why, pull it."

"O. K.," said Tony, "but for God's sake, Rico, no gunwork."

Otero said:

"You leave Rico alone. He does what is right."

Whistles were blowing all over town. They walked up the carpet which was laid across the pavement under the canvas marquee. Inside there was a blaze of lights and they could hear the music. The lobby was deserted except for two check girls, one waiter, a cigar clerk, and the cashier, a pale woman with a green eyeshade, who was perched on a stool. Joe Massara, in a big ulster and a derby hat, was standing at the cigar counter, kidding the clerk. He saw them out of the corner of his eye and nodded twice.

They came in quickly, Rico in front with his big automatic at ready, Otero slightly behind him and to the left, carrying the sawed-off shotgun hip-high, Tony in the rear, his hand in his overcoat pocket.

Before Rico could say anything, Joe Massara faced them, put his back up against the counter and raised his hands.

"My God," he cried, "it's a holdup."

One of the check girls screamed piercingly. The waiter's knees buckled and he almost fell. The others stood petrified.

"You're goddam right it's a holdup!" shouted Rico, trying to intimidate them, "and it ain't gonna be no picnic. Get that, all of you birds. I got lead in this here rod and my finger's itching. One crack out of any of you and they'll pat you with a spade. All right, Tony."

Tony, white as chalk, took the sacks out of his pocket and walked over to the cashier's desk. The cashier was standing behind the register, hands raised. When Tony came up she said:

"Take anything you want, only for God's sake don't touch me."

"O. K.," said Tony, "clean out the box but don't get funny."

Tony held the sacks while the cashier scooped the money into them. Tony saw pack after pack of wrapped greenbacks drop into the sacks. He began to feel a little better.

Rico left the cashier to Tony, but looked at each of the others in turn, his eyes, under his tilted hat, intimidating them as successfully as the big Luger in his hand. Otero stood behind him and a little to the left, impassive, the riot gun hip-high.

The manager opened the door of his office and with a dazed look hesitated for a moment, then, with a great sigh, put his back against the wall and raised his hands. He was a Czech with a swarthy complexion which gradually turned greenish.

Rico glared at the manager.

"Stay put, you!" he said.

"All right, all right," said the Czech.

Joe Massara said:

"Jesus, my arm's paralyzed."

"Yeah," shouted Rico, "well, don't let it drop."

"All set," cried Tony.

Otero was busy at the door with a man in a top hat who had just come in. The man couldn't believe his eyes and kept muttering:

"Good Lord! Good Lord!"

Otero backed him against the wall.

In the club proper, beyond the big arched doorways, the band was playing loudly, horns were tooting, people were shouting.

"All right," said Rico, "get out your gat, Tony. I'll tap the box inside."
"God," said Tony, "it'll take too long."
Rico looked at him. Tony, holding the sacks in one arm, pulled out his gun. Rico walked over to the manager.
"Listen," he said, "I want action. Go in and open that box and slip me the jack. One funny move and I'll blow your guts out."
"Oh, my God!" cried the Czech.
They disappeared. There was a dead silence in the lobby. One of the check girls began to cry.
"Nice little holdup," said Joe.
Nobody said anything.
"Yeah," said Joe, nonchalant, "fine little holdup."
He smiled at the waiter, who looked hastily away and turned agonized eyes on Tony as if to say: "Look, I can't help what that bird's saying."
Two more men came in the street door and were backed up against the wall by Otero. The seconds seemed like hours to Tony, who was slowly losing his nerve.
The manager reappeared, followed by Rico, who had his gun pressed against the manager's back. Rico's pockets bulged.
"Good Lord," hissed Tony, "let's go."
Three men and two women came out into the lobby from the club proper. They stopped, petrified.
The strain was beginning to tell on Rico, whose face was ghastly.
"Stick up your hands, you," he cried, "and don't move."
Two of the men and both of the women put up their hands, but the third man, burly and red-faced, hesitated.
"Good God," said Joe, "it's Courtney, the bull."
Joe's mask of nonchalance slipped from him instantly; he dropped his hands and reached for his gun.
"Beat it," cried Rico to Tony and Otero.
They made a break for the door. One of the women with Courtney fainted and fell hard, hitting her head.
"Don't touch her," cried Rico, "my finger's itching."
Joe followed the others, backing out with his gun in his hand.
Courtney's face was purple. He glanced at his wife, lying pale and unconscious on the floor, then, shouting "you dirty bums" reached for his gun. Rico fired. Courtney took two steps toward Rico, staring. Then he fell heavily, his arms spread.
At the door Rico collided with a drunken man, who was just entering. The man tried to hug him, but he knocked him down with a blow of his fist.
Rico jumped on the running board and bellowed:

"Open her up, Tony. This ain't no picnic." Tony was unnerved and tears were dripping down onto his hands. Joe and Otero sat silent in the back seat. Otero rolled a cigarette between his palms. Nobody said anything.

Tony took a corner, careening. The wind had died down a little and it had begun to snow again, a thin, cold, powdery snow. The whistles were still blowing, but fainter now, one leaving off, then another.

"Well," said Rico, "I plugged him."

"Yeah," said Joe, "I seen him fall. Like a ton of bricks."

"Well," said Otero, "what can you do? The fool, pulling a gat!"

Tony said nothing, but sat with his eyes fixed.

"It's our hips for this," said Joe.

Otero shrugged and lit a cigarette.

"Losing your guts, Joe?" asked Rico.

"Me!" said Joe.

Tony turned into the alleyway back of The Palermo. Rico put the sacks under his coat and jumped out. Otero and Joe followed him.

"Tony," said Rico, "ditch that can, then come back for your split. Hear what I say. Ditch it good and proper. We'll wait."

"Look," said Joe, "I got to have my split now. I'm on at one-twenty. Boy, I can't miss that turn."

"O. K.," said Rico.

Tony drove off down the alley. Rico knocked at the door and Carillo let them in.

II

When they came in Vettori was standing in the middle of the room mopping his forehead with his big white silk handkerchief. Beads of sweat stood out all over his swarthy, fat face.

Rico threw the sacks on the table and began to empty his pockets.

"Well," said Vettori.

"There's the dough," said Rico, "looks like a good haul."

Joe sat down at the table under the green-shaded lamp without taking off his hat or coat. Otero took the riot gun from under his coat and locked it up in a cupboard. Vettori knew there was something the matter. His eyes narrowed.

"Well," he said again.

"Everything was O. K.," said Rico, "only I had to plug a guy."

Vettori fell down into a chair and stared out the window.

"Yeah," said Joe, trying to smile, "and the guy was Courtney."

Vettori put his head on the back of his chair and stared at the ceiling. Then he sat up suddenly and banged on the table with both fists.

"Goddam!" he cried, "what did I tell you, Rico! What did I tell you! Love of God, didn't I tell you no gunwork?"

Rico was white with rage.

"Listen, Sam, you think I'm gonna let a guy pull a gat on me. What the hell! Any more of them cracks and this is my last job."

Vettori made an elaborate, tragic gesture. "Yeah, you bet this is your last job."

Joe took off his derby and put it beside him on the table. His face was dead white.

"You said it," said Joe, "they'll get us sure for this."

Vettori shook his big head slowly from side to side.

"They'll get us dead sure for this."

Rico began to comb his hair.

"Maybe you better go over and give yourself up," he said; then dropping his sarcastic tone, "listen, how the hell they gonna get us? Why, you're the finest bunch of yellow bastards I ever seen."

"Not me," said Otero.

Joe tried to smile.

"Wait till you see the papers."

Rico came over and leaned on the table.

"Listen, don't they always play that stuff up in the papers. Courtney's the only guy in the place that ever seen one of us before. Come on, snap out of it. And split the dough."

But Vettori sat inert, mopping his face. Suddenly he asked:

"Where's Tony?"

"He's ditching the can," said Rico.

"Suppose they pick him up?"

Rico began to open the sacks.

"That'll be just too bad," said Joe.

Rico laughed.

"A fine bunch of yeggs!"

Vettori got to his feet in a fury.

"You, Rico! Shut your mouth. You think I want to hang because you get yellow and shoot somebody."

Rico, very calm, put his hand in his pocket and said:

"Sam, you get funny with me and you won't get no split at all. Only a horseshoe wreath."

"Oh, hell, Sam," said Joe, "we're all in it, ain't we? Come on, split the dough."

Vettori sat down. Otero stood a little behind him, watching.

"Since you want it, Sam," said Rico, his face pale and drawn, "you're gonna get it. Listen, you split even, that's all. Hear me! You get an even split."

Vettori said nothing. Joe sat rigid, ready to dive under the table. For months Scabby had been predicting this break; now it had come. Joe feared Vettori and Rico equally, but something told him that Rico would win.

Vettori let his hands fall on the table.

"All right, Rico," he said, "I split even. Sit down and we'll divvy."

But Rico didn't move.

"You got a gun on you, Sam?" he asked.

Vettori looked up at him.

"Sure I got a gun on me."

"Well, don't try to use it."

"No," said Otero, "don't try to use it."

Vettori's face went slack. He sat tapping on the table with his fat fingers.

"Rico," he said, finally, "I split even on the square."

Rico's victory was complete. Joe looked at him with admiration. Sam was a tough bird, but Rico was tougher.

Vettori got up, walked across the room and stood looking out the window.

III

Joe handed Rico a sheet of paper full of figures. Rico read: 9331.75.

"All right," said Rico, "split it five ways and we'll make up Scabby's split between us."

Otero sat with his chair tipped back against the wall, smoking a cigarette with his eyes closed.

Vettori was playing solitaire and swearing softly to himself.

Joe looked at his watch.

"Quarter till. I got to beat it. Say, Sam, call Carillo and let him get me a cab, will you?"

Sam heaved himself to his feet and called Carillo. In a moment the bouncer put his flattened face in the door.

"Three dicks downstairs, boss."

"Who are they?" asked Vettori.

"Flaherty and two guys I don't know, boss. They want to see you."

Vettori stood looking at the floor. Carillo jumped in and shut the door.

"Christ," he said, "they're coming up."

Rico leapt to his feet, ran across the room and opened a panel in the wall.

"Come on, Joe," he said, "you can slip out the back way. Stay where you are, Otero, and go right on smoking. Send Joe's cab around in the alley, Bat."

Vettori looked at Rico.

"You suppose they know something, Rico?"

"Not unless they picked Tony up. You don't know nothing, Sam, see? I'll be right here listening, and if there's any trouble, why, it'll be tough on the dicks."

Vettori scooped up the money, wrapped his coat around it, and handed it to Rico. Joe went through the panel, followed by Rico. There was a knock at the door.

Vettori nodded and Carillo opened the door. Two plainclothes men stepped in and stood looking around the room. One was tall and burly in a huge ulster; the other was short and very young. They both had their right hands in their overcoat pockets.

"All right, Carillo," said Vettori, "go ahead. That's all."

"Wait a minute," said the burly one, "tell Flaherty we'll be down in a couple of minutes, for him to wait."

"Sure, sure," said Carillo.

He went out closing the door softly.

"Well," said Vettori, "you want to see me?"

"Yeah," said the burly one, who did all the talking, "we want to see you, Vettori."

"Well, here I am!"

Otero opened his eyes long enough to look at them, then closed them again and went on smoking.

"Vettori," said the detective, "we want some information."

"Well?"

Vettori sat down at the table and began to shuffle the cards.

"There's a big Cadillac draped around a pole a couple of blocks down the street and we just wondered if you knew anything about it."

Vettori began to lay out a game of solitaire.

"How should I know anything about it? Ain't it got no license plates on it?"

"Sure, but they're phony."

"Yeah?"

"Yeah. It was stolen about eight o'clock tonight on the North Side and we got a pretty good description of the guy that stole it."

"Well," said Vettori, "I got a good business. What the hell'd I be doing stealing automobiles."

He laughed and shook his head.

"Oh, you got me wrong," said the detective with elaborate innocence. "You see, it's piled up right straight down the street from here and I thought maybe it was some of the guys from your joint, see? I mean some of the young guys that come here to dance."

"Well," said Vettori, "how would I know?"

The detective took out a cigar and began to chew on it.

"Wasn't there nobody in it?" asked Otero.

"Yeah," said the detective, "one guy. But he beat it."

"I don't know nothing about it," said Vettori.

"Well, no harm in asking," said the detective. "Come on, Mike, let's get going. I guess Vettori don't know nothing about it."

The two of them walked slowly to the door. The big one turned.

"Say, Vettori," he said, "did you hear the news?"

Vettori looked up.

"What news?"

"Why, some bastard bumped Cap Courtney off over at the Casa Alvarado."

"Yeah?" said Vettori, "some guys are sure careless with the lead. That's a tough break."

The young detective opened the door and they started out.

"Ain't it?" said the big one. "Well, so long."

As soon as the door closed, Vettori went over and shot the bolt, then peeped out through the shutter. Rico came out of his hiding place.

"Well," said Vettori, glancing at Rico, "things ain't going so good."

Rico shrugged.

"They don't know nothing. Just feeling around. Listen, Sam, where's your guts? We got to stick together on this."

"I know," said Vettori, falling back into his chair, "but I never seen things break so tough."

Rico held out a roll of bills.

"Here's your split, Sam."

Vettori took the bills and stuffed them into his pocket. Rico handed Otero his. Otero got up and put on his overcoat.

"I think I go see my woman," he said.

When he had gone Rico went over and sat down beside Vettori.

"Listen, Sam," he said, "I been taking orders too long. We're done. Get the idea? But we got to see this through. We get a break and we'll come clean. Only we got to shoot straight. See what I mean? I got a rope around my neck right now and they can only hang you once. If anybody gets yellow and squeals, my gun's gonna speak its piece."

"That's O. K. with me," said Sam.

They sat silent. Down stairs the jazz band was playing and the saxophone was sending vibrations along the floor. Vettori laid out another game of solitaire.

"Funny for Tony to crash," he said.
"He lost his nerve," said Rico.
"You suppose he'll show?"
"Not till tomorrow if he's got any sense. I'll leave his split with you."

IV

Rico went over to see Ma Magdalena, the fence. Her fruit store was still open and her son Arrigo was sitting half-asleep beside a pile of oranges.

"Hello," he said.

"Where's Ma?" asked Rico.

Arrigo pulled a cord which rang a bell in the rooms beyond the store. Ma, leaning on her stick, came out into the store. Seeing Rico, she said:

"Oh, it's you! Well, well! Come back. Come back."

"Can I come too, Ma?" said Arrigo.

"You stay and mind the store, you lazy loafer," said Ma, shaking her stick at him.

Arrigo sat down once more by the pile of oranges.

Rico followed Ma Magdalena back into her little office. She pulled up a chair for him and he sat down, then she got out a bottle.

"You talk, I drink," she said, sitting down beside him and pouring herself a drink.

Rico took out his split, peeled off a few bills and handed her the rest.

"Plant it," he said.

She took the roll, counted it, and put it down inside her dress.

"Had a big New Year's Eve, did you?"

"Yeah," said Rico, "plenty big. There'll be lots of fun tomorrow."

"Well, well," said Ma, "that's the way it goes."

She poured herself another glass of wine, then she reached over and touched Rico with her stick.

"Look, Rico, you ain't got a nice little girl who wants a big diamond ring, have you?"

"Me, buy a diamond ring for a skirt?"

Ma Magdalena made a clucking noise and shook her head.

"You are cold, Rico. Don't like wine. Don't like women. You are no good, Rico."

Rico smiled.

"Me, I like women once in a while, but I ain't putting out no diamond rings."

Leaving Ma Magdalena's Rico went in the direction of Sicily Pete's. The wind was blowing hard and Rico, turning up his overcoat collar, leaned against it. It was after three o'clock and the streets were empty. Southward the lights of the Loop made a reddish glow in the sky.

At Sicily Pete's the mechanical piano was playing. Three men, all Italians, and two girls, both Americans, were sitting at a front table. They were drunk. They played with their food, spilled their coffee, and banged on the plates with their knives. Pete stood behind the counter, scowling.

When Rico came in he said:

"Hello, my friend, where have you been keeping yourself?"

"I haven't been around lately. Got some noisy birds, ain't you?"

Pete shrugged his shoulders.

"Yes, the fools. They drink gin. That is no drink for an Italian."

Rico took out his cigarettes and offered Pete one. They stood smoking. One of the girls pulled up her dress and fixed her garter. Rico smiled.

"Get an eyeful of that, Pete."

"Yes, yes," said Pete, "that's all I get, an eyeful. Every night I stand here while other people have a good time."

The girl looked up at Rico and he winked at her. She said to one of the men:

"Look at that smarty over there. He thinks he's cute."

The man looked foggily at Rico. Pete put his hand on Rico's arm.

"My friend, don't start no trouble, please. That's all we have around here, trouble. With one thing and another, I think I go back to Italy."

Rico turned his back on the girl.

"O. K.," he said.

While Pete was getting Rico a cup of coffee, a newsboy came in:

"EXTRA! EXTRA! All about the big holdup."

Rico bought a paper and glanced at the three-inch headlines.

THUGS KILL CAPTAIN COURTNEY
IN CASA ALVARADO HOLD-UP

Rico showed Pete the paper.

"Another killing," he said.

"Yes," said Pete, "kill, kill, that's all they do. I wish to God I was back in Sicily. The Mafia, what is that? That is a kindergarten."

One of the Italians bought a paper and started to read the account of the holdup aloud. All the people round the table stopped eating to listen. Rico sipped his coffee and watched them.

V

Tony hadn't slept all night. He lay in the cold dark room, sweating. The covers felt heavy as lead and from time to time he tossed them off, only to pull them over him again as the lake wind, streaming in the window, made him shiver. At intervals he would fall into a doze. Then he would see a windy street, feel a car skidding under him, feel a sickening jolt. He would wake with a start and sit up in bed.

"They'll get us for this," he kept repeating, "they'll get us sure."

Unable to control his imagination, he saw the high forbidding walls of the State Prison, the tiny death cells with their heavily grated windows; then in the prison yard, the gallows. He remembered what Rico had said about Red Gus, on the night of his execution: "Well, they're gonna put a necktie on Gus he won't take off!" Yeah, they sure put a necktie on Gus.

Tony smoked cigarette after cigarette. In his despair he cast about for someone to put the blame on. It was all Midge's fault. Wasn't she always after him to make more jack so she could put on the dog? Hadn't he tried to go straight and drive a taxi and make an honest living? Yeah, and hadn't Sam Vettori and Rico offered him money to quit his job and give them a lift on their stickups? Well, you couldn't quit a gang; once you were in, you were in!

Tony sat up in bed and looked out across the roofs outside his window. The sun was coming up and a cold, windy winter morning was dawning. Of a sudden he began to feel sick at his stomach. He lay down, but that didn't help him, then he tossed from side to side.

He heard his mother moving about in the next room. She was getting dressed to go to work. An alarm clock in a room across the court rang, then there was some loud swearing, and a window was slammed.

Tony had to vomit. He jumped out of bed and ran for the bathroom. When he came out his mother was lighting the stove. She acted as if she didn't see him. He went back to his room but stopped in the doorway.

"Hello, mom," he said.

His mother paid no attention.

"Say," said Tony, "what's the matter?"

His mother turned and with her hands on her hips stared at him.

"Go back to bed, you loafer," she said, "I am sick of you. You are no good on earth. Just like your father."

"Aw, mom," said Tony.

"Don't try to salve me," said Tony's mother. "You go back to bed and get sober. You think I don't know nothing, don't you? Just like your father."

"I'm not drunk," said Tony, "I'm sick."

His mother turned her back and went on with her cooking. Tony went into his room, slammed the door, and got back into bed. A deadly depression settled on him. The world looked black.

He heard his mother go out, then he got up, dressed and made himself some toast and coffee. Anyway, he wanted his split.

On the way to Vettori's he met Father McConagha. The priest was a big man with a big, pale face. He walked with a rolling gait and there was something arrogant about him. Tony took off his hat.

"Good morning, Father."

"Good morning, Antonio," said Father McConagha. "Where have you been, my boy? I haven't seen you for months."

"I been working," said Tony.

"What sort of work?" asked Father McConagha, putting his hand on Tony's shoulder.

"I been driving a taxi."

The priest nodded his head slowly.

"That is good work, Antonio."

Tony couldn't look at Father McConagha and kept twisting his hat in his hands and staring at it. Father McConagha talked to him for a minute or two about the rewards of honesty and the happiness to be derived from doing your work faithfully, then he said:

"Antonio, one day your father asked me to look out for you. Your father was a good man, but weak. Remember this, Antonio, if you are ever in any trouble I am the one to come to."

Tony flushed and said:

"Thank you, Father."

When Father McConagha had gone, Tony began to speculate. Did he know anything? Why, on this very morning, had he said something about being in trouble? Tony respected and admired Father McConagha. He felt that he could always turn to him.

Talking with the priest had made him feel stronger, but now that the priest had gone all the hopelessness of the night before rushed back on him. He took out a cigarette and lit it with shaking hands.

"They'll get us sure for this," he said.

Then once more he began to think about Red Gus and what Rico had said about him.

VI

Seal Skin couldn't get Otero sober. She made him eat tomatoes and she gave him a cold bath, but nothing seemed to do him any good. He walked about the flat in his underclothes singing songs in bastard Spanish and bragging about what a great, brave man he was. Only one man in the world braver: Rico.

Seal Skin was dead for sleep, but she didn't shut her eyes for fear Otero would do some crazy thing like shooting out the window at the street light (he had done this one night) or going out in his underclothes.

Otero sat at the table with his automatic beside him, singing at the top of his voice.

"Look," he cried, "I am Ramón Otero, a great, brave man. I ain't afraid of nobody or nothing. I can drink any man in the world under the table and I can outshoot any man that walks on two legs. Only Rico; he is my friend. He is a great man like Pancho Villa and I love him with a great love. I would not shoot Rico if he shot me first. Rico is my friend and I love him with a great love."

Then he got up and, snapping his fingers, began to dance, stamping with his heels, wiggling his hips, till Seal Skin nearly fell out of her chair laughing.

Toward morning he went to sleep with his head on the table. Seal Skin picked him up and carried him to bed (he weighed about a hundred and fifteen pounds), then, too tired to take off her clothes, she climbed in beside him.

VII

Rico bought all the papers he could find and went up to his room to read them. He sat at his table, his hat tilted over his eyes, with a pair of scissors in his hand, cutting from the papers all the articles dealing with the holdup and the killing of Police Captain Courtney. He arranged the clippings in a neat pile, then read them over and over.

One said:

> ... the thug who shot Police Captain Courtney was a small, pale foreigner, probably an Italian. He was dressed in a natty overcoat and a light felt hat.

Another:

... Courtney's murderer was described by one eyewitness as a small, unhealthy-looking foreigner."

Rico tore up this clipping.
"Where do they get that unhealthy stuff!" he said. "I never been sick a day in my life."

PART III

I

Sam Vettori's heavy, dark face looked puffy and his eyes were swollen. He hadn't been sleeping well lately and he had been drinking whiskey. As wine was his usual drink, the whiskey indicated a state of mind the reverse of calm. He sat chewing a cold stogie and from time to time pouring himself a shot from the bottle at his elbow. Rico was playing solitaire, his hat tilted over his eyes. The Big Boy sat opposite Vettori, his derby on the side of his head, and his huge fists, fists which at one time had swung a pick in a section gang, lying before him on the table.

The Big Boy shook his head from side to side slowly.

"Not a chance, Sam," he said, "I can't do nothing for you. Why, you must be out of your mind. Listen, they're after me hot and heavy. I got all I can do to take care of number one, see? Things was running too good for you, Sam. That's your trouble. You thought I was God himself. But listen, I ain't no miracle man. A stickup more or less, what's that? But when it comes to plugging a bull like Courtney, that's out! No, Sam. You're on your own now. It ain't gonna be none too healthy for none of us for a while. Just don't lose your nerve, that's the main thing. Just hang on and watch the guys that are in the know."

"You leave that to me," said Rico without looking up.

"O. K.," said the Big Boy, "I think you're the goods, Rico. But don't get nervous with that gat of yours, or they'll put a necktie on you. Get this. No more stickups. No more jobs. Just lay low, all of you. If you run out of jack, I'll stake you. Now I got to beat it. Don't call me up no more, Sam. Because I can't do nothing for you and it might give the bulls an idea."

The Big Boy got to his feet and stood leaning his huge hairy paws on the table.

"Why, you guys are lucky and don't know it. Wood's manager got so goddam rattled he identified one of the plainclothes men as the guy that did the inside stand. Jesus, but it was rich! Spike Rieger was boiling. Pretty soon he pinned the manager down and the damn dummy said that the guys that did the job were Poles. So they went out and grabbed Steve Gollancz. Steve and his bunch had just tapped a bank and Steve thought they had the goods on him. It was funny as hell!"

The Big Boy put his head back and brayed. Sam Vettori drummed on the table irritably.

"All right, laugh," said Sam.

"Sure, I'll laugh," said the Big Boy; "if you'd seen Steve's face when he found out what it was all about you'd split your pants laughing."

"Steve's the goods," said Rico.

"You said a mouthful," said the Big Boy, "he's got them eating out of his hand. Well, I'm gonna beat it. You guys lay low and it may blow over. If things get hot, I'll tip off Scabby and then you all better hit the rods. So long."

The Big Boy went out slamming the door. They heard him go downstairs; he walked as heavily as a squad of police and banged each step with his heels.

Rico went on with his game of solitaire.

"Well," said Vettori, "something just tells me we're gonna get ours."

"Oh, hell!" said Rico, pushing the cards away from him, "I'd like to get the guy that invented that game."

Vettori swore softly to himself at Rico's indifference, then, pouring himself another drink, he said:

"You think Joe's safe, Rico."

"Yeah," said Rico, "as long as they don't nab him and put it to him. He can't stand the gaff."

"How about The Greek?"

Rico laughed.

"Safe as hell. Only thing with Otero, he gets lit and wants to raise hell. I had to knock him down a couple of times last night. He gets a little money and he goes nuts. That goddam greaser never saw over five dollars all at once till I picked him up in Toledo. But he's safe."

"How about Tony?"

Rico didn't say anything for a minute but picked up his cards and began to shuffle them.

"I don't know about Tony."

Sam Vettori got up and walked back and forth, mopping his forehead at intervals with his big white silk handkerchief.

"Love of God, Rico, we can't take no chances with him."

Rico dealt out a couple of poker hands and began to play an imaginary game.

"You leave that to me, Sam," he said.

Vettori put his hand on Rico's shoulder.

"That's the talk, Rico. We get a break we may come clean."

Vettori dropped back into his chair and poured himself another drink, but Rico reached across the table and pushed the glass off on the floor.

"Slow down on that stuff, Sam. You got to keep your head clear."

Vettori looked at Rico in a fury, then he lowered his eyes. "You got the right dope, Rico. That stuff don't do nobody no good." Vettori took the whiskey bottle and locked it up in a cupboard.

II

About nine o'clock Carillo put his head in the door. Downstairs the jazz band had just started to play.

"Well?" demanded Vettori, getting to his feet.

"Blackie wants to see you," said Carillo.

"All right."

Carillo went out.

"What you suppose he wants?" said Vettori.

Rico, who was sitting with his chair tipped back against the wall reading a magazine, shook his head without looking up or answering. He was deep in the reading of a story about a rich society girl who fell in love with a bootlegger. Rico read everything he could find that had anything to do with society. He was fascinated by a stratum of existence which seemed so remote and unreal to him. The men of this level were "saps" and "softies" to him, but he envied them their women. He had seen them getting out of limousines at the doors of Gold Coast hotels. He had seen them, magnificently dressed, insolent, inaccessible, walking up the carpets under the canvas marquees. The doormen would bow. The women would disappear. Rico hated them. They were so arrogant and self-sufficient, and they did not know that there was such a person in the world as Rico.

Blackie Avezzano, who managed Sam's garage, came in and shut the door behind him. He was small and bowlegged, and he was so dark that he had been taken for a mulatto many times.

Vettori impatiently exclaimed:

"Well, what's on your mind, Blackie?"

Rico went on reading his magazine. Blackie sat down at the table and seemed to be making an effort to collect his thoughts.

"All right, spit it out," said Vettori.

Blackie couldn't speak very good English, but as Rico didn't know a word of Italian and Vettori preferred to speak English, he did the best he could.

"Tony he took sick. Listen, I tell you, Tony he no know what. He took sick. I see him, listen, I tell you, what-you-say, he no got his guts. The Madre she send me call the doctore. Listen, he say, Tony, what-you-say, you been a drink. Now listen, you cut out a drink. That's all. Tony he no drink. What a hell! One bottle of beer he can no drink. He no got his guts, that's all."

Vettori looked at Rico, who went on reading.

"Rico," he said.

"I heard him," said Rico, "I ain't deaf."

Blackie got up and stood twisting his cap in his hand. Vettori took out his billfold and handed Blackie a ten.

"Blackie," he said, "keep your eyes open, understand?"

"All right," said Blackie, "I watch, see, I know. Tony no good. All right, I watch."

When he had gone Rico said:

"Well, that's that."

"We can't take no chances," said Vettori.

"I'll give him till tomorrow," said Rico; "he can't go far wrong with Blackie watching him. After that if he don't settle down, there won't be no more Tony."

III

Tony had always been of a rather easy-going nature and took things as they came. His emotions, it is true, were very unstable; with him anger was almost immediately followed by a grin, and depression lasted only long enough for him to recognize that he had felt such an emotion. No, he had never before experienced the loneliness which is the result of continued despair. Now he felt it and it was too much for him. He looked back on the past as a sort of fabulous period when he had had peace of mind.

He could enjoy nothing. The fear of arrest and hanging dogged him even at the movies, formerly his chief pleasure, and in the company of Midge, his woman, he was so preoccupied that she thought he had a new woman and treated him accordingly. Even the presence of his mother, who had begun to realize that something was wrong, did not tranquilize him. He drank, played pool, rode about in an automobile, but fear pursued him and he could find no rest.

Then he began to have attacks of acute indigestion, and it got so bad that the very sight of food was repugnant to him. He lost weight rapidly.

There was nothing he could do. He could not find one avenue of escape. But little by little the thought of Father McConagha took possession of him. Tony was too unintelligent to know that what he needed most of all was someone he could unburden himself to. But he blundered toward that solution.

Blackie's solicitude helped some. Blackie came to see him every night; and once, when Tony's indigestion had been worse than usual, he had even gone for the doctor.

Tony's mother put her hand on his shoulder.

"Antonio," she said, "I think I'll go over across the street and see Mrs. Mangia. She is having a new baby. Only think! That will be twelve."

Tony tried to smile.

"Twelve!" said Tony's mother, shaking her head slowly from side to side, "and one is too much."

"A bad egg like me is."

"You ain't a bad egg, Antonio," said his mother, "you are only lazy."

Tony said nothing.

"Listen, Antonio, I left some spaghetti on the stove. If you feel better eat some. You don't want to get all run down."

"All right," said Tony.

Tony's mother went out. As soon as the door was shut, Tony wished that she hadn't gone. He was afraid. At the sound of footsteps in the corridor, he felt his hair rise and beads of sweat stood out on his forehead. He got to his feet and began to walk up and down. A fury seized him; he cursed Rico and Vettori aloud. Then suddenly the anger left him and the fear returned.

Blackie put his head in the door.

"How you feel, Tony?" he asked.

"Hello, Blackie," said Tony, "come on in and have a smoke."

Blackie took a cigarette from the proffered pack and sat down. While he smoked he kept glancing at Tony.

"Whatsa mat, Tony?" said Blackie. "You ain't look so good."

Tony stared at Blackie for a moment, then he began to shake all over.

"Jesus, Blackie," he cried, "I can't stand it. They'll get us sure. Have you seen tonight's paper?"

Blackie shrugged.

"I can no read."

"It's all up with us," said Tony. "My God, I don't see how Rico stands it."

"Rico no scared."

"Well, he ought to be. He's the one that done it."

Blackie shrugged.

"No can help. What-you-say, Cortenni pull a gat. No can help."

Tony got very pale of a sudden. He heard an automobile stop in the street below. He ran to the window and looked down, then he turned and came back.

"I thought it was the cops," he said.

"Look," said Blackie, "you no better be sick. Listen, you no got your guts, Tony. Rico say, be a man. That is good. Be a man, Rico say. You no better be sick."

"The hell with Rico," said Tony.

Blackie shrugged.

Tony stood in the middle of the room for a minute or two looking at the floor, then, suddenly making up his mind, he went over to the hat rack and got his hat.

"Where you go?" asked Blackie.

Tony hesitated.

"I go too," said Blackie.

"No, you go home," said Tony, then looking steadily at Blackie he said: "Me, I'm going down to St. Dominick's and see Father McConagha."

"What," cried Blackie, leaping up in alarm. "Tony, my God, you no tell him nothing."

"I got to," cried Tony vehemently.

Blackie took hold of Tony's arm.

"Tony, my boy, don't go. Listen, Tony, you no sick. Be a man. Hear what I tell you. You no live, see, you no live. Be a man."

Tony pushed him away.

"You go home, Blackie."

Tony went out. Blackie heard him walking slowly down the corridor. When he could no longer hear his footsteps, he leapt to his feet, opened a back window, went down the fire escape, and took a short cut through the alleys. He knocked at the back door of the Palermo and Carillo let him in.

IV

Vettori stared at Rico, who said nothing. "Crazy! Crazy!" said Blackie. "I tell him, be a man, be a man. But he say, I got to, I got to."

Rico hastily put on his overcoat.

"Well, I guess that's it," said Sam Vettori.

"Yeah," said Rico, "that's it. Now get yourself a can, Sam, and let's go. We ain't got any time to waste."

Vettori rubbed both hands over his face.

"Not me," he said.

Rico looked at him.

"Take Blackie," said Vettori.

Blackie implored them with his eyes. "Blackie's no good," said Rico.

"No," said Blackie, "I no good."

Carillo put his head in the door.

"Reilley's downstairs, boss."

"Take Carillo," said Vettori.

Carillo stared at them suspiciously. Rico leapt across the room and grabbed him by the arm.

"Listen, Bat, can you drive a can?"

"Sure."

"Will you let her out when I office you?"

"Sure."

"All right, let's go."

"Take that black roadster, Carillo," said Vettori, "but for God's sake don't smash it up."

Carillo ran out leaving the door open. Rico walked over and closed the door, then he said:

"Sam, you ain't got any more guts than Tony. Now listen, get down there and talk turkey to Reilley. Get that! By God, I guess I got to boss this job myself."

Vettori looked at Rico with hatred. But he said:

"All right, Rico, you're the boss now."

Rico went out. Blackie said:

"Goodbye Tony!"

Carillo was waiting with the black roadster in the alleyway. Rico jumped in and the roadster leapt away. Carillo took a turn on two wheels.

"It's a cinch he went the shortest cut," said Rico.

"Sure," said Carillo, "I know what I'm doing."

"All right," said Rico, "do it."

The wind had risen and it began to snow, big, heavy flakes which sailed past the street lights. In a few minutes the ground was covered.

Carillo took the shortest cut and Rico, holding his big automatic on the seat beside him, sat straining his eyes. But there was no sign of Tony.

"If we miss him I'll kick hell out of Blackie," said Rico.

"Keep your shirt on, boss," said Carillo.

The tall spires of St. Dominick's rose before them at the end of the block. The street was deserted. Carillo drove slowly now, hugging the curb. In a moment he pointed:

"There's a guy."

Rico leaned forward.

"Take it easy, Bat," he said, "I think it's Tony."

Carillo throttled down to five miles an hour. The man, a dim black figure in the falling snow, stopped in front of the cathedral and looked up. When the automobile came abreast of him he turned.

"Tony," called Rico.

"Yeah?" came Tony's voice. "Who is it?"

Rico fired. A long spurt of flame shot out in the darkness. Rico emptied his gun. Tony fell without a sound.

"All right now, Bat," said Rico, "let her out."

V

Joe and Olga were sitting in a quiet corner of a Gold Coast hotel dining room. They were waiting for their dessert. Joe, comfortably full and inclined to be amiable, sat looking at Olga. She was the goods. Of course he stepped out with other broads occasionally when Olga was busy, but that didn't count. Olga was the goods and she was his woman. Other men didn't rate with her, that's all. He studied her. There she sat with her round dark face, her high cheekbones, and her dark mascaraed eyes. Her long thin fingers covered with rings fascinated him. Her slimness, her elegance made him feel very uncouth and protective and masculine.

"Well," said Olga, "take a good look."

"Listen, baby," said Joe, "you got it. I ain't kidding. You got everything. There ain't a woman in Chicago that's got half your stuff. You make 'em all look silly."

Olga reached across the table and patted his hand.

"I don't believe it, but say it again. I like it."

"No fooling."

"What a line," said Olga.

The waiter brought their dessert.

"I'll tell you," said Olga, looking at her wrist watch, "let's go to a movie. I got time."

Joe didn't like movies very well; all that sappy love stuff! But now he wanted to please Olga.

"All right. Where'll it be?"

Olga turned to the waiter.

"Bring us a paper, please."

The waiter brought a paper and handed it to Joe. He unfolded it and started to turn to the theatrical page, but instead he read with absorption an article on the front page. Olga saw him swallow several times. When he glanced up at her there was a bewildered look in his eyes and his face had begun to get pale.

"What's wrong?" she asked.

"They got Tony," said Joe.

"Who?"

"I don't know. Rico, I guess. He must have turned yellow."

Joe ran his hand across his forehead, then he took out his gold cigarette case, but without ostentation this time, and lit a cigarette. Olga took the paper from him. She read:

ANOTHER GANG KILLING

Antonio Passalacqua, known as Tony Passa, reputed to be a member of the Vettori gang, was found dead near the steps of St. Dominick's Cathedral ... as far as the police can ascertain no one saw him killed ... when questioned Sam Vettori denied all knowledge of the shooting and intimated that it was the work of a rival gang ... police say that this is likely.

"Jesus!" said Joe.
Olga turned quickly to the theatrical page. "Joe, honey," she said, "there's a good comedy at the Oriental. What do you say?"
Joe crumpled up his cigarette and put it in the ashtray.
"Boy, Rico didn't waste no time with him."
"Joe, don't you want to see that comedy?"
"Sure," said Joe, "let's go see it."
Joe sat silent in the taxi all the way to the theatre. As they were getting out, he said:
"Boy, that Rico is sure careless with a rod."
"Forget it, honey," said Olga.

VI

When Rico came in Seal Skin was sitting in a chair by the window and Otero was lying on the bed without his shirt, singing loudly. Rico walked over and put his hand on Seal Skin's shoulder.
"Listen," he said, "I thought you told me you was gonna look after The Greek?"
"I can't do nothing with him," said Seal Skin.
Rico went over to the bed and looked at Otero.
"Señor Rico," cried Otero, "listen, I will sing for you."
Rico turned.
"Seal," he said, "that bird's gonna spill something if you don't keep him sober."
"Listen," said Seal Skin, "I ain't no nurse. A guy ought to look out for himself. What the hell can I do, anyway? I can't knock him cold."
"You never did have much sense," said Rico.
"All right, wise boy. Let's see what you can do."
Rico took off his overcoat.
"Got any ice?"

"Sure," said Seal Skin without moving.

"Well, goddam it, get on your feet and get it."

Seal Skin was afraid of Rico but she didn't want him to suspect it. She got to her feet leisurely, picked up one of Otero's big cigars, lit it, and stood puffing. Then, having demonstrated her lack of fear, she went to the kitchen for the ice.

Rico went over to the bed.

"Otero," he said, "have you got any liquor around here?"

"What do I care for liquor!" cried Otero. "I will sing for you."

Rico slapped Otero's face.

"A hell of a crew I'm mixed up with," he said.

Otero looked at him, startled.

"What is wrong with me?"

"You're a dirty yellow bum."

"I am not a yellow bum," cried Otero, trying to sit up.

Rico struck him hard this time, knocking him back on the bed. Otero put his hand to his face and looked at Rico.

"If you got any more liquor here you better tell me where it is," said Rico.

Otero reached under his pillow and pulled out a quart bottle over half full. Rico slipped it into his pocket.

Otero's face got red.

"Rico," he said, "you give me back my liquor."

He tried to sit up but Rico hit him and he fell back. Seal Skin came in with a couple of pieces of ice wrapped in a towel.

"What the hell you want to beat him up for?" she said.

"I'm gonna get him sober and keep him that way."

"Yeah? Well, you're gonna have a full-time job."

Rico took the ice, a piece in each hand, and began to rub it over Otero's face and chest. He rubbed hard and it hurt Otero, who struggled.

"Rico," he said, "what have I done to you? Rico, you are my friend. Why do you treat me this way?"

"He'll be bawling next," said Seal Skin.

Of a sudden Otero got angry and struggled so fiercely that he threw Rico off and climbed out of bed. The ice clattered to the floor. Rico took one step toward him and set himself for a punch, but Seal Skin grabbed his arm.

"For God's sake let up on him," she cried, "ain't he in bad enough shape?"

Rico was furious. He slapped Seal Skin across the face with his open hand.

"A fine bunch of yellow bellies and squealers I'm mixed up with," he cried. "Listen, idiot, ain't he a meal ticket? You want the black wagon to come and haul him away?"

Otero reeled across the room. Rico leapt after him and knocked him to the floor. Otero raised his head.

"Rico," he said, "what have I done to you?"

Rico picked up the ice and kneeling down beside Otero began to rub him with it, harder than before. Otero gasped.

"Listen," said Rico, "you got to get sober. I'm your friend, Otero. I don't want to see you get us all hung. Listen, Otero, do you get what I'm saying? You got to sober up and stay that way."

Tears ran down Otero's cheeks.

"All right, Rico," he said.

In half an hour Rico had him sober. Seal Skin was sitting with her feet on the window sill, smoking one of Otero's big cigars. Otero sat pale and shaken, looking at Rico.

"Well, big boy," said Seal Skin, "I got to hand it to you. You done it."

Rico smiled. Then he took out his billfold and handed Seal Skin a ten.

"There's a little cush for you. You ain't sore at me cause I socked you, are you? I got red hot mad, that's all."

"You didn't sock me hard," said Seal Skin, "but it was ten dollars' worth."

Otero didn't have much to say. He sat looking at the floor, ashamed of himself.

"How do you feel?" asked Rico.

"Me, not so good," said Otero.

"Want a little drink?"

Otero looked at Rico, not trusting him, then he nodded. Rico handed him the bottle.

"I said little drink," cautioned Rico.

Otero took a swallow and handed back the bottle.

"Now," said Rico, "get your clothes on and we'll take a look at Tony."

VII

There were many rumors in Little Italy about the passing of Sam Vettori. The full truth, of course, was only guessed at, but the simple facts were known. Sam Vettori's star was setting, Rico's was rising. Rico had always been right; there was never any question of that. Rico had always inspired fear. But now, as the probable head of a big minor gang whose activities were varied and whose yearly income was enormous, his potentialities were prodigiously increased and he was treated accordingly.

When he entered Tony's flat several members of the Vettori gang, sitting near the door, got up and offered him their chairs. He merely shook his head and walked across to where Sam Vettori was sitting. Otero, who had entered a little behind Rico, stopped to talk with Blackie Avezzano.

Carillo brought a chair for Rico and Rico sat down beside Sam Vettori.

"We're going to plant the kid right," said Vettori, "that'll look good."

Rico stared across the room at a large horseshoe wreath which bore the single word: Tony. That was his contribution.

"Sure," said Rico.

He was a little uneasy. Not that he felt any remorse. What he had done was merely an act of policy. A man in this game must be a man. If he gets yellow, why, there's only one remedy for it. No, Rico was never likely to err on the side of contrition. It was the massed flowers; their sickly and overpowering odor made him vaguely uneasy.

"They sure fix 'em up good now," said Vettori, nodding in the direction of the coffin; "he don't look dead. He looks like he was asleep."

"Yeah?" said Rico.

"It beats me how they do it," said Vettori.

Carillo came across the room and whispered to Rico and Vettori.

"Two bulls in the hallway."

"They coming in?" asked Rico.

"No, just standing there."

"All right."

There was a movement at the door. Mrs. Passalacqua came in between two of her friends. She had been at St. Dominick's for over an hour. Rico got up and offered her his chair. One of the women helped her off with her hat. She sat down. Her gray hair was parted in the middle and drawn tightly down; her face was a dead white. She was wearing a plain black dress and she sat with her hands in her lap. She looked at no one, but fastened her eyes on the coffin.

Rico walked over to look at Tony. At the head of the coffin were two big candles, one of them leaning a little and dripping tallow. Tony lay with his hands folded. Rico looked down. Somehow he had expected Tony to be changed. He was not. Here lay the same Tony who used to play poker with such fury. The same Tony, yes, only dead. Rico saw the rigidity of the face, the parchment skin. He stood there, looking.

Carillo put his hand on Rico's shoulder.

"Bulls want to see you, boss."

Rico nodded.

"They want you to come out in the hall."

"All right," said Rico, turning away from the coffin, "tell Otero."

Otero came over beside Rico and stood looking at Tony.

"Listen," said Rico, "this may be a pinch. I don't know. If it is, I'll go with them. They ain't got nothing on me. But if there's any trouble, Scabby'll keep you posted. Ma's got my jack, see?"

"All right," said Otero.

Rico started across the room and Otero followed him. Before Rico reached the door Tony's mother suddenly put her hands to her face and began to sob wildly.

"Oh, Tony, Tony!" she cried.

The women who had come in with her tried to quiet her, but she pushed them away, and, rising, walked over to the coffin and stood looking down at Tony. Then, still sobbing, she let the women lead her into the next room.

"That's a woman for you," said Rico.

"Well," said Otero, shrugging, "Tony was her son."

The hallway was lined with poor Italians who, not knowing the Passalacquas, had come out of curiosity. They stood in silent groups, trying to peep in through the open door. Women in disreputable housedresses carrying dirty children; pregnant women; old men with crinkly gray hair and seamed brown faces; young girls trying to look up-to-date and American. When Rico came out they all stared at him.

Flaherty took hold of his arm.

"Rico," he said, "come down to the end of the hall. I want to see you a minute."

"Is this a pinch?" asked Rico.

Flaherty laughed.

"Got a bad conscience, have you? Well, you ought to have."

Rico noticed that the other detective, whom he had never seen before, kept staring at him. Rico planted his feet firmly and stared back.

"What's the big idea, Flaherty?" he asked.

"Well," said Flaherty, "just to put your mind at rest I'll tell you, this ain't a pinch. It ought to be, but it ain't. Now will you take a walk …?"

"Sure," said Rico.

Otero came out into the hallway and stood watching them. Rico went down to the end of the hall with the two plainclothes men. Some of the poor Italians followed them and stood staring. But Flaherty motioned them off as if he were shooing chickens.

"Beat it," he said; "go tend to your own business."

They moved away slowly, looking back.

"All right," said Rico, "let's have it."

Flaherty took out a big cigar and began chewing on it. The other man kept staring. Rico was puzzled and wondered what the game was;

then he noticed that the light at their end of the hall was good, much better than any other place in the hall. The once-over? Well, what then?

"Listen, Rico," said Flaherty, "I like you and I'm going to give you a tip. It's going to be tough on you birds from now on. The Old Man's got his back up. Now get this. If you got anything on your mind, you better spill it." Flaherty paused to light his cigar. The other detective watched Rico intently. "Because it's going to be easy for the bird that spilled it first. But God help the rest of them."

Rico smiled slightly.

"Quit stalling," he said.

Flaherty glanced at the man with him, but the man shook his head. Flaherty said:

"Well, I'm giving you a friendly tip."

"Yeah," said Rico, "you bulls always was friendly as hell. I spent two years once just thinking how friendly you was. Listen, I ain't got nothing to spill. What the hell's wrong with you, Flaherty? Did I ever do any spilling?"

Flaherty laughed.

"Well," he said, "there's a first time for everything. All right, Rico, you can go."

The two plainclothes men pushed their way through the crowd and went down the stairs. Rico went back into Tony's flat. Sam Vettori and Otero were waiting for him. Vettori was mopping his face with his big white silk handkerchief.

"Well?" he demanded.

Rico shrugged.

"Just stalling."

"What's the game?"

"You got me. I guess Flaherty wanted this other bird to give me the once-over."

"Things getting pretty hot, Rico."

"Don't beef, Sam. We're gonna come through."

Otero said:

"The old lady sure is taking it hard."

They could hear Tony's mother sobbing loudly in the next room.

PART IV

I

For three or four years Bat Carillo, once a third-rate light-heavyweight, had been the leader of one of Vettori's gangs of hooligans. The members of this gang specialized in strongarm stuff and intimidation; they threw bombs; they smashed up barrooms and vice joints operated by rival gangs. They were, in other words, Vettori's shock troops. Carillo was an excellent lieutenant, as he always carried out orders to the letter; and was congenitally incapable of imagining himself as chief in his own right. A good honest subordinate without ambition. Vettori trusted him.

In Carillo's attitude since the killing of Courtney, therefore, Vettori saw the most unmistakable symptom of his own passing. Carillo had attached himself to Rico and called him "boss." Carillo was not careless with the word "boss"; it was not a conventional expression; when he said "boss" he meant it. Aroused, Vettori saw similar manifestations all around him; in Blackie Avezzano, in Killer Pepi, in a dozen others.

Vettori had always disliked Rico. Now he hated him. If Carillo or Killer Pepi had remained faithful he would have had one of them kill him and damn the consequences. But there was no question of that now. He knew that he was whipped and he saw the necessity of a compromise. Hanging was just over the horizon and Rico's gun promised an even more certain death. Vettori had never split with anyone. He had always taken with both hands and given as little as possible. But it was split now or die and Vettori could not contemplate the prospect of dying with any degree of complacency. He sent for Rico.

A new Rico appeared, followed by Otero, Carillo, and Killer Pepi. Rico was wearing a big ulster like Joe's and a derby also like Joe's. He had on fawn-colored spats drawn over pointed patent leather shoes; and a diamond horseshoe pin sparkled in a red, green and white striped necktie.

Vettori looked him over and winked at Killer Pepi, but Killer Pepi's face was stony. Carillo got a chair for Rico.

"What's on your mind, Sam?" said Rico, sitting down, throwing back his ulster and pulling up his trousers to preserve the crease.

Vettori hesitated.

"I want to see you alone," he said.

"No," said Rico, "I think I know your game, Sam, and I want the boys to get an earful. Go ahead and spill it."

Vettori began to sweat. Killer Pepi said:

"Yeah, we know."

"You know a hell of a lot, don't you?" said Vettori.

"We know, all right," said Pepi.

Nobody said anything. Rico took off his hat and began to comb his hair. Vettori got out his cards and began to lay out a game of solitaire.

Pepi said:

"We know you went yellow, Sam, when Tony blew his top and started after Come-To-Jesus McConagha. We know all right."

Vettori looked up at him.

"What the hell I got you guys for anyway! Who hands out the cush?"

Rico paused in the combing of his hair.

"Don't get rough, Sam."

Killer Pepi went over and stood with his back against the door. Otero sat down opposite Vettori.

"Well," said Rico, "if you want to see me, spill it quick because I ain't got all night."

Vettori sighed profoundly, then he put down his cards and looked at the men around him. He saw four hostile faces.

"All right," said Vettori, "but why the strongarm stuff, Rico? Sit down, you guys, and I'll have some drinks sent up."

The three men looked at Rico.

"All right," he said, "go bring up some drinks, Bat."

Carillo went out. Nobody said anything. Outside, a winter dusk settled and the big electric sign on a level with the windows was switched on. They sat looking at the sign.

CLUB
P
A
L
E
R
M
O
DANCING

Carillo brought in the drinks and they all sat around the table under the green-shaded lamp. Otero, Carillo, and Killer Pepi drank whiskey;

Vettori wine; Rico pop.

Vettori put down his glass.

"Well, Rico," he said, "I got a proposition to make you."

"All right," said Rico, "spring it."

"Listen," said Vettori, "I'm getting old. I'll never see forty-five again and when a guy's that old he ain't worth much."

"You ain't getting old, Sam, you're losing your guts," said Rico.

Killer Pepi laughed out loud and banged his fist on the table. But Vettori swallowed this insult.

"All right, Rico," he said, "that's your story. Well, here's how it is. I need a partner. You're young, Rico, and you got the guts. All the guys like you and they'll do what you say. I got the lay-out and you're looking for a chance to be a big guy. Well, here's your chance." Vettori thought for a moment, then he said: "I'll split the works with you."

Carillo and Pepi exchanged a look. Otero began to hum to himself. But Rico said:

"I'll think it over."

Vettori began to sweat again. Was Rico going to get rid of him?

"Well," he said, putting on a front, "you can take it or leave it. I like you, Rico, and I'm doing you a favor. Who's got the money? Who's got the pull? What the hell would you guys do if you didn't have the Big Boy to pull you through?"

"I'm O. K. with the Big Boy," said Rico; "he was up to see me this morning."

"Yeah," said Pepi, "I brung him."

Vettori laid out a new game of solitaire.

"Here's the thing," said Rico: "you're trying to hang on, Sam. You must think we're dumb as hell. You want me to do the work so you can take it easy. And you call that an even split. Hear what I say! That ain't my idea of a split."

"Well, I ain't handing out charity," said Vettori, losing his temper.

Rico got to his feet and buttoned up his ulster.

"All right, Sam."

Vettori slammed down his cards.

"What do you guys think?" he demanded of Carillo, Pepi and Otero. They just looked at him.

"Ain't that a fair split?"

"No," said Rico, "I guess we can't do no business."

Rico put on his hat and walked toward the door. The other three got up and followed him. Vettori stood up.

"Well," he said, "you gonna try to run me out, Rico?"

Vettori was panicky. Rico stood at the door and looked at him.

"I was just figuring I'd open a joint across the street," he said.

Vettori knew what that meant. He had been through half a dozen gang wars, but that was long ago when there were at least five separate gangs in the neighborhood. Things had been comparatively quiet for over three years. Vettori regretted the past bitterly. He regretted having taken up with Rico, an unknown Youngstown wop.

"Well," he said, "Rico, you're young and you ain't got any too much sense. What the hell! With things the way they are, we wouldn't none of us last a month. Listen, Rico, what's your idea of a split?"

Rico took off his hat and scratched his head, but carefully so that his hair wouldn't be disarranged.

"I'll hand you this, Sam," said Rico, "you got the lay-out. The split's good that way. But you got sense enough to know that no two guys can run things. The lay-out split is O. K. with me, but I got to have the say, get that!"

Vettori looked at the others.

"What do you guys say?"

"We're in with Rico," said Killer Pepi.

Otero and Carillo nodded. Vettori brought his hand down on the table with a smack.

"O. K.," he said.

II

The gang gave a banquet for Rico in one of Sam Vettori's big back rooms. The table was fifteen feet long and was covered by a fine white cloth. Red, green and white streamers hung from the chandeliers and Italian and American flags were crossed at intervals along the walls. At eleven o'clock the notables began to arrive. Killer Pepi in a blue suit and a brown derby, with his woman, Blue Jay, on his arm. Joe Sansone, gunman and ex-lightweight, in a tuxedo, followed by his shadow Kid Bean, a Sicilian, dark as a negro. Then Ottavio Vettori, Sam's cousin, not yet twenty-one, already famous as a gunman and spoken of as a potential gang chief. Then Otero, Blackie Avezzano and Bat Carillo, all with their women. They stood about stiffly, a little uncomfortable in their fine clothes, and tried to make conversation. The men, like all specialists, talked shop. Ottavio Vettori declared that the police were a bunch of bums. Killer Pepi agreed that they were. Joe Sansone said that the Federal men were just as bad, only smarter and crookeder. Killer Pepi agreed that they were. Ottavio Vettori didn't agree. He said that the Federal men were dumber and harder to fix. This brought on an argument.

When Sam Vettori came in the men were all shouting.
"What the hell!" said Sam, "ain't this a fine way to act at a banquet? You act like a bunch of gashouse micks. Cut the chatter."
Ottavio made a noise like a goat.
"Baa! Baa!"
Everybody laughed. Otero took out a quart bottle of whiskey, drank from it and passed it to Seal Skin; she drank and passed it to Ottavio. The bottle circled the room and returned empty.
"You sure came prepared, you birds," said Sam. "Did any of you guys bring a lunch?"
"Baa! Baa!" bellowed Ottavio.
"My God, ain't that cute!" said Killer Pepi's girl.
"Hell, that ain't nothing," said Pepi, "listen." Pepi put three fingers in his mouth and blew a blast that made their eardrums ring.
"Lord," said Ottavio, "the cops! Baa! Baa!"
Three waiters came in, each carrying two quarts of whiskey. They put the bottles on the table and went out.
"That's an appetizer," said Sam.
"Apéritif," Joe Sansone corrected.
Ottavio slapped him on the back.
"What's that, little Joe? What the hell lingo is that?"
Joe pushed him away.
"You dumb birds don't know nothing. Swell people don't say appetizer; they say apéritif."
"The hell they do! Well, I expect you know all about it. You used to be a bellboy at the Blackstone."
Everybody laughed. Killer Pepi blew a blast on his fingers. His girl looked at him admiringly.
"How the hell you ever learn to do that?"
"Aw, that ain't nothing."
"Say, Sam," said Carillo, "when do we eat?"
"When the boss gets here," said Pepi.
"Well, he better step on it because I'm so hungry I could eat dynamite," said Ottavio.
"Keep your shirt on," said Pepi.
"Haven't got an old soup sandwich in your pocket, have you?" asked Ottavio.
Everybody laughed. Ottavio was the recognized wit of the Vettori gang. All that he had to do to get a laugh was to open his mouth.
Sam Vettori took one of the quarts from the table and sent it round the room. It came back empty.
"What the hell you suppose is keeping Rico?" asked Carillo.

"Keep your shirt on," said Pepi.

"I go see," said Otero.

As he went out, the Big Boy came in. He had on a big raccoon coat and his derby was on the side of his head. Sam Vettori rushed over and shook hands with him.

"What the hell you doing here?" he demanded.

"Me, I came to see the fun. Things are looking up, Sam. Things sure to God are looking up. I think we got 'em whipped."

Sam Vettori smiled broadly and poured the Big Boy a drink. Well, well! If the Courtney business blew over he was sitting pretty. All things considered, he hadn't done so bad. Time after time he had seen old gang leaders go down before younger men. But here he was hanging on, getting a 50-50 split, and taking no chances. Rico was the goods. Goddam him and all his kind, but he was the goods.

"Yeah," said the Big Boy, "you got the Old Man on the run and Flaherty's about ready to do the Dutch Act. It's gonna blow over, Sam. You heard me speak. It's gonna blow over. I want to see Rico."

"He ain't showed yet," said Sam.

"Damn smart boy," said the Big Boy.

Sam smiled.

"Yeah," he said, pouring the Big Boy another drink, "damn smart kid. He's young yet, but I can show him the ropes."

The Big Boy didn't say anything. He just looked at Vettori.

Otero came running in, followed by two waiters, one of whom was carrying a big ulster and a derby; the other was carrying a woman's fur coat.

"Here he comes," cried Otero.

Kid Bean, who had collected a crowd in the middle of the room, and was walking on his hands to amuse them (he had once been an acrobat), jumped hastily to his feet and backed up against the wall. The crowd followed him. Killer Pepi said:

"All right now. Everybody yell like hell when he comes in."

Rico came in slowly, talking to Blondy Belle, the swellest woman in Little Italy. She was a handsome Italian, bold and aquiline. Her complexion and eyes were dark, but her hair, naturally black, was blondined, and this gave her an incongruous and a somewhat formidable appearance.

Rico was greeted by an uproar, pierced by Killer Pepi's shrill whistle. The Big Boy went to meet Rico and shook hands with him. Sam Vettori smiled and nodded, very affable, then went out to get things started. The Big Boy said to Blondy Belle:

"Got yourself a regular man, did you?"

Blondy took hold of Rico's arm.

"Surest thing you know."

The Big Boy laughed.

"What'd you do with Little Arnie?"

Rico took out a cigar and bit off the end.

"She ditched him," he said.

The Big Boy meditated. Blondy Belle had been Little Arnie's woman for a long time. Little Arnie ran the biggest gambling joint on the North Side, but he had been slipping for a year or more. He wasn't right; nobody could trust him.

"How did Little Arnie take it?" asked the Big Boy.

"He took it standing up," said Blondy Belle.

"Well, what could he do?" said Rico.

Killer Pepi, Ottavio Vettori and Joe Sansone, as the most important men in the gang next to Sam Vettori, came over to shake hands with Rico.

"A million dollars ain't in it with you," said Pepi, looking his boss over.

Rico was wearing a loud striped suit and a purple tie. He still had on his gloves, yellow kid, of which he was very proud, and his diamond horseshoe pin had been replaced by a big ruby surrounded by little diamonds. Ottavio envied him his gloves. But Joe Sansone was not impressed; he knew better.

"Yes sir, boss, you sure are lit up," said Ottavio.

"Here's the half-pint," said Killer Pepi, pushing Joe Sansone forward.

Joe shook hands with Rico.

"Yes sir," said Ottavio, "the half-pint's a good boy, but he and Gentleman Joe're too swell for us."

Rico looked around the room.

"Joe Massara here?"

"Ain't seen him," said Pepi.

"He won't be here," said Joe Sansone; "he's busy."

Rico didn't say anything. Blondy took hold of his arm.

"I want a drink."

Rico looked at Pepi.

"Get her a drink," he said.

The Big Boy took Rico aside and said:

"I want to see you a minute, Rico."

Rico said:

"Listen, if you see Joe Massara tomorrow you tell him to look me up. I got something to say to that bird."

"I'll be seeing him maybe," said the Big Boy. "I got a date with his boss tomorrow morning. There's a square guy, Rico. DeVoss is a square guy all right. Never have to nudge him for dough."

Rico seemed in a bad humor.

"They tell me you lined up something good," said the Big Boy.

Rico nodded.

"Yeah, it's gonna be a money maker. Little Arnie wised me up. I'm gonna give him a split. That's the game now. Sam never had sense enough to get in on it."

"Little Arnie, eh? That guy'd double-cross his grandmother."

"He'll only double-cross me once," said Rico.

"I believe you," said the Big Boy; then, putting his hand on Rico's shoulder, he went on: "Funny for you to split with Arnie. How about Blondy?"

"Arnie don't give a damn. He's all shot to pieces. He can't do a woman no good."

"No wonder," said the Big Boy, "with a woman like that."

Rico grinned.

"Ain't she a bearcat!" he said; then his face clouded. "Wonder what the hell Joe Massara's game is?"

The Big Boy looked at Rico for a moment.

"That little hunky dancer over at DeVoss's has got him down. They tell me he's going straight."

Rico laughed unpleasantly.

"Yeah? Well, I'll have to go over and give that bird an earful."

"Better stay out of that end of town, Rico."

"To hell with that."

Sam Vettori came in, followed by three waiters bringing the soup.

"All right," said Sam, "we're all set."

Rico took his place at the head of the table. The Big Boy sat on his right and Blondy Belle on his left. The gunmen and their women arranged themselves according to rank. Blackie Avezzano sat at the foot of the table.

III

When the meal was over the Big Boy asked Rico to make a speech. There was a prolonged clamor. Rico got up.

"All right," he said, "if you birds want me to make a speech, here you are: I want to thank you guys for this banquet. It sure is swell. The liquor is good, so they tell me, I don't drink it myself, and the food don't leave nothing to be desired. I guess we all had a swell time and it sure is good to see all you guys gathered together. Well, I guess that's about all. Only I wish you guys wouldn't get drunk and raise hell, as that's the way a lot of birds get bumped off."

Rico sat down. The applause lasted for over a minute. Then Ottavio got up with a bottle in his hand.

"Here's to Rico and Blondy and the Big Boy."

Everybody shouted and made a grab for bottles and glasses. Blackie Avezzano fell under the table and stayed there, lying on his face. After the toast was drunk, Killer Pepi and Kid Bean began to quarrel. The Kid picked up a plate and struck at Pepi, who threw a bottle at the Kid, missing him by a fraction of an inch.

Rico banged on the table.

"Cut it out, you guys. Ain't that a hell of a way to act?"

Pepi and the Kid shook hands and another toast was drunk.

A waiter came in the door and went over to Rico.

"Couple of newspaper guys, boss. They want to take a flashlight."

"What's the idea?" the Big Boy inquired.

"Send 'em up," said Rico.

"We're gonna get our mugs shot," cried Blondy Belle.

"Maybe we are," said Rico.

"What's the idea?" the Big Boy reiterated.

"We ain't got nothing to hide," said Rico.

The waiter returned, followed by two newspaper men, one of whom was carrying a big camera. Rico motioned them over.

"Who sent you?" he asked.

Sam Vettori came in and went over to Rico.

"They're O. K., Rico," he said, "they been here before."

"Sure, we're O. K.," said the photographer, a little intimidated by Rico's manner.

"Well, spill it," said Rico, "what's the idea of the flashlight?"

"Well, we got a section in the Sunday paper about how different classes of people live in Chicago. See? Last week we featured Lake Forest. Had some pictures of the swells, see, and the dumps where they lived. This Sunday we want Little Italy. We just heard about the banquet they was giving you, Mr. Rico, so we kinda thought ..."

"O. K.," said Rico, "but make it snappy."

"I'm out of this picture," said the Big Boy, rising and walking over to the doorway. Sam Vettori took his place.

After maneuvering about for a few minutes the photographer got the correct slant. He put the powder on the little tray.

"Now!" he cried.

Rico sat with his thumbs in the arm holes of his vest, looking very stern. There was a blinding flash. Ottavio Vettori leapt into the air and crying "My God, I'm shot" fell face down across the table. Everybody laughed.

When the newspaper men had gone the Big Boy came over and put his hand on Rico's arm. "They may pick you up on that."

"Who the hell's gonna see it."

"You don't know who's gonna see it. That was a bad play, Rico."

Rico laughed.

"If they pick me up, I'll alibi them to death."

When the banquet was over Rico had Otero call him a cab. Blondy Belle was a little drunk and Rico had to support her as they went down the stairs. As she weighed about twenty pounds more than he did, this was not an easy job. As they were going out the side entrance, Flaherty left his table in the club and came over to them.

He put his hand on Rico's shoulder.

"Getting up in the world ain't you, Rico?"

Rico looked at him.

"Don't you know your old pal Jim Flaherty?"

"Sure I know you. What's the big idea?"

"Go chase yourself around the block, flatfoot," said Blondy Belle; "if I ain't getting sick of seeing bulls."

"Hello, Blondy," said Flaherty, "you and Rico hitting it off, eh? That's the old ticket. Rico's a good boy, but he's young. If they don't put him behind the bars, he'll be a man yet."

"What's the idea, Flaherty?" asked Rico.

"Why, I don't want you to forget that I'm your friend," said Flaherty. "I got my eyes on you, Rico. I like to see a young guy getting up in the world."

"Yeah?" said Rico.

The cab was waiting at the curb and one of the waiters went out and opened the door for them. Rico boosted Blondy Belle into the cab. Flaherty stood in the doorway and watched them drive off.

"The nerve of that Irish bastard," said Blondy.

But Rico had forgotten Flaherty. He sat thinking about Joe Massara. Gentleman Joe was getting too good for them, eh? He was going to turn softie.

"Well, I guess not," said Rico.

IV

The sound of the pianola woke Rico. He sat up and looked at his wrist watch. It was 2 o'clock in the afternoon. He had slept twelve hours.

Rico lived at a tension. His nervous system was geared up to such a pitch that he was never sleepy, never felt the desire to relax, was always keenly alive. He did not average over five hours sleep a night and as soon as he opened his eyes he was awake. When he sat in a chair he never thrust out his feet and lolled, but sat rigid and alert. He walked, ate, took his pleasures in the same manner. What distinguished him from his associates was his inability to live in the present. He was like a man on a long train journey to a promised land. To him the present was but a dingy way-station; he had his eyes on the end of the journey. This is the mental attitude of a man destined for success. But the resultant tension had its drawbacks. He was subject to periodic slumps. His energy would suddenly disappear; he would lose interest in everything and for several days would sleep twelve to fifteen hours at a stretch. This was a dangerous weakness, and Rico was aware of it and feared it.

Rico leapt out of bed and hastily put on his clothes.

"Twelve hours, boy," he said to his reflection in the mirror, as he stood combing his hair, "that'll never do."

He had been seeing too much of Blondy Belle; that was the trouble. Rico had very little to do with women. He regarded them with a sort of contempt; they seemed so silly, reckless and purposeless, also mendacious and extremely undependable. Not that Rico trusted men, far from it. He was temperamentally suspicious. But in the course of his life he had discovered a few men he could trust, but no women. What he feared most in women, though, was not their treachery, that could be guarded against, but their ability to relax a man, to make him soft and slack, like Joe Massara. Rico had never been deeply involved with a woman. Incapable of tender sentiments, he had escaped the commoner kind of pitfalls. He was given to short bursts of lust, and, this lust once satisfied, he looked at women impersonally for a while, as one looks at inanimate objects. But at times this lust, usually the result of an inner need and not the outcome of exterior stimulus, would be aroused by the sight of some particular woman. This had been the case with Blondy Belle; she was big, healthy and lascivious. This exactly suited Rico's tastes; she excited him, and for that very reason he was on guard against her.

"Yeah," he said, "I got to lay off Blondy for a while."

She wanted him to come and live with her, but he refused. The offer tickled his vanity, though, for Pepi or Joe Sansone would have jumped at the chance. But not Rico. He fought shy of any kind of ties. A slight relaxing of this principal and you are tangled up before you know it. The strong travel light.

He went out into the living room. Blondy, in a cerise kimono, was pedaling the pianola and singing loudly. The room was in disorder.

Stockings hung from the backs of chairs, the dress Blondy had worn the night before was suspended from the chandelier on a coat hanger, and there was a pile of clothes in the middle of the room.

Blondy turned around and smiled at him, pedaling the piano at the same time.

"What the hell kind of a piece is that?" asked Rico.

"That's an Eyetalian piece," said Blondy. "Ain't it swell?"

"No," said Rico, "I like jazz better."

Blondy stopped the pianola and back-pedaled the roll.

"I got it yesterday because I thought you'd like it," she said.

"Hell, quit kidding," said Rico.

"I sure did. It's from an Opera."

"Yeah? Say, what's wrong with you?"

Blondy looked at him. She had pretensions. Ten years ago she had been a lady's maid and she felt that she was somewhat cultured. One summer she had even made Little Arnie take her to Ravinia Park to hear the Opera. The soprano impressed her by her loud singing; the tenor by his beautiful legs.

"You'd think I was a regular wop to hear you talk," said Rico; "say, I was born in Youngstown and I can't even speak the lingo."

"Well, I guess I wasn't born in the old country either," said Blondy.

She put a new roll on the pianola and Rico sat smoking, while she played it. Rico had no ear for music; he couldn't even whistle, or distinguish one tune from another. But he liked rhythm. There was something straightforward and primitive about jazz rhythms that impressed him.

"That's a good one," he said, when the roll was played through.

"Want to hear some more?"

"No," said Rico, "I got to go."

He rose and went over to the closet for his overcoat, but Blondy said: "Listen, Rico, I want to see you a minute before you go."

"What about?"

"About Little Arnie."

Rico stared at her.

"What's the idea? To hell with Little Arnie. As long as he's straight with me I ain't got no interest in him at all."

"He ain't straight with nobody."

Rico just looked at her.

Little Arnie had played his hand badly. At first he hadn't minded losing Blondy Belle in the least; she cost him a good deal of money and she bored and irritated him. But he had been kidded unmercifully. As he had no sense of humor whatever and was very touchy in a personal matter, this eventually angered him. In revenge, he talked. He told all who would listen that Blondy Belle was a liar, a crook, and had certain unnatural appetites. Killer Pepi was one of the auditors and he immediately repeated Little Arnie's assertions to his woman, Blue Jay, who ran at once to Blondy Belle. Yes, Little Arnie, who was fifty percent fool, had played his hand badly.

Blondy lit a cigarette and lay down on the davenport.

"Come over here and sit down," she said; "I'll give you an earful."

"I ain't got no time," said Rico.

Blondy blew out a cloud of smoke.

"Arnie's double-crossing you right now!" said Blondy.

"What you got on your mind?" said Rico; "spill it."

"All right," said Blondy. "Arnie's giving you a split on the house, ain't he? What's the split?"

"Thirty percent."

"How do you know you're getting thirty?"

"I look at the books."

Blondy laughed.

"Them books is crooked."

"Straight dope?" asked Rico, his face hardening.

"Sure," said Blondy, "I wasn't gonna say nothing. It wasn't none of my business, but Arnie's been peddling a lot of loose talk about me and I don't take that."

"All right," said Rico, "now you know so damn much, how we gonna prove it?"

"It's a cinch," said Blondy; "hand Arnie's boy, Joe Peeper, some dough and he'll spill the news. Joe hates Arnie."

"Good!" said Rico, banging the table with his fist; "I'll run Arnie out of town and declare you in, Blondy. You got brains."

Blondy looked at him.

"You stick to me, boy, and we'll own the town."

"Don't get swelled up," said Rico, "just because you happened to be in the know."

That's what she liked about Rico. He was hard to impress.

"Hell of a lot of thanks I get for it," said Blondy.

"Don't worry about that," said Rico, his head buzzing with projects, "you'll get something better than thanks."

Rico went to the closet and got his coat and hat.

"Wait a minute, big boy," said Blondy, "you ain't heard it all. Listen, that joint of Arnie's is worth plenty of dough. He ain't gonna give it up without a battle."

"Hell," said Rico, "he's yellow."

"Sure he is. But he's tricky. Rico, if you can't work the Joe Peeper stunt, here's a lever. Remember Limpy John?"
"Sure," said Rico, "they bumped him off."
"Who did?"
"The cops."
Blondy laughed.
"They thought they did. Arnie bumped him off."
Rico grinned.
"I got you."
Rico put on his overcoat.
"Be round tonight?" asked Blondy.
"No, I got business."
"Monkey business."
"No, I got to go cross town. I'll give you a ring tomorrow."
Blondy lay back on the davenport.
"You'll sure be missing something," she said.
"I'll ketch up," said Rico.
When Rico had gone, Blondy played a couple of rolls on the pianola, then she drank half a pint of liquor and went back to bed.

V

Rico found the door of his apartment unlocked. Before entering he unbuttoned his overcoat and took out his automatic. Only one person had a key to his apartment except himself: Otero. If Otero wasn't in there then whoever was in there was in trouble. Rico opened the door slowly. Otero was sitting with his chair tipped back against the wall, smoking a cigarette and dozing.
"Otero!"
Otero opened his eyes.
"Hello, boss."
Rico locked the door behind him.
"Listen, don't you know better than to leave that door open?"
"I forgot, Rico."
Rico took off his overcoat and hat.
"You better keep your head working, boy," said Rico, "or you'll get your neck stretched. What you doing here, anyway?"
Otero got up from his chair and stood dangling his hat.
"I want money."
Rico looked at him.
"I'm broke, boss. I ain't got a cent."
Rico laughed. Otero seemed so helpless.

"You mean to tell me you ain't got a cent out of that Casa Alvarado split?"

Otero shrugged.

"What in hell did you do with it?"

"Well, Seal she spends money, spends money. I take it out of my pocket till I ain't got any more." Otero shrugged and rolled a fresh cigarette.

Rico took out his billfold and handed Otero a fifty.

"I'll take that out of your next split."

Otero smiled.

"That's all the same to me, boss."

He was speaking the truth. He hadn't the slightest conception of the value of money. He spent till what he had was gone, then he asked Rico for more. Rico shook his head.

"Listen, Otero, ain't you never gonna get no sense! You got over a grand and a half out of that Casa Alvarado stand. And here you are broke. Why some guys work a whole year for less than that."

Otero shrugged.

"I have worked for two pesos a week."

Rico took some small change out of his pocket and handed it to Otero.

"Go down to the corner and get a couple of *Tribunes*. Get three."

"Three of the same kind?"

"Sure."

Otero went out. Rico opened the window a few inches and sat down beside it. There was a touch of Spring in the air and it made him feel restless. He wanted to be doing things. In a week or less, he'd have Little Arnie's big gambling joint. That meant dough and plenty of it. He'd turn it over to Sam Vettori and let him run it. Sam was looking for something to do. Then maybe he could muscle in on the North Side graft. That wasn't easy. Pete Montana was a wise bird and he had the North Side tied up. Well, maybe the Big Boy could help him there. Rico jumped to his feet and began to pace up and down.

Otero came in with the papers. Rico took them from him and tore one of them apart till he came to the magazine section. There it was. Big type proclaimed:

ITALIAN UNDERWORLD CHIEF
GIVEN BIG FEED

Otero, looking over Rico's shoulder, saw the flashlight picture. In his excitement he pushed Rico aside and placing his finger on a section of the picture, cried:

"There I am!"

Rico took the other two papers apart and got out the magazine sections. Then he put the three sections side by side and compared them.

"All too dark," he said.

Nevertheless, having chosen the clearest one of the three, he took his scissors and cut it out.

"I want one too," said Otero.

"All right," said Rico, "help yourself."

VI

DeVoss was standing in the lobby when Rico came in. DeVoss looked him over thoroughly, positive that he was out of his element in an atmosphere as exclusive as that of The Bronze Peacock. Not that Rico looked the least bit shabby. If anything, he was dressed more carefully than usual, from his modish derby to his fawn-colored spats. The big ulster he was wearing hid the loud striped suit and a plain dark muffler hid the loud striped tie. No, sartorially Rico could pass at The Bronze Peacock. But there was something vulgar and predatory about him that did not escape DeVoss.

"That's a bad one there," he told himself.

Rico glanced about the lobby, taking everything in from habit. It was not a good plant but it could be worked. Not that he had any intention of working it, but you never know. He came up to DeVoss and said:

"Excuse me, but where'll I find the manager of this place."

DeVoss looked at him coldly.

"I'm the manager."

Rico grinned.

"Well," he said, "I guess we got a mutual friend. The Big Boy tells me you and him does business together."

DeVoss's manner changed abruptly.

"Oh, yes. You're one of his friends, are you? What can I do for you?"

"I want to see Joe Massara."

"That's easy," said DeVoss, "he's back in his dressing room. I'll take you back."

Rico followed DeVoss and they went up a few steps at the end of the lobby and came out into the club proper. It was empty except for a couple of electricians who were working on the stage spotlights.

"So you're one of the Big Boy's friends," said DeVoss, curious.

"I'm Rico."

DeVoss looked at him, startled.

"Oh," he said, "you're Rico."

All the way up the rear corridor DeVoss kept looking sideways at Rico. One of Little Arnie's men had told him about the new Vettori gang chief. Dangerous as dynamite! He congratulated himself on his acumen. By God, he kept repeating to himself, I knew he was a bad one.

DeVoss knocked at Joe's door. Someone called "come in." DeVoss opened the door and Rico followed him into the room. Joe was sitting in his shirt sleeves, his vest off, displaying a pair of fancy suspenders. (Rico made a mental note of the suspenders. His taste ran more to fancy sleeve garters. But if men like Joe were wearing fancy suspenders, why, he'd have to get himself a pair.) Olga Stassoff, in a black, red and gold Japanese kimono, was lying on a lounge, holding a Pekingese on her chest and rubbing its face against her own. A big man in evening clothes was standing with his back to the door. When Joe saw Rico he got to his feet in a hurry and stood smiling a little uneasily. The big man turned around.

"Mr. Rico wants to see you, Joe," said DeVoss; then he put his hand on Rico's arm and said: "When you get done with Joe, why, come up to the office and we'll have a little drink."

"Sorry," said Rico, "I don't use it. But thanks just the same."

DeVoss's eyebrows rose.

"You mean you don't drink!"

"Rico drinks milk," said Joe, trying to be funny.

But Rico didn't even smile.

"Yeah," he said, "sometimes I drink milk."

"Well, drop in anyway on your way out," said DeVoss.

DeVoss closed the door. Rico noticed that the girl in the Japanese kimono was staring at him. She didn't look like much to him; too skinny; all the same he insolently ran his eyes over her. The big man said:

"I guess there's no use for us to offer you a drink."

Joe took Rico by the arm.

"Olga, I want you to meet Rico. Rico, this is Olga Stassoff."

"Pleased to meet you," said Rico.

Olga sat up and tried to smile, but it was no use. Rico was repulsive to her, principally because she was certain that he had killed Joe's friend, Tony, but also because he stared at her insolently with his small, pale eyes.

"This boy here," said Joe, taking the big man familiarly by the arm, "is Mr. Willoughby, the millionaire."

"Why bring that up?" said Willoughby.

Rico had an instinctive respect for wealth. Money was power. He smiled affably and offered his hand.

"Pleased to meet you," he said.

Willoughby shook hands strenuously, then he inquired:

"Have you got some private business with Joe?"

"Yeah," said Rico, "but there ain't no hurry about it."

"That's all right," said Willoughby. "Olga and I'll go over next door. Eh, Olga? When you get through, why, give us a rap and we'll come back. Don't suppose I could persuade you to join us in a little supper before the show?"

Rico was flattered.

"Well," he said, "I might."

"Good," said Willoughby; then taking Olga by the hand he pulled her to her feet. But Olga hesitated and stood looking from Joe to Rico.

"Run along, baby," said Joe.

"Well, don't take all night about it," said Olga.

"I won't keep him long," Rico put in.

When Olga and Willoughby had gone Rico said:

"Flying pretty high, ain't you, Joe?"

"Willoughby's just one of Olga's fish. He's gonna back her in a big show."

"Yeah? Well, if that bird's got a million bucks you both better clamp onto him. Nice little Jane you got, Joe."

"Olga's O. K.," said Joe.

Rico unbuttoned his ulster to display his finery. He had on one of his striped suits. It was dead black with a narrow pink stripe. The color scheme was further complicated by a pale blue shirt and an orange and white striped tie adorned with the ruby pin.

Joe stared at him.

"All lit up, ain't you, Rico?" he said.

Rico nodded, pleased.

"Yeah, I kind of got it into my head I ought to dress up now."

"They tell me you crowded Sam out," said Joe.

Rico looked at him.

"Didn't nobody tell you the boys was giving a banquet for me?"

"Yeah, they told me," said Joe, hurriedly, "but it was on at the wrong time for me."

Rico took out a cigar and bit off the end of it.

"I ain't seen you since the big stand."

"No," said Joe, looking at the floor. "I been laying low. They had me scared."

Rico banged his fist on the arm of his chair.

"Goddam it, Joe, what you got up your sleeve?"

Joe looked startled. He sat silent and from time to time raised his eyes to glance at Rico, who was staring at him.

"Spill it, Joe," said Rico.

"Well," said Joe, "I been making pretty good money with my dancing. Olga and me has got a turn together that's going over big. They want to put us in a show. Listen, Rico, I got enough of the racket. This last stand damn near fixed me. Jesus, but we was lucky."

"We ain't out yet," said Rico, "and we don't want no softies spoiling things."

Rico and Joe stared at each other for a moment. Joe began to get pale.

"You ain't dumb, Joe," said Rico, "what the devil! You mean to tell me you're gonna quit the racket. Why, boy, you ain't seen nothing yet. In a couple of weeks I'm gonna take over Little Arnie's joint. The Big Boy even wants to be declared in. Listen, Joe, you're a smart boy and I can use you. To hell with that dancing stuff. As a front it's O. K., but no man's gonna make his living that way."

Joe slumped down in his chair.

"I got your number, Joe," Rico went on, "it's that damn skirt. She's making a softie of you, Joe."

"Lord, Rico," said Joe, "can't a guy quit? I ain't gonna spill nothing. You think I want to get my neck stretched?"

"Yeah? Look at Tony. He turned soft and they patted him with a spade. Once a guy turns soft he ain't no good in this world. Didn't Humpy get soft on Red Gus and turn State's? Yeah! Who got the neck stretching? Red Gus. Humpy got fifteen years and he'll be out in half of that."

Joe slumped further down in his chair. "Rico, you know I ain't yellow."

"All right," said Rico, "if that's the dope, I can use you. Ottavio and me has been figuring on a little stand that won't be half bad. I need a good inside man, Joe. A cut will be worth two grand at least."

Someone knocked at the door. It was DeVoss. He came over to Rico and said:

"Mr. Rico, there's a couple of dicks out in the lobby. When I asked them what they wanted, they said they was just looking around."

Rico said:

"Two bits it's Flaherty. All right, Mr. DeVoss, thanks."

DeVoss went out. Joe got to his feet and turned agonized eyes on Rico.

"What did you have to come clear across town for, Rico? Can't you let me alone?"

Rico paid no attention to him.

"There's one Irishman," he said, "that ain't long for this world."

"Rico," said Joe, "for God's sake stay over in your own end of town. I don't want the bulls coming here."

"Listen," said Rico, his eyes glowing, "if I hear any more of this softie stuff I'll only be back once more."

Willoughby and Olga came in.

"Didn't you rap for us?" asked Willoughby.

"No, that was DeVoss," said Rico, "but we're done. Say, Mr. Willoughby, I sure am sorry but I got to pass up that invitation of yours. I got some important business with a couple of guys."

"Sorry," said Willoughby.

"Yes, we're sorry," said Olga, trying to be affable on Joe's account. Rico shook hands with Joe.

"I'll be seeing you."

"All right, Rico," said Joe.

When Rico emerged he saw DeVoss coming down the corridor. He looked somewhat agitated.

"They're sure enough looking for you, Mr. Rico. For Lord's sake don't cause no trouble in my place."

Rico grinned.

"There won't be no trouble unless them damn dummies out there start it."

Rico followed DeVoss back through the club. On the stage the orchestra was tuning up and a few early couples were sitting at the tables. When they got to the lobby Rico saw Flaherty and another detective. Flaherty came over to him.

"Well, Rico," he said, "kind of out of your territory, ain't you?"

"What the hell of it?"

Rico buttoned his ulster and carefully arranged his muffler.

"Oh, nothing. Don't you remember I told you I was keeping an eye on you? Sure thing. I'm interested in young guys that want to get up in the world."

"Aw, can that," said Rico.

He noticed that people were coming into the place; in the club the orchestra had begun to play. He remembered what the Big Boy had said about DeVoss.

"Let's get the hell out of here," he said, "no use causing DeVoss no trouble. You bulls got about as much regard for a guy as a couple of hyenas."

"You're long on regard yourself, ain't you, Rico?" said Flaherty, laughing.

Rico nodded to DeVoss and went out. Flaherty and the other detective followed him. Rico was standing at the curb under the canvas marquee. They came up to him. He stared at Flaherty.

"Listen, Flaherty," he said, "did you ever stop to think how you'd look with a lily in your hand?"

"I never did," said Flaherty, with a sneer. "I been at this game for twenty-five years and I've got better guys than you hung, and I never got a scratch."

Rico took out a cigar and lit it. A taxi drew up at the curb.

"Well, here's my wagon," said Rico, "want to take a ride?"

"No," said Flaherty, "when we take a ride together I'll have the cuffs on you."

"No Irish bastard'll ever put no cuffs on Rico!"

Flaherty's face got red, but he turned on his heel and was about to go when Rico said:

"And another thing, Flaherty, you was always O. K. with me, see, but now you ain't. You ain't got nothing on me and you ain't got no business trailing me every place I go. Take a tip. Sam and me 're getting tired of seeing you guys climb the stairs. The first floor's open to anybody, they even allow cops in there, but the upstairs is private."

"Yeah?" said Flaherty, who had succeeded in controlling his temper.

"Yeah. Someday one of you wise dicks is gonna make a one way trip up them stairs."

"Getting up in the world, ain't you, Rico?" said Flaherty, "maybe you better run for mayor."

Rico slammed the door of the cab. Flaherty turned to the man with him and said:

"I'll get that swell-headed Dago if it's the last thing I ever do."

PART V

I

There were quite a few wise boys in Little Italy who thought that Rico's sensational rise was a fluke. The matter was talked about a good deal and he was unfavorably compared with Nig Po and Monk de Angelo, former leaders, and there were even those who considered him inferior to Killer Pepi, Ottavio Vettori, and Joe Sansone. This confusion arose because Rico was not understood. He had none of the outward signs of greatness. Neither the great strength and hairiness of Pepi, nor the dash and effrontery of Ottavio Vettori, nor the maniacal temper of Joe Sansone. He was small, pale and quiet. In spite of his new finery he wasn't much to look at. He did not swagger, he seldom raised his voice, he never bragged. In other words, the general run of Little Italians could find nothing in him to exaggerate; they could not make a legendary figure of him because the qualities he possessed were qualities they could not comprehend. The only thing that redeemed him in their eyes was his reputation as a killer.

Rico was brave enough, but he did not flaunt his bravery like Kid Bean. Rico was cunning enough, but cunning was not an obsession with him as it was with Sam Vettori. Rico was capable of sudden audacity, but even his audacity had a sort of precision and was entirely without the dash of Ottavio's.

Rico, while he was small and pale, was capable of great endurance, but this endurance of his was nothing compared to Killer Pepi's inhuman vitality. Rico's great strength lay in his single-mindedness, his energy and his self-discipline. The Little Italians could not appreciate qualities so abstract.

The men that were considered his rivals were really not to be compared with him. Killer Pepi was strong and courageous, but he was very erratic and a drug addict. Ottavio Vettori was daring enough and cool in a tight place, he could shoot straight and he feared nothing, but he was light-minded, dissipated his energies on all sorts of follies, and ran after every woman that looked at him. Joe Sansone, though brave enough and dependable when it came to a sudden action, was a periodic drunkard, and, generally speaking, nervous and unreliable. Sam Vettori, a good man once, had let his congenital lethargy and his congenital love of trickery overcome him; he had become petty and had entirely lost the initiative which, years ago, had put him at the head of the gang. Now he was not even taken seriously by the men he had once led, and but for Rico's authority, he would have sunken into obscurity.

The case of Sam Vettori was a strange one, without its parallel in gang annals. In Little Italy there is no such thing as abdication unless it is accompanied by flight. The old gang leader who is superseded has two alternatives: flight or death. Sam had escaped both. His growing inability to make decisions had lost him his power, but it had also saved his life. Rico did not consider him dangerous. But that was not all. Rico considered him useful. That saved him from flight. With the proper guidance, Sam Vettori was an asset to any gang. He was wise and he knew the ropes.

Sam was docile; not that his hatred for Rico had abated; but things were breaking good, money was rolling in, and Sam loved money above all things. The Vettori gang had never known such prosperity before. Sam was quick to see where his advantage lay. Rico could be killed. Scabby, who hated Rico for some fancied slight and who, for this reason, was faithful to Sam, would have done it. But what would have been the good of that? Sam knew that he was through as a gang leader. With Rico dead, there would be a mad scramble for leadership. Besides, Rico had the devil's own luck, and Scabby might fail. If he failed, Scabby's life and his own wouldn't be worth a plugged dime. No, Sam Vettori accepted a somewhat odd situation philosophically and prospered.

II

Blondy Belle lolled back in her chair and put her fat hands on the table. Rico sat opposite her with his hat tilted over his eyes.

"Well," said Blondy Belle, "I guess that's it, ain't it, Rico?"

Rico nodded.

"I told you not to give that bird a chance. He thinks you're soft."

Rico smiled and twisted his diamond ring round and round.

"He raised the split to fifty percent, and the books were straight."

"Well," said Blondy, "he couldn't stand prosperity. Listen, you're gonna let him have it, ain't you?"

Blondy hated Little Arnie so that she couldn't sleep at night. She couldn't understand Rico's lenience.

"No," said Rico.

"Hell," said Blondy, "you're getting soft."

"Aw, can that," said Rico; "you want me to get my neck stretched over a dirty double-crosser that ain't worth a good bullet? Listen, I'm gonna run that bird out of town."

Blondy was disgusted. She started to get to her feet, but Rico reached across the table and pushed her back into her chair.

"Sit down," he said, "and cut the funny stuff. If you women ain't awful! Use your head, that's what you got it for."

Blondy sulked. Across the room the orchestra started up and couples crowded out into the roped-off dance floor.

"Don't they ever get sick of dancing?" said Blondy, in a bad temper.

Rico got to his feet.

"Listen," he said, "get yourself a cab and beat it. Go home and take some aspirin and hit the hay. If you'd lay off that bad liquor you wouldn't always be beefing."

Blondy looked at Rico for a moment, then she said:

"Aw, sit down, Rico. I'll snap out of it."

"No," said Rico, "I got business to look after and I'm getting sick of this beefing. See, I'm getting sick. Any more of this kind of stuff and I'm gonna get me another woman. Hell, I might as well talk to Flaherty as you."

Blondy got to her feet without speaking. Rico never kidded; he meant what he said. Blondy was not used to men like Rico. She often wondered why it was she couldn't seem to get any hold on him.

Silently they walked around the little, roped-off dance floor. Rico told one of the waiters to get him a cab, then, to pass the time, he started putting nickels in a slot machine. After the third nickel, the bell rang and Rico won fifty cents; on the sixth nickel he won again.

"Ain't that good!" said Rico.

He called the man behind the counter.

"Say," he said, "have you seen anybody fooling with this machine?"

The man nodded.

"Yes, sir," he said, "I seen Ottavio doing something to it."

Rico laughed.

"Can you beat that petty crook! He'll be robbing blind men next. Say, tell Sam to get all the machines overhauled. What the hell! He might as well hand out nickels over the counter."

Blondy laughed, glad of this opportunity to put on a change of front.

"Boy, you don't miss anything," she said.

"Well," said Rico, serious, "what's the use of letting somebody gyp you?"

The waiter they had sent for the cab came to tell them that it was outside.

Blondy put her hand on Rico's arm.

"Listen, wise boy," she said, "you got the right dope about that Little Arnie business. Run him out, that's O. K., but do it up brown."

"You watch," said Rico.

He put her in the cab.

"Gonna give me a ring tonight, Rico?" she asked.

"Can't say."

"Well, don't let me ketch you with any more dark hairs on your coat."

"Can that!" said Rico.

Blondy slammed the cab door. Rico stood and watched the cab till it disappeared. Blondy was just like any other woman. Now she had got to the grand rush stage. Always beefing about something. Rico stood looking down the street. It was hot and the city sweltered, but now and then you could feel a breath of lake wind. He looked up at the sky. Stars everywhere.

"It's a swell night," said Rico.

Contrary to custom, he decided to walk down to the newsstand and get a paper. Since his rise, he seldom went out unaccompanied; never at night. Otero, Killer Pepi and Bat Carillo had constituted themselves his bodyguard and one of them was always within calling distance. They were jealous of this privilege and sometimes quarreled among themselves. But the night tempted Rico; the atmosphere of The Palermo was vile, and the lake breeze was fresh and cool.

He had gone scarcely half a block when a large touring car with the curtains closed passed him. He saw the car, noticing especially the closed curtains and the fact that the driver was hugging the curb, and, fearing the worst, he looked about for a shelter, but, as the car passed him and went on, he paid no further attention to it. Stopping in front of a lighted drugstore window he took out his watch and looked at it. One o'clock! Kid Bean and the Killer ought to be back any minute now. Suddenly he looked up. The big touring car had turned and was coming back at full speed with its exhaust roaring. Rico cursed himself for his carelessness and reached under his armpit for his gun. But the car was abreast of him now and three guns blazed. Rico felt a searing pain in his shoulder and fell to the ground. His gun was stuck in its holster and he couldn't get it out. One of the men leaned out of the car and emptied his gun at Rico, who, helpless on the ground, heard the bullets sing.

"A goddam fine shot you are!" said Rico.

The big touring car turned a corner and disappeared. Rico got to his feet and walked into the drugstore. The screen door banged behind him and the clerk, who had been lying down behind the counter, got unsteadily to his feet.

"My God," he stammered, "what was all the popping for?"

Then he noticed that there was a torn place on the shoulder of Rico's coat.

"Was they after you, mister?" he asked.

"Yeah," said Rico, "I got brushed. Give me a roll of bandages."

The clerk stood there with his mouth open. People began to come into the store. Some of them knew who Rico was and stood staring at him.

"They put a bullet through my window," said the clerk.

"Listen," said Rico, "go get me a package of bandages."

The clerk finally came to himself and went for the bandages. A crowd had gathered in the street and now there were so many people in the drugstore that the people on the outside couldn't get in. Rico stood with his back to the counter, watching. Blood had begun to drip from his coat sleeve. Before the clerk returned with the bandages, Jastrow, the famous Little Italy cop, pushed his way through the crowd, followed almost immediately by Joe Massara.

"Well," said Jastrow, "somebody finally put one in you, did they, Rico?"

"Yeah," said Rico.

Joe Massara came over and put his hand on Rico's arm. Joe's face was white.

"Hurt you much, boss?"

"No," said Rico; "what the hell you doing way over here?"

"I got tipped off," said Joe. "I couldn't get you on the phone and I began to get nervous. We'd 've made it only my cab driver got hooked for speeding."

"Who gave you the tip?" Jastrow demanded.

"Go press the bricks," said Rico, "this ain't your funeral."

Jastrow laughed.

"Rico," he said, "don't you know that the Old Man's taken an awful interest in you?"

"Well, tell him the cops couldn't get me no other way so they hired a couple of gunmen."

Joe laughed. Jastrow laughed also and taking out his notebook began to write in it. The clerk came with the bandages. Joe took them from him and paid him. Before they could get started, Killer Pepi and Otero came shoving their way through the crowd.

"Hello, boys," said Jastrow, looking up from his little book, "your boss got nudged by a hunk of lead."

"So they tell me," said the Killer.

Rico said:

"Let's get the hell out of here."

Jastrow went in front, clearing the way, followed by Otero and Killer Pepi, who had Rico between them. Joe brought up the rear. People were lined to the car tracks; lights blazed in all the houses along the street, and men hung from the lampposts. When they came out of the store, the crowd was so thick that they were unable to get any farther. Jastrow took out his nightstick and flourished it, but the sight of it was enough, the crowd made a path.

As they walked along Joe came up close to Rico and whispered: "Little Arnie."

Rico nodded. Pepi heard Joe.

"Yeah," he said, "and I'm gonna plug him tonight."

"There won't be no plugging," said Rico.

"Aw, hell," said Pepi.

Otero was excited.

"Yes, yes, Rico," he cried.

"Shut up, you birds," said Rico; "who the hell's running this show?"

A crowd was waiting for them in front of The Palermo. Bat Carillo and Ottavio Vettori began to yell as soon as they saw that Rico was on his feet.

Jastrow turned around.

"Well, I guess I done my duty."

"Sure," said Rico, "come in and have a drink."

"Nothing doing," said Jastrow, then he shouted: "You birds quit your damn yelling and get in off the sidewalk."

Everybody laughed. They all liked Jastrow, who had the reputation of being on the square. Rico went in escorted by a mob of Little Italians. In the club people were standing on the tables; the orchestra was playing loudly; and Sam Vettori, in the middle of the deserted dance floor, was waving his arms wildly and bellowing.

When they saw Rico there was a tumult.

"Rico! Rico! Rico!"

Killer Pepi and Otero, intoxicated by the excitement, grabbed each other and began to dance. Joe waved the bandages. Rico took off his hat and smiled.

On the way up the stairs Rico turned to Joe and said:

"Go get The Sheeny."

Killer Pepi took Rico by the arm.

"He's upstairs now, boss," he said; "the Kid got plugged."

"How'd you make out?" Rico inquired.

"O. K.," said Killer Pepi; "we was making a getaway on the third stand when one of the guys plugged the Kid. He ain't hurt much. Just skinned him."

Killer Pepi and Kid Bean had robbed twenty-five filling stations in the last two weeks.

"All right," said Rico, "you guys have been on the up and up. Split the money two ways."

"That's the talk, boss," said the Killer.

Otero knocked at the door. Joe Sansone's face appeared at the grating, then the door swung open.

The Sheeny was working on Kid Bean. The Kid was lying on the card table, smoking a cigarette. His shirt was off and there was a smear of blood on his hairy chest. When he saw Rico he said:

"They damn near hit the target, boss."

He pointed to a pierced heart tattooed on his chest. He was as proud of his tattooing as a Maori chief.

"The boss got plugged," said Pepi.

"What!" yelled the Kid, sitting up; "go fix him up, Sheeny."

He gave The Sheeny a push. But Rico said:

"Finish up the Kid first. I can wait."

"Only jist got to bandage him yet," said The Sheeny with his ingratiating smile.

The Sheeny was a graduate doctor, but he had been sent up for an illegal operation and his license had been revoked. He said his name was Lazarro, but nobody believed him and everybody referred to him simply as The Sheeny.

Rico took off his coat and shirt, and sat waiting. His wound had stopped bleeding.

Joe Massara came over and stood by his chair. Joe's big cut for an inside job had pulled him back to the fold. He never talked anymore about quitting the racket. The Courtney affair had blown over apparently, and he had regained his confidence.

"Joe," said Rico, "how come they gave you the tip?"

"Well," said Joe, "I ain't sure, but I think it was an outsider that didn't know nobody but me. He sure had the dope all right. He said the guys were gonna park at twelve. They didn't expect you out till two or three."

"A fine bunch of gunmen Arnie picked!"

"Yeah," said Joe.

The Kid climbed off the table and stood feeling his chest.

"Boy, I thought I was plugged for sure."

"They just bounce off of you," said Pepi.

The Sheeny began to bathe Rico's wound.

"'Tain't much," he said, "but it pays to be careful."

When The Sheeny had got Rico bandaged, Rico put on his shirt and sat smoking. Bat Carillo and Ottavio Vettori, whom he had sent for, came in and sat down beside him. The Sheeny put on his hat.

"Well," he said, smiling at Rico, "I guess I'm done. If you guys have any trouble with them wounds let me know."

Rico got his billfold and gave The Sheeny a fifty.

"Thank you! Thank you!" said The Sheeny, bowing.

Joe Sansone let him out.

Rico said:

"Now, listen, you birds, tonight's the big cleanup. If these guys want trouble, why, that's just what we're looking for."

"You bet," said Killer Pepi.

"Now," Rico went on, "I got things fixed with Joe Peeper and I'm gonna to give Little Arnie the grand rush right away. I want Killer Pepi and Otero and Ottavio to go with me."

"How about me?" demanded Joe Sansone.

"You too, Joe. And you, Bat, I want you to take your gang and smash up Jew Mike's. Run everybody out and then smash the place. If Little Arnie wants trouble, why that's what we got the most of. Got it?"

"O.K.," said Bat, "how about the rods?"

"Don't use 'em," said Rico; "Jew Mike's yellow and he won't put up no fight."

"Them guys of mine sure are hard to hold on to," said Carillo, grinning.

"That's your job," said Rico. "We got to watch this plugging stuff with Flaherty on our trail."

"O. K., boss," said Carillo.

III

When the doorman saw Rico get out of the automobile he stood stunned, then, pulling himself together, he made an attempt to run. But Pepi crossed the pavement in two strides, grabbed him by the collar and pushed him ahead of him up the stairs.

"Listen, Handsome," said Pepi, "you tell the lookout we're O. K. or they'll bury you."

At the head of the stairs the doorman spoke to the lookout through the shutter.

"These birds are all right," he said.

The lookout opened the door and Pepi shoved a gun against him.

"Turn your back, Buddy," said Pepi, "and march straight ahead of me."

Rico, followed by Joe Sansone, Ottavio Vettori, and Otero, climbed the long flight of stairs and entered the lobby. The lobby was deserted except for two or three couples. Beyond it, through a big arched doorway, they could see the crowded roulette wheels. Rico caught up with Pepi and said to the doorman:

"Where's Joe Peeper?"

The doorman had an agonized look. He was sure they were going to kill him. He just stood there, unable to force himself to speak.

"Say," said Pepi, "speak up."

The doorman pointed to a door.

"He's in with the boss, is he?" said Rico.

The doorman nodded.

"Yeah," said the lookout, eager to get in good, "Joe's in there with the boss and a couple of other guys."

"All right," said Rico, "now, Pepi, if the door's locked, do your stuff."

Pepi could force the heaviest door with his shoulder.

Joe Sansone tried the door; it was locked.

"Now," said Rico, "Pepi'll force the door. You cover him, Joe, in case somebody in there gets nervous and pulls a gat. I'll follow you. Otero, you stay out here and don't let nobody in. You watch this pair of hard guys here, Ottavio." Rico jerked his thumb toward the lookout and the doorman.

"You don't have to watch us," said the doorman.

They all laughed.

"All right, Pepi," said Rico.

Pepi hunched his shoulders and flung himself against the door. It opened with a crash. They saw four startled men rise half way out of their chairs and stand staring. Joe Peeper cried:

"It's Rico!"

Pepi was on his hands and knees in the middle of the room, but Joe Sansone stepped in behind him and covered the four men with his big automatic. Rico came in, took off his hat and bowed.

"Hello, Arnie," he said; "how's business?"

Little Arnie sat with his mouth slightly open. As a rule Little Arnie was imperturbable. He hid an excess of both cunning and timidity behind a cold, repellent, sallow Jewish mask. But this cyclonic entry was too much for him. His mask had slipped, revealing a pale, terrified countenance.

"Well," he said, "what's the game?"

Joe Peeper, who was in Rico's pay, said: "Pull up a chair, you guys."

Pepi found two chairs. Joe Sansone and Rico sat down; Pepi stood behind Rico's chair.

Little Arnie turned to the two men sitting beside him. They were strangers to Rico and they looked tough.

"I don't know what this is all about," said Arnie, "but it's a private row, so you guys better beat it."

Rico said very quietly:

"Nobody's gonna leave this room."

One of the toughs shouted:

"Think not, wop! Well, who the hell's gonna stop us?"

Before Rico could reply, Joe Sansone said: "Me, I'm gonna stop you, see! And I ain't gentle. I'm just itching to put some lead in a couple of hard guys."

"Yeah," said Rico, smiling, "you guys are invited to this private party." The two men looked at Arnie, who sat tapping his desk with a pencil.

"Say," said one, "you sure got a fine bunch of friends, Arnie."

"Yeah," said Arnie.

Pepi laughed and said:

"Yeah, he sure has. Arnie, you ought to had better sense than to get a couple of outside yaps to bump Rico off."

Nobody said anything. Arnie took out a cigar and lit it. The two strangers sat staring at Rico. Pepi sat staring at them. Finally he asked:

"Where you guys from?"

The men looked uneasily at Arnie. Little by little they were losing their nerve.

"Speak up," said Pepi, "where you guys from?"

"We're from Detroit," said one of the men.

"Where the hell's that?" Joe Sansone inquired. "I never heard of it."

"Say," said Pepi, "don't you know that tough guys like you oughtn't to be running around loose. No sir. You're liable to get arrested for firing a rod in the city limits."

"Listen," said one of the men from Detroit, "what you guys got against us? We ain't done nothing. We just got in."

They were thoroughly intimidated.

Arnie, who had recovered his poise, said:

"Well, Rico, what's the talk? Let's have it."

Pepi and Joe Sansone both started to talk at once, but Rico motioned for them to be quiet.

"Arnie," said Rico, "you're through. If you ain't out of town by tomorrow morning, you won't never leave town except in a box."

Arnie said nothing but sat staring at the smoke rising from his cigar.

"In the first place," Rico went on, "you been double-crossing me for two months. In the second place you hire these bums here to pop me. Now I guess that's about all."

Arnie laughed.

"Rico," he said, "somebody has sure been stringing you. Why, you ought to know I wouldn't double-cross you. Hell, that wouldn't help me none."

"Can that," said Rico. "Your number's up, Jew. Take it like a man."

Arnie's face got red.

"Listen, Rico, if you think you can muscle into this joint you're off your nut."

"All right, Joe," said Rico, jerking his head in Joe Peeper's direction, "spill it."

Joe Peeper looked sideways at Arnie.

"The books're crooked, Rico," said Joe Peeper; "he's been gypping you out of half your split every week."

The Detroit toughs began to shift about uneasily.

"Well, you two-timing bastard," said Arnie.

Rico laughed.

"Arnie," he said, "that's that. Here's the dope. You get your hat and beat it. Leave the burg. If I ever hear about you being in town again, why, I'm gonna turn the Killer loose on you."

"Yeah," said Pepi, "and I never did like kikes."

"I ain't any too fond of them, myself," said Joe Sansone.

Arnie meditated. Rico said:

"I been square with you, Arnie, but you couldn't stand prosperity, that's all. So take it standing up."

"What the hell else can he do?" Pepi demanded.

"I'll tell you what I can do," said Arnie, "I can have a talk with Mr. Flaherty."

Arnie studied Rico carefully to see what effect this would have. But Rico merely smiled at him.

"Getting pretty low, Arnie," he said, "when you take the bulls in with you." Then he paused and leaned forward in his chair. "If you go to see Mr. Flaherty you better have an alibi because he might ask you about Limpy John."

Arnie dropped his cigar and sat staring into space, his hands lying palms up on the table.

"All over but the shouting," said Joe Sansone, "somebody better throw in a towel. But I don't suppose the dirty bums in Detroit ever heard of towels."

"Aw, lay off of us," said one of the Detroit toughs.

Joe Sansone stared at him.

"Say, Gyp-the-Blood, I bet they think you're a pretty hard bird where you live, don't they?"

Arnie turned to Joe Peeper.

"Well, Joe," he said, "you sure put the skids under me."

"Sure I did," said Joe Peeper; "you thought you could bat me around and make me like it."

Pepi laughed.

"Arnie," he said, "you better go back to Detroit with your boyfriends."

When Rico and his men left Arnie's joint Joe Peeper followed them. As soon as they reached the pavement, Joe walked up to Rico and said:

"You sore at me, Rico?"

All Rico's men stopped and stood staring at Joe, wondering what his game was.

"You guys get in the car," said Rico.

They all got in except Pepi, who stood with his back against the car, his right hand in his pocket. Pepi didn't trust anybody who had ever been mixed up with Little Arnie.

"What's on your mind, Joe?" Rico demanded.

"I thought you acted like you was sore at me," said Joe Peeper; "honest to God, Rico, I didn't know nothing about them Detroit bums. I didn't know what Arnie was up to. Lord, you know I wouldn't double-cross you after all you done for me."

"Well, who said you did?"

"Nobody," said Joe, "only it looked funny, and I thought maybe you guys had got a wrong notion. I'd be a sap to pull anything like that."

Rico laughed.

"Forget it," he said.

Rico started to get into the automobile, but Joe took hold of his arm.

"How about me, Rico?" he said. "If I stick around here they'll bump me off sure."

"Yeah?" said Rico; "say, them guys wouldn't bump nobody off now. But get in. I can use you, Joe."

Joe got in the back seat with Otero and Ottavio Vettori. He talked to them all the way back to The Palermo, trying to get in good with them but they said nothing.

IV

The next day in the society column of one of the Chicago papers there appeared a small item, which read:

> "Mr. Arnold Worch, of the North Side, has just left for Detroit where he intends to spend the summer. He was accompanied by two of his Detroit friends, who have been in Chicago for a short stay."

This was the work of Ottavio Vettori. The underworld was convulsed and thousands of extra copies of the paper were sold. The clipping was to be found pasted up in all the barrooms, gambling joints, and dancehalls. Rico and Ottavio Vettori had become famous overnight.

Little Arnie wasn't the only one who left town. Several of Little Arnie's henchmen, who had been closely connected with the attempted killing, followed him into exile. Joseph Pavlovsky, the doorman, who had driven the car, went to Hammond, where, on the money Arnie had given him, he opened a speakeasy. Pippy Coke, who with the two Detroit gunmen had done the shooting, went with Pavlovsky, and they were followed by two croupiers, who had shadowed Rico.

Arnie's gang was smashed and the Little Italians took over a territory they hadn't controlled since the days of Monk De Angelo.

Arnie had come to Chicago from New York about five years ago. His reputation had got so bad in New York that no one would do business with him. He came west with a small stake and was lucky enough to arrive at just the right time. Kips Berger, also formerly of New York and once one of Arnie's pals, had gone broke and was willing to sell out his big gambling joint for practically nothing. Arnie bought it and prospered. This gambling joint was in a neutral zone, touching Little Italy on the south and the vast territory that Pete Montana controlled on the north. Arnie was acute enough to see his advantage. He worked hard at his job and in a little while had consolidated his territory. But he was not a good gang chief: first, because he was a coward, second, because his closest associate couldn't trust him, third, because he was inclined to lose his head in an emergency. His lieutenant, Jew Mike, was a tougher and more violent replica of his chief. Between them they bossed the territory, but under them the gang never prospered and their hold was at best precarious. They held on only because there was little or no opposition. Their gangsters were a poor lot and were content to take small splits. On the south, Sam Vettori was slipping and his lethargy prevented him interfering; on the north the great Pete Montana was magnificently indifferent.

Arnie had been slipping for the last year or so, and Rico's sudden rise had accelerated his decline. Arnie, fearing the worst, committed blunder after blunder; first, he made advances to Rico, then, getting Rico's protection for a thirty percent split, things looked too easy and he began to double-cross him. Lastly, although he should have known better, he made the tactical error of trying to get Rico killed. If he had succeeded his position would not have been improved; he would have been worse off, because the Vettori gang would have made short work of him.

No one regretted the passing of Little Arnie. He had never been straight with anybody. No one could depend on him and he had none of the qualities that go to make up a good gang chief. The wonder is that he lasted as long as he did.

Arnie's fall was the signal for a series of minor tumbles. Jew Mike, whose joint Bat Carillo and his gang had demolished, fled to the South

Side, where he opened a couple of vice joints. Kid Burg moved to Cicero, and Squint Maschke, after a short exile, offered his services to Rico, who gave him twenty-four hours to make a second disappearance. With the fall of Arnie's three lieutenants, the last vestiges of his rule vanished.

V

Otero helped Rico out of his coat, then, while Rico doused his face at the washstand, he sat down, tipped back his chair and rolled himself a cigarette.

"You better lay down, Rico, and get some rest," said Otero; "you ain't looking so good."

"I'm O. K.," said Rico.

But this was bravado. He had slept only four hours in the last two days; his face was pale and drawn and he suffered from an intermittent fever. His wound, though a slight one, was not healing properly, and The Sheeny had warned him that he had better take it easy. Inactivity at any time was abhorrent to Rico; now it was impossible. His big chance had come. Nothing could stop him now but a hunk of lead in the right spot.

Rico, a little unsteady on his legs, stood staring at Otero.

"You're sure making yourself at home," he said.

"Well," said Otero, "I think I stay."

Rico laughed.

"Listen, I don't need no nurse. Beat it."

"No," said Otero, tossing away his cigarette and starting to roll another one, "I think I stay."

Rico walked over to the bed and stood staring at it. If he had been alone he would have flopped down and been asleep in an instant.

"Think I'll catch a little sleep," he said; "you beat it, Otero."

Otero didn't say anything. He finished rolling his cigarette, lit it, and tipped his hat down over his eyes.

"Goddam it," cried Rico, "beat it! I'm sick of you trailing me like a Chicago Avenue bull. I ain't gonna drop in my tracks."

"All right," said Otero, "you lay down. I finish my cigarette."

Rico threw himself on the bed, fully dressed except for his coat. He put his hands under his head and tried to keep awake by staring at the ceiling. But in a moment he was asleep.

Otero sat looking at his chief. All along he'd known. Rico was a great man like Pancho Villa. Even in Toledo when he and Rico were sticking up filling stations, he knew. A little, skinny young fellow with a little mustache, sure, that's what everybody saw. But everybody didn't have the eyes of Otero.

Otero flung his second cigarette on the floor and rolled another one. Rico turned from side to side in his sleep and mumbled. His face was white and drawn. Otero got to his feet and went over to look at him. No, Rico was not well. Otero put his hand on Rico's forehead. Fever! He stood looking down at his chief, shaking his head.

"Like hell!" cried Rico; "you can't hand Rico none of that bunk. No Irish bastard'll ever put no cuffs on Rico."

Otero went back to his chair and sat dozing under his big hat, while Rico tossed from side to side and talked.

Someone knocked at the door. Otero was slow in opening his eyes, but Rico sat up, stared for a moment, then jumped out of bed and got his automatic.

"Go see who it is," he said to Otero; "don't open the door. Ask them."

Otero went over to the door and called:

"Who's there?"

There was a short silence, then a voice with a marked Italian accent said:

"A couple of right guys. We want to see Rico."

Otero turned and looked at Rico, who came over to the door.

"Listen, you right guys," said Rico, "I'll give you a one-two-three to get out of that hall and then I'm gonna start pumping lead. Got it?"

There was a pause.

"Rico," said another voice, a deeper voice with no trace of an accent, "you don't know me, but I'm Pete Montana and I want to talk turkey."

Otero and Rico exchanged a stupefied look.

"Pete," said Rico, "do you know the Big Boy?"

"Sure."

"What's his name in full?"

"James Michael O'Doul."

"All right, Otero," said Rico, "let 'em in."

Otero unbarred the door. Rico, with his gun still leveled, stood a little behind the door, watching.

Pete Montana, followed by Ritz Colonna, his lieutenant, came in. Montana, in private life Pietro Fontano, was a big, solemn, respectable-looking Italian. He was dressed very quietly, wore no jewelry, and carried a cane. Colonna, once a ham prizefighter, was a small, bull-necked man with a battered, dark face. His clothes were shabby and he wore an old cap on the side of his head.

Montana and Rico stood measuring each other. Rico looked small and frail beside the robust Montana, but Rico wasn't impressed, for Montana looked fat and puffy, like Sam Vettori. Otero barred the door.

"Get a couple of chairs, Otero," said Rico.

Otero dragged up the only two chairs in the room and Montana and Colonna sat down. Otero squatted on his heels with his back to the wall and Rico sat on the bed.

Montana took out a monogrammed cigar case and passed it around, then he selected one of the cigars himself and cut off the end with a little gold cutter on his watch chain.

"Mopping up, ain't you, Rico?" asked Montana, who kept his eyes lowered.

"Well," said Rico, "Arnie was double-crossing me."

"He wasn't no good," said Colonna; "I was just aching to bump that bird off."

Montana motioned for him to be quiet.

"They slung some lead, didn't they, Rico?"

"Yeah, and I stopped some of it. Nothing to shout about."

"If he'd 've got you, his number was up," said Montana, "you know, I been watching you ever since you muscled in on Sam Vettori."

"Yeah?"

"Sure thing. We been taking an interest in you, ain't we, Ritz?"

Ritz grinned.

"That's the word," he said.

"Sure," said Montana, "you're on the up and up with us."

"Well," said Rico, "that's O. K. with me."

Montana looked up at Rico suddenly.

"Any guy that can muscle in on Sam Vettori and Little Arnie is on the up and up with me. The Big Boy's with me there."

Rico smoked and said nothing. But he wondered what the game was. Was Pete Montana getting soft like Sam Vettori? Could it be possible that the great Pete Montana was turning sap? All this palaver and softie talk. Rico's head began to buzz.

"Look," said Montana, "I used to work Arnie's territory myself, but it slowed down, you know what I mean. It wasn't worth nothing when Kips Berger had it, and after Arnie got it I didn't pay no attention. I got all I can handle, ain't I, Ritz?"

"That's the word," said Ritz.

"Yeah," said Montana, "by rights that territory's mine, get the idea? I could get all the protection I wanted, but I don't muscle in on no right guy, see? Kiketown's yours, Rico."

"Much obliged," said Rico; "I ain't looking for no trouble with you, Pete."

"That's the talk," said Montana; then he turned to Ritz: "see, Ritz, you had the wrong steer."

"Yeah, I had the wrong steer," said Ritz.

Montana turned back to Rico.

"Yeah," he said, "some wise guys was giving Ritz a lot of bull. Ritz said you was trying to muscle in on my territory."

Rico thought he was dreaming. So this was the great Pete Montana. A guy that couldn't turn over in bed without getting plastered all over the front page. All that softie stuff was a front. Pete Montana was scared.

"No," said Rico, "them guys don't know what they're talking about."

Montana smiled blandly.

"Maybe we can team up on a job or two, Rico. I like your work. The Big Boy's no fool and he thinks you're the goods. Yeah, maybe we can team up, but I ain't making no promises. Only this. I ain't looking for no split on Arnie's layout. She's yours."

"Don't forget the hideout, chief," said Ritz.

Montana smiled again.

"By God, I sure enough did forget it. Yeah, Rico, some of Ritz's boys has got a hideout a half a block from Arnie's joint. That's O. K., ain't it?"

Rico's manner changed. He lost his affability and his face became serious.

"Well," he said, "as long as there ain't no cutting in. I won't stand for no cutting in."

Montana looked at Ritz. Ritz said:

"Hell, there won't be no cutting in."

"What do you say, Pete?" asked Rico.

Montana meditated, pulling at one of his thick lips. Otero sat watching Rico. Caramba! Here was little Rico telling the big Pete Montana where to get off. Otero never took his eyes off Rico's face.

"Well," said Montana, "they're my men and I'm behind them. If there's any cutting in, why, I'll settle with you, Rico. Christ, no use for us to fight over a little thing like that. Anyway, if we get along, I'll put you in on the alcohol racket."

"All right," said Rico, "you and me can do business, Pete."

Montana got up and offered Rico his hand. They pumped arms briefly. Then Pete said: "Well, I guess we'll saunter. But let me give you a tip, Rico. You're getting too much notice, get the idea? You got the bulls watching you. I know a new guy has always got to expect that, but take it easy for a while. They'll go to sleep; they always do."

Rico admired Montana's shiftiness, but he wasn't fooled. Pete was trying to tie him up, make him leery.

"Much obliged," said Rico; "a new guy has got a lot to learn."

Montana smiled blandly, certain he had scored. "Well," said Montana, "so long. Maybe I'll drop down to your new joint and give it the once over some night."

"All right," said Rico, "just let me know."
Otero unbarred the door. Montana started out; Ritz offered his hand to Rico, then followed his chief. Otero barred the door.
Rico stood in the middle of the room, staring into space. Otero said: "He ain't so much."
Rico laughed out loud.
"Otero," he cried, "you said a mouthful."

PART VI

I

Rico felt small and unimportant in the Big Boy's apartment. He was intensely self-centered and as a rule surroundings made no impression on him. But he had never seen anything like this before. He sat in the big, paneled dining room, eating cautiously, dropping his fork from nervousness, and looking furtively about him. From time to time he pulled at his high, stiff collar, and when he caught the Big Boy's eye he grinned.

Joe Sansone had dressed him so that he would look presentable. It had taken a good deal of management and tact, but Joe Sansone was a stickler for clothes and persevered with Rico, who swore at him at first and wouldn't listen.

"Look, boss," he said, "you're getting up in the world. Ain't none of us ever been asked to eat with the Big Boy at his dump. Hear what I'm telling you. Nobody's ever crashed the gates before but Pete Montana. See what I mean? You don't want the Big Boy to think you ain't got no class."

Joe had his own dress suit cleaned and pressed, and punctually at five he presented himself at Rico's door with the outfit under his arm. Rico had resisted from the beginning; first, he balked at the suspenders, then the starched shirt. Joe, laboring with the studs, the buttoned shoes, the invincible collar, cursed and sweated. Rico resisted. But Joe won.

As Joe was ten pounds heavier than Rico, the dress suit was not precisely a perfect fit, but as Joe said "men are wearing their clothes a lot looser now." To which Rico sardonically replied: "Yeah? Say, they rig you up better than this in stir."

Finally Joe got Rico into his harness. Rico stamped about declaring that he'd be goddamned if he'd go out looking like that. Why, the Big Boy would think he was off his nut.

"You look fine, boss," said Joe.

"Yeah," said Rico, "all I need is a napkin over my arm."

But Joe moved Rico's bureau out from its corner and tipped the mirror so Rico could get a full length view of himself. He was won over immediately. Why, honest to God, he looked like one of them rich clubmen he read about in the magazines. The enormous white shirtfront, the black silk coat lapels, the neatly-tied white tie dazzled him.

"I guess I don't look so bad," he said to Joe; "we got plenty of time, let's go down to Sam's place for a while."

Rico played with his dessert and looked about the room. The Big Boy ate with gusto, smacking his lips. The magnificence of the Big Boy's apartment crushed Rico. He stared at the big pictures of old-time guys in their gold frames; at the silver and glass ware on the serving table; at the high, carved chairs. Lord, why, it was like a hop dream.

He shook his head slowly.

"Some dump you got here," he said.

"Yeah," said the Big Boy, glancing negligently about him, "and I sure paid for it. See that picture over there?" He pointed to an imitation Velásquez. "That baby set me back one hundred and fifty berries."

Rico stared.

"Jesus, one hundred and fifty berries for a picture!"

"Yeah," said the Big Boy, "but that ain't nothing. See that bunch of junk over there?" He jerked his head in the direction of the serving table. "That stuff set me back one grand."

Rico stared.

"One grand for that stuff?"

"Sure," said the Big Boy, "that's the real thing. Only what the hell, I say! A plate's to eat off of, ain't it? What's the odds what it's made of? But I got a spell about two years ago. I had a pot full of money and I thought, well, other guys that ain't got as much dough as I got put on a front, so why shouldn't I? Sure, I could buy and sell guys that's got three homes and a couple of chugwagons. So I got a guy down at a big store, you know, one of them decorators, to pick me out a swell apartment and fix it up A-1. So he did. I got a library too and a lot of other stuff that ain't worth a damn. I was talking to a rich guy the other day and he said I was a damn fool to buy real books because he had a library twice as big as mine and dummy books. What the hell! If a guy's gonna have a library, why, I say do it right. So there you are. I got so damn many books it gives me a headache just to look at 'em through the glass. Shakespeare and all that stuff."

"Yeah?" said Rico, stupefied.

A servant took away their dessert and brought coffee. Then he passed a humidor full of cigars. Rico took one of the fat, black cigars, lit it, and tipped his chair back. What a way to live!

"Yeah," said the Big Boy, "I got a lot of dough tied up in this dump. I get rent free, though. Eschelman, the contractor, owns this dump and he knows how I stand in the city. Boy, he puts up what he pleases and gets away with it. See the idea, Rico? If a guy stands in with me, he owns the burg."

"Sure," said Rico, "you're a big guy."

"I get him contracts, too," said the Big Boy; "course I get mine out of it, but I made that guy. When he come here from down state he didn't have an extra pair of pants, now he's climbing. Yeah, if I had a wife and a couple of kids, why, I'd build me a big house out in some swell suburb, but as it is, I'd just as leave be here on one floor. I got everything I need and then some."

"Sure," said Rico.

"Let's go in the library," said the Big Boy, "it's more comfortable in there."

The Big Boy told the servant to take their coffee into the library. Then he got up and Rico followed him. The Big Boy put his hand on Rico's shoulder.

"Kind of lit up yourself tonight, ain't you, Rico?"

"Yeah, I thought I better put on the monkey suit."

"That's right, Rico. May as well learn now."

"Sure," said Rico.

The Big Boy motioned Rico to a chair, then sat down. Rico looked about him at the great expanse of glass guarding tier after tier of books. Lord, if a guy'd read that many books he'd sure know a lot!

"Rico," said the Big Boy, "let's talk serious."

"All right," said Rico.

The Big Boy leaned forward in his chair and stared at Rico.

"Listen," he said, "I'm gonna talk and you ain't gonna hear a word I say, see, this is inside dope and if it gets out it'll be just too bad for somebody."

"You know me," said Rico.

"All right," said the Big Boy; "get this: if I didn't think a hell of a lot of you I wouldn't be asking you to eat with me. You're on the square, Rico, and you're a comer, see. You got the nerve and you're a good, sober, steady guy. That's what we need. Trouble with most of these guys they ain't got nothing from the collar up. O. K. Now, listen. Pete Montana's through."

Rico nearly leapt out of his chair.

"Yeah?"

"Now don't get excited," said the Big Boy, "because, when it gets out, there's gonna be hell to pay. Ritz Colonna and a couple of other lowdown bums is gonna make a rush, see, and that means that somebody's gonna get hurt."

"Sure," said Rico, settling back.

"But not you," said the Big Boy; "you're gonna lay back and let them dumb eggs bump each other off, then we'll get our licks in, see? Pete's through. The Old Man's gonna have a talk with him tomorrow or the next day and Pete's gonna mosey. He's all swelled up, thinks he's king and all that stuff, but wait till the Old Man gets through with him. Why, he can hang that guy. Besides that, he can turn the Federal guys loose on him for peddling narcotics. And boy, how he peddles them! He built that big house of his on 'em. Well, see how things are? I can't spill no more."

"Well," said Rico, "I'm on."

"All right," said the Big Boy, "but listen: I'm doing a hell of a lot for you and when I get you planted I want plenty of service."

"You'll sure get it," said Rico.

Rico, with the Big Boy's cigar still between his teeth, lay back in the taxi and stared out at the tangle of traffic on Michigan Boulevard. Things were sure to God looking up! Five years ago he wasn't nobody to speak of; just a lonely yegg, sticking up chain-stores and filling stations. Chiggi had sure given him the right dope. He remembered one night in Toledo when he was pretty low. There was a blonde he used to meet at one of the call-houses and she sure did satisfy him, but, boy, she had to have the coin on the nose or there wasn't nothing doing. Well, he didn't have a red. He was just sitting there in Chiggi's thinking about the blonde, when Chiggi came over and said: "Listen, kid, you got big town stuff in you. What you want around here? Get somebody to stake you or hit the rods. Hell, don't be a piker." Well, Chiggi staked him, but he blew the stake on the blonde, oh, boy what a couple of days, and then he hit the rods with Otero. Little Italy sure looked good to them. They didn't have a good pair of pants between them, and a bowl of mulligan tasted better than the stuff he'd ate at the Big Boy's. Well, here he was riding taxis and hobnobbing with guys like James O'Doul, who paid one grand for a bunch of crockery. Yeah, here he was!

Rico saw nothing but success in the future. With the Big Boy behind him he couldn't be stopped, and when he once got some place he knew how to stay there. Play square with the guys that are square with you; the hell with everybody else.

Rico smoked his cigar slowly (he had six more of them in his pocket), and looked absently at the jam of traffic: taxis, Hispano-Suizas, Fords, huge double-decked buses, leaning as they turned corners. Rico dropped the cigar butt out the window. Lying back in his seat he observed:

"And I thought Pete Montana was such a hell of a guy!"

II

Olga was only partly dressed when Joe burst in on her. She looked at him, startled. "My Lord," she said, "what makes you so pale, Joe?"

"Got any liquor?" demanded Joe.

Olga opened a drawer and handed him a flask. He tipped it up and took a long pull, then he stood with the flask in his hand staring at the wall.

"Joe," Olga insisted, "what's wrong with you?"

Joe came to himself, screwed the top on the flask, and handed it back to Olga.

"Boy, I got a shock," said Joe.

Olga came over and put her arm around him. "Tell Olga all about it."

"Well," said Joe, "I was finishing up my Pierrot dance, see, and you know when it's dark and they got the spot on you you can't see nothing. Well, I was circling the outside of the floor like I do before I take that last leap when some dame at a corner table gives a yell, a hell of a yell. Sibby hears the yell and switches on all the lights and here I am, right in front of a dame that looks like she's off her nut. She was standing up and she had her hands on the table and she was staring right at me. If I didn't feel funny, boy! Well, there was a guy with her and he kept asking her what was the matter, but she wouldn't say nothing. I thought she was gonna jump right on me, she looked so funny, yeah, that dame sure looked funny."

Joe paused and meditated. Olga laughed.

"Listen," she said, "you better lay off the liquor."

"No, straight," said Joe, "you know I kind of got the idea she recognized me or something, but, hell, I never seen her before. She's an old dame, about forty, and she's got peroxide hair. There was a guy with her, a nice-looking guy, and he kept saying, 'What's the matter, Nell, what's the matter, Nell,' but he couldn't get nothing out of her."

Olga laughed again.

"Well, this ain't nothing to write home about," she said. "I thought I was gonna get a thrill. We better change bootleggers, Joe."

"Aw, lay off," said Joe. "I'm telling you, you'd 've got all the kick you're looking for if you'd heard that dame yell."

"Well, what happened?" demanded Olga, who was getting impatient.

Joe got out the flask and took another pull at it before he answered her. The color had come back into his face now and he felt much better.

"Soon as the boss found out there was something wrong he came in and asked this dame if he could do anything for her. And she says, 'Yes, get me a taxi.' The guy with her says, 'What the devil, Nell.' And she says, 'I want to go home.' So they went out. Boy, the way that dame looked at me, like I was, God, I don't know what!"

"Say, listen," said Olga, "you been hitting the pipe?"

"Aw, lay off," said Joe; "that dame's got something on her mind, see. She's got something on her mind."

Someone knocked. Olga called "come in" and a waiter opened the door and bowed.

"Mr. Willoughby wants to know if we can bring the table in now, Miss Stassoff."

"Sure," said Olga, "bring it in."

"Yes, ma'am," said the waiter, then he cupped his hands and called down the corridor: "Allez!"

Joe lay down on the lounge and lit a cigarette. Olga went over to her dressing table, made up her face, and put on her Japanese kimono.

Two waiters came in carrying a table; a third followed with a cloth and silver. When the table was set one of the waiters said:

"Mr. Willoughby wants to know if he can come back now."

"Sure," said Olga, "tell him to come right back."

"Shall we start to serve?"

"Yeah," said Olga, "right away."

When the waiters had gone, Joe said:

"I'm getting fed up with this Willoughby guy. He's a dumb egg."

"Sure he's dumb," said Olga, "but I don't hold that against him. What I like about that bird is that he don't get his hand stuck in his pocket when the boy comes around with the bill."

"He sure don't, that's a fact," said Joe, laughing.

"Well, then don't be so particular," said Olga; "guys like him are few and far between."

Willoughby tapped lightly on the door and then came in. He was freshly shaven and he looked chubby and boyish.

Joe got up and shook hands with him. Olga said:

"Was you out front?"

"Yes," said Willoughby; "by the way, Joe, what was all the commotion?"

"See," said Joe, turning to Olga. "She thought I was making it up, Mr. Willoughby."

"No, he wasn't making it up," said Willoughby, serious. "I never heard such a scream in my life."

"Don't remind me," said Joe; "boy, my hair stood straight up."

A waiter came in carrying a wine bucket, followed by another waiter carrying the soup.

"Well," said Willoughby, "shall we monjay, as they say in France?"

"Oui, monsieur," said Olga.

"Sure," said Joe, "I'm ready for the feed bag in any language."

They sat down. One of the waiters poured the wine. Willoughby held his glass up to the light.

"I hope you like this stuff," he said, "it's out of my own cellar."

"I'd like to sleep in that cellar," said Olga.

"Well," said Willoughby, "you have a standing invitation."

They ate in silence for a moment, then Joe said:

"Say, Mr. Willoughby, what you suppose was the matter with that dame?"

"I couldn't say."

"Oh, forget it, Joe," said Olga, "she was probably full of hop."

III

Willoughby passed the cigarettes and they all left the table. Joe went back to the lounge, Olga sat in one of the armchairs, and Willoughby pulled up an ottoman and sat facing her.

Willoughby hesitated before he said:

"Olga, when we going to take that little trip?"

"I don't know," said Olga.

"What little trip?" asked Joe, looking at Olga.

"Why, I got a cabin up in Wisconsin," said Willoughby, "and I thought before it got cold it would be nice for Olga to go up and take a rest."

"Yeah?" said Joe.

As soon as Willoughby lowered his eyes, Olga winked at Joe.

"Maybe I could pull it," said Olga.

"Sure," said Joe, "Olga works too hard, that's a fact. A little rest wouldn't hurt her none."

"That's just what I was thinking," said Willoughby. "She could sure get a rest up there. I got a couple of nice motor boats and the fishing's great."

"Fishing!" said Olga, looking at Joe.

"Well," Willoughby considered, "maybe you wouldn't care for that, but there are any number of things you could do. Anyway, the air's great, nothing like this Chicago muck."

"Sounds good," said Olga.

The waiters came in to take away the table, but they were immediately followed by DeVoss, who motioned them out. There was something so strange about DeVoss's actions that Joe sat up and stared at him. DeVoss said:

"Joe, there's a couple of guys looking for you."

"Yeah?" said Joe. "What kind of guys?"

"Bulls," said DeVoss, "what you been up to?"

Olga got to her feet and stood staring at DeVoss. Willoughby exclaimed:

"What's all this! What's all this!"

Joe took an automatic from his hip pocket and put it in Olga's dressing table. Olga took hold of DeVoss's arm and said:

"Tell them Joe ain't here. Joe, honey, beat it. I'll see if I can find out what it's all about."

Willoughby was staring stupefied at Joe. He pointed to the dressing table.

"What do you carry that thing for?" he demanded.

Olga said:

"Oh, be quiet!"

Joe grinned at Willoughby.

"Just in case," he said.

"Listen, Olga," said DeVoss, "this is serious. I could tell the way they acted. I told them I didn't think Joe was here but they just laughed."

Joe stood undecided.

"Joe," DeVoss went on, "remember that time Mr. Rico was over here and a couple of bulls shadowed him? Well, the big one's here."

"Flaherty!" cried Joe.

Olga gave Joe a push.

"Beat it, Joe. You know them bulls. They'll frame you."

"O. K., honey," said Joe.

"Why, Joe," said Willoughby, "you mean to tell me you're in some kind of trouble?"

"Oh, be quiet," said Olga.

Joe grabbed his hat from a chair and started for the door.

"Goodbye, honey," he said to Olga, "you'll hear from me."

"Better face the music," said Willoughby.

"Go out through the kitchen," said DeVoss.

Joe opened the door but closed it immediately and said:

"It's all up. Here they come."

He looked in agony at Olga. Wasn't this just his goddam luck! Penned up in a room three stories above the pavement. He made a dash for the dressing table, but Olga grabbed his arm.

"For God's sake, Joe," said DeVoss, "don't cause no trouble in my place. I don't know what they want you for and I don't give a damn. I'll get you a lawyer and see you through, but, for God's sake, don't do no shooting in my place."

Willoughby, stunned, sat staring till his cigarette burned his fingers, then he said:

"Don't worry, Joe. I'll see you through, too."

"Goddam it," cried Joe, "you think I'm gonna let 'em take me like I was a purse snatcher on his first stand."

He pushed Olga away from him and was pulling at the dressing table drawer, when the door opened and Flaherty came in, followed by Spike Rieger. Flaherty had his right hand in his coat pocket.

"Joe," said Flaherty, "step away from that drawer and make it snappy."

Joe knew Flaherty's reputation. That boy used his rod and argued afterwards. Joe moved away from the dressing table and stood staring at the floor.

"What's the idea, Flaherty?" he demanded.

"Well," said Flaherty, "we got a big audience here and I ain't much on embarrassing people, so you better just come along and we'll have a nice little talk."

"Aw, can that," said Joe.

Willoughby walked over to Flaherty.

"My name's Willoughby," he said, "John C. Willoughby. I suppose you've heard of me. Say, what's this all about anyway? Why, I've known Joe for nearly a year and as far as I know he's a nice young fellow."

"Yeah," said Flaherty, "Joe's a pretty smooth young fellow, but we caught up with him."

"Well," said Willoughby, "I don't know what he's done, but I'm willing to go on his bail."

Flaherty turned to Rieger.

"I don't suppose there'll be much talk about bail, do you, Spike?"

Rieger grinned and shook his head.

"No bail!" Willoughby exclaimed.

"Aw, it's just one of their wise frame-ups, Mr. Willoughby," said Joe, but his face was white.

"Well, we'll see about this," said Willoughby. "I'll have my lawyer down in half an hour."

"Listen," said Flaherty, "there ain't nobody gonna see this bird for twenty-four hours."

Olga flung herself on the lounge and began to cry.

"And let me give you an earful, Mr. Willoughby," said Flaherty; "for a guy of your class you sure ain't very careful about who you mix up with. These two birds here are taking you, see, and if I was you I'd snap out of it and forget all about getting a lawyer."

"If that ain't a bull for you," said Joe.

"Don't pay no attention to him, Jack," said Olga.

"Certainly not," said Willoughby.

"All right, Spike," said Flaherty, "I guess we wasted enough time on these birds. Put the cuffs on him."

Olga jumped up and made a grab for Rieger, but DeVoss caught her from the back and held her.

"You can't do nothing that way, Olga," he said, "you'll just make it tough for Joe."

Olga screamed with rage and kicked back at DeVoss.

"Ain't dames awful?" said Flaherty.

Willoughby went over to Olga and tried to talk to her, but she continued to struggle. Rieger took out his handcuffs and walked over to Joe.

"Wait a minute," said Joe, "you can't put no bracelets on me. Where's your warrant?"

Rieger took the warrant out of his pocket and handed it to Joe. Joe read it slowly, then, without comment, handed it back.

"Well, Joe," said Flaherty.

Joe didn't say anything; he just held out his wrists.

"What do they want you for, Joe?" cried Olga.

"Never mind," said Joe, "they ain't got no case."

Olga stopped struggling.

"You mean it, Joe?"

"Sure," said Joe, "they ain't got no case at all. I'll be out in twenty-four hours."

"Shall I get my lawyer?" asked Willoughby.

"Ain't much use," said Joe.

DeVoss came over to Flaherty and said:

"Listen, Mr. Flaherty, take him out through the kitchen, can't you? I can't have cops coming in here pinching people."

"You got a nerve," said Flaherty; "why, I ought to pull you in for complicity. Didn't you come back here and tip Joe off?"

DeVoss got pale.

"Honest to God, I didn't tip him off. I just told him a couple of guys wanted to see him."

"Pipe down," said Flaherty. "Come on, Joe, let's take a ride."

Joe's face was ghastly, but he grinned.

"O. K.," he said; "it's the first ride I ever took with any of you birds."

"Well, I hope it's the last," said Flaherty.

"Want me to come down and see you, Joe?" asked Olga.

"No," said Joe.

They put Joe between two policemen in the back seat of the police car. Rieger and Flaherty sat in front. The traffic was light as it was nearly three o'clock in the morning. Rieger drove carelessly, one hand on the wheel most of the time, and talked to Flaherty.

"Boy," said Joe, "that bird don't care how he drives."
"You ain't got far to go," said one of the policemen.
"No, but I ain't sure of getting there."
The policemen laughed.
"Say," said Joe, "can I smoke?"
One of the policemen leaned forward.
"Say, chief, can this bird smoke?"
"No," said Flaherty; "what the hell you think this is, Joe! Maybe we better pick up a couple of girls for you."
The policemen laughed.
"Funny thing," said Joe, "you know, Flaherty, a friend of mine told me the other day that he didn't think you'd live long."
"Yeah," said Flaherty, "I know that friend of yours. He ain't looking any too healthy himself."

For as late as it was there was a good deal of activity at the station. A dozen plainclothes men were waiting in the big room, when they brought Joe in, and the Assistant County Prosecutor was standing at the desk talking to the sergeant.
"Looks like big doings," said Joe.
"Shut up," said Flaherty; "recess is over. You open your mouth again and I'll close it for you."
They took Joe up to the desk to book him.
"Well, you got him," said the prosecutor, looking Joe over.
"Yeah, we got him," said Flaherty. "Did you chase the newspaper guys?"
"Yeah," said the prosecutor, "there won't be no leaks to this."
"O. K.," said Flaherty.
The sergeant nodded to him.
"All right, chief."
Flaherty took Joe by the arm.
"All right, Joe," he said, "we're gonna give you a nice little room."
"With bath?" asked Joe.
"Listen, boy," said Flaherty, "we're gonna take all that smartness out of you."
Joe didn't say anything. He was trying to keep up his front until they locked him in his cell, but he was ready to drop. They had him; they sure to God had him.
The turnkey swung the big barred door wide. Flaherty took Joe to the door of his cell, unlocked the handcuffs, and gave him a push.
"All right, boy," he said, "I'll be back later."
"Listen, Flaherty," said Joe, "can't I even have a smoke?"

Flaherty laughed, motioned for the turnkey to lock the cell door, and disappeared down the corridor.

"Say, buddy," said Joe to the turnkey, "can't you get me a pack of cigarettes?"

"Nothing doing," said the turnkey, "not for fifty bucks. I got strict orders on you, boy."

The turnkey went away. Joe stood in the middle of his cell for a moment, then he climbed up on his bunk and looked out the window. Far away down a side street he saw a big electric sign: DANCING.

Joe flung himself down on his bunk. They had him; they sure to God did.

"If I can only stick it out!" he said.

IV

Joe awoke from a doze and turned to look out the window. Still dark. He couldn't have been asleep long. Wasn't it never going to get light! He got up and walked to the front of his cell. It wouldn't be so bad if there were some other guys to talk to; but the cells on either side of him were vacant; also the ones across the corridor.

"They sure ain't taking no chances with me," said Joe.

He began to feel very uneasy. Something seemed to be dragging at his stomach and he had a rotten taste in his mouth.

"Some of that high-hat grub I et," said Joe.

The turnkey came down the corridor and stopped in front of Joe's cell.

"Say, buddy," he said, "they'll be wanting you up front pretty soon."

"Yeah?" said Joe. "Listen, can't you do me a favor and get me a pack of cigs. I got plenty of money. Ask the sergeant."

"Can't cut it," said the turnkey.

"What's doing up front?" asked Joe.

"A show-up."

"Yeah?" said Joe; then, "listen, I'll give you a couple of bucks for some cigs."

The turnkey laughed.

"Say, there's a guy in 18 that'd give me a hundred berries for some snow. Not a chance. They sure are putting the clamps on us now. It's that goddam Crime Commission business. Tough on you birds."

"Ain't it!" said Joe.

The turnkey went away. Joe threw himself down on his bunk. Yeah, now it was coming. That goddam peroxide dame had sure put the skids under him. Well, there you was! Can't tell how things are going to break. If he'd 've been wise he'd 've sent Olga to see the Big Boy or

Rico. But then there's no use letting a dame get too familiar with everything. Anyway, he had an alibi. But Flaherty was a rough agent and you could never tell what he would pull. Joe felt mechanically for his absent cigarette case.

"Hell," he said, "I lost my head! I lost my head! Rico ought to put a hunk of lead in me. As long as I been in the game and then don't know no better. God, but I was dumb."

He turned over irritably and sat up. He heard the keys clanking down the corridor. A policeman stopped in front of his door and called:

"All right, dago."

Joe got up. The turnkey unlocked the door. There were two policemen and a plainclothes man standing a little way down the corridor. When Joe came out one of the policemen said:

"There's the guy that plugged Courtney."

They stared at him. Joe felt sick at his stomach.

"Yeah," said the plainclothes man, "they won't do much to that bird."

The turnkey took Joe by the arm.

"All right, kid," he said.

Joe walked between the turnkey and the policeman, who had called him. They took him into a big room where there were three policemen and about a dozen prisoners. Joe saw Bugs Liska, Steve Gollancz's lieutenant. They exchanged a glance.

A police sergeant got to his feet and shouted: "All right, you birds, let's go."

The turnkey pushed Joe into line. A big door was swung open and he saw a small, brilliantly lighted room with a crowd of people lining the walls. Joe looked for the peroxide blonde. There she was, pale and hardboiled, between two bulls. Joe started. God, he had her now. She was standing side of Courtney when he dropped. Joe began to sweat.

The line in single file was herded in. Bugs Liska, who was in front of Joe, whispered:

"Say, what's this all about?"

The sergeant heard him and leaping across the room grabbed him by the shoulder.

"Any more of that," said the sergeant, "and some of you bad eggs is gonna get cracked."

"Drop dead," said Liska.

Joe found himself face to face with the blonde. She stared at him. Flaherty walked along the line and examined the prisoners. When he got to Joe, Joe looked away.

"How's that bath?" asked Flaherty.

"O. K.," said Joe.

Liska said:

"Say, Irish, what's this all about?"

"Shut your dirty mouth," said Flaherty.

A man Joe had never seen before, a big husky man with curly gray hair, went over to the blonde and said:

"Is he in that bunch, Mrs. Weil?"

The blonde nodded.

"Well, Mrs. Weil, this is a very serious matter so don't make any mistakes. Now if you're sure he's in that bunch, point him out."

The blonde compressed her lips and walked over to Joe.

"There he is. There's the dirty skunk."

"Jesus," said Liska, glancing at Joe, "it's your funeral, hunh?"

The blonde stood glaring at Joe.

"I hope they hang you," she cried, "shooting a guy like Jim Courtney."

"I never shot him," said Joe.

"Shut up," said Flaherty. "All right, sergeant, march 'em out."

In the big room Liska said:

"Joe, it sure looks tough for you."

"They can't prove nothing," said Joe.

The sergeant rushed at them.

"Where do you birds think you're at!" he cried.

Stepping back, he struck Joe a hard blow with his fist. Mechanically Joe set himself and raised his hands, then, coming to himself, he dropped his hands and stood looking at the floor. Liska said:

"Say, sergeant, I guess I can go home, can't I? My old mother'll be worried to death."

The sergeant stared at Liska, then he laughed.

"I'm gonna hang on to you just for fun," he said.

"Yeah?" said Liska. "Well not long, cause Steve's gonna spring me."

The sergeant motioned for the turnkey.

"Lock the dago up," he said; "you plant yourself over there in a chair, Bugs."

Joe lay down and tried to sleep. Over his head the barred window began to get gray. Morning sure was slow in coming.

Of a sudden he thought of Red Gus. He got to his feet and began to walk back and forth. Yeah, they sure put the rope on old Gus and there wasn't a tougher guy in the world. Yeah, he was so tough he didn't die right away and kept kicking. Cops fainted and all that stuff. Joe climbed up on his bunk and stood tiptoe to look out the window. Morning was coming. He saw a milk wagon passing the jail. How come he had to think of Red Gus?

He thought he heard a noise and turned around. There were two cops standing in front of his cell, looking at him. Joe felt uneasy.

"Want me?" he called.

They didn't say anything; they just stood there looking, then went away.

Joe got down from the window and sat on his bunk. No use trying to sleep. Down the corridor someone began to scream. The turnkey passed his cell on the run. Joe felt his hair stirring and sweat stood out on his forehead.

"Christ," he said, "it's only that dope."

In a minute the turnkey came back and stopped at Joe's door.

"Couple of guys coming back to take a look at you," he said.

"Yeah?" said Joe; "say, what was all the noise?"

"The dope blew his top again," said the turnkey; "the Doc's gonna give him a shot pretty soon."

The big man with the curly gray hair, Flaherty, and two policemen came down the corridor.

"All right," said Flaherty, "let him out."

The turnkey unlocked the door and pushed Joe into the corridor. They all stood staring at Joe; nobody said anything.

Finally the gray-haired man said:

"Well, it's too bad. Nice-looking boy."

"Yeah," said Flaherty, "but he's hell with a gun."

Joe didn't say anything. But Flaherty said:

"Joe, I never thought you was the kind of a bird that'd shoot a guy in the back."

Joe didn't say anything.

"Hanging's too good for you, Joe."

"Poor old Jim never even had a gun on him. You lousy dago!" cried one of the policemen, and took a step toward Joe.

Flaherty motioned him back.

"Just let the law take its course, Luke," he said, "they'll hang this baby sure."

"Will they?" said Joe.

The gray-haired man shook his finger at Joe.

"Yes, my boy, I'm afraid they will."

"They can't prove nothing on me," said Joe; "I wasn't even in that end of town the night Courtney was bumped off. That dame's full of hop."

One of the policemen stepped past Flaherty and knocked Joe down. Flaherty grabbed the policeman and pushed him back. Joe got to his feet and stood holding his jaw.

"I'm gonna put it to you birds for this," said Joe.

Both of the policemen made a rush at Joe, but Flaherty held them back.

"Well," said Flaherty, "got an eyeful, Mr. McClure?"

Joe stared at the gray-haired man. So this was the Crime Commission guy that was kicking up all the row. Joe took a good look at him so he'd know him the next time he saw him. Maybe, if things broke right, he could deliver a nice package at that bird's house some morning.

"Yes," said Mr. McClure, "lock him up, turnkey."

The turnkey took Joe by the arm and flung him into his cell. Joe fell on his hands and knees.

"Say," said Joe, "what's the idea?"

The turnkey came over and put his face against the bars.

"Orders, buddy," he said, then he went away.

Yeah, it was orders all right. They wasn't going to let up on him till he spilled something. Joe felt panicky. He flung himself face down on his bunk and began to sob.

"Won't I never get out of here?" he said.

They had been questioning Joe for over two hours. He sat under a blazing light and they sat round him in the darkness. Joe was so thirsty that he could hardly swallow. They took turns at him: first, Mr. McClure, then Flaherty, then Rieger. Flaherty sat near him and when he was slow with his answers rapped him over the knuckles with a ruler. But Joe stuck it out.

The turnkey took him back to his cell and gave him some water. Joe took a big drink then lay down on his bunk and tried to sleep, but it was no use. He felt hot all over and his tongue was swollen.

He put his hands under his head and lay looking at the square spots of sunshine in the dark corridor.

"God," he said, "I can't stand much of this."

In five minutes the turnkey came back.

"They want you again, kid," he said.

"God, I can't move," said Joe.

The turnkey unlocked the door and came into the cell.

"Get on your feet," he said, "and snap it up. The prosecutor's in there now and you're gonna ketch hell."

Joe got slowly to his feet and the turnkey led him down the corridor.

V

Sam Vettori sat half-dozing in an armchair watching a crap game. It was about eleven o'clock in the morning and most of the blinds were still down. All the wheels were covered and the chairs were piled up on the tables. The game was desultory as nobody had much money. As it wasn't a house game, but merely some of the Vettori gang amusing themselves, Sam occasionally staked one or another of the players.

Since the rise of Rico, Sam had confined his efforts to the managing of Little Arnie's old joint. He was making money hand over fist and he was content to sit all day in his armchair and superintend the work of his employees. He drank wine by the gallon and ate plate after plate of spaghetti. In a month he put on fifteen pounds. As he was fat to begin with, this added poundage made him immense. His aquiline features were puffed out nearly beyond recognition and there were rolls of fat at the base of his skull. Sam had loosed the reins and gone slack. Formerly, effort had kept him in better condition, but now, perfectly at ease, free of responsibility, the deadly lethargy which had threatened him all his life took possession of him.

Sam crossed his legs with difficulty and took out a stogie. The crap game had ended in an argument. Kid Bean loudly contended that he had been gypped.

"Shut up, you guys," said Sam, "I'm doing you a favor to let you shoot in here. Any more of this kind of stuff and you don't do it no more. If you guys'd save your money you wouldn't have to be fighting over two bits."

"Aw, rest your jaw," said Kid Bean.

Joe Peeper took the dice and flung them out the window.

"Them babies'll never bother me no more," said Joe.

"Can you beat that!" said Kid Bean.

"Well," said Sam, "since Blackie's got all the jack, the rest of you guys can pitch pennies. Listen, Kid, don't forget you owe me two bucks."

"You can take it out of my hide," said the Kid.

"Your hide ain't worth it," said Sam.

Chesty, the doorman, came out of Sam's office rubbing his eyes.

"Sam," he said, "Scabby wants to see you."

"Tell him to come out here," said Sam.

"No," said Chesty, "he wants to see you private."

"Hey, Sam," said Kid Bean, "give us a deck of cards, will you?"

"No," said Sam, "you don't even know what they're for." He pulled himself slowly to his feet and turning to Chesty went on: "Get these guys a pack of cards and lock 'em up some place. They'd bump each other off for two bits and I don't want this nice carpet spoiled."

Yawning and stretching, Sam went into his office and shut the door. Scabby was standing in the middle of the room, biting his nails.

"Want a bottle of wine or something, Scabby?" asked Sam.

"Christ, no!" cried Scabby.

Sam stared at him, then dropped into a chair. "Well," he said, "you look like you got something on your mind, so spill it."

Scabby was so nervous that he couldn't control the muscles of his face.

"You're goddam right I got something on my mind," said Scabby, "Joe spilled the works."

Sam opened his eyes wide.

"Joe who?"

"Joe Massara," said Scabby, "they nabbed him on the Courtney business and he squawked."

Sam's jaw fell and he ran his hands over his face in a bewildered way. "Yeah?" he said.

"It's the God's truth," said Scabby; "boy, the bulls sure played this one slick. Listen, I didn't even know nothing about it. They kept the newspaper guys out and when a couple guys who were in the know came looking for Joe they told them that they must have him at the Chicago Avenue station. And out at Chicago Avenue they sent 'em someplace else. Yeah, it's all over now."

This was too much for Sam. He just sat there staring at Scabby.

"God, Sam," said Scabby, astonished, "don't you get me? It's all over. Listen, if it wasn't for you I'd be on my way right now. I don't know whether I'll be named or not, but I ain't taking no chances. Love of God, Sam, don't just sit there. You got to do something."

"Joe spilled everything?" asked Sam, taking it in slowly.

"Yeah, he stuck it out for four hours, but he didn't have a chance."

There was a flash of the old Sam Vettori. He got up and took Scabby by the arm.

"Is Rico wised up?"

"No," said Scabby.

"All right," said Sam, "you keep your mouth shut."

"You don't have to tell me," said Scabby.

Sam looked about him, bewildered.

"But, good God," he cried, "what am I gonna do?"

"Well," said Scabby, "I got a can down here and I'm hitting East. Want to go with me? I'll take a chance."

Sam looked his bewilderment. Things were moving too fast for him. Why, he hadn't been out of Chicago for twenty years. He hadn't been out of Little Italy for over five. Just pick up and beat it.

"What the hell!" said Sam, "I got a good business.... God, what am I gonna do?"

Scabby stared at him.

"Why, Sam," he said, "you must be losing your mind."

Sam wiped the sweat from his face and sank back into his chair.

"Joe spilled it, hunh? Rico said he'd turn yellow."

Scabby took him under the arms and tried to pull him to his feet, but Sam pushed him away.

"No use running," he said, "they'll get you sure. I ain't gonna go running all over hell and back and a bunch of bulls chasing me."

Scabby swore violently in Italian.

"No," said Sam, "no use running."

"Well," said Scabby, "this bird's gonna pull his freight. Sam, you must be full of hop."

Sam sat staring at his shoes.

"Listen," said Scabby, "I can't waste no more time. Are you gonna pull out or ain't you?"

Sam didn't say anything.

"O. K.," said Scabby; "I'm moving."

"Wait," cried Sam. "Scabby, listen to me. I been good to you, ain't I?"

"You sure have."

"I give you the money to bring your old man over here, didn't I? And I give you the money to bury him, didn't I?"

"You sure did."

"Well, listen, Scabby, if Rico gets away, pop him. Goddam him; he's busted us all. Pop him, Scabby, for old Sam."

"He won't get away," said Scabby.

"You don't know that guy," said Sam, getting shakily to his feet; "sure to God as I'm a Catholic, you don't know that guy. He's got a run of luck and it may last."

"If he gets away I'll pop him," said Scabby.

The door was flung violently open and Killer Pepi stepped in.

"I heard you bastards," he said. "The Kid told me there was something up. Double-crossing the boss, hunh?"

"Go to hell," said Sam.

Scabby raised his gun but it missed fire. The Killer shot from his hip, then ran out, slamming the door.

"Did he plug you, Scabby?" cried Sam.

"No," said Scabby, "but I heard her sing."

The window behind Scabby had a bullet hole in it.

"He'll spill it sure," said Sam, his face puckered.

"Won't do him no good," said Scabby, "'cause the bulls are on their way. Well, Sam, I'm moving."

Sam just looked at him. Scabby raised the window and climbed out on the fire escape.

"Love of God, Sam," said Scabby, "you got to do something."

Sam took his hat from the hook.

"I'll go see the Big Boy."

"It won't do you no good, Sam."

They heard someone running down the hall, then, there was a shot, followed by a rush of feet. Chesty flung open the door.

"The bulls!" he cried.

Scabby disappeared down the fire escape. Sam took out his automatic and put his back against the wall. Spike Rieger put his head in the door, then drew it back hastily.

"Sam," he called, "better give up."

"All right," said Sam, flinging his gun on the floor.

Spike Rieger came in followed by two policemen.

"Put the cuffs on him," said Spike.

Sam held out his hands and one of the policemen snapped on the handcuffs.

"Spike," said Sam, "did you pick the Killer up on the way in?"

"No," said Spike, "we don't want him for nothing." Turning to the policemen Spike said: "All right, put him in the wagon."

"Listen, Spike," said Sam, "did you get Rico?"

"I don't know," said Spike. "Flaherty's after him. I guess you know Gentleman Joe squawked, don't you?"

"Yeah," said Sam, indifferently, "but you ain't got no case against me."

Spike laughed.

VI

The Killer knocked at Rico's door but got no response. He knocked again and again, then, getting impatient, he put his shoulder to the door and flung it open. No Rico. The Killer stood in the hall, wondering where Rico could have gone. From the landing above him, the landlady yelled:

"Hey, what did you do to that door?"

"The hell with the door," said Pepi; "do you know where the guy that lives there is?"

"No," said the landlady, "but I seen him go out with a fellow."

"What kind of a fellow?"

"A little fellow."

Otero! Killer took the stairs at a jump but slowed his pace as he reached the main floor. There was a police car at the curb. Flaherty got out leisurely and stood talking to one of the policemen in the front seat. Pepi went over to him.

"Looking for the boss?"

"Yeah," said Flaherty, "the Big Boy sent me down. I want to have a talk with him."

"Yeah?" said Pepi. "Getting wise to yourself, hunh?"

"Rico was always O. K. with me."

"That's the talk," said Pepi. "Well, the boss is upstairs by himself."

When Flaherty and one of his men had gone into the building, the Killer grinned at the others and walked slowly away, but, as soon as he had turned the corner, he broke into a run.

There were two little Italian kids sitting on the steps of the stairway that led up to Otero's. They made way for Pepi.

"Otero upstairs?" he asked.

One of the kids said:

"That funny little guy?"

"Yeah," said Pepi.

"I think I seen him go up."

"Yeah," said the other kid, "I seen him."

Pepi took the stairs at a run and rapped at Otero's door. Seal Skin opened it a few inches but Pepi pushed her aside and walked in. Otero was sitting with his feet on the bed, smoking a big cigar.

"Where's the boss?" asked Pepi.

"At Blondy's. What's the matter?"

"Joe squawked," said Pepi, "and the bulls is looking for Rico. Get your coat on and beat it, Otero. I'll go after the boss."

Otero leapt to his feet and struggled into his coat.

"Bulls looking for me too?"

"Sure," said Pepi, "it's the Courtney business. You beat it, Otero. This ain't no picnic."

"No," said Otero, "I go with Rico."

"You damn dummy," said Seal Skin.

"Yeah," said Pepi, "you beat it, Otero. Get out of town. They don't want me for nothing. I'll see if I can't get Rico on the phone; if I can't I'll go after him. Listen, the bulls is over at Rico's right now."

"Caramba!" cried Otero, and, slipping his automatic into his coat pocket, he ran out into the hall and down the stairs.

"The damn dummy!" said Seal Skin.

Pepi stood looking at Seal Skin then he said:

"Sure he's a damn dummy, but he's right."

Before Otero had gone half a block in the direction of Blondy's, he saw a police car coming toward him. He ducked into a drugstore. It was empty except for a clerk who stood staring at Otero.

"Show me the back way out, you!" said Otero.

"Say!" said the clerk.

Otero took out his gun. The clerk threw himself down behind the counter. Otero ran out through the prescription room and found the back door, which opened into an alley. One end of the alley was blind, the other came out onto a busy street. Otero ran toward the open end, praying in Spanish.

All along the curbs on both sides of the street pushcarts were drawn up and peddlers were calling their wares. A slow-moving crowd of Little Italians blocked the pavements. Otero, because of his size, disappeared into the crowd, and, although he was forced to go slowly, he was safe from observation. Half a block from Blondy's he ducked down an alley, crossed a long cement court and climbed the fire escape.

Blondy's bedroom window was locked. Otero beat on it with his fist. For a moment there was no response, then he saw the bedroom door open slowly and Blondy's face appeared. She ran over and unlocked the window, then she turned and called:

"Rico, it's The Greek."

Rico came into the bedroom. He had his hat on. "Did Pepi get you?"

"No, what the hell?"

The phone rang and Blondy went to answer it.

"They got Joe and he squawked," said Otero.

Rico looked at him. Blondy came running back.

"My God, Rico," she said, "the bulls're after you. Joe squealed. You ought to plugged that softie, Rico. You ought to plugged him."

Rico stood in the middle of the room, staring.

By an effort of the will, he rid himself of an attitude of mind which had been growing on him since his interviews with Montana and the Big Boy. He was nobody, nobody. Worse than nobody. The bulls wanted him now and they wanted him bad. Goodbye dollar cigars and crockery at one grand, goodbye swell food and tuxedos and security. Rico was nobody. Just a lonely Youngstown yegg that the bulls wanted. His face was ghastly.

He swung his fist at the air.

"I ought to plugged him! I ought to plugged him!"

Otero stood staring at Rico. Blondy was putting on her hat.

"All right," said Rico, "let's go."

Blondy said:

"Take me, Rico."

Rico shook his head.

"Nothing doing, Blondy. I'm traveling fast and I can't be bothered with no dame."

"Jesus, Rico," said Blondy, unable to realize what had happened, "everything was going so nice."

"Sure," said Rico, "but it's all over now and that's that. You stay planted, Blondy, and as soon as I get a chance I'll send you a stake."

Otero crawled out the window onto the fire escape and Rico followed him. Blondy began to scream.

"Shut your mouth," said Rico, "and if the bulls come up the front way kid 'em along. Make 'em think you got me hid, see?"

"O. K., Rico," said Blondy.

Otero and Rico went down the fire escape. They stopped at the foot of the fire escape and Rico took Otero by the arm.

"Listen," he said, "here's the dope. We got to get to Ma Magdalena's. She's got most of my jack and a good hideout. It ain't gonna be easy, because the bulls're probably scattered all around. But once we get there, we're O. K."

"All right," said Otero.

They started. Rico knew every alley in the district, and he led Otero by such a safe route that they were soon within a block and a half of Ma Magdalena's without having crossed a main thoroughfare.

"Now," said Rico, "we got to watch our step. If the bulls are cruising, they're cruising this street sure."

"All right," said Otero.

"Listen," said Rico, "don't be afraid to use your gat if the fun begins. They can only hang you once."

"I ain't afraid," said Otero.

They left the alley and were half way across the street when somebody shouted at them to halt. Without turning, they broke into a run.

"It's only one bull," said Rico.

A bullet sang over them and they heard the blast of a policeman's whistle. Otero stopped in his tracks, turned, took a steady aim and fired.

The policeman staggered forward three or four steps and fell to his knees.

"Got him," said Otero.

Rico turned. The policeman was kneeling in the middle of the street, trying to steady his hand for a shot.

"Duck," cried Rico, simultaneously with the firing of the policeman's gun.

Otero twisted sideways, looked at Rico with surprise, then dropped his gun, and began to walk up the alley holding his stomach. Rico put his arm around him and, pulling him over to the side of the alley where he could keep a telephone pole between them and the policeman, guided him along. But after a few steps, Otero pulled away from Rico and cried:

"Run, Rico, run. They got me sure. I can't feel nothing."

Rico grabbed him and tried to pull him along, but he resisted.

"Goddam you, Rico," cried Otero, "run! I can't go no farther. I'm done for."

Rico heard the roar of a police car. He released Otero, who staggered away from him and then fell flat on his back.

"Run, Rico," said Otero.

Rico climbed a fence, ran up through a filthy backyard, and in at an open back door. There was a young Italian girl sweeping in the hall. At Rico's sudden appearance, she dropped her broom and flattened herself against the wall. Rico took her by the arm.

"Listen, sister," he said, "the bulls're after me. I'm going out the front way, see, but if the bulls come through here you tell 'em I hopped the fence next door and doubled back. Got it?"

"Yes sir," said the girl, then looking up at Rico, "I know you."

"Yeah?" said Rico. "Well, do your stuff then, sister."

In the alley behind the house there was a shriek of breaks and someone cried in a loud voice: "He went in that way!"

The girl picked up her broom and went on sweeping. Rico ran out through the front hall, down the long flight of stone steps, and crossed the street leisurely.

VII

Ma Magdalena let him in at the alley door.

"Well, Rico," she said; "got yourself in a nice fix, didn't you?"

Rico grinned.

"Yeah," he said, "who told you?"

"The bulls were here and searched the place."

"Didn't find the hideout, did they?"

Ma Magdalena laughed.

"What a chance!"

Rico followed Ma down into the basement. She led him through a short tunnel and back into the hideout. A small, round opening just large enough to admit one person had been pierced in a heavy stone wall. In front of the wall rows of pine shelves had been built and these were filled with canned goods. The section of the shelves which hid the opening was hinged and could be swung open.

Rico followed Ma through the opening and came out into a little room with a cot in one corner, a table, and one chair. Rico took off his hat and sat down.

"They got The Greek," he said.

"Yeah?" said Ma.

Rico took out a cigar and lit it.

"Listen," he said, "I want to stay here a couple of days. Then I'm gonna pull out. Get me some magazines and keep me posted."

"All right," said Ma, "but it's gonna cost you, because I'm taking chances, see, I'm taking big chances."

"Well," said Rico, "you got my roll, help yourself."

Ma Magdalena smiled broadly.

"That's the talk, Rico. Old Ma'll sure take care of you."

"O. K.," said Rico; "now, get this: in two days I want a car."

"Arrigo's got a car. If we go hooking one, it might spoil your getaway."

"That's good," said Rico; "all right, I want a jumper suit, you know, one of them suits like a garage mechanic wears, and a razor."

"All right," said Ma Magdalena.

When she had gone, Rico took off his coat and shoes, and lay down on the cot. His nerves were jumpy and he couldn't seem to get settled. He flung his cigar away and turned his face to the wall.

"Just when I thought things was on the up and up," he said.

Rico felt resentful, but his resentment was not directed at any specific group or person; it was vague as yet. He turned from side to side on his cot, then he gave it up.

Ma Magdalena came back with a big mug of coffee and a couple of papers. Rico sat down at the table.

"They got Sam," said Ma.

"Well," said Rico, "that's hips for Sam."

Rico took the papers from her and glanced at the headlines.

GENTLEMAN JOE WILTS
GANG CHIEF NAMED AS SLAYER

Ma Magdalena went out. Rico sat reading the paper and sipping his coffee.

> Gentleman Joe Massara looks more like a movie actor than a gunman. When arrested he was wearing an expensive tuxedo and the rings that were taken from him are valued at $3000.

"To hell with that," said Rico. He read on:

> Cesare Bandello, known as Rico, the Vettori gang chief, was named as the actual slayer of Courtney....

"Yeah," said Rico, "and I'm the only one they ain't gonna get."

PART VII

I

It was dark when Rico reached the outskirts of Hammond. He drove into a field, took the license plates off and buried them, and got out of his jumpers. Then he took some clean waste from the tool box and wiped the grease from his face.

"What a cinch," he said.

Things had gone a lot better than he had expected them to. There hadn't been a hitch of any kind. A motor cop out in Blue Island had waved to him even. Rico laughed. You never know. When you're looking for things to go right they never do. When you're looking for trouble, why, things are O. K. Yeah, funny!

Rico walked to the car line. He was wearing a plain, dark suit and an army shirt Arrigo had given him. He had shaved off his mustache and the hard, short bristles on his upper lip worried him. Rico felt very proud of his escape. It was a good idea to dress himself up like a garage mechanic and drive across town in broad daylight. Yeah, it was a good idea and if things broke right he'd write to one of the papers and tell them all about it. Only the postmark would give him away. Not so good. Well, anyway, he could tell Sansotta about it.

Rico got on a streetcar.

"Well, how's things?" he said to the conductor.

"All right," said the conductor; "getting cooler, ain't it? Reckon we'll have winter before we know it."

"Yeah," said Rico.

II

Rico went up the alley at the side of Sansotta's place and knocked at the back door. It was a long time before somebody came and took a look at him through the shutter. A voice with a marked Italian accent said:

"Who are you?"

"Where's Sansotta?" asked Rico.

"What do you care?"

"Listen, buddy," said Rico, "don't get all het up. I'm right. Go tell Sansotta that Cesare wants him."

In a few minutes the door opened and a hand motioned for Rico to come in. The hall was dark and Rico stumbled going up the stairs. The lookout took hold of his arm.

"The boss's up in his room. I'll take you up. Where you from, buddy?"

"Youngstown," said Rico.

"Where's that?"

"Over east."

The lookout led Rico down a long, dark hallway and to a door at the end of it. Light showed over a transom. The lookout knocked three times and the door was opened. Rico went in.

"Well," said Sansotta, locking the door, "here you are?"

"Yeah," said Rico.

Sansotta was a small, bowlegged Italian with a dark, scarred face. He had on a striped suit, brown and red, and a stiff collar the points of which were so high that his chin rested on them. There was a big diamond stud in his shirtfront.

"You must've got a break," said Sansotta.

Rico explained how he had got away.

"Pretty nifty," said Sansotta; "I got to hand it to you on that, Cesare."

"Yeah," said Rico, "it was a good idea."

Sansotta went over to a table, opened a drawer and took out a handbill which he gave to Rico. Rico smiled.

"Raised the ante, did they? Last I heard it was five grand."

Rico read the handbill over and over and stared at the Bertillon pictures.

"Them pictures don't look like me," he said.

Sansotta pursed his lips and scrutinized them.

"Not since you got the tickler off. No, and you look thinner in them pictures. How long ago was they taken?"

"About seven years ago."

The handbill read:

> Wanted for murder: Cesare Bandello, known as Rico. Age: 29. Height: 5 ft. 5 in. Weight: 125. Complexion: pale. Hair: black and wavy. Eyes: light, gray or blue. His face is thin and he walks with one foot slightly turned in. Does not take up with strangers. Solitary type, morose and dangerous. Reward: $5000, offered by management of Casa Alvarado. $2000, offered by City of Chicago, for capture dead or alive.

"Well," said Sansotta, "where you headed for?"

"I'm gonna stick around here for a while," said Rico.

"Yeah?" said Sansotta; "pretty close to trouble, ain't it?"

"I don't know," said Rico, "they ain't got any idea which way I went. I got a big stake and I don't have to worry none."

"You sure went up fast over in the big burg," said Sansotta, looking at Rico with a sort of awe.

"Yeah," said Rico, "and the hell of it was, I was just getting started. Everything was on the up and up when one of the gang turned softie. Ain't that hell?"

Rico had been very much elated over his escape from Chicago, so elated in fact that he had forgotten all about his troubles; but, now that the excitement of the escape had passed, the thought of how much he had lost struck him full force. He felt resentful.

"Yeah," said Sansotta, "that's the way it goes. It's a tough game. They picked up two of my men last night."

"That so?" said Rico, paying no attention.

Sansotta got up.

"Well, Cesare," he said, "I got business or I'd stick around and chin with you. Want to stay here with me till things blow over?"

"Yeah," said Rico.

III

Night after night Rico lay awake looking at the arc light outside his window. His mind was filled with resentment and he went over and over the incidents which had led to his fall. Now that it was too late, he saw the mistakes he had made. He should have plugged Gentleman Joe; that's all. When a guy begins to turn softie, why there ain't no good in him. Yeah, he had been too easy. Another thing. He should have played Scabby up; that guy was in a position to do him all kinds of favors. But Scabby was a hard guy to get along with; he always thought somebody was trying to make a fool of him and he always had a chip on his shoulder.

Sometimes Rico would fall asleep for a little while, but his sleep was full of dreams and he would toss from side to side and wake up with a start. Then he would get up and smoke one cigarette after another and think about Montana and Little Arnie and the Big Boy. Often, in these short naps, he would see The Greek lying on his back in the alley, or the little Italian girl sweeping the hall, or Ma Magdalena helping him put the grease on his face. Then he would awake in confusion and stare at the unfamiliar arc light a long time before he could realize where he was.

In the day time it wasn't so bad. He could play cards with Sansotta and some of his gang, or shoot crap on a pool table in the back room. Rico always played to win and while the game was in progress he forgot his troubles. But even this was but a partial alleviation. He was nobody. Just an unknown wop who seemed to have unlimited resources. Sansotta was the only one who knew who he was. He had taken his uncle's name, Luigi De Angelo, and around Sansotta's he was called Youngstown Louis, or usually plain Louis. No, he was nobody. When a card game got hot and one of the players thought he was getting gypped, a look from Rico did not quiet the tumult as it had done in Little Italy. A look from Rico meant nothing. He was cursed with the rest of them. Often the desire to show these two-bit wops who they were yelling at would make him writhe in his chair, and his hand would move toward his armpit, but he couldn't risk it. He had his neck to think about, and there was Sansotta, a good guy, doing what he could for him. Rico kept saying to himself, you are nobody, nobody, but it was galling.

Sometimes he would go to his room early and just sit in the dark and think. He would imagine himself in the Big Boy's wonderful apartment; he would see the big pictures of the old-time guys in their gold frames, the one grand crockery, and the library full of books; or he would recall the night when Little Arnie's Detroit toughs tried to bump him off and how when he came back to The Palermo the people stood on the chairs and shouted: "Rico! Rico!" God, it was hard to take!

The stories in the magazines about swell society people that he used to read with such eagerness failed to interest him now. After a paragraph or two he would fling the magazine aside and swear.

"Yeah," he would say, "ain't that great! The damn dressed-up softies. Got everything in the world and never had to turn a hand for it."

Rico was filled with resentment and when he spoke, rarely now, it was to denounce or ridicule something. The wops around Sansotta's, though they were obtuse enough, were not long in noticing this, and Rico began to be known as Crabby Louis.

They would say: "Well, Crabby Louis, it's your shot;" or "All right, Crabby, deal the cards."

The only thing that really interested Rico was the trial of Sam Vettori. Joe Massara, who had turned State's evidence, had been sentenced to life. "Lord," said Rico, when he read Joe's sentence, "I never thought they'd give Gentleman Joe a jolt like that after he turned State's. Them boys means business." Sam's trial had been rushed because of the hubbub raised by Mr. McClure and other influential men, and the outcome was never in doubt. Sam Vettori was sentenced to be hanged.

When Rico read the verdict he lay back in his chair and looked at the wall.

"Well, old Sam had a long whack at it," he said; "never seen the inside of a prison in his life. A guy's luck's bound to turn."

Then he went over in his mind the robbery of the Casa Alvarado and all the steps which had led to his own rise and fall.

"It made me and it broke me," he said.

On New Year's Eve Rico dressed up more than usual and went down into Sansotta's cabaret. It was jammed and unable to get a seat he went into Sansotta's office and had one of the waiters bring him a meal. He sat with the door open and watched the antics on the dance floor. There was plenty of liquor about and the crowd was pretty rough. Rico saw a big blonde dancing with a fat Italian. She gave him a look and he motioned for her to come in the office. She nodded. Rico got up and closed the door. In a few minutes the Blonde came in.

"Well, kid," she said, "what's on your mind?"

"I got a room upstairs," said Rico, "that ain't occupied."

"The hell you have," said the Blonde.

"Yeah," said Rico, "and I got a bank roll that ain't got any strings on it."

"Now you're talking," said the Blonde, putting her arm around Rico.

"Well," said Rico, "let's go."

"Listen," said the Blonde, "I'll be back after while. I got a guy out here that's plenty tough and I got to humor him."

"Aw, hell," said Rico, "I'll take that toughness out of him. Stick around."

The Blonde looked at Rico and laughed.

"Say," she said, "you ain't big enough to talk so big."

"No," said Rico, resentful, "I ain't so big."

"Listen, honey," said the Blonde, "this boy would eat you alive."

"Yeah?" said Rico.

The fat Italian opened the door and came in.

"What's the idea, Micky?" he said to the Blonde.

"Why, I just happened to bump into an old friend of mine," said the Blonde, scared.

Rico got up and stood looking at the fat Italian.

"What's it to you!" he said.

"Why, listen, kid," said the fat Italian, "you better go get your big brother cause if you make any more cracks I'm gonna dust off the furniture with you."

The Blonde took the fat Italian by the arm.

"Come on, Paul," she said, "let's go dance."

"Yeah," said Rico, "take that bird away before something happens to him."

The fat Italian pulled away from the Blonde and started toward Rico.

"That's one crack too many," he said.

But Rico, standing with his back against Sansotta's desk, perfectly calm, reached under his armpit and pulled his gun. The fat Italian hesitated and looked bewildered.

"Well," said Rico, "kind of lost your steam, didn't you?"

The fat Italian turned and looked at the Blonde.

"That's a nice boyfriend you got," he said.

The Blonde stood there with her mouth open.

"All right, big boy," said Rico, "we can get along without you."

Sansotta opened the door and stood looking from one to the other.

"What's the matter, Paul?" he inquired.

The fat Italian pointed at Rico.

"That bird there tried to grab my girl, and when I told him about it he pulled a gat on me."

Sansotta's face darkened.

"Put that gun up, Louis," he said, staring hard at Rico; "where you think you're at? Listen, Paul, Louis's a new guy here and he don't know the ropes."

"Well," said the fat Italian, "he sure is quick with a gun."

"That's all right, Paul," said the Blonde, laughing, "he needs a handicap."

Rico, furious, put on his hat and started to go. But Sansotta said:

"Wait a minute, Louis, I want to see you." Then turning to the fat Italian: "I'm sure sorry this happened, but you know how it is when a guy don't know the ropes, he'll butt in where it ain't healthy to butt in, see? Louis's all right, but he's got a bad temper."

"Ain't he!" said Paul. "Well, I guess we better be moving uptown. I ain't any too anxious to hang around where you're liable to get bumped off."

"Aw, stick around, Paul," Sansotta implored; "you won't have no more trouble."

"No," said Paul, "I'll be moving. Come on, Micky. I seen about all of your boyfriend that I want to see."

Sansotta followed them out into the cabaret, trying to persuade them to remain, but Paul went over to the check-window and got their wraps. Rico sat down and went on with his meal. Sansotta came in and slammed the door after him.

"Goddam you, Cesare," he cried, "why don't you be more careful? That guy is Paolo, the political boss. He can close me up tomorrow if he wants to."

"Take it easy," said Rico; "how the hell did I know? You think I'm gonna let a guy take a bust at me?"

Sansotta took out a cigar and began to chew on it.

"Cesare," he said, "you got to be moving. I can't have you hanging around here no more. It's too dangerous."

Rico dropped his fork and stared at Sansotta.

"Giving me the go-by, hunh?"

"Yeah," said Sansotta, "you got to be moving."

Rico got to his feet and stood looking at Sansotta.

"Just on account of a small-town ward heeler," he said; "why that guy couldn't boss a section gang. You're a hell of a guy, Sansotta. After all the jack I spent in this dump."

"I can't help that," said Sansotta, "you got to be moving right away."

Rico laughed.

"Don't get funny," he said.

"Don't you get funny," said Sansotta; "you ain't in no shape to get funny."

"Maybe you better call the bulls and turn me up," said Rico.

"Well," said Sansotta, "you got to be moving, that's all."

IV

Rico was acutely conscious of his position. A lonely Youngstown yegg in a hostile city without friends or influence. Yeah, funny! Just a no-account yap in a burg like Hammond and not four months ago he had been a big guy in a big burg.

He put on his ulster and went out. The wind was cold and it was snowing. He walked around for a while, keeping to the dark streets, then, chilled through, he went into a little Italian restaurant for a cup of coffee and a sandwich.

The waiter, an Italian boy with a handsome dark face, brought Rico his food. When he set it down on the table he grinned and said:

"Well, happy New Year."

Rico looked up in surprise.

"Yeah," he said, "thanks."

He felt better. This anonymous friendliness cheered him up. While he was eating, he watched the Italian boy, who was wiping off the counter and singing.

"Nice kid," thought Rico.

When Rico had finished his coffee, he lit a cigarette and sat smoking. He felt comfortable. Looking around the restaurant, he saw that there was a mechanical piano up front. Like Pete's!

"Say," he called, "let's have a little music."

"Sure," said the boy.

He put a slug in the piano. It played "Farewell To Thee" in tremolo. Rico felt sad. He called the boy back and gave him a dollar.

"Keep the change, kid," he said.

The mechanical piano stopped on a discord, and Rico got to his feet. While he was putting on his coat two men came in the front door. One of them went up to the counter and ordered a cup of coffee, but the other stopped and stood staring at Rico.

Rico, noticing the man's scrutiny, put his hand inside his coat and started out, but the man touched him on the shoulder and whispered:

"Things ain't going so good, are they, Rico?"

Rico stared at the man and demanded: "Who the hell are you?"

Then he recognized him. It was Little Arnie's doorman, Joseph Pavlovsky, one of the guys he had chased.

"I'm one of Arnie's boys," said Pavlovsky; "I been in Hammond ever since you gave us the rush."

"Yeah?" said Rico.

"Straight," said Pavlovsky. "I been in the beer racket over here and I cleaned up. I'm going back to the big burg next month."

Rico envied him.

"Yeah?" said Rico.

"You sure pulled one on 'em, Rico," said Pavlovsky; "you always was a smart boy, Rico."

"Aw, can that," said Rico, and, pulling away from Pavlovsky, he went out.

The wind was blowing hard now and it had stopped snowing. Rico turned up his coat collar and started toward Sansotta's. But he hadn't gone half a block when he realized that he was being followed. He turned just in time to see two men pass under an arc light.

"It's Little Arnie's boy," he said, "looking for seven grand."

Rico took out his gun, got behind a telephone pole, and fired a warning shot. The two men ran for cover and Rico ducked down an alley, ran for two blocks, then turned up another alley and doubled back. He had lost them.

When the lookout let him in he said:

"Louis, the boss wants to see you."

Rico went up to Sansotta's room.

"Well?" he said to Sansotta.

"Cesare," said Sansotta, "a friend of mine is pulling out for Toledo tomorrow night. He'll take you for fifty bucks."

"What's his game?"

"Running dope."

"It's O. K. with me," said Rico.

Rico went up to his room, took off his overcoat, and flung himself down on the bed. He'd have to pull out now whether he wanted to or not.

V

The dope-runner dropped Rico at the edge of town. It was about five o'clock in the morning and still dark. A heavy fog had come in from Lake Erie and a damp, cold wind was blowing. Rico walked up and down to keep warm while waiting for a car. He felt pretty low.

"Yeah," said Rico, "right back where I started from."

The headlight on the streetcar cut through the fog. The motorman didn't see Rico and ran past him.

"Ain't that a break?" said Rico.

There wouldn't be another car for half an hour. Rico decided to walk. He turned up his coat collar against the damp wind and lit a cigar. His mind was full of resentment. Yeah, by God, a lousy streetcar wouldn't even stop for him.

Rico got a room at a bachelor's hotel on the waterfront, and went to bed. It was about five o'clock in the evening when he woke up. He doused his face at the washstand, put on his overcoat, and went out.

He ate at a little Italian restaurant where he and Otero used to split a bowl of soup when things were going bad. But the place had changed. New management, new waiters, new everything. Toledo seemed small and dingy and quiet to Rico. He was a little bit puzzled.

"Didn't used to be like this," he said.

As soon as he finished his meal he walked over to Chiggi's, which was about two blocks away. But the place was dark and when Rico went up to the door to peer in he saw that it had been padlocked by the Federal Authorities.

"Ain't that a break?" he said.

He had no place to go.

There was a fruit store next to Chiggi's and Rico went in. A little Italian girl came to wait on him.

"Listen, sister," said Rico, "you know where Chiggi is now?"

"I get my grandfather," she said.

She went into the back of the store and returned with an old Italian who had crinkly gray hair and wore earrings.

"Listen, mister," said Rico, "could you tell me where Chiggi is now?"

The old man just looked at him. Rico felt a little uneasy.

"No speak English?" he asked.

"Yes," said the old man, "I speak good English. What do you want with Chiggi?"

"Well," said Rico, "Chiggi used to be a pal of mine, but I been away for three or four years and now I don't know where to find him."

"Chiggi has had trouble," said the old man; "he is in the prison."

"Yeah?" said Rico. "Atlanta, hunh?"

"Yes," said the old man, "Chiggi is in Atlanta. It is too bad. Chiggi was good to the poor. When my wife was sick and my business was not going good, Chiggi gave me money."

"Yeah," said Rico. "Chiggi staked me too."

Rico took out a cigar and gave it to the old man.

"Listen," he went on, "do you know where any of Chiggi's old bunch is?"

"Yes," said the old man, "Chiggi's boy has got a place a couple of blocks from here."

The old man wrote down the address for Rico.

Young Chiggi was a dressed-up wop and thought he was a lot better than his father. He wouldn't even wait on a customer but sat all day in the back of his joint reading the *Police Gazette* or playing solitaire. Things were breaking good for Young Chiggi and he was thinking about selling out and going to Chicago or Detroit.

He had been in the beer and alcohol racket for over three years, first with his father, then by himself, and now with Bill Hackett, known as Chicago Red. He bought diamonds and automobiles and he kept his woman in a big apartment.

When Rico was shown into his office by one of his bartenders, he didn't even look up but went on with his game of solitaire. The bartender went out and Rico sat down across from Young Chiggi.

"Chiggi," said Rico, "I want to talk to you a minute."

Chiggi didn't look up.

"All right," he said.

"Listen," said Rico, "put them cards down. I want to talk business."

Chiggi looked up and stared at Rico.

"Say," he said, "where the hell do you get that stuff! I don't know you."

"Your old man was a pal of mine," said Rico.

"Well, Buddy," said Chiggi, "that don't help you none with me, 'cause me and the old man had a split-up. He thought he was so damn wise, see, but they got him behind the bars and I'm running loose."

"Yeah?" said Rico, "well, that's a tough break for the old man. You see, your old man staked me once and I thought I'd look him up and get even. I'm pretty well-heeled right now and I'm looking for a place to lay in."

Chiggi looked at Rico with interest.

"Looking for a place to lay in, hunh? Bulls after you?"

"Yeah," said Rico.

Chiggi put his cards away. Then he took out a couple of cigars and offered Rico one. They sat smoking.

"Well," said Chiggi, "maybe I can take care of you."

"That's the talk," said Rico; "got some rooms up above?"

"No," said Chiggi, "but a friend of mine's got a boarding house next door that's O. K. Now about that jack the old man staked you to, you can give it to me, 'cause he owes me plenty."

Rico said nothing, but took out his fold and counted out a hundred and fifty dollars. He knew he had to buy his way in.

Rico selected his room carefully. It was on the side of the house and could not be reached from the outside as there were no porches near it. It had two doors, one opening into the front hall, one into the back hall. The doors themselves were heavy and could be barred from the inside. It was a good hideout.

Rico's plans were vague. He had plenty of money and if he went easy with it he would be able to live a year or more in comparative comfort. But Rico could not bear the thought of a year of inactivity. What would he do with himself? He had no vices. He couldn't amuse himself by getting drunk, or taking dope, or playing faro. He didn't mind losing a couple hundred dollars gambling occasionally, but you can't put in a whole year gambling. He thought if things went right that maybe he'd move on to New York, but that would be risky and one slip and he was gone. No, he didn't see much ahead of him.

Rico spent most of the day in his room, lying on the bed reading, or else going over and over in his mind the episodes leading to his rise and fall. The resentment he had been experiencing ever since he got to Hammond had grown till it had become almost an obsession. He was never in a good humor. When he was not reading or thinking about Chicago he would pace up and down his room and wait for night. He got so, finally, that he could sleep twelve hours every day and this helped some.

At night he would go down to Chiggi's and play pool or shoot crap. Sometimes there would be a big poker game and he would sit in. He was known as Youngstown Louis and nobody in the place had the slightest idea who he really was.

Everything was against Rico. The very virtues that had been responsible for his rise were liabilities in his present situation. He had no outlet for his energy; the self-discipline which had marked him out from his fellows was of no use to him here; and the tenacity of purpose that had kept him at high tension while he was the Vettori gang chief had no object to expend itself on.

"I am nobody, nobody," Rico would say.

Sometimes at night he would go to one of the call-houses on a nearby street and spend a couple of hours with one of the women. But he got very little pleasure from these infrequent debauches. He used to wonder what had happened to the blonde he had spent old Chiggi's stake on, and was positive that if he could find her it would do him a lot of good, but she had disappeared and nobody had any idea where she had gone.

Rico tried to buy his way in. Chiggi was agreeable but Chicago Red was not. Chicago Red had taken a dislike to Rico from the first and never missed an opportunity of bullying him. Chicago Red had left Chicago under a cloud. There was a rumor that he had got in bad with a South Side gang over there and had left to keep from getting bumped off. Red was over six feet tall and weighed about two hundred pounds; he had muscles like a wrestler, a bull neck, and enormous hairy hands.

Rico kept away from him as much as possible to avoid trouble. But Red seemed to take a delight in worrying Rico, probably because, despite the fact that Rico never argued with him, always let him have his way, he felt that Rico was not impressed.

One night there was a big poker game going on in Chiggi's back room. Rico was winning. About midnight Red came in and wanted to sit in, but there was no place for him.

"Louis," he said, "get the hell off that chair and let a man get in the game."

"Not a chance," said Rico.

"Listen, Dago ..." said Red.

"Don't call me, Dago," said Rico, looking hard at Red.

"Get off that chair or I'll throw you off," said Red starting toward Rico.

But Chiggi grabbed Red from behind and pulled him into the next room.

When the game broke up, Chiggi came in and said to Rico:

"When you get settled up, come in the office."

After the other players had gone Rico went into Chiggi's office. Red was sitting with his feet on the desk and Chiggi was walking up and down.

"Well, Dago," said Red, "did you clean 'em?"

"Yeah," said Rico.

"Sit down, Louis," said Chiggi; "we want to talk to you."

Rico sat down.

"Louis," said Chiggi, "I don't know whether you're wised up or not, but we been hitting the rocks. The bulls got two of our men and a big load of alcohol, and a couple of days ago another one of our carts got hijacked at Monroe. See, so we're pretty low."

"Yeah?" said Rico.

"Well," said Chiggi, "we want a stake, don't we, Red?"

"Yeah," said Red, "and we ain't any too particular where we get it."

"Well," said Rico, getting up, "you got a lot of guys around here. Ask them."

"Listen, Red," said Chiggi, "you keep your goddam lip out of this."
Red got to his feet suddenly and stood glaring at Chiggi.
"Why, you lousy small-time wop, I guess you don't know who you're talking to, do you?" He raised his arm and pointed at Rico. "You see that guy there, he thinks he's the best there is, got it? He thinks he's the biggest dago outside of Italy, and here you go honeying after him like we couldn't get a stake no place else. But I ain't begging no goddam dago to stake me."
Chiggi looked helplessly at Rico.
"Yeah," said Red, "and while we're talking, I'm getting sick of the way that bird there sits around and don't say nothing and acts like he was God-only-knows-who. Yeah, I'm getting good and sick of it, Chiggi."
"Well," said Chiggi, "when you get real sick of it, why beat it."
Red laughed.
"Gonna stick to your dago buddy, are you? Well, he's got the jack. But what're you gonna do when you need a guy that's got the guts?"
This was too much for Rico. He said:
"What do you know about guts? I guess you ain't so tough or they wouldn't've run you out of Chi."
"Will you listen to that!" said Red; "all right, buddy, you said your piece and you sure spoke out of turn. Why, dago, where I come from you wouldn't live five minutes. Now I'm gonna show you how they treat smart dagos in Chi."
Red made a motion toward his coat pocket, but Rico beat him to it. He pulled his gun from the holster under his armpit and covered Red.
"Red," he said, "in Chicago I wouldn't let you rob filling stations for me."
Red stood with his hands up, looking from Rico to Chiggi.
"Don't bump him off, Louis," said Chiggi.
"I wouldn't waste a bullet on him," said Rico; then glaring at Red he went on: "You been getting away with this rough stuff too long, Red. I'm Cesare Bandello!"
Red's mouth fell open and he stood staring at Rico. Chiggi took Rico by the arm.
"Are you Rico?" he cried.
Rico nodded and put up his gun. Red dropped his hands, sank into a chair and wiped the sweat from his face.
"You sit down, Chiggi," said Rico, "and I'll do the talking."
Chiggi sat down.
"Lord," said Red, "so you're Rico? Steve Gollancz told me you was a big fellow."
"Steve never seen me," said Rico.
Chiggi leaned forward eagerly.

"You gonna put in with us, Louis?"
Rico said:
"I'll put in a third, but I got to boss the works or I won't put in nothing."
Chiggi looked at Red.
"That's O. K. with me," said Red.
Chiggi got to his feet and danced a few steps.
"Hurray for us," he cried.

VI

Under Rico's guidance Chiggi's gang prospered. Chicago Red, impressed by Rico's reputation, carried out his orders and never argued; Chiggi also. And Chiggi's men were influenced by the attitude of their former bosses. Rico made decisions quickly, seldom asked for advice, and was nearly always right. Chiggi and Red were used to doing things on a small scale and hated to split with the authorities, but Rico had been in the game long enough to know that to make money you've got to spend money. Through Antonio Rizzio, one of Old Chiggi's friends, now a minor politician, Rico got in touch with some of the high-ups and bought protection. Chiggi's alcohol runners were no longer picked up and in a little while Chiggi's business had doubled. But, due to this increase in business, a new difficulty had risen: hijackers. They waylaid Chiggi's men and robbed them of their cargoes. There was a well-organized gang of them around Monroe, Michigan, and they began to cut into Chiggi's profits. Rico tried rerouting his runners and this was successful for a month or two, but the Monroe gang soon got on to it, and the trouble started over again. Rico took a chance. He ordered three sho-sho guns from a firm in Chicago. These small automatic rifles, as formidable as machine guns, were concealed in special cases under the seats of the trucks. Rico instructed his runners in the use of them and after a few encounters the Monroe gang decided that it would be more lucrative and also safer to confine their hijacking to smaller bootleggers who were not equipped with artillery.

Rico was pleased with his success, but hardly satisfied. This was small stuff and, as he could take no active part in it, he had a good deal of time on his hands. Of course he was a pretty big guy for Toledo and around Chiggi's he was king, but, after all, Chiggi's boys were a mighty poor lot, worse even than Little Arnie's, and their adulation wasn't worth much.

But that wasn't the worst of it. Rico knew that he had blundered badly in revealing his identity to Chiggi and Chicago Red. Neither of them was very dependable. Chiggi talked incessantly, contradicting himself, forgetting what he had said two minutes after he had said it; and all this talk was directed at one object: self-glorification. An association with Cesare Bandello, of Chicago, was something to brag about and Rico knew it. Chicago Red as a rule was not very talkative, but when he got drunk he would boast about his former connection with Steve Gollancz. Rico feared them both. Sometimes when the three of them were alone together he would caution them. There was only one thing that reassured Rico. Chiggi's prosperity depended on him, and Rico knew that both Chicago Red and Chiggi were aware of it.

At about seven o'clock one night Rico went out for supper. He ate at the little Italian restaurant where he and Otero used to split a bowl of soup when things were bad. He always sat facing the front door at a table in the back of the place. In this position he could see everyone who came in and also he could keep an eye on the people at the tables. On his right and a couple of feet ahead of him was a little window which looked out on an alley. While Rico was finishing his coffee he happened to glance at the window. When he did, a face which had been pressed against the window pane was hastily withdrawn. Rico got up, put on his hat and paid his check.

"I'm going out the back way," he said to the counterman.

"O. K., boss."

"If anybody comes in here and asks for Louis De Angelo take a good look at him."

"All right, boss," said the counterman.

Rico went out through the kitchen door, which opened onto a little cement court where the refuse from the restaurant was dumped. The big garbage cans along the wall were in the shadow and, as Rico stepped out, a man jumped up from behind one of the cans and put a gun against him. Rico threw himself to the ground, the gun exploded harmlessly, and the man made a break for the alley, stumbling over the cans. Rico fired from a prone position and missed. Then he jumped to his feet and ran out into the alley. The man had disappeared.

"God," said Rico, "if that boy didn't almost pull one on me."

One of the cooks opened the back door and put his head out.

"What the hell!" he said.

"Damned if I know," said Rico; "a couple of guys was popping at each other out here in the alley."

"Some of them bootleggers," said the cook.

Rico took a cab back to Chiggi's. He was very much perturbed. Whoever that boy was he certainly meant business.

"Well," said Rico, "somebody has sure spilled something."

As soon as he came in Chiggi rushed up to him and grabbed him by the arm.

"Louis," he said, "Red's drunk and we can't do nothing with him."

Rico stared at Chiggi.

"Where's he been?"

"Why," said Chiggi, "he's been on a bat with some Chicago guys."

"Hell," cried Rico, "where is he?"

Chiggi led Rico back into one of the private rooms. Red was sitting at a table with a half empty quart of whiskey on the table beside him. When he saw Rico he cried:

"If it ain't old Rico himself! By God, I been drinking all day. I can hardly see but nobody can put me under the table, ain't that so, boss? Yes sir, I'd like to see the bastard that could drink Rico's buddy under the table."

Rico turned to Chiggi.

"A guy tried to pop me over at Frank's. This bird has spilled something. I got to be moving."

Chiggi's eyes got big.

"You gonna pull out, Louis?"

"I got to," said Rico; "somebody's looking for that seven grand."

"Jesus, Louis," said Chiggi, "what we gonna do without you?"

"Best you can," said Rico. "Go get me a cab, Chiggi, I'm moving right now."

Chiggi went out of the room. Rico took Red by the shoulders and shook him. Red blinked his eyes.

"Red," said Rico, "was you on a bat with some Chicago guys?"

"Was I?" cried Red; "spent a hundred bucks on them birds."

"Any of them know me?"

Red rolled his head from side to side, and sang, then he smashed his fists down on the table.

"Rico," he said, "old Red's going back to the big burg, yes sir, old Red's tired of this tank town. Old Red's got a good stake now and he's moving. They run me out once but I ain't scairt of them no more. I'm going back and show 'em who Red Hackett is. Yeah bo!"

Rico shook him.

"Listen, Red," he said, "did any of them birds know me?"

Red lolled his head, trying to focus his eyes on Rico.

"One of them guys was a personal friend of yours," said Red; "fact, he asked me if you wasn't laying up here, see, he knew all right; wasn't no harm in telling him nothing."

"Who was he?" shouted Rico.

Red thought for a moment then he said:

"I can't seem to remember. He's a wop, all right, a bald-headed wop."

"Scabby!" Rico exclaimed.

Good God, wasn't that a break! Scabby hated him and Scabby would sell his own mother out for a split on seven grand. Rico felt resentful. Just his damn luck to get mixed up with a bunch of yellowbellies and softies.

Chiggi came in.

"Cab out in front, Louis," he said.

Rico pointed at Red.

"That guy spilled the works. For two bits I'd bump him off."

Rico was furious. He made a move toward his armpit, but one of the bartenders opened the door and yelled:

"The bulls!"

"What!" cried Rico.

The bartender was trembling all over and his face was white.

"Police car out in front, boss."

Rico made a dive for the door but Chiggi grabbed him by the arm.

"Out the back, Louis."

Chiggi leapt across the room and pulled a switch and all the lights in the place went out. Then he took Rico by the arm and led him through the hall and out into a little court at the rear.

"So long, Louis," he said.

Chiggi slammed the door. Rico was in utter darkness.

"A hell of a chance I got," he said.

He stepped cautiously out into the alley back of the court and took a look around. The alley was blind to his right; to his left it came out onto a main thoroughfare and there was a bright arc light at that end. Rico took out his gun and moved slowly toward the arc light.

"You can't never tell," he said; then, in an excess of rage: "They'll never put no cuffs on this baby."

When he was within fifty feet of the main thoroughfare a man appeared at the end of the alleyway, a big man in a derby hat. He saw Rico and immediately blew a blast on his whistle. Rico raised his gun and pulled the trigger; it missed fire.

Rico was frantic. He wanted to live. For the first time in his life he addressed a vague power which he felt to be stronger than himself.

"Give me a break! Give me a break!" he implored.

The man in the derby hat raised his arm and Rico rushed him, pumping lead. Rico saw a long spurt of flame and then something hit him a sledgehammer blow in the chest. He took two steps, dropped his gun, and fell flat on his face. He heard a rush of feet up the alley.

"Mother of God," he said, "is this the end of Rico?"

THE END

The Silver Eagle
W. R. BURNETT

To the
Wilson and Oak Gang
1915-1918

It is a strange desire, to seek power and to lose liberty: or to seek power over others and to lose power over a man's self. The rising unto place is laborious; and by pains men come to greater pains; and it is sometimes base; and by indignities men come to dignities. The standing is slippery, and the regress is either downfall or at least eclipse, with is a melancholy thing.
—FRANCIS BACON

PART ONE

ONE

Michaelson laughed, and knocked the ashes from his cigar with his little finger, in order to show off a big diamond ring. Stein glanced across the room at Harworth and sat tapping with his cane.

"All right," said Harworth; "but talking about it is one thing, and collecting is another."

Michaelson leaned forward in his chair and shook his finger at Harworth.

"Sure, but I collect. I don't take no chances with big accounts. Hell, life's too short. Them kind of accounts ain't no good, anyway. Once you get the money that's all you need to worry about."

Harworth turned the check Michaelson had given him over and over, but said nothing.

"See what I mean?" Michaelson went on. "The guys that run accounts, big accounts, are squawkers. All they're looking for is a chance to welsh. Once you got their dough, give 'em the boot."

"Don't let 'em get in you in the first place," said Stein; "that's the best way to save a lot of trouble."

"Sure. Sure." Michaelson replied. "Sounds easy, but when a guy's lost his roll, maybe five, maybe ten grand, and he asks you if you can't stake him to a grand or so, what the hell! He'll play it back."

"Well," said Harworth to Michaelson, "all I got to say is, I wish I had a couple more men like you, Sam."

Stein looked up but said nothing. His face was dark and melancholy and seamed. His hair was grizzled and there was something patriarchal in his expression.

"Oh, I do my best, Mr. Harworth," said Michaelson, flushing with pleasure. "Look," he went on, "you gave me a break when I needed one damn bad. What I say is, play square with a square guy. Give me a chance and I'll double our take next month."

"How's the protection?" asked Stein.

"I'm looking after that," replied Michaelson sharply.

"I asked you a question."

Michaelson turned his sharp, pale, hawklike face toward Harworth.

"Well?" Stein insisted.

"Look," said Michaelson, "don't you trust me on that angle, Mr. Harworth?"

"Sure," said Harworth.

Michaelson threw a triumphant glance at Stein, but Stein said: "Who said anything about trusting! I asked you a plain question. I'm managing things here till I get further notice. I looked that expense sheet over and I didn't see no mention of money spent that way."

"Well," said Michaelson, looking at the carpet, "I don't keep no account of it, see; I can't. Bourke gets his fifty bucks a day and I got to take care of the dicks, a little at a time."

"Wait a minute, August," Harworth put in. "Don't go so fast. The take this month is away over last month. What you kicking about?"

"Sam," said Stein, "I want that protection money accounted for next month."

"Can you beat that!" exclaimed Michaelson. Then he addressed himself to Harworth: "I guess he thinks I'm crooked!"

Stein laughed, a single snort, then turned away and lit a cigar. Michaelson looked from one to the other.

"Jees! Can you beat that!"

"Never mind," said Harworth, getting to his feet and looking at his watch. "What time you got, August?"

Michaelson hastily pulled out an expensive watch, platinum, thin as paper and with his monogram in gold on the back.

"Five till three, boss," he said, displaying the watch.

"I'm going to give that bohunk a going over. I told him two-thirty. I guess he thinks all I've got to do is sit around and wait for him."

Harworth took a cigarette from a humidor on the table beside him and lit it. Stein said:

"He's a busy guy, Frank."

"Is he? Busy doing what? Telling everybody what a great man he is!"

Michaelson laughed and got up.

"Through with me, Mr. Harworth?"

"No. I want to ask you one question."

"Shoot."

"How did you collect from Joe Bergson and Faro Welch?"

Michaelson waved his cigar.

"It's a business secret."

"Well?"

Stein sat looking up at Michaelson, tapping with his cane. Michaelson rubbed his chin for a minute, looking from one to the other, then he said:

"Mr. Harworth, how many big accounts you got standing out at the Casa Alvarado and The Machine?"

"Plenty."

"Big ones?"

"Five or six in the thousands."

"How about your restaurants?"

"None there."

"All right. I'll collect every big account you got for ten percent."

Harworth said nothing but turned to look at Stein. Stein shrugged.

"What's your system?" he asked.

"Never mind. Never mind. I ain't asking for a thing; just ten percent. And I ain't taking it out. When you're satisfied you pay me. Is it a go?"

"Why not," said Harworth.

"Well," Stein smiled. "Sounds all right. Going to sic Canovi on 'em?"

Michaelson started and Stein smiled again.

"It's a bum system."

"They pay just the same," said Michaelson, "and that's the main thing. Canovi just has a quiet little talk with 'em and they pay. Sometimes they leave town and someone pays for 'em, that's all. See?"

"Nothing doing," said Stein. "We don't need money that bad."

Harworth stood looking from one to the other, perplexed.

"Say, let me in on this."

"Well," said Stein, "Sam here's got a nice little gentleman friend named Canovi. When people don't pay up he drops round to see them and asks them how they'd like to stop a few bullets!"

"Yeah, but it's just a stall. He don't even pack a heater."

"Don't what?"

"He don't carry a gun. It's all a bluff. It's the old run around."

Harworth's face hardened.

"Why not," he said. "It's better than suing. I'll send you a list, Sam; and the ten percent goes."

"Frank," Stein put in, "that's a bad move. You don't need the money."

"It's settled. I'm sick of carrying a half dozen rich mugs on my books. Let 'em pay up; they've got it."

"It's a cinch," said Michaelson, picking up his hat. "Rich guys 're always the hardest to collect from. They got it, and they know you know they got it. They can afford to stall. All right. Send me the list. I'll clear up your books in thirty days."

"Well," said Stein, "I wouldn't stand for murder myself."

Harworth started slightly, but said nothing.

"Jees!" exclaimed Michaelson, "listen to the guy. Say, them guys never take a second look at Canovi. They pay up. Canovi's got eyes! Jees, he looks like he ate rattlesnakes for breakfast, but he's as nice a guy as you'd want to meet."

"You bet!" said Stein.

There was a knock at the door and Joseph came in.

"Well?" called Harworth.

"Mr. Hrdlicka wants to see you, Mr. Harworth."

"All right."

"I'm on my way," said Michaelson. "See you soon."

"Wait a minute."

Joseph opened the door for Hrdlicka, a big, dark, powerfully built Bohemian, who was wearing a short black double-breasted coat, striped trousers and white spats. He bowed.

"I'm very late, Mr. Harworth. I was detained."

"Detained, eh? Goddam it, when I say two-thirty I mean it! You expect me to wait around here all day!"

Hrdlicka flushed, but said nothing.

"Hello, Anton," said Stein.

"Hello, August."

Hrdlicka took a chair beside Stein and handed him a big envelope containing the monthly account.

"Anton," said Harworth, "give Sam those six big accounts. He's going to collect them."

Hrdlicka looked at Michaelson for a moment, then took a second envelope from his pocket and handed it to Harworth, who gave it to Michaelson.

"It's all there," explained Hrdlicka. "Addresses, references and all. I thought you were going to sue."

"We'll try this first," said Harworth.

"It's a cinch." Michaelson walked to the door and then added: "Goodbye, boss."

Joseph showed him out and they heard him talking and laughing in the hall; then the door slammed. Stein tapped the paper he had in his hand.

"That's what I call a real account. You're making money hand over fist there, Frank."

"Business is good," said Hrdlicka. "Both places are packed every night but Monday. On Saturday we turn 'em away."

Harworth shrugged.

"August, when you get through with Hrdlicka come back to my room. I want to see you."

Then with a curt nod he went out. Hrdlicka rose half out of his chair to acknowledge the nod, then sank back with a profound sigh. Stein bent over the accounts, but Hrdlicka demanded:

"What did I ever do to Mr. Harworth?"

"Nothing, nothing, It's because you was late, see? He's awful damn touchy about things like that. He thinks you done it on purpose, trying to make him look small. He's a funny boy, that way."

"I couldn't help it."

"Never mind. Just remember: when he says two-thirty make it a quarter past and then he'll be all smiles, see?"

"I like him," said Hrdlicka. "He's a very interesting young man. So successful at his age."

"Well," Stein looked up over his glasses, "he's earned it. He was kicked around like a football. Never had a chance. His old man run one of the toughest saloons in Ohio. But that's between us, see? Don't never let him find out I told you!"

"Not for anything," said Hrdlicka.

TWO

When Stein came in, Harworth was sitting with his feet on the window sill, reading a newspaper. It was summer and the window was wide open. A strong, cool breeze was flapping the curtains and far away over the housetops Stein saw Belmont Harbor full of moored sailboats and launches, and beyond, the open lake, deep blue in the early evening.

"Hello, August," said Harworth, turning.

He was smiling now and his habitual set, harsh expression softened.

"Hello, kid," said August, putting his hand on Harworth's shoulder. "How you making out? I'm hungry."

"It's only about six-thirty," said Harworth, but he rang for Joseph, who appeared almost immediately.

"Yes sir," said Joseph.

"Tell Ella to hurry things up. August is starved."

"Yes sir," said Joseph, hesitating.

"Well?"

"I don't want to bother you, Mr. Harworth, but I wonder if ... I mean my wife's sick and it's been a big expense to me and I was just wondering. I didn't want to bother you but ..."

"Need money?"

"Yes sir."

"All right. Fix him up, August."

Joseph bowed slightly then he said:

"Excuse me, Mr. Harworth. But we was talking last night. All of us, I mean: Sandy and Ella, and we was saying we ought to thank you for the way you treat us."

"All right, Joseph," said Harworth, irritably. Joseph went out.

"Just because I play fish for that bunch of chiselers," said Harworth, laughing. "Only I know what it means not to have money."

"They swear by you, kid."

Harworth got up and stood looking out the window. August took out one of his big black cigars and lit it.

"Frank," he said, finally, settling himself into a big chair, "I don't like your friend Michaelson. He's tough."

"He gets results."

"Sure. But how? You know I never wanted you to get mixed up in that gambling racket, anyway. You're making enough money legitimately."

"Enough?" Harworth turned. "What do you mean enough! I want to make millions. Hell, this is piking."

"Well," said August, "I've seen the day when a five-spot looked pretty good to you."

"All right! All right. You knew me 'when,' didn't you!"

"Sure."

"Listen. I'm not started yet. I haven't begun to open up. This is pocket money."

August laughed, but said nothing.

"No kidding. I'd like to get into the big money."

"Well, you're in bigger money right now than I ever hoped to see. Nine to ten thousand a month don't look bad to me if you'd only keep some of it."

"Yeah, but it comes in dribbles. You know. You never feel like you've got anything."

"How about your investments?"

"I don't think that way. Money is money. A house is a house."

"A nigger financier," said August, laughing. "He's got to have spot cash or he thinks he's broke. How you made all this dough in the first place is a puzzle to me!"

"Well, just like any other guy that makes money. I got the breaks. That Zimmerman Point proposition put me up in the good money class." He came over and put his hand on Stein's shoulder. "And I had plenty of good advice."

"Thanks for the compliment. But why don't you take my advice anymore?"

"What do you mean?"

"About Michaelson. He's a crook. And about that strongarm stuff. You'll get somebody killed and wouldn't that be nice."

"No danger." Harworth thought for a moment then said: "You can't just kill a guy."

"Can't you?"

Joseph came in.

"Dinner's ready, Mr. Harworth."

"Thanks."

Joseph went out. As soon as the door was closed, Harworth seized Stein by the wrist and pulled him to his feet.

"Come on, August, you old glutton."

THREE

Hrdlicka opened the door of the dressing room and came in. Lily was lying on a couch at the side of her dressing table reading a magazine. Campi, in evening clothes, was walking up and down, smoking.

"Just had a call from Stein," said Hrdlicka; "Harworth's on his way down here."

"Thanks, Anton," said Lily, lowering the magazine.

She was small and slight with blondined hair and dark eyes. Her feet were small and well-arched and her hands were long and slim. Her face was heavily made up as she was ready for her first number.

"We'll move the first number up five minutes," said Hrdlicka; "he probably wants to see you."

Campi shrugged and turned away. He had a narrow dark face and patent leather hair. He was tall and slender and looked well in clothes, except that he was usually overdressed. He was very nervous and couldn't stay in a chair any length of time. His eyes were big and dark and his black eyebrows met above his nose.

"How's the crowd?" he asked.

"Good. Very good," said Hrdlicka.

When Hrdlicka had gone Campi laughed and turned to Lily.

"Well," he said, "get all set."

"He makes me sick," exclaimed Lily, throwing her magazine on the floor.

"Oh, yes," said Campi.

"Well, he does."

"It's a free country."

"Is it?"

"That's what they tell me."

Lily got up and stood with her hands on her hips, looking at Campi.

"Now don't start that."

Campi swore under his breath and turned away.

"Who got me into this?" she asked.

"Well, it's good dough, isn't it? We're fixed. Getting twice what we're worth."

"Think so?"

"Sure. You belong in a chorus; back row."

"Shut up."

Campi shrugged and taking out a flask drank from it.

"Just as long as you can put your feet under a table and buy liquor you're satisfied," said Lily.

"Well, what more could I want?"

He laughed, put his flask away and sat down on the couch. Lily went to the dressing table and began to dab powder on her face.

"He's a big chump," said Campi. "How he ever made all that dough I'll never tell! He don't know straight up." He got suddenly to his feet, went to the door and came back, imitating Harworth, with a set, harsh expression on his face, swinging his arms as he walked and swaggering.

"Hello," he said in a slightly hoarse voice, nodding curtly.

Lily leaned against the dressing table, laughing. Campi shrugged and sat down on the couch again.

"You don't know him like I do," said Lily.

"I hope not."

"Say, don't get smart. I mean he's bugs, off his nut. What does he want to wear a monocle for and all that stuff? Why, he looks to me like he ought to be shoveling coal with them shoulders of his, but here he is all dressed up like a chorus man."

"He thinks he's society," said Campi, then he bit his thumb at the wall and made a derisive noise with his lips.

"And that ain't all," said Lily, but turned back to the mirror without going on.

"Come on," said Campi; "let's have it."

"No, you wouldn't understand."

"But you do, eh? Jees, that's a compliment."

"All right, brainy."

There was a knock at the door. Beyond the dressing room a jazz band began to play.

"Your number, Miss Devereaux," someone called from the hall.

"O.K."

Lily bent over and kissed Campi, then she went out. Campi stretched out on the couch and closed his eyes.

In a few minutes, Cassella the headwaiter opened the door and hissed:

"Giovanni! Beat it! Here comes Harworth."

Campi leaped to his feet and hurried out into the hall, where he stood talking with Cassella. Harworth was coming down the hall with Hrdlicka, who was walking beside him, talking deferentially. Harworth was in evening clothes and carrying a top hat; he had a monocle screwed into his right eye. He looked slighter in dark clothes, but his enormous shoulders bulged under his coat.

"Hello," he said, nodding curtly.

"Hello, Mr. Harworth," said Campi. "Haven't seen you for a long time. We missed you around here."

"Been busy."

"Can I get you something?" asked Cassella. "A drink?"

"Don't use it."

"Of course not," said Hrdlicka, frowning at Cassella. "Go look after things, Louis. I'll take care of Mr. Harworth."

Cassella went back into the club. Harworth jerked his thumb toward Lily's dressing room.

"I'll wait here. Say, Hrdlicka, Lily's through for the night."

Hrdlicka and Campi exchanged a glance.

"She's got two more numbers," said Campi; "one with me."

"What of it?"

"We'll fix it. We'll fix it," said Hrdlicka. "You dance the Apache with Miss Raymond, Campi."

Campi set his jaw but said nothing. Harworth took out his billfold and offered Campi a fifty. Campi smiled and bowed, taking the bill.

"All set," he said.

Harworth nodded and went into Lily's dressing room. Hrdlicka and Campi stood looking at each other.

"Well," said Hrdlicka, "it's his place."

"Sure," said Campi, "but why don't he unscrew his face a little and smile; it wouldn't hurt him none."

"Quiet," Hrdlicka whispered, glancing apprehensively at Lily's door.

Harworth stood looking out the window of Lily's apartment. A cool breeze had sprung up and it felt good beating against his face. The clock was striking two. Lily sat watching him, her face pale and drawn. Why didn't he go?

"Well," he said, turning.

"I'm tired."

He nodded but didn't move. He stood looking at the floor. In repose his face was much softer, sad even. Lily had noticed this many times and was always puzzled by it. She thought of him as brutal; even Campi had tender moments and sometimes would tell her that he loved her (even if he didn't mean it), but Harworth was always taciturn, never expansive as a man should be at certain times. Often when she was lying with him there was a cold ferocity in his face. He had no idea of pleasure, he never relaxed.

"I'm going," he said.

She got up and came toward him. He picked up his hat from a chair and started for the door.

"Frank," she said, trying to make her voice tender, "you know what you promised me."

Harworth smiled.

"Well, it goes." He stood thinking for a moment then he said: "It all comes down to that, doesn't it?"

"What?"

"Never mind." He went out into the hall and opened the door. "I'll have Hrdlicka make you out a check. Good night."

"Aren't you going to kiss me?"

"What for?"

He went out.

She went back into the bedroom and, shrugging, began to get ready for bed; then suddenly she burst out crying.

Harworth had Sandy drive him down to Stromberg's, an all-night restaurant in The Loop. When he got out, he said to Sandy:

"Hungry?"

Sandy smiled.

"Yep."

Harworth handed him a bill.

"Get yourself something across the street."

Sandy took the bill but said:

"Nope. I'll go in with you and sit at the counter. This joint's tough this time of night."

Harworth looked at Sandy. He was big, redheaded and freckled; back in '17 he had been a pretty good middleweight, but he had gone across during the war and got himself shot up. Now his left arm wasn't any good. Harworth liked Sandy.

"All right," he said.

He went in and Sandy followed him. The cashier, an Italian, glanced up from his paper, then stared at Harworth, who had put his monocle into his eye and hadn't taken off his top hat. The cashier winked at one of the waiters, who grinned.

"Right this way, sir," said the waiter, bowing and winking at a group of men at a big table in the center of the room.

"Whoops!" said one of the men, "look at Algy."

Sandy stood leaning on the front counter, meditatively rubbing his chin. Harworth took off his hat and sat down.

"What'll it be?" asked the waiter.

Harworth ordered a sandwich and a cup of coffee, then took out a cigarette and lit it.

"Oh, girls!" said one of the men at the big center table.

There was a roar of laughter. Harworth glanced at them, then looked away, averting his eyes. They nudged each other.

The restaurant was crowded; all the booths along the walls were full and there was a steady murmur of conversation. Harworth smoked and glanced over the restaurant. It was a pretty tough-looking crowd.

"What a nice boy!" said one of the men loudly.

Harworth grew pale, shifted uneasily, then called:

"Talking to me?"

All the men at the big table turned suddenly to look at him.

"Oh, girls," said one of them, an Italian with a low, wide brow and a brutal, dark face, "he's alive."

"Pipe down," said Harworth, calmly.

Sandy sauntered back through the restaurant, rubbing his chin and watching the men at the big table. There was a long silence and people at the other tables began to crane their necks. Some men in the back stood up. The cashier came back quickly and whispered to the Italian, but he pushed the cashier away. Turning he called to Harworth:

"Nuts, you!"

The waiter came with Harworth's order, then hurried away. Sandy leaned against a booth and stared at the Italian.

"Look," said one of the men, "he's got his army with him."

"Oh, girls!" said the Italian.

Sandy yawned loudly. The proprietor, a tall Swede, with reddish hair and a big mustache, came out of his office and hurried back to the big table. The Italian saw him coming and got up.

"How'd you like a punch in the nose," he shouted at Harworth.

"Sit down," said Sandy; "you just think you're tough."

The proprietor came over to Harworth and said:

"Don't get mixed up with that man. He's a bad one. When he's sober he's bad enough. I'm always having trouble with him."

"Who is he?" asked Harworth.

The proprietor called the cashier and asked him who the Italian was.

"Don't know," said the cashier, "but I see him in here with Sam Michaelson off and on."

The restaurant was in confusion now. Men were standing up calling to the proprietor, demanding to know what was the matter. Women were looking apprehensively at the Italian, who, a little unsteady on his feet, was walking toward Harworth. Sandy got in front of Harworth's booth and stood rubbing his chin with his left hand, carrying his right low, ready for a sudden uppercut.

"Call a cop!" yelled somebody.

But Harworth stood up and motioned for the Italian to come over. The Italian turned to stare at the men he was with, then he went over to Harworth's table and leaned on it. Sandy looked at Harworth, puzzled.

"Say! ..." the Italian began.

But Harworth said:

"Wait a minute. You know Sam Michaelson, don't you?"

"Sure," said the Italian, blinking. "I work for him."

"All right," said Harworth, "he works for me."

The Italian blinked.

"Yeah? You own The Burgoyne, hunh?"

"Yes."

"Oh, well," said the Italian, grinning. "'Scuse me."

"What's your name?" asked Harworth.

"Canovi."

Harworth studied him, then he said:

"All right. Go back to your table and behave yourself."

"Say! ..." said Canovi.

Then he stood staring at Harworth's pale, set face.

"Go on."

Canovi shrugged and, turning, went back to his table.

"Jees! What a tough-looking mug," said Sandy.

The proprietor and the cashier stood staring at each other. Gradually the clamor subsided; waiters hurried about among the tables, carrying loaded trays. Sandy walked back to the counter and ordered. The men at Canovi's table sat whispering among themselves and from time to time one of them turned to look at Harworth.

When Harworth was finishing his coffee, one of the men with Canovi got up and came over.

"Mr. Harworth," he said, "Canovi's ginned up. He didn't mean nothing. He was just fooling."

"That's all right," said Harworth.

The man went back and nudged Canovi, who grinned at Harworth and nodded.

On the way home, Sandy opened the glass panel behind him and said:

"Boss, that mug's poison. He was packing a gun. I seen the strap under his vest."

"He's tough, all right," said Harworth.

Harworth woke with a start. The sun was up now, sending a blinding beam through his curtains. He was sweating clammily and every nerve in his body was tense. His head ached dully.

"What a face! What a face!" he thought.

He had been dreaming about Canovi.

The morning wind sent his curtains flapping and bellying and there was the reassuring clamor of traffic in the street below, but he lay for a minute or two with his mind in confusion and his pulses racing.

Then he jumped up, stripped off his pajamas and took a shower. The cold water made his body glow; he felt fit and young, glad to be alive on this bright morning. But he couldn't fight down a feeling of uneasiness.

He was getting in with a bad bunch. Maybe August was right.

FOUR

Harworth was alone in the library when Joseph came in. August was out in Stony Island going over the books of Harworth's far South Side restaurant: one of a chain, known as STEIN'S.

"Well?" asked Harworth, looking up.

"A man named Joyce wants to see you," said Joseph.

"Joyce? I don't know anybody by that name."

Joseph gave Harworth a card. It read:

ROBERT OGDEN JOYCE

The name was vaguely familiar and Harworth sat tapping the card against his thumb and looking off across the room.

"Oh, well," said Harworth. "I'll see him."

Joseph went out. Harworth sat thinking. The name was familiar, still he was sure the man was not known to him personally. He must have read the name some place, but where? Suddenly he sat up. R. O. Joyce! Why, good Lord, he'd seen it in the society column (which he never failed to read). Sure, that was it. Just the other night he had seen the name in the list of guests at a big, swanky wedding. He got up hastily, smoothed out his coat and screwed his monocle into his eye. Then he lit a cigarette and stood waiting, pleased and perplexed.

Joseph opened the door and a tall, young man with light hair, a small mustache and very blue eyes, stepped in. Joseph closed the door. Joyce stood hesitating.

"Want to see me?" asked Harworth.

"Are you Frank Harworth?"

"Francis Harworth."

"Well ..."

"Sit down."

Joyce sat down and accepted a cigarette.

"Want to see me on business?" asked Harworth, slightly embarrassed by Joyce's very apparent bewilderment.

"Yes, in a way," said Joyce, clearing his throat and glancing about Harworth's library, with its tier after tier of books.

"Drink?"

"Well," Joyce smiled slightly, "I never refuse."

Harworth nodded and rang for Joseph, who came in immediately.

"Yes sir," said Joseph.

"Make Mr. Joyce one of those orange blossoms. It's a specialty with him," Harworth went on, smiling.

Joseph went out. Joyce sat, puzzled, looking at the magnificent big room, at the books, at Harworth's monocle.

"To tell you the truth," said Joyce, "I didn't expect anything quite like this. What a wonderful place you've got here."

"It's not bad."

"No, really. I wish I could afford a place like this."

Harworth laughed shortly.

"It sure sets me back, that's a fact."

Joyce smiled slightly, but said nothing.

"But when you got it, spend it, that's what I say."

"You're making a lot of money, aren't you?"

"Can't complain."

Joyce hesitated for a long time, then he said:

"Mr. Harworth, I had a very unpleasant experience this morning."

"That so?"

"Yes. A man named Canovi came in my place and threatened me."

"Oh, yes."

"It's about a bill I owe Mr. Hrdlicka at the Casa Alvarado. I went to see Mr. Hrdlicka, a nice fellow, by the way, and he told me I was to see you."

"That's right."

"But good Lord, Mr. Harworth, aren't there other ways of collecting bills?"

"That's out of my hands. One of my men's handling that for me. Why don't you pay?"

Joyce sat clasping and unclasping his hands. At first he had been perfectly at ease with Harworth, though puzzled, had felt, if anything, a slight contempt for this man who sported a monocle and bragged about how much he made; but now, noting the harsh, pale face and the steady stare, he felt very uneasy and wished he had turned the whole business over to his lawyer.

Joseph came in with the orange blossom on a tray and Joyce took it, with a nod of his head. Joseph went out.

"Won't you join me?" asked Joyce.

"I never touch it."

Joyce sipped his drink.

"Excellent," he said; "very good."

Harworth lit another cigarette and sat with his legs crossed, watching Joyce. Finally he said:

"You're Thomas Joyce's son, aren't you?"

"Yes. Know him?"

"No. But I used to see his name in the paper. He had the rapid transit business tied up, didn't he?"

"Yes. He was a good business man. Nothing like me."

Joyce finished his drink and put the glass on the table beside him. There was a short silence, then Harworth asked:

"How much do you owe?"

"About three thousand dollars, I think. I'm perfectly good for it. But you see I have a set income from Father's estate and I live it up."

Harworth said nothing, but in spite of the fact that he was awed by Joyce's position in society, he felt somewhat contemptuous of him. A plain parasite.

"When can you pay?"

"Not for thirty days. Even then it will strain me."

Joyce smiled slightly and looked away.

"All right," said Harworth. "I'll take care of it. You're directly responsible to me, understand?"

"Fine," said Joyce, rising; "thank you."

Harworth got up also and offered his hand. They pumped arms briefly, then Joyce said:

"What a lot of books you've got."

"Yes," said Harworth, looking proudly at his books.

"Do you mind if I look? I read a lot."

"No," said Harworth, smiling. "Help yourself."

Joyce walked over to one of the larger shelves and began to read the titles: *Paradise Lost, The Divine Comedy* in translation, *Shakespeare's Plays, Shelley's Poems*, all the usual library stuff in tooled calf. He turned to Harworth.

"Frankly now, do you read these?"

Harworth flushed slightly but said:

"No."

"Good. If you'd said yes I wouldn't have believed it. I've tried them all.

I used to think it was obligatory, you know. What nonsense!"

Harworth smiled and warmed up.

"They fill up space," he said, "and they look good. My stuff's over here."

Joyce followed him to a little book case in a dark corner, expecting the cheapest fiction, but, bending down, discovered *Casanova*, three lives of Brummell, Goldsmith's *Beau Nash, Caesar's Commentaries,* Suetonius's *Lives of the Twelve Caesars, Plutarch*, and a half dozen lives of Napoleon. He looked up in surprise.

"Well!" he said.

"I like that kind of stuff," said Harworth, flushing slightly. "Biography, you see."

"I suppose you got the taste in college," said Joyce, getting up and looking at Harworth, greatly perplexed.

Harworth hesitated, but said:

"No, I never even graduated from high school."

"Oh."

There was a long embarrassed silence, then Joyce spoke.

"Here I am taking up your time. I'd better run along."

Harworth wanted Joyce to stay; he wanted somebody he could talk to; he wanted to invite him to dinner, but he said nothing.

"Thanks for all your trouble," said Joyce.

Harworth rang for Joseph.

"No trouble at all."

Joseph opened the door and stood waiting. Joyce hesitated.

"Why don't you drop around and see me some time, Mr. Harworth? I live right near you. Toward town a couple of blocks on Rush Street."

Harworth was deeply pleased and smiled, but said:

"I might. Thanks."

As soon as Joyce had gone, Harworth called Michaelson and told him that he was looking after Joyce's account.

"But, boss," said Michaelson, "you already turned him over to me. Is that business?"

"I'll send you a check for the ten percent."

"That's different."

"Any news from the others?"

"Three paid. Ask Hrdlicka."

"All right. But that's the last of that. I bumped into Canovi the other night."

"He told me," said Michaelson. "Jees, I'm sorry about that. He was plastered."

"Can't you make him lay off the liquor? He'll get you in trouble some time."

"Don't you worry. Just leave everything to me. I can handle that egg. I got plenty on him."

Harworth was taking a shower when August came in. August opened the bathroom door and called:
"Frank! All set. The books are straight."
"Good," called Harworth.
"I guess Rieger beat it on account of his wife. He was having trouble with her. Ain't men silly! Throwing up a job like that! I gave Schultz a shot at it."
"Fine. How's last month's take?"
"Away up."
Supporting himself with his cane August limped to a big chair and sank into it. He had been drinking and felt mellow. He lit a cigar and puffed meditatively, waiting for Harworth. After a moment he began to sing.

"Sweet Rosie O'Grady,
My wild Irish rose ..."

Harworth shouted:
"What do you know about the Irish, you kike!"
"All right! All right!" said August, laughing.... "But the Irish ain't so much. I notice you changed your name."
"Not so loud," said Harworth.
August sang a few more bars, then called:
"All right, Mr. Keogh."
"Say," said Harworth, putting his head in the door, "not so loud, August."
"Ashamed of a good Irish name like Keogh."
Harworth hastily threw on his underclothes and a bathrobe and ran out into the bedroom. He stood in front of August, with his hands on his hips, laughing at him.
"What a bun you got," he said. "Don't kid me. You can't get that way on beer."
"*I* can," said August.
Harworth sat down and lit a cigarette. He looked at August for a moment, then he said:
"Honest, August, do you enjoy that stuff? I mean do you like to get woozy?"
"I do. Pleasantly so. I hate crying jags, and fighting jags. A man should get tight in a civilized manner. Drink beer and ale. Look, when

I was a young fellow, I used to fight it. You know what I mean. I drank hard liquor; kept at it steadily all day long. One night they started to come up over the foot of the bed after me; snakes. So I been drinking beer ever since."

"I don't like it," said Harworth. "I saw too much of it. My old man used to have a bouncer named West and I used to see him bouncing poor bums out on their tails at all hours of the night. Where's the percentage?"

"That's it. There ain't no percentage. That's why it don't appeal to you."

Harworth looked at the carpet and said nothing.

"Frank, don't you ever have a good time? Don't you ever say to yourself, 'well, here goes,' and cut loose?"

"Well, I have a pretty good time."

"No; you think about yourself too much. You can't have a good time that way. Look, all you think about is making money."

"Well," said Harworth, flushing, "somebody's got to think about it."

"Now, now," said August; then keeping time with his cane, he went on with his song. His voice was deep and rich, pleasant to listen to. "You see," he said when he had finished, "that's how I feel with a couple gallons of beer under my belt. The world looks like a new place."

Harworth got up and began to dress. Suddenly he turned to August.

"Say, guess who was here this afternoon?"

"I give it up."

"R. O. Joyce."

"Joyce?"

"Yeah. His old man owned all the L lines."

"Did he? What did he want?"

"It was about an account at the Alvarado. But he invited me over to his place, see? He's a swell."

"Well, well."

"You don't know about things like that. It means something to be invited out by a guy like that."

"Does it?"

"Sure. He comes from an old family."

"Well, so do you. I've heard your old man tell many a time how he was descended from an Irish king."

"Quit kidding!"

"I ain't kidding. Your old man used to say: 'I'm descended from an Irish king and I kin lick any man in Cleveland.'"

"Say, lay off my old man."

August lay back in his chair, laughing. Harworth said nothing for a long time and August sat humming to himself.

"August," said Harworth, finally "if you was me what would you do? Would you call Joyce up and invite him over here? Or should I wait till he calls me?"

"Don't ask me. Etiquette is one thing I don't know nothing about. If he's a good guy, call him up; if he ain't, forget it. Just because his old man was so and so, don't mean anything. He may be a louse for all you know."

Harworth stared at August but said nothing.

Joseph knocked and came in.

"Dinner in fifteen minutes, Mr. Harworth."

"All right."

"Good! Good!" cried August, pounding with his cane.

FIVE

"Look at that rain," Joyce called from the window seat. "What a night!"

"Oh, well," said Richman, "I wasn't going any place, anyway."

Richman was a short young man, already corpulent, with a fat, pale face and a bull neck. He was lying on a lounge with his hands under his head, looking at the ceiling. He wrote special articles for a newspaper and occasionally had a story published. He leaned toward satire, and mildly satirical in ordinary life, in print he was ferocious.

The phone rang and Richman made a move to answer it, but Arthur Burne, who had been sitting at the piano, pecking at the keys, beat him to it.

"Who is it?" shouted Joyce. "If it's a woman I'm not here."

"It's your cousin," called Burne; "she's coming over with Larsen."

"Oh, Lord," said Joyce.

"He'll be delighted," said Burne over the phone; "we all will." Hanging up the receiver he added: "And I mean it."

"What you see in her is beyond me," said Joyce. "Nice enough looking, but what a disposition!"

Without speaking, Burne went back to the piano, and began pecking away again; he played a certain progression over and over and as it ended on an excruciating dissonance, Joyce finally called:

"Good Lord, Arthur!"

Burne turned.

"Does that make your flesh creep?"

"It does."

"Good."

Richman sighed and closed his eyes. Joyce got up and began to walk back and forth. The rain drummed steadily and occasionally a gust caught it and flung it against the window with a splash.

Burne went over and over his progression, bending down from time to time to listen. He was a small man, swarthy and hairy, with heavy eyebrows and soft, irregular features. He was very alert and agile, moved quickly, and was very restless. His face was lean and healthy, his glance keen.

"There," he said, raising his hands from the piano; "for muted strings, oboe and English horn. It's fine!"

"Short, isn't it?" asked Richman without smiling.

"That wasn't funny," said Burne.

"Play something! Play something!" Joyce's voice sounded tired.

"Oh, have a drink," put in Burne, getting up and crossing to a chair, where he sat, smoking and swinging his feet.

"If I had any money, I'd go East for a couple of weeks," said Joyce; "this place is getting on my nerves."

"I like it," said Burne.

"So do I," Richman agreed. "It gives you perspective. If you live here long enough any place will look good to you."

"No, I really like it. It's the rawest town in the world."

"I don't like 'em raw," said Richman; "I was born in Arkansas."

"Well, I was born here," Joyce yawned, "and it's always been this way."

"I hope it stays this way," said Burne.

Richman yawned and sat up.

"If I stay here much longer I'll be asleep."

"So'll I," said Joyce.

"Oh, look here," said Richman, "let's talk."

"I've heard everything you've got to say."

"A perfect host!" laughed Richman.

He got up and walked around the room humming, looking indifferently at the pictures and fingering the magazines.

There was a long silence and then the doorbell rang. "Oh Lord!" said Joyce, "it's Louise and Olaf." Burne went to the door and opened it. Louise Joyce ran in, shaking water from her hat which she was carrying.

"Hello," said Burne.

"Look at me," cried Louise. "I'm dripping. It's a wonder that they wouldn't have a marquee here."

"They have," said Joyce. "Where are your eyes?"

"No they haven't," said Larsen, coming in and shaking water from him like a dog; "it blew down."

"Oh, well," said Richman.

Louise turned to him.

"Don't say 'Oh, well,' Berg. I've heard you say that a thousand times."

"Now, now," Burne put in. "Berg accepts the universe and that's his way of saying so. No matter what happens he says 'Oh, well!'"

"Thanks," said Richman.

Louise threw her coat and hat on a chair, sat down and accepted a cigarette. She was very slender with ash-blond hair, which she wore long, and large blue eyes with black lashes. She was broad-shouldered and narrow-hipped and had long, slender, well-shaped legs.

"Drink?" asked Burne.

Louise looked at her cousin, who was lying on the lounge.

"What's the matter, Bob, bored again? Yes, I'll have a drink."

Burne went to get the drink and Joyce said: "Tolerably."

"Well, it's no wonder. The company you keep."

"What's wrong with us?" Richman demanded. "Eh, Larsen?"

Larsen had sat down across from Louise and was looking at her. He was a big young man with white-blond hair and a red face. He started at the mention of his name and said:

"Sure."

"I don't mean you," said Louise. "Don't be so touchy. I mean a certain brunette who shellacs her face."

"Her name is Gladys," Joyce explained.

"We saw you at the Drake."

"Who's we?" asked Joyce.

"Helen Magnussen and I. You might at least 've taken her some place else."

"That's where his money goes," sang Richman.

"Well, who's Helen Magnussen, anyway!" Joyce demanded. "She's not so particular. Gladys is all right. Her husband left her."

Richman burst out laughing.

"No wonder," said Louise.

Burne came back with a tray full of drinks and passed them around.

"What do you get for this?" Richman inquired.

"The pleasure," Burne replied. "Somebody's got to do it. Bob won't move. And his Filipino boy left him since he stopped paying wages."

"I made my own bed this morning," said Joyce.

"Well, you've got to start to work some time," laughed Louise.

"I'm up to my neck in debt right now."

"You've got company," Richman put in.

"Sure," said Larsen. "I owe."

There was a long silence and they all sat sipping their drinks. The rain had slackened a little and the wind had died down. Joyce opened a panel of the window and fanned the smoke out. In the stillness they heard the siren of a lake boat. Then Richman spoke. "'He knew the melancholy of packet boats.' That's a quotation from Flaubert. Say what is a packet boat, anyway, and why are they melancholy?"

No one answered. Burne got up and went over to the piano bench but sat without playing, looking at the keys and sipping his drink. There was a prolonged silence then Richman said:

"Let's play post office."

"There isn't a man in this room I'd kiss," said Louise.

Joyce laughed shortly.

"There are men in this room you have kissed."

"Who?" demanded Larsen, opening his eyes wide and looking around.

Louise laughed, then she smiled at Larsen.

"Thanks for that laugh, Olaf."

Larsen smiled and studied the toes of his shoes.

"Well," said Richman, "let's get back to Gladys."

"Fine," Joyce agreed. "I think I'll call her up and have her come over. When she gets a few drinks you'd be surprised."

"Oh, no you won't," said Louise, "not while I'm here."

"Aren't women funny?" said Richman.

Burne began to play a Chopin waltz, but after a few bars he struck some discords and changed to "Oh, how I miss you tonight." Then he stopped and turned round on the bench, facing the rest. In the stillness Larsen's stomach rumbled loudly and he flushed painfully and cleared his throat.

"How's the portrait coming, Olaf?" asked Burne, feeling sorry for him.

"Fine," Larsen replied; "only," he went on, pointing at Louise, "she won't sit still. She wiggles, wiggles."

"I sit still as long as I can," said Louise; "but when Olaf gets to work he forgets all about you; he thinks you're a piece of bric-a-brac."

"Oh, not you," said Larsen; "others, yes."

"I've got it!" cried Joyce, leaping up.

"Keep it!" said Richman.

They all stared at Joyce, but Louise said:

"Berg, why will you say those silly things?"

"It's a form of insanity."

"Listen," Joyce went on, "I know you won't believe this, but listen, anyway." Then lighting a cigarette and pacing up and down he told them how he had run up a huge bill at the Casa Alvarado (principally lobster salad, mushrooms and oysters for Gladys), and how he had put off paying the bill, in fact throwing the letters containing the bills in the wastebasket unopened, until one day a man called on him and told him to pay up or else.

"Honestly," said Joyce; "I couldn't believe my ears. He was an Italian and he had the most murderous face I ever saw on a human. I thought it was a joke; it wasn't."

"Why didn't you call the police?" asked Larsen.

"Olaf," said Richman, "what police?"

"Anyway," said Joyce. "I thought I'd better take it seriously, so I went to see the manager of the place, and he referred me to the owner. Now, wait! You haven't heard anything yet."

Then, flushing and dropping his bored, listless air, he told them how he had gone to see Harworth, expecting a tough or at least a smart Jew, and had found a magnificent apartment, a servant in livery, a very cold and polite young man, who wore a monocle, didn't drink, and read *Caesar's Commentaries* and Suetonius.

They all stared at Joyce, stupefied. Then Richman said:

"Drop down and see Doc Herman tomorrow. He's the best neurologist in town. Have you started to buy pink silk shirts by the gross yet? That's the way De Maupassant began."

"Really, Bob?" Louise demanded.

"Really," said Joyce, smiling. "He's tall and he has very broad shoulders. He talks slang and says 'sure' and 'yeah.'"

"Who doesn't?" Richman demanded.

"I know," said Joyce; "but it's the way he says it."

"How old is he?" asked Louise.

"Well, about thirty-five I'd say, maybe older."

"What you think of that!" said Larsen. "Wears a monocle? Is he a foreigner?"

"No; plain American. Very plain."

Burne whirled around on the bench and began to play loudly and discordantly.

"Arthur!" called Louise.

"Well," said Burne, stopping, "we might as well all go crazy at once."

"I don't believe it!" snapped Richman.

"You don't?" cried Joyce. "I'll bet you fifty dollars."

"I'm not that skeptical. Anyway, who would I collect from?"

"He was very nice," said Joyce; "he took personal charge of my account. And I'm going to pay him."

"Now I know you're losing your mind!"

"All right," said Joyce; "I'll invite him over. I told him to drop in on me some night."

"Do it, Bob," cried Louise. "Invite him over right now."

Joyce looked at his watch.

"It's ten o'clock."

"He's backing water," cried Burne.

Without another word, Joyce went out into the hall and shut the door. They all sat looking at each other.

"Well," said Louise, "this is something like it."

In a few minutes Joyce came back laughing: "He's coming."

"Good," said Louise.

Joyce went on laughing, then he said:

"What do you think he asked me? 'Shall I dress?' says he in a nice, polite voice. 'No,' says I, 'this is very informal!'"

"Oh, Lord," exclaimed Richman; "I'll bet this will be terrible."

But Louise got up and went into Joyce's bedroom to fix her hair.

When the doorbell rang, Joyce hurried to answer it. Louise lit a cigarette and lay back in her chair. Larsen and Richman got up and stood waiting, but Burne remained on the piano bench, swinging his feet.

Joyce opened the door. It was Sandy, the chauffeur.

"'Scuse me," he said. "Is this where Mr. Joyce lives?"

"Yes," said Joyce.

Sandy turned.

"Here you are, boss."

Harworth came down the hall hurriedly and offered his hand to Joyce. He was dressed in a double-breasted gray suit, a soft silk shirt with a dark tie, and he had a soft light hat crushed in his right hand. As soon as he had shaken hands he put his monocle in his eye and said:

"I forgot your number, and we couldn't find your name downstairs. All right, Sandy."

"Too bad," said Joyce; "come in."

He stood aside and Harworth came into the hall and stopped. Richman and Larsen stood in the doorway, looking. Joyce introduced them and Harworth, shook their hands and made them each a bow, a Prussian military bow he had seen in the movies.

Larsen smiled, very friendly, but Richman, turned and stared at Joyce behind Harworth's back with his mouth slightly open.

"The rain's stopped," said Harworth.

"Really?" exclaimed Richman.

Joyce scowled at Richman, then he took Harworth into the library. Burne got to his feet, acknowledged Harworth's bow from across the room and sat down again.

"And this," said Joyce, "is my cousin, Louise. I was saving her till last."

Louise reached up to shake hands and smiled at him. Harworth held her hand for a moment, then said:

"You look something alike, you and Mr. Joyce."

"Thank you," said Joyce, laughing.

Harworth flushed.

"I mean, well, you know. There's a family resemblance."

"That's interesting," said Louise. "Sit down."

She indicated a chair beside her. Harworth stood uncertainly turning his hat in his hand. Joyce said:

"Give me your hat, Mr. Harworth."

He took Harworth's hat and Harworth sat down. There was a prolonged silence. Louise sat smoking and watching the smoke curl up from her cigarette. Larsen and Richman sat down on the lounge, both of them looking at Harworth, each in his own way: Larsen staring stolidly, Richman glancing at him, then averting his eyes. Harworth began to shift uncomfortably and finally dropped his monocle from his eye, caught it deftly and put it in his vest pocket.

"You do it well," said Richman.

Joyce cleared his throat nervously.

"I'll mix some drinks. What will it be, Mr. Harworth?"

"I'll take some ginger ale, or some White Rock with lemon." Then he turned to Louise. "I don't drink, you know."

"So Bob said." She turned and looked at him. "Why not?"

"I try to keep fit."

"Why?"

He was somewhat surprised by the question and didn't answer immediately.

"Well," he said, finally, "I like to keep fit."

"That's an interesting explanation," said Richman, turning to Larsen.

Harworth glanced over at Richman and their eyes met. Richman felt uncomfortable; Harworth's eyes were dark, keen and hard. Richman understood immediately that Harworth had caught the purpose of his remark. He said:

"I wish I had enough backbone to give up drinking."

"Not me," said Burne. "I like drinking, and I manage to keep pretty fit."

This sounded like a challenge to Harworth, who turned to look at Burne.

"You look fit," he said. "Box?"

"No, I don't do any of the prescribed things. I just sit around and fill up on liquor. It keeps me fit."

"You'll feel it someday."

"I doubt it."

"You will," said Larsen. "That's right. I wrestle to keep in shape. It's great."

Harworth smiled at Larsen, who seemed sympathetic.

"Who do you wrestle with?" demanded Richman. "Your models?"

"Of course not," replied Larsen, scowling.

Burne and Richman laughed. Louise said:

"What a simple soul. He paints, Mr. Harworth. Very well, too. He's making a portrait of me."

"I'll buy it," said Harworth.

There was a short silence, and Louise turned to look at Harworth, noting the broad pale face with the high cheekbones, the thick, curved eyebrows and the heavy jaw and neck.

"I wouldn't sell it," said Larsen. "It's for Louise."

"That's why he can't pay his rent," explained Louise.

"Sometimes I pay," said Larsen.

Everyone laughed but Harworth, who sat with his arms folded looking grave. He was all at sea with these people; the people he had known never talked about not paying rent; that would be a disgrace.

"One time Olaf painted a picture of The Loop in winter," Louise said to Harworth. "It was very good. A man who owned a restaurant wanted to buy it to put in his window, but Olaf wouldn't sell."

"Why should I?" Larsen demanded. "That picture is not for a restaurant window."

"Did he offer you a good price?" Harworth inquired.

"Very good."

Harworth said nothing, but looked from one to the other. Joyce came in with the drinks on a tray and passed them around. Then he sat down.

Finally Burne said:

"Speaking about keeping in shape, do you box, Mr. Harworth?"

"Yeah. Every day. My chauffeur is an ex-pug. He got wounded in the war, but he can still step."

"Really?" said Louise. "Do you like boxing? I've always wanted to see a real match, but no one would ever take me."

"I'll take you," said Harworth.

There was a short silence and Joyce stared hard at his cousin, but she said:

"All right. When?"

Burne got to his feet and walked over to Louise. "But, Louise," he said, "you don't want to go to a fight. That's no place for you."

"Why not?"

"The best people go," said Harworth.

"Do they?" asked Burne. "And who are the best people?"

"Well," said Harworth shifting. "Society, I mean."

Louise laughed but said nothing. There was another silence, then Burne said:

"You're joking, Louise. But if you must go, I'll take you."
Harworth hesitated.
"I've got a boy fighting Friday night. Both of you go along with me."
They all turned to look at him.
"A boy?" Louise demanded. "What boy?"
"A boy called Red Cannon. He's under contract to me. I mean, of course, I don't pay any attention to what he does; he's got a manager. But I lent him the money to get started. He's fighting his first main-go Friday night."

"We'll do it," said Louise.

Burne looked over Harworth's shoulder at Joyce, swearing under his breath.

"If anything should happen that I couldn't get away, I'll send one of my cars after you and turn up later."

"It's a go," said Louise.

Her eyes met Harworth's and held. He flushed slightly and looked away. He had never seen such a beautiful woman before; he wanted to reach out and pull her toward him. The impulse was so strong that he looked resolutely off across the room and did not look in her direction anymore when she talked. But he carried in his mind an image of her with her ash-blond hair shining under the lights, her head tilted back, her throat curving.

At twelve o'clock Harworth got up to go. Joyce protested out of politeness, but Harworth said:

"I want to get a good sleep tonight. I've got to get up early."

He shook hands with the men and murmured a few off-hand, conventional phrases; then he turned to Louise and when she offered her hand he took it and said:

"I'm going to look forward to Friday night."

"All right," she said; then she asked: "Are the fights very brutal?"

Harworth laughed.

"No; not anymore. Nowadays the fighters are business men."

He nodded to the rest, said good night to Louise, and went out, followed by Joyce.

When he heard the door shut, Richman exclaimed:

"Well, that's that."

"Oh, no," said Burne, "that isn't that. Louise wants to see him again. She always did have a taste for low company."

Louise looked around the room.

"That's right."

Larsen said:

"Nice fellow. I like him."

Joyce came back and sank into a chair.

"Well," said Richman, "your skyrocket was a fizzer."

"He's dull as the deuce," Burne agreed.

"I like him," said Larsen. "He has a Roman head. Strong. I would like to paint him."

"Nonsense!" cried Burne, making a gesture of disgust.

"By the way, speaking of Romans," said Richman, "what about Suetonius and *Caesar's Commentaries?* He looks to me like he was raised on Emily Post and *What Every Boy Should Know.*"

Burne burst out laughing, but Joyce asked:

"Well, did you expect him to come in carrying them under his arm?"

"Yes. Now that I've seen him."

"And why the monocle?" asked Burne.

"I think he looks fine wearing a monocle," said Louise.

"Women's opinions never matter."

"All the same," said Larsen, "I'd like to paint him."

They all sat looking at each other; then Louise said: "I'd enjoy the fights much more if you didn't go, Arthur."

"But I'm going."

Louise stretched lazily and got up.

"Come on, Olaf."

"I'll run along with you," said Burne.

At ten o'clock the next morning someone knocked at Louise's door. Her maid opened it and Burne stepped in. Louise recognized his voice and called:

"Arthur."

He went into the living room, dangling his hat. Louise was lying on the lounge, reading.

"Well?" she said.

He waited till the maid had closed the door.

"I didn't sleep a wink."

"Oh, don't start all over again."

Burne sat down and she noticed that his hands were trembling and that his swarthy face was drawn.

"Louise," he said, "marry me."

She sat up, shaking her head. "Arthur, you haven't a cent and neither have I."

"But, I'll get going before long."

"I can't risk it."

Burne sat staring at the carpet. Suddenly he burst out:

"I'm a damned fool to want to marry anybody. Least of all, you."

"Thanks."

"Well, you know it's true. You think money's to play with."

"What is it for?"

"It's an armor against the world."

"You sound just like Berg Richman."

"Oh, Louise! Can't you take a chance?"

"No. I'm tired of being afraid to go to the door. It's lovely to say that money doesn't matter and all that. But it does. No one is half decent to me anymore. Helen Magnussen is the only one who ever calls me up. Have I changed? Father went bankrupt. That's an offense against the Holy Ghost."

"I had quite enough of that last night."

"Wouldn't I be in a lovely position if it weren't for what Uncle Thomas left me!"

"Oh, let's go someplace," said Burne. "Let's get out in the air."

"I don't mind."

They walked down Division Street and took a bus north. It was a bright summer day and they sat on top. A steady breeze was blowing in from the lake. The beaches were crowded and, far off, sailboats were skimming over the water. Lincoln Park looked green and tranquil in the sun. They got off at the bus stop across from the Lion House and waited in a pedestrian traffic lane for the policeman's whistle.

"What a day!" exclaimed Burne.

Louise put her hand on his arm.

"Look!"

A Rolls Royce limousine had drawn up at the white traffic line; it was all a-glitter in deep maroon and silver and there was a liveried chauffeur at the wheel. Harworth, in a Panama, his monocle gleaming, was sitting back talking to a well-dressed woman with blondined hair and a small determined face.

Burne and Louise crossed to the park in silence; then the policeman blew his whistle and turning, Louise saw the limousine move off. Harworth hadn't seen them.

At the entrance to the Lion House, Burne spoke: "He's filthy with money."

"He earned it, Bob says."

"Well, all you need to earn money is cunning and lack of scruples."

Louise didn't reply. She stood leaning on the rail looking at a huge African lion, which was pacing up and down behind the bars.

"Louise, don't go to that fight. Harworth's a tough. He owns a gambling house."

Louise thought for a while then she said:

"I've been thinking it over. I'm not going."

"Good."

They walked along arm in arm, looking into the different cages. Two black panthers, male and female, magnificent animals with blunt, strong heads and glossy coats, were rolling on the floor of their cage, playfully biting and striking at each other.

"Look," cried Louise, "the male has a head just like Harworth."

Burne turned to stare at her, but said nothing.

Harworth sat with his hands resting on his desk, looking at Canovi. The Italian had discarded his old cap and his baggy clothes and was dressed in a striped suit and a pink silk shirt. He was leaning slightly forward with his chin thrust out.

"Molina'll give you an awful cut, boss," he said. "You can't pass that up."

"I've already passed it up," said Harworth, harshly. "There'll be no booze sold in my places. I'm making too much money legitimately. I don't want a padlock slapped on."

"No danger. No danger."

"It's settled."

Canovi looked at the floor, smiling slightly, and took out a cigarette which he rolled between his palms.

"Couldn't you use twenty grand?" he demanded; "that's only pledge money, see?"

Harworth started slightly but said:

"No."

Canovi had noticed the start and, smiling, got to his feet.

"All right, I'll tell Molina. He ain't used to being refused, but he's a good guy. No hard feelings, boss."

"Don't call me 'boss'."

Canovi stood looking at Harworth for a moment. "Boss, could you let me have fifty dollars?"

Harworth took out his billfold and sat holding it.

"Canovi," he said, "you think you're tough don't you?"

"Me?" Canovi was smiling.

"Well, drop the boss stuff. I'm not your boss and I never will be."

"No use to get sore about it. I might come in mighty handy someday. Who knows?"

Harworth took out a fifty and handed it to Canovi, who took it and crumpling it into a wad, shoved it into his vest pocket. Then he stood looking around the room.

"Some joint you got here," he said.

The phone rang.

"Well, I'm on my way. Maybe Molina'll drop round and talk things over."

Harworth said nothing, and with a nod Canovi went out. But Harworth was flattered. Molina was a millionaire bootlegger and as well publicized as a prima donna. It meant something to have Molina looking you up.

The phone rang again and Harworth answered it. "Mr. Harworth?"

"Yes."

"This is Louise Joyce."

Harworth nearly dropped the receiver.

"Oh, yes, Miss Joyce."

"I'm awfully sorry, but I won't be able to go to that fight."

Harworth's face fell. He had been looking forward to that evening! But he said negligently:

"Sorry."

"I have to go out of town."

"That's too bad."

"It was nice of you to ask me."

He wanted to say "Oh, have a heart!" Her voice came to him faintly over the wire as if she were very tired. He liked her voice; it was nothing like Lily's.

"Not at all."

"Well, maybe some other time."

"Don't worry about it."

"Goodbye."

He hung up the receiver and sat staring at the wall for a moment, then he got up in a rage, and looked about the room for something to break. But presently he sank back into his chair and said:

"I'll bet Burne talked her out of it."

PART TWO

ONE

The evening of the fight Harworth was restless and couldn't find anything to hold his attention. He paced up and down the library, whistling aimlessly, saying nothing and barely nodding when Stein spoke to him. Stein sat reading an evening paper with his glasses nearly to the tip of his nose. Finally he said:

"I'm hungry, Frank. What's holding things up?"

"I don't know," said Harworth. "I think I'll go out and eat."

Stein put down his paper and looked up.

"Say, what's wrong with you?"

"Nothing. Nothing."

"Well," said Stein, "you're giving a great imitation of a guy with something on his mind."

Harworth shrugged.

"I heard you walking around last night," said Stein; "it must've been three o'clock."

"I read late."

"Yeah?"

Harworth turned and looked at Stein.

"You keep tab on me like a Dutch uncle, don't you?"

"Well, I been doing it for a good many years. What about it?"

Harworth frowned, then smiled.

"Nothing, August," he said. "I'd be a damn lonesome guy if I didn't have you around."

"Never mind," said Stein, pleased. "I'm a pretty lucky old bird, with a berth like this. I was headed for the poorhouse back in '19."

"No, you're too smart for that."

"Well," said Stein, "I'll admit I never sold pencils on the street, but smartness don't cut no ice if you don't get the breaks."

"That's a fact," said Harworth. "I remember once when I tried to borrow fifty dollars at the 1st National back in Cleveland and I couldn't get a cent."

"You didn't have no security. I've heard this before."

"That's all right. I knew the guy."

Stein laughed but said nothing.

"Yeah. I had a hot tip but I was broke and couldn't scare up a cent. It was Gascon Cadet. He finished four lengths to the good and paid ten to one. With that five hundred dollars I could have put in with Tod Murray's faro game. He cleaned up afterwards. You sure have to get the breaks."

"Frank, you never forget things, do you?"

"How do you mean?"

"You've told me that story a dozen times."

"Well, it was the way Manning turned me down on that fifty. His old man used to work for mine. Young Manning went to night school and got away from the neighborhood, but my old man kept his family once for nearly a month when he was out of work. And here he turns me down for fifty bucks."

Stein laughed.

"It's the way of the world," he said. "A guy as smart as you ought to know that. Gratitude's a thing you don't find very often. It kind of surprises you when you do, or it ought to."

"I know," said Harworth. "And how about that time I lent Joe Edwards two hundred dollars when I only had four hundred to my name!"

"Joe Edwards?"

"Yeah. The fellow who married that rich woman down in Wheeling."

"Oh, yeah."

"Well, I was broke in Wheeling one time and he wouldn't speak to me on the street."

Stein laughed.

"Is that what's the matter with you now?"

"Well, I just got to thinking, that's all. Those 're the kind of things that makes a guy tough."

"Why not?" said Stein. "It don't hurt anybody to be tough, if he's tough in the right way. A guy that hands out his money promiscuous is a fool. Some people call it generosity, especially people who haven't got any money of their own."

"Sure," said Harworth, "only ... look, August, everybody isn't that way. I mean, there must be people that aren't. I mean, what's it all about, anyway, if that's all people think about?"

"Don't get deep," said Stein, looking up in surprise at Harworth. "Go get your dinner some place and then go see the fights. You're getting stale, that's all."

Harworth took out a handkerchief and mopped his face.

"I guess I'm getting soft."

"Don't do it," said Stein. "It's a hard world. But, look here, Frank, it seems to me you ought to be pretty well satisfied with things as they are."

"Well, I'm not."

Stein took off his glasses and put them in a case, then he shook his finger at Harworth.

"You're one of the luckiest guys in the world. Five years ago the seat was out of your pants and now look; you're getting so rich that pretty soon you'll have to hire people to help you spend it."

Harworth said nothing and there was a long silence. Several times Harworth opened his mouth to say something, but thought better of it, and checked himself. He felt the impossibility of making Stein understand him. He wanted to say that things looked wonderful till you got them; he wanted to say that people seemed fine till you knew them; he wanted to give some kind of expression to an attitude of mind which had been growing on him and which had been further aggravated by his meeting with Joyce and his friends. Instead, he said:

"Well, I think I'll go over to the Drake and get my dinner."

"Sure," said Stein.

"Good evening, Mr. Harworth," said the headwaiter. "All by yourself tonight?"

"Yeah," said Harworth. "I want to sit over in the corner, away from the orchestra."

"Right this way."

Harworth followed the headwaiter across the long dining room, but before he reached his table he saw Louise Joyce. She was sitting with a pretty, dark-haired woman, who looked up at him tentatively, then looked away. Louise had seen him; he was sure of that, because she had turned her face away as if to avoid him. He had known she was lying to him about having to go out of town; but he felt hurt just the same. He went on a step or two, but she turned and called to him:

"Mr. Harworth."

With a start, he came back to their table and bowed. "This is Mrs. Magnussen," said Louise.

"How do you do," said Harworth, bowing; then he took out his monocle and hastily put it in place. Helen looked at Louise, then smiled up at Harworth. He thought she was very good-looking with her dark face, her big dark eyes, her white teeth.

"I didn't go out of town after all," said Louise.

"I see," said Harworth.

Louise flushed slightly and Helen Magnussen looked from one to the other, puzzled. Louise had mentioned Harworth to her casually and told her that he was very rich but slightly ridiculous. Helen didn't think he was at all ridiculous, quite the opposite, and she glanced suspiciously at Louise.

"I didn't find out till just a little while ago," said Louise.

"It doesn't matter," said Harworth. "I understand."

She knew that he did from the tone of his voice, and lowered her eyes uncomfortably. Helen said:

"Louise tells me you own the Casa Alvarado. What a wonderful place."

"It's nice," said Harworth. "Ever been to The Machine?"

"That's on the North Side, isn't it? No. But I've heard about it, what an original place it was. Is that yours too?"

"Yes."

"Are you going to the fight?" asked Louise.

"Yes. I haven't anything better to do. The main-go ought to be good."

"I love fights," said Helen. "My brother took me once or twice to The Garden when we were in New York."

"Was it brutal?" asked Louise.

"Sort of. But it was fun."

There was a short silence, then Harworth bowed.

"I think I'll go eat. Very glad to have seen you."

When he had gone Helen looked at Louise for a long time before she spoke.

"Well," she said, "I like him."

"Oh, I guess he's all right," said Louise. "But he's always pretending. I mean, the monocle and the bowing. I'd like to know what he's really like."

"I don't care a bit. He'd be fun."

"Maybe. But Arthur and Bob got on their high horses, so I thought I'd better not disgrace the family."

Louise smiled. Helen said:

"I wish he'd ask me some place. I haven't anything to lose. Divorcees aren't quite nice anyway."

Louise looked at Helen thoughtfully. Helen had put her head on one side to get a better view of Harworth, who was ordering.

"Arthur and I saw him the other day. He was in his car with a woman."

"What kind of a woman?"

"An actress, or something."

The waiter came with their dessert and for a little while they ate in silence, then Louise said:

"I wish we hadn't come here. I felt queer, running into him."

"That's what you get. Now you can spend the evening with Arthur and listen to a lecture on music from Bach to Prokofiev."

"Oh, Arthur's all right. And everyone thinks he has talent; even Berg Richman."

"Well, I wouldn't know."

"I wouldn't either. I haven't any ear for music, so Arthur says. Oh!" she burst out suddenly, "I'm sick of everything."

Helen was watching Harworth and said nothing.

When they had finished Louise asked for the check and they got up to go. Louise opened her purse and took out some money, but stopped and looked at the check again, then flushing she said:

"Helen, this is awful. I haven't enough money."

Helen smiled.

"Give me the check, dear. I'm rich today. Mr. Alimony dropped round to see me."

"But I invited you."

"That doesn't matter."

Louise said:

"A perfect day all around."

When they were crossing the room Helen turned to smile at Harworth, who bowed gravely. Louise did not turn. Harworth watched Helen cross the room; she was wearing a yellow silk dress which was very tight at the hips.

"Well," thought Harworth, "that one's not so uppish."

The semi-windup was dull. Harworth sat at ringside with Curran from the *Examiner*, who kept falling asleep and at the end of each round asked Harworth how it was going. In the tenth round the fight livened up a bit, and the favorite knocked his opponent into the ropes. But Curran yawned, wakened by the yelling and said:

"What a life! What a life! I ain't seen a good fight in two years."

When the referee held up the hand of the winner there was some feeble cheering which was nearly drowned by the boos.

Then the principals climbed into the ring. Maginnis, Red Cannon's manager, put his stool beside Harworth who had an aisle seat in the first row.

"It's in the bag," he whispered. "It won't go five rounds."

"Crooked, you mean?"

"No," said Maginnis, "Red's all hopped up. He'll lick this wop in jig time."

Red turned and waved a glove at Harworth who nodded.

"This fight's worth about three grand to you, Mr. Harworth," said Maginnis. "We got a lump sum and a small cut at the gate. It's a sellout."

Harworth nodded. Someone touched him on the shoulder and turning, he saw Faro Welch, a gambler who lost all he won on prizefights playing faro at The Burgoyne.

"Three grand even money on the Sailor."

Harworth nodded. Maginnis turned around laughing.

"Kiss it goodbye, Faro."

"I already have," said Faro. "Harworth's the luckiest guy in town."

The first round was too fast, the pace too hot for a ten-round bout. Red fought in a crouch which bothered the Sailor, whose best bet was a terrific right hand. Red threw overhand lefts up out of his crouch and at the end of the fourth round he had the Sailor groggy. Dancing back to his corner, Red grinned at Harworth who nodded. At the beginning of the fifth the Sailor caught Red coming in and sent him back on his heels with a right. Red's eyes were glazed but he kept on his feet and putting his head against the Sailor's chest body-punched him groggy. In the sixth round the Sailor went down under a series of sharp lefts and didn't get up.

The gallery howled and newspapers sailed down. Faro Welch put his hat on the floor and jumped on it, then he leaned forward and handed Harworth a wad of bills.

"I'll get that back tomorrow night," he shouted, above the uproar.

Red spoke a few words over the radio, then Harworth got up and shook hands with him. Red had a big purplish bruise on his left cheekbone, but he was grinning. Over in the Sailor's corner they were giving him the ammonia and he was demanding to know why the fight had been stopped. He was still out.

"Well," said Curran, "somebody got knocked out anyway. It wasn't the usual waltz."

"What do you think about Red?" asked Harworth.

"Good boy. I think he likes to fight, which is very, very unusual."

Curran yawned and stretched, then said:

"Well, so long. I wish my mother had made a preacher of me like she wanted to. I'm tired of work."

Harworth shook hands with Maginnis, then he followed the crowd up the aisle and into the big cement corridor. Someone touched his arm and said:

"Hello. I won three leaves on your boy."

It was Canovi and he was grinning.

"Hello," said Harworth.

"Look," said Canovi, "Molina's right over there with some of his boys. Want to meet him?"

"Not now."

"Say," said Canovi, "he can put you 'way up in the bucks. Come on, meet him. He told me he'd heard you was a swell guy."

"Well."

Molina was standing at the door of the promoter's office and he was surrounded by half a dozen men. He was tall and fat with a flabby, dark face, a double chin and a heavy jaw. His fat hands were covered with rings and he was flourishing a big cigar in an amber holder.

"That's how it is, see, that's how it is," he was saying to the promoter, who was standing with his head inclined deferentially and a foolish smile on his face.

"Joe," called Canovi, "here's Mr. Harworth."

"Hello, hello," said Molina, very cordial. "I'm sure pleased to meet you, yes sir. I heard a lot about you. And I used to spend a lot of money over at the Alvarado. Swell dump."

They shook hands. Molina's hand was soft and moist; he winced slightly under Harworth's grip.

"Jees, what a hand," he said, looking from one to another of his men, who all had their eyes fastened on his face, waiting for his next word.

"This guy's got a hand," said Frankie Dean, Molina's chief bodyguard. The other men nodded and looked at Harworth.

"What do you think of Cannon?" asked Harworth, a little uneasy.

"Good boy," said Molina. "Got an interest in him, ain't you? Want to sell it?"

"No," said Harworth, "he made six grand for me tonight."

"Not bad," said Molina, negligently. "Eh, Frankie?"

"No, not bad," said Frankie, in the same tone of voice.

"Well," said Molina, "I'm shoving off. I want to see you some time, Harworth. We ought to get together."

"All right," said Harworth, not wanting to refuse.

Molina nodded, put his cigar in his mouth and walked off down the corridor, surrounded by his men, who shouldered the crowd out of his way.

"Great guy, eh?" said Canovi, jerking his thumb toward Molina.

"Great guy," said the promoter hurriedly.

Harworth stood talking to the promoter. Canovi had gone and the crowd was thinning out. The promoter was telling Harworth what a good drawing card Red Cannon had become, but stopped suddenly and said:

"My God! What's that!"

They listened; there was a rattle of gunfire down the street, then a silence, followed by shouts and the screaming of a police siren.

"They got Molina," said the promoter, paling. "I bet they got Molina."

In a moment Frankie Dean came running back, his hat off and a big cut on his forehead. He was followed by a milling mob which a lone policeman was trying to hold in check.

"Where's a phone! Where's a phone!"

The promoter, pale with fright, pointed to his office. Canovi pushed his way through the mob and came over to Harworth.

"Jees," he said, "what a nerve! They sideswiped his car and then let him have it. Jees, they sure fixed that car up pretty."

"Did they get him?" asked the promoter.

Canovi grinned.

"Naw! They'll never get him. He's lucky, that guy, but they bumped his chauffeur and another bird."

Harworth was shaking with excitement and Canovi, noticing how pale he was, said:

"Jees, you're taking it hard. It ain't your funeral. Wait till tomorrow. They'll be some pretty bumping tomorrow. Molina's sore as hell. Sure."

When Harworth got down town the extras were already on the street and everybody was talking about Molina's narrow escape.

TWO

Harworth had just got home from Lily's. Stein was in bed, and the house was quiet. He took off his coat and vest, unfastened his collar and, opening a window, sat down. He was tired and disgusted. Lily did not interest him anymore; he went to see her out of boredom and habit. She was cold, though she tried to appear cheerful and willing. She no longer sang when she was with him; she no longer kept up a steady fire of amusing chatter. When she was not in bed with him, she sat silent or else made a labored effort to listen or to be funny. She was no longer natural in her words or actions. It was a business.

Harworth turned to stare out the window. He remembered when he had first seen Lily. She was working with two other girls and Campi in a dancing act Hrdlicka had picked up some place. She was small and slim and blond and she sang popular songs in a high weak soprano; a voice greatly at odds with the costume, the music, the general atmosphere of a night club. Though she seemed very young, very alert and very assured, there was something pathetic about her voice. At first she kidded him unmercifully and because of this he wrote her one or two silly letters; he shifted uncomfortably thinking about those letters. Then one night she took him home with her. She lived in a one-room apartment on the near North Side. The windows looked out onto a fire escape and a deep dark court. There was no wind and it was sweltering hot. Lily started a tiny electric fan and they laughed about it. In the court cats began to yowl; heads were thrust out of court windows and tin cans began to rattle on the pavement below. They laughed some more; then Lily made coffee on a little electric heater.

She had seemed very timid to Harworth and this had increased his liking for her and his pleasure. But it was all over now.

He got up and stood looking out the window. A strong, steady wind was blowing in from Lake Michigan. Far off he saw the boulevard lights of the Lake Drive, in a curving parallel northward; beyond was the quiet lake, and at the far point of some pier a winking beacon, alternately red and white. The city was very still; occasionally a taxi stopped with a shriek of brakes, or hooted crazily on the drive; westward, he could hear the elevated trains stopping and starting at the Chicago Avenue station; but between these sounds there were long gaps of utter silence.

He turned from the window. His nerves were jumpy and he felt very tired, but not sleepy. For a while he walked up and down the room trying to figure out what it was he wanted. He felt stale, slack, bored. He wasn't hungry, he wasn't thirsty; his senses were quiet. What was wrong with him?

Aimlessly, he walked about lighting lights, looking at his apartment, which once had seemed so magnificent to him. He looked at the furniture, the rugs, the pictures, the bookcases with their tier after tier of books he had never read; then he went to his desk in the library and unlocked a drawer in which he kept his letters, his souvenirs, everything which would remind him of what he had come from and where he had got to. He glanced through his account books, his bank books, his list of investments; but there was no thrill in it. He read a few letters from a pile he kept tied with a ribbon; but they were mostly requests for money from men who, in the days when he was drifting broke and hopeless, would have grumbled about giving him a cigarette. He never answered these letters, but kept them to remind him of his increasing power and of the venality of men generally.

On one envelope he had written in pencil: "Money is power." The letter was from a man his father had done business with once. The man had turned out to be a crook and had bilked his father out of two thousand dollars, an enormous sum then. Now the man had written him that Tom Keogh (Harworth's father) had died owing him money, that he was broke and had a family on his hands. Harworth answered this letter, threatening the man with criminal action if he did not at once pay him the two thousand dollars he had embezzled from his father. He never heard from the man again.

One day he said to Stein:

"It's funny how they get my name and address."

But Stein said:

"Cats find fish no matter where you hide it."

Harworth choked at the word "fish," but Stein had intended no double meaning, and Harworth agreed with the truth of the maxim.

Naturally careless and generous, he had trained himself to hardness. With men he trusted he could be generous enough, but with others, with all others, he was stingy and had acquired a reputation for being tight-fisted. With his servants he was too generous and spoiled them, as Stein was always pointing out; but with the men who worked for him and were not in personal contact with him, Hrdlicka, Pierce at The Machine, all his restaurant managers, he was ruthless; paid them as little as possible and expected miracles.

His whole success, his triumph over his naturally lazy and careless disposition, was due to a will he had not started to cultivate till he was nearly twenty-four. Until that age he had drifted, had worked as a clerk, a tout, a stevedore, a carpenter's helper, a marker in a brokerage house, an engineer's helper on a lake boat, a super on the stage, and once as a waiter in a waterfront joint in Toledo. As fast as he made money he spent it; he was always playing the horses, always, when he could raise funds, putting in with a faro game, betting on prizefights, shooting crap.

But he was never satisfied. Unlike the men he knew, he was unable to swallow insults or to bow to humiliations. He began to understand that if you've got money, no matter how you got it, you are deferred to, respected; if you haven't you're under the lash. It was merely a matter of dollars and cents. Luckily he made a killing on the Kentucky Derby and instead of feeding it across the faro board as he would formerly have done, he put it in the bank, settled down to work and began to save. His first venture was enormously profitable; he bought a half interest in an amusement park which had been mismanaged. Zimmerman, the man who took it over, was a German and work-broken early; he worked day and night and in one season had the park going full blast. He was an honest fellow and liked Harworth (who was known as Frank Keogh then) and was grateful to him, as Harworth was the only one who believed in Zimmerman's ability enough to put in with him. At twenty-four Harworth was broke; at twenty-eight he had over a hundred and fifty thousand dollars.

It was during the four years at the park that Harworth had begun to read. Before, he had read nothing but magazines, principally Wild West fiction and Detective stories. But they had never satisfied him; he had wanted something else from reading, but there was no one to advise him. One day Mrs. Mahaffy, who ran one of the better park hotels, gave him Suetonius's *Lives of the Twelve Caesars*; a man had left it in his room. Harwood ate it up and wanted more. He drove into Cleveland and consulted a librarian, a little man with a pale, thin face and thick-lensed glasses, who was very puzzled and superior, but helped him. For two years he read incessantly, and was jeered at by Stein and Zimmerman, who thought he was losing his mind.

The books had a queer effect on him. He was not content to live vicariously; he was not soothed by reading about the successful lives of Napoleon, Julius Caesar, Octavius, Antony, Charles XII and Marlborough; he wanted to emulate them; but Capt. Jesse's *The Life of Brummel* and Casanova's *Memoirs* affected him most deeply, and changed him, in a few months, from a rather tough young man who used his fists and argued afterwards, into an exaggeratedly polite young man who had his clothes made by the best tailors and wore a monocle. Everybody laughed at him and said he was crazy; but they generally laughed behind his back. Stein, a shrewd man, was puzzled and Zimmerman was worried. But Harworth would say to himself: 'if they (meaning his heroes) could do it, why can't I?'

Harworth locked his desk and put the key in his pocket, then he walked over once more to the window and stood looking out. Far off, the red and white beacon was still winking. He felt tired and lonely. He did not know what was the matter with him.

THREE

It was a terrifically hot day and Harworth was sitting at his desk in his shirt sleeves. Stein with his collar unfastened was lying on a couch under an electric fan. Michaelson had a silk handkerchief stuffed down inside his tall, stiff collar, and Canovi sat complaining about the heat and sweating profusely.

Finally Harworth raised his eyes.

"Sam, I hate to take a loss like that."

Canovi said:

"But, you don't have to. Jees, it's a cinch. Molina can fix it."

"Sure," said Michaelson, "it's a shakedown. We're making too much money out there and Bourke wants to cut in. But a grand a day, boss; you know that's ridiculous!"

"Give me Bourke's number," said Harworth.

"All right," said Michaelson, handing Harworth a slip of paper, "but it won't do no good."

"That guy ought to get taught a lesson," said Canovi, thrusting out his chin; "the dirty double-crosser. Him a reform candidate! Ain't that pretty!"

"It won't do him any good to kill him," said Stein. "That's always poor business."

Canovi turned and stared at Stein, who was laughing. Canovi laughed too and said:

"Sure. But somebody might tap him one just for luck. You know, just playful-like. A headache might do that guy some good."

"Be quiet," said Harworth; "he's on the line."

Stein sat up and they all stared at Harworth.

"Oh," he was saying, "you don't want to talk about it, eh? Well, listen here ..."

Harworth slammed up the receiver.

"He hung up," said Harworth, flushing.

There was a long silence and they all sat avoiding each other's eyes. Then Harworth said:

"August, I'm not going to close that place up. It's worth too much."

"Well, I hope not," said Michaelson.

"Well," said Stein, "I'm out of this. I was against it in the first place. But think it over, before you do anything."

Harworth got up and began to pace the floor. Canovi said:

"Let me call the Big Boy, boss. He can fix it. Say, if Bourke knew Molina was behind you, he'd turn a handspring and crawl up here on his hands and knees."

Harworth turned and said:

"Do it."

Michaelson and Canovi exchanged a glance, but Stein said:

"Think it over, Frank. You know what this means."

Harworth got very red in the face and shouted:

"I know! I know! I'm running this."

Canovi said:

"I'll have to call him on another line, boss. I can't give his number away."

"All right. Go in my bedroom."

Canovi went out. Stein said:

"This means plenty of grief, Frank."

"Why?" Michaelson cut in. "Joe Molina's as square a guy as there is. All that newspaper stuff's the bunk. He's got him a wife and a kid. He's a good guy."

"I'll take a chance," said Harworth.

In a few minutes Canovi came in grinning.

"Well," said Harworth.

"O.K.," said Canovi. "I talked to Frankie Dean. The Big Boy was sitting right there. He said he'd fix it. So I asked Frankie what it was worth and he asked Joe. Know what Joe said?"

"What?" Harworth demanded, apprehensive.

"He said it wouldn't cost nothing. He said he was doing it as a favor."

"Yeah," said Stein; "a favor with a string to it."

Canovi glanced at Michaelson, who said:

"No, you got Joe wrong. He's a good guy and if he likes you he'll go the limit. He took a shine to Mr. Harworth here."

"Sure," said Canovi, "he says to me: 'That guy's the nuts. He's got a grip like Strangler Lewis.'"

Harworth smiled and passed out cigars. The phone rang and Canovi laughed.

"Just answer it," he said; "and see how Joe Molina does things."

Harworth answered the phone. It was Bourke; he was very nice, too nice, and said that he had reconsidered things and had decided to take a chance on the protection even if he was a reform candidate; but he wanted one hundred a day. Harworth said that fifty was all they were willing to pay, and Bourke, after many protestations and a long explanation of how much he needed for his campaign, accepted.

While Harworth was talking Canovi sat grinning. When he hung up, Canovi said:

"See?"

Harworth smiled.

"There ain't anything that guy can't do," said Michaelson. "Well, that's that."

"Yep," said Stein, "that's that."

FOUR

Harworth in his shirt sleeves was going over restaurant accounts with Stein when the phone rang. It was about seven o'clock and they had just finished dinner.

"Answer it," said Harworth, deep in a calculation which made him sweat; he was slow at figures.

Stein obeyed.

"Frank," he said, holding his hand over the receiver, "it's a woman."

"If it's Lily, I'm not here," said Harworth, then he began to count on his fingers, staring at the ceiling, his face puckered.

"Frank, it's somebody's maid."

Harworth looked up. Stein was speaking into the phone:

"Mrs. Markle? Mrs. Magnussen? Just a minute."

Harworth snatched the receiver from Stein. It was Mrs. Magnussen's maid speaking; Mrs. Magnussen wondered if it would be possible for him to come to her house that evening; she was having some people in.

Harworth flushed with pleasure, but said:

"Tell Mrs. Magnussen I'll call her in an hour. I'm not certain."

But the maid said "wait a minute" and Mrs. Magnussen came to the phone.

"Mr. Harworth? It's not nice of me calling you up at this short notice, but I'm just having a few people in. Can you come?"

He liked her voice; there was vitality in it. He thought of Louise Joyce, whose voice sounded so weary, so faraway; of Lily, whose voice, over the phone, was harsh and insistent.

"I think I can arrange it," said Harworth. "I'm tied up right now. Business. I could call you in an hour."

"Try and make it," said Mrs. Magnussen. "I'm counting on you."

Harworth hung up the receiver and sat smiling at Stein.

"Well, well, well," said Stein.

"I'm getting in right," said Harworth. "That girl's away up there. She was Richard Magnussen's wife; you know, the guy who made all that money in lumber. He built the Triangle Building on part of it. What a building."

Stein sat tapping with his cane and looking at Harworth.

"Well," he said, finally, "that's what you been wanting, Frank. And I guess it's as good an ambition as any. Just don't take it too serious; don't never take anything too serious."

"That's pretty good," said Harworth, paying no attention to Stein. "Yes sir. That's pretty good her inviting me like that. I liked her the minute I saw her."

He rang for Joseph and when Joseph came in he said:

"Call Mrs. Magnussen, Mrs. Richard Magnussen, at eight o'clock and tell her that I'll be able to get away. Find out what time I'm to go to her house."

"Yes sir," said Joseph, then he looked from Stein to Harworth and went out.

Stein went back to the books, but Harworth got up.

"Frank," said Stein, "let's finish this."

"Not tonight. I don't feel like working now. Can't you do it?"

"Yes. But I want your O.K."

"O.K. it for me, August. Hell, don't kid me. I'm just in your way, anyhow."

He threw back his head and laughed.

"Keep it up! Keep it up!" said Stein; "I ain't seen you laugh like that for two years."

Harworth went into his bedroom and shut the door.

Stein took off his coat and unfastened his collar; then he sat bent over the mass of reports, trying to concentrate. But he heard Harworth banging around and occasionally singing. Harworth had a queer voice which alternated between bass and tenor, as if, at adolescence, it had never changed properly. He had a good sense of pitch but his singing was terrible as he would jump from octave to octave. But Stein sat smiling. He was glad Harworth was singing.

Stein turned from the reports and sat looking off across the room. He remembered when he had first seen Harworth. He was making a small book then and Harworth came in to place a two-dollar bet. Harworth was a broad-shouldered, pale, surly young man. He walked with a swagger and never smiled. But Stein liked him. He came to realize that the surliness and swagger were assumed; that underneath, Harworth was just an overgrown kid, generous and easily hurt. They got to be good friends.

A few years later Stein was hit by an automobile and, as he had dropped all his money meanwhile, he was taken to a charity hospital. All his friends had disappeared; no one came to see him. He was very much depressed and didn't care whether he lived or died. One day Harworth came to see him. He had been out of town and had just found out that Stein was in the hospital. He gave Stein a good cussing for not letting him know, then he told him that he was having him moved to the best hospital in town. Harworth had made a lot of money and was itching to spend it. Stein protested, but it was of no use; he was moved into a private room at a big hospital. When he recovered he went to work for Harworth and had been with him ever since.

"But he ain't my boss," he would sometimes explain, "I'm his. He's like a son to me."

Stein thought there was nobody in the world quite like Harworth.

When Harworth came out to get into the car, Sandy touched his cap and said:

"Frank, I mean, boss, I want to see you a minute."

"All right," said Harworth, smiling: "Are you in another jam?"

Sandy ducked his head and grinned.

"No; it's this way. Somebody's tailing you."

"I don't believe it."

"Sure as shooting," said Sandy. "There's been two guys watching you for three days."

Harworth didn't say anything.

"Sure," said Sandy. "I don't know for certain, but I don't think they're dicks. It's funny."

Harworth stood with one foot on the running board, wondering.

"Look," said Sandy, nodding his head cautiously in the direction of the apartment house entrance.

Harworth looked. A man with a slouch hat over his eyes was standing in the shadows watching them.

Sandy put his hand on Harworth's arm.

"Listen," he said, "send me back for something. Make it loud. We'll buzz this bird."

"Better let it go."

"Say," said Sandy, "you don't know what this means. Let me handle this."

"All right. But you're probably making this up. Still on the gin?"

"Never mind," said Sandy, and turning he took a short, blunt automatic out of a vest pocket.

"What you got that thing for?" Harworth demanded, taking a step backward.

"I bought it yesterday," said Sandy. "I ain't taking no chances. Do your stuff, boss!"

Harworth hesitated then he said loudly:

"Sandy, go get my gloves, will you?"

"O.K., boss."

Sandy touched his cap, then turned and hurried back toward the apartment house entrance, but instead of going in he veered suddenly and shoved his gun against the man in the slouch hat.

"Don't bump me," said the man, panting. "This is square, O.K. Take me out to Mr. Harworth."

Sandy nodded, but made the man walk in front of him. Harworth was sitting in the car but had left the door open. The man took off his hat.

"Mr. Harworth, you got me wrong, I guess. Your boy here shoved a gat up against me."

"What are you following me for?" Harworth demanded.

"Listen," said the man, "this is square, take it from me."

"Better get the police," said Harworth.

The man laughed.

"Say, they wouldn't pinch me. I work for Number One. On the level, Mr. Harworth, don't do nothing silly. This is square."

"Well," said Harworth, "speak up then."

"Look," said the man, "Number One put us on this job. He told us to look after you and see that nothing happened to you. That's all. It's square."

Sandy looked at Harworth, who was bewildered.

"Who's Number One?" he demanded.

The man laughed.

"It ain't hard to guess, is it? I ain't saying a word."

"Molina?"

"Maybe, maybe," said the man. "Look, Mr. Harworth, this is square. Number One sure has took a big interest in you. Jees, you're a lucky guy."

"Sounds funny," said Sandy.

The man put his hand on Harworth's arm and whispered:

"Get in touch with Canovi."

Harworth thought for a little while, then he said to Sandy:

"I guess it's all right. Let's go."

Sandy shook his head, but said nothing, and got into the driver's seat. The man put his hat on and smiled at Harworth. Then they drove off.

Harworth was puzzled and uneasy, and all the way to Helen Magnussen's apartment he sat wetting his lips, and staring out at the traffic. It had rained and the headlights of the automobiles made a glare on the wet pavement.

When they drew up in front of the apartment house, a big black touring car drove slowly past, and a man leaned out, looking back.

"Keep your eyes open, Sandy," said Harworth.

"O.K.," said Sandy. "Boss, if I was you I'd be careful, the way they been bumping people off!"

Harworth said nothing.

Harworth looked off over the room. Burne was playing and everybody was listening, or pretending to. From time to time Helen looked in Harworth's direction, but he avoided her eyes. She didn't know what to make of him; he seemed very distant. Once she noticed that for some reason he had flushed and his usually pale face turned nearly brick red; she was still wondering what had caused the flush when suddenly he stiffened in his seat and put his monocle in place.

She lowered her eyes and thought:

"He's shy, poor thing. He's having one hell of a time."

Louise was very pale and silent and sat looking at the carpet. Harworth had hardly spoken a word to her all evening. She didn't blame him, but she blamed Helen. Why invite him? He didn't fit in. Burne had gritted his teeth when he found Harworth with Helen; then, barely nodding to Harworth and Helen, he had whispered to Louise: "I always told you what she was!" Arthur was so possessive; he even objected to her women friends! She turned to look at him. He sat with his head bent over the keys, his big, bony hands going full tilt. He played very well; everybody said so.

Larsen and Richman were sitting on a lounge together, silently contemplating their shoes. Each had a half empty glass in his hand. Joyce was sitting in a big armchair with his eyes closed. He always listened to music with his eyes closed; it gave him a good excuse for napping.

Harworth, very self-conscious, sat avoiding everyone's eyes, trying to follow the music, but it was too intricate and peculiar for him. He had never heard such music before. It confused him.

Finally Burne stopped and whirled around. "I'm sick of that sugar," he said.

"I like Debussy," said Richman; "his music is primitive. What was that?"

"*L'Ile Joyeuse*. Primitive, my hat!"

"It is," said Richman. "The whole-tone scale is primitive in itself. Shepherds' pipes, see?"

"Oh, nonsense," snapped Burne. "If that sweet stuff's primitive, I'm a nigger. It's sugar water, romantic junk."

"Play us one of yours," said Richman, with a cruel smile.

Burne, ruffled, turned to Harworth.

"What do you think of Debussy, Mr. Harworth?"

Everyone turned to look at Harworth. He hesitated a moment, then he said:

"I don't know Debussy from Adam."

"Neither does Berg Richman," laughed Helen, "only he's not so honest."

"Me!" cried Richman. "Say, I've sung Debussy. He's my favorite composer. Don't know him! I wrote one of the first articles about him ever printed in a Chicago newspaper."

"That proves it," said Burne.

"Play something! Play something!" called Joyce.

"Wait," cried Richman; "want to hear me sing *Beau Soir*?"

"No," said Burne.

"Shall we eat?" asked Helen.

"No," said Joyce; "I want to hear Arthur's latest. Tell them the title, Arthur. That's the best part of the piece."

"*Nein*," said Burne.

But Richman, Larsen and Joyce began to shout, so Burne turned back to the piano and struck a few chords.

"This opus," said Joyce, "is entitled the 'Death of a Prostitute.'"

Harworth sat up suddenly and stared. Helen said:

"You ought to sell that title to the movies."
Louise said:
"It's just some of his nastiness. He likes to shock people."
"Thanks," said Burne.
Then he started to play. Richman got up and poured himself another drink. Harworth sat stupefied. Was Burne serious? It sounded like a series of reiterated discords to him; it made him feel queer. He looked at the others; they were all listening. The piece, a short one, ended with a burlesque funeral march, built on a popular tune, then trailed off. Burne got up and stood looking at Louise.

There was a short silence, then Richman called:
"You've got something there."
"I know it," said Burne.
"Let me have a copy of that," said Richman; "I'll see what I can do."
"I'm not ready yet."
Everybody began to talk at once. Harworth watched them, feeling remote. Then Helen came over and sat beside him.
"Arthur's very talented, I guess. I don't know," she said; "but he's so silly. He won't let anybody see his work."

Harworth cleared his throat but said nothing. He liked Helen; she was not like the others; she was friendly.
She smiled at him.
"Are you very bored?"
He hesitated, stammering slightly, and lowering his eyes, said:
"Oh, no. Not at all. Only it's all new to me. You see, I never had any education."
She smiled.
"But Bob told me that you read a lot."
"Oh, I read. But that's not like going to college, is it? I mean I know a lot about history and stuff like that, but I never had anybody to show me how to study."
"I like you," said Helen, suddenly. "You don't put on."
"I put on a lot. But not about some things."
"We all do. For instance, I'm bored stiff right now."

Harworth looked up. Louise was staring at them. Her eyes were narrowed and there was a set, determined look on her face. Harworth shifted about uneasily, avoiding her eyes. Burne was talking with Richman in a corner; Larsen was pouring himself another drink.

"After that music I guess I better drink," he said. "What music! It makes me itch all over."

"You're one of the great unwashed," said Richman; "you need insect powder."

"Say," said Larsen, "I take a cold shower every morning."

"Olaf," exclaimed Louise, "won't you ever learn! Come here and sit by me."

Larsen forgot his drink and, grinning with pleasure, went to sit beside Louise.

Harworth hated Larsen now. He watched him as he leaned over Louise's chair, grinning. He had shoulders like an ox and big red hands covered with yellow bristles. Louise looked so frail beside him; like very fragile china. He glanced at her slender, silken legs; at her small, high-heeled shoes. Then he flushed and shifted at a sudden ugly thought. If that big bird'd ever get her alone and get a notion! "I'd break his goddam neck!" thought Harworth, automatically clenching his hands.

"And I feel sorry for Louise," Helen was saying. "She's every bit as bored as I am. But what can she do? She hasn't any money. She goes where she can."

Harworth thought he detected malice and glanced up at Helen, but her smile reassured him.

"Money's pretty important," he said. "I know."

"You've made lots, haven't you?"

"Quite a lot."

"And all yourself. You must be very young."

"I'll be thirty-four."

"When?"

"Next month. Twelfth."

"I'll remember that."

Harworth looked up at her.

"Why?"

"Because."

He hesitated for a long time, then he said:

"Let's have dinner together some night!"

"All right, let's. What night?"

"Tomorrow night. Seven. I'll come after you."

Helen smiled and put her hand on his arm.

"It's a go."

He glanced across at Louise. She was staring, but quickly looked away. Helen got up.

"Come on, people. We'll eat."

Harworth was the first to leave. They all got up and murmured politely, but Helen said:

"Tomorrow night, then."

"You bet. Good night."

When he had gone, Richman exclaimed laughing:

"A new victim for Helen."
Louise said:
"Arthur, let's go. It's after one."
"No," said Richman, "don't go. Now that Helen's parlor Hercules has gone, I want to hear some more of Arthur's music."
"I'll take you," said Olaf.
"All of you go," said Helen; "I'm dead tired."
"Need a little beauty sleep for tomorrow night, eh?" Richman demanded.
"Are you really going someplace with him?" asked Burne.
"Certainly. Why not? It seems to me he's very nice."
Louise bit her lip.
"I think you'd better not, Helen. He might misunderstand."
"He owns a gambling house," said Joyce, getting to his feet. "Really, he does."
"I was going to a prizefight with him," said Louise, "but I changed my mind."
"I believe you told me that before, dear, several times," said Helen smiling.
Louise shot a look at Helen, then turned and left the room. Burne and Olaf followed her out. Richman said:
"Well, well." Then he stared at Helen for a moment and went out into the hall where Helen's maid was helping Louise on with her coat.
"Helen," said Joyce, "I saw your husband yesterday."
"My ex, you mean. Is he in town again?"
"He was tight as a drum. I ran into him at the Lake Michigan Club. He asked about you. What ails him?"
"Don't ask me."
"Really, Helen, I think he's very much in love with you."
Helen laughed and walked out into the hall with Joyce.

FIVE

Canovi sat with his watch in his hand, glancing up from time to time at Harworth, who was trying to concentrate on a newspaper.
"What time?" demanded Harworth, finally.
"Seventeen till. He's only a little over ten minutes late. He'll be here."
"Well, I'll give him till six, then I've got to get dressed."
"You got to wait now, boss. You can't turn him down and him running clear across town to see you. Jees; you don't seem to realize what a big guy he is! Say, he don't need to run after nobody."
"Well," said Harworth, frowning, "do I?"

"No, of course not," said Canovi. "But, listen; Joe can do you a lot of good. Take a tip from me, I know. Say, didn't I get myself in a jam and didn't they railroad me and wasn't I out in no time? What's the answer? Joe Molina."

The phone rang and Canovi answered it.

"He's on his way up. I'll go show him in. Joseph's out, ain't he?"

"Yes, but Sandy's looking after things."

"I'll go anyway," said Canovi, hastily. "Joe likes to be showed around, you know. He rates it, see?"

Canovi went out. Harworth sat gripping his newspaper, trying to appear at ease. In a moment he heard some loud talking in the hall, then the door opened and Molina came in, followed by Canovi and Sandy. Harworth got up against his will, but before he could speak, Molina turned and said:

"Beat it, you guys."

Sandy looked at Harworth but didn't budge. Canovi said:

"Aw, Joe; ain't I in on this?"

Molina merely looked at Canovi.

"O.K. I'm going."

Harworth said:

"Look after Canovi, Sandy."

"You, Canovi," said Molina, "go downstairs and talk to Frankie. He's waiting in the lobby."

When they had gone, Harworth and Molina shook hands, then they sat down.

"I'm late, I guess," said Molina, smiling. "Sorry, but the bridge was up. It's a wonder they wouldn't get a high-level bridge in this man's town, ain't it?"

"Yes," said Harworth.

Molina offered Harworth a cigar and they sat smoking. In the long silence that followed Molina sat chewing on his cigar and running his eyes over the room, noting the bookcases, the rugs, the furniture, the pictures. Too conservative, he thought. Harworth studied Molina out of the corner of his eye. He had heard so much about him; everybody had; he was sure-fire for the newspapermen, who had made his name known all over the country. He was a big man, corpulent, with a fat, bland face, a heavy jaw, and a double chin. He was quietly dressed in dark clothes and he looked very neat and well-groomed. He was wearing three diamond rings on his plump fingers.

Molina finally broke the silence by leaning forward and saying:

"I've been having you tailed."

Molina had just come from a barber shop; Harworth caught a sweetish odor of hair tonic and talcum powder.

"I know," said Harworth.

Molina grinned.

"So I hear. The chauffeur packs a rod, eh? Not a bad idea. But you ain't expecting no trouble, are you?"

Harworth was staring at his desk but he felt Molina's eyes on his face.

"No. Why should I? He did it on his own hook. He knew we were being followed."

Molina smiled and settled himself comfortably.

"That's it, eh? I thought maybe you was in a jam of some kind. Course, I don't see why a guy like you'd be in a jam but you never know in this man's town."

Harworth said nothing. Molina made him uneasy. At first glance he was merely a big, rather fat man, verging on middle-age; at certain angles his face looked round and jovial, but after a moment you realized that he was neither bland nor good-natured, but tough, determined and dangerous. When he talked his thick lips turned upward in nearly comical fashion, but his eyes, small and dark, narrowed in a peculiar way.

"How's The Burgoyne? Ain't had any trouble with protection since I gave Bourke a going-over, have you?"

"No. Everything's fine."

"Good. Good," said Molina, nodding. "Whenever you want any of them grafters nudged, let me know. They're hell if they think they got a lever to pry you loose with. I know. I ain't always been on top of the heap."

Harworth looked at his watch. Molina said:

"Got a date?"

"Later."

"Well," said Molina, "let's get down to business." Then he laughed and went on: "I wouldn't want to be keeping a young guy like you from his woman. My chasing days are over. I'm married. But I know, I know."

"Canovi tells me you've got a little boy," said Harworth politely.

Molina grinned and reaching across the desk patted Harworth's arm.

"Got a little boy, eh? Say, I got a great big boy. Damnedest kid, I ever seen. We can't do nothing with him. He's just like his old man."

He took a picture from his pocket and handed it to Harworth.

"Take a slant at that."

Harworth saw a plump, dark-haired, serious-faced little boy in a sailor suit.

He glanced up at Molina.

"He looks just like you."

Molina swelled out his chest.

"Don't he! Don't he! The missus says he looks like her connections. Like hell he does."

He took the picture and put it back in his pocket, then he sat smiling at Harworth; he had dropped his slightly suspicious, calculating air. Harworth had touched his weak spot, and knew it.

"That kid's going to have everything," said Molina. "Yes sir. When I kick off, and we all got to kick off someday, he's going to have plenty. Not like me, out on my own when I was twelve years old. But," he said, catching himself up hurriedly, "I'm taking up a lot of time here and getting no place."

Harworth said nothing. Molina sat fiddling with his cigar.

"Canovi says you're set against selling booze in your places; the Alvarado and that place up north. Is that right?"

"That's right."

"Well," said Molina, "I ain't blaming you. You got big investments there and you never know when some government dick is going to kick over the traces. Money or no money. You can't trust 'em. A padlock wouldn't help you a bit. Let's forget it."

"All right."

"Now," said Molina, "how do you stand on restaurants?"

"The same goes there."

"Sure; but I been looking them restaurants of yours up. You ain't getting rich off of 'em."

"No," said Harworth, "but we make a pretty good profit."

"I'll buy 'em."

Harworth said nothing and Molina took a big black wallet out of an inside pocket and counted out seventy-five one-thousand-dollar bills.

"Here's pledge money. I'll pay your price providing it ain't a holdup. And I ain't even looking for a receipt for this dough. I think you're a right guy."

"I'd like to talk it over with my manager."

"All right," said Molina. "Here's the pledge money. You'll sell to me, won't you? All you got to talk over with your manager is price."

Harworth hesitated for a long time.

"Any stipulations?"

"Any which?"

"Any strings to this?"

Molina rubbed his chin.

"Well, not exactly."

"What do you want with these restaurants?"

Molina leaned forward.

"Brother," he said, "I ain't in the habit of spilling my business, but you look good to me. Listen, I've been looking your restaurants over for a long time and you got 'em placed just right. Depots, that's the answer. Booze depots. Here's a tip. I'm taking over the city. It'll cause me a lot of grief, but I been piking compared to what I'm going to do."

"Well," said Harworth, "it doesn't make any difference to me, as long as the price is right."

Molina stared at the tip of his cigar for a while. "All right. But you got to keep right on handling these places like they was yours."

Harworth smiled.

"So that's it!"

"That's it."

Harworth said nothing but sat vigorously shaking his head. Molina laughed.

"Smart guy, ain't you?"

"Too smart for that. I'm no sucker."

Molina threw back his head and laughed.

"By God, I knew you was a smart guy. Last night I was saying to Frankie 'that Harworth guy belongs on big time.' Yes sir."

"The deal's off then?"

"Hell, no. I was just kidding. I got a hundred guys that'll take over them restaurants and put their names on 'em."

Molina glanced at his watch and got up. Harworth got up also. Molina shoved the bills across the desk.

"When you and your manager decide, call Canovi. The price don't matter; on the square, unless it's a hold up. I know my way around. So don't try to pry me loose for three times what they're worth."

"No danger."

"I believe you."

They shook hands, then Molina said:

"If any of that North Side bunch tries to get in touch with you, don't talk. You're dumb, see? You don't know nothing. I ain't the only guy that had his eyes on them restaurants."

"The North Side bunch?"

"Sure. Monahan's mob. What do you think I was having you tailed for?"

"I don't get you."

"Well," said Molina, puffing on his cigar, "I was kind of figuring maybe Monahan'd get to you before I did, see? So I wasn't taking no chances."

Harworth felt a wave of nausea, but said nothing.

"If they bother you, call Frankie or Canovi. We'll settle 'em." Harworth saw the bland face suddenly transformed; Molina looked murder. Harworth drew back a step, but smiled.

"I'll take a chance."

"Sure you will," said Molina. "I know guys, see? I picked you the first time I seen you. 'There's a guy that'll stand the gaff,' I said to Frankie. Sure; you stick to me. I know a right guy when I see one."

He nodded and went out.

Harworth sank into his chair and sat looking off across the room. His nerves were jumpy and he felt very tired. He wanted to lie down and sleep off this sudden fatigue, but the sight of the thick stack of greenbacks quieted him somewhat. He got up and locked the money in a safe. Lord, if that wasn't easy money! And before long he'd have more, lots more, all cash; a tremendous roll.

He went to look out the window. The late summer day was failing and as he watched, the boulevard lights came on, pale in the twilight. A huge sweep of cloud over the lake was rosy in the sunset. A far-off beacon began to wink.

Suddenly he started and glanced at his watch, then, swearing, he ran to the phone and called Helen Magnussen.

"I'm sorry," he said, "but I won't have time to dress unless you want to wait."

"Don't dress. Come right over."

There was something in her voice, something more than friendly. His heart began to beat fast. Maybe she was falling for him! He opened the door and shouted:

"Sandy, get the Rolls right away!"

Then he left a memorandum for Stein and went out.

They had just got back to Helen's apartment when the phone rang. The maid answered it and came into the hall where Harworth was helping Helen off with her coat.

"For you, Mrs. Magnussen."

"Go in and sit down, Mr. Harworth," said Helen.

He went in but didn't sit down. He was too excited. Helen had been so friendly, so sympathetic, and when he had suggested going to a show she had replied that she preferred to spend the evening at home, talking. Talking? Harworth couldn't decide whether Helen was plain friendly or something else. She had been divorced from her husband for nearly a year; was, practically, a widow, and widows, especially handsome, young widows, were, Harworth speculated, not exactly famous for continence. The thought excited him further and his face grew hot. He walked up and down impatiently, waiting for her to finish her telephone conversation.

She came in frowning.

"Some people are coming over. It doesn't matter, only I thought we could have such a nice talk together."

"It's too bad," said Harworth; "but tomorrow's another day."

Helen sat down across the room from him.

"Are you inviting me some place?"

"Any place."

"All right. Casa Alvarado."

"Fine," said Harworth. "I hardly ever go there anymore."

He hesitated, thinking of Lily, and finally said: "But let's go to The Machine. It's much nicer."

"And I haven't been there. All right."

She was smiling now. He liked her smile; there was warmth in it.

"Dinner, too?"

"Sorry. I'm going to dinner with Louise; then she's going to a concert with Arthur. I was invited, but I don't like concerts."

"I never went to one."

"Never, went to ... Oh, well; you haven't missed much."

"But I'd like to go."

She looked at him for a moment, puzzled.

"Well, I suppose we could go there."

"Not tomorrow night," said Harworth, smiling.

"It's our own little party."

"Yes," said Harworth, shifting uncomfortably. He wanted to walk across the room and put his arms around Helen. He was certain that was what she wanted him to do. But the place was brilliantly lighted. The maid was in the next room; he could hear her moving about. There were too many hazards. And then if he had misjudged her entirely, what a mess! He crossed his legs and looked uneasily at the carpet.

Helen said:

"You'd never guess who's coming here tonight."

"Who?"

"My ex: Dick Magnussen."

Harworth shifted, swallowed, and flushed.

"What are you blushing about?" demanded Helen, laughing. "It's perfectly all right. He's bringing a cute little girl with him. Jo Paul. She's quite a celebrity. She can drink with Dick."

"Oh, he's a drinker."

"That's too mild. He's hardly ever sober. It caused all our trouble, that and gambling."

She lowered her eyes.

"That's too bad."

"Oh, don't feel sorry for me. I was never happier in my life."

Her face was serious, but she was pouting and looked like a child. In a moment she smiled.

"I'm awfully glad I met you," she said. "I was tired of everybody I knew. I was lonesome."

Harworth sat up and leaned toward her.

"I was lonesome, too. Lonesome as the devil."

"Was that why you invited Louise to the prizefight?"

Harworth hesitated.

"Well, in a way."

"Louise is a lovely girl. I feel so sorry for her. Her father died bankrupt, you know. She used to have scads of money."

"Oh," said Harworth.

"Frankly," she said, "I think she's wasting her time with Arthur Burne. He has a bare living. He'll never make money with his music."

Harworth said nothing.

"Louise is very unhappy. I'm practically the only person she sees anymore."

Harworth could think of nothing to say and sat staring at the carpet. It was a shame she didn't have any money, a wonderful girl like her!

Helen sat watching him.

The doorbell rang and the maid went to the door.

Magnussen came in with a shout, followed by Louise and Larsen, and a slim, childish-looking little girl with brilliant yellow hair.

"Helen," cried Magnussen, "look who I found on your doorstep!"

He pointed to Louise and Larsen.

"We were out walking," said Larsen, grinning. "Today I finished the great portrait. Oh, hello, Mr. Harworth."

Helen introduced Josephine Paul and Magnussen to Harworth, who came to attention and bowed stiffly.

Louise said:

"Hello, Mr. Harworth," and offered her hand.

She seemed friendly. He smiled.

"Hello. I'm very glad to see you."

But Helen took him by the arm.

"Come over here and talk to Dick, Frank. He wants to know all about prizefighting."

Harworth was puzzled. Why did she call him Frank? Glancing at Louise he saw that she was frowning, and before he could say anything to her, she turned away. Helen put her arm through his and guided him over to where Jo and Magnussen were sitting.

"First," said Magnussen, a handsome, dark, little man of about forty, "I want a drink."

Helen went out to see about the cocktails and Harworth sat down near

Magnussen and Jo.

"Helen tells me you're interested in fighting," said Magnussen. "I'm crazy about it myself, but I always bet on the wrong man."

"Yes," said Jo, "and he always buys the wrong stocks, and bets on the wrong horse, but what lovely alibis he thinks up!"

"You need a drink," said Magnussen.

"Naturally."

"Any game's hard to beat from the outside," said Harworth.

"Certainly," said Magnussen; "but what fun! You haven't a professional interest in boxing, have you?"

"Not exactly, but I like it as a sport."

"Well," said Jo, "men have funny ideas. They like the funniest things. I went to a prizefight once and before it was over I was exhausted. It was so monotonous; all they did was hug each other and dance around."

"It's no place for women, anyway," said Magnussen. "I know it's fashionable, but men ought to have some place where they can go and have a good time unmolested."

"Why?" Jo demanded.

Magnussen looked at Harworth and winked. Harworth smiled. He was having a wonderful time. Imagine him hobnobbing with Richard Magnussen! He thought of the great Gothic doorway of the Triangle Building, Magnussen's folly they used to call it till it panned out. He thought of how many times he had read Magnussen's name in the society column; and he thought also how one time back in '20 he had come into Chicago on a freight and had been arrested by yard bulls. Magnussen's offhand manner put him at ease. He forgot to sit up straight and look stern and impressive; he felt no need to mask his self-consciousness with a monocle.

The maid came in with the drinks on a tray. When Harwood said "no, thanks," Magnussen looked up.

"Not drinking tonight?"

"I never drink."

"Good gracious," said Jo, "what you miss!"

"Oh, I don't know," said Magnussen, looking dubiously at the cocktail in his hand. "Sometimes I wish I liked lemon pop. Life would be much simpler."

"It's too simple now," said Jo, then she turned and called: "Turn on the radio. Let's dance."

"Oh, Lord," said Magnussen.

"But he'll dance with me, won't you?" said Jo, smiling at Harworth.

"Certainly."

Helen turned on the radio. Harworth and Jo began to dance, then

Larsen and Louise. Helen went to sit with Magnussen, who sank back and comfortably crossed his legs.

"Helen," he said, "you wouldn't dance with me if I asked you, would you?"

"No," said Helen, looking off across the room at Jo and Harworth.

"Good. We should have got along better."

She said nothing and he watched her for a moment.

"Are you interested in that young man with the big shoulders, what's-his-name?"

"Oh, I like him."

"Where did you find him?"

"Louise introduced me."

"Louise introduced …! Good for Louise. Her taste is improving."

"You like him?"

"Yes. What on earth does he do?"

"He owns things."

"What an occupation!"

"Well, he owns the Casa Alvarado and The Machine on the North Side and a chain of restaurants and I don't know what all. He's very rich."

"Amazing," said Magnussen. "I'll bet Papa didn't leave them to him."

"Why do you say that?"

"Well, I'd say off hand that he was a self-made man. It's strange, but I can always tell them. There's a certain similarity in the architecture."

"Don't try to be smart. I thought you liked him."

"I do. I do."

When Burne came in an hour or so later, Harworth was dancing with Louise and Larsen with Helen. Jo was sitting on the lounge with Magnussen who was teaching her a song.

"Well, well," said Magnussen. "How are you, Arthur? Haven't seen you for nearly a year."

Burne came across and gloomily shook hands. Jo said:

"Hello, Arthur. Why so sad?"

"I'm tired."

"Did you get my letter?" asked Magnussen. "I wrote you from Vienna about an opera I'd heard. I thought you'd be interested."

"I got it. Thanks."

"What about your music?"

"Well, I haven't taken up writing popular songs yet, so I haven't anything to report."

"Now, now," said Magnussen.

"But why don't you write a nice popular song, Arthur?" asked Jo.

"I may yet."

The music stopped and the dancers came over to speak to Burne. Larsen shook hands with him vigorously.

"Arthur, today we finished the portrait."

"Yes? I was up to your place and couldn't get in."

"Hello, Mr. Burne," said Harworth.

"Hello," said Burne, turning away without offering his hand.

Helen said:

"Have a drink, Arthur?"

"No," said Burne; "not tonight. I've got some work to do later."

Louise turned to Harworth.

"He works terribly hard. All hours of the night. He's orchestrating something, I don't know what for. I mean it'll probably never be played. It's too bad."

Harworth was still smarting from Burne's rebuff, and said nothing.

Helen came over to him, glanced sharply at Louise and said:

"Another drink, Louise?"

"No thanks."

Helen hesitated for a moment.

"Frank and I had dinner at the nicest little place. The food's very good and you get wine with your meals."

"Frank?"

"Mr. Harworth."

"Oh."

Harworth had decided to go and was at the point of telling Helen so, when Magnussen came over and took him by the arm.

"Now that Burne's here," he said, "there are plenty of men. Helen doesn't care much about dancing, so everything works out fine. Want some excitement?"

Harworth was puzzled but he said:

"Sure."

"All right. Come with me."

He took Harworth by the arm. Helen and Louise were talking but Helen turned.

"Where are you going?"

"We'll be back; we'll be back," said Magnussen.

Harworth bowed and followed Magnussen back through the hall and into a bedroom. Magnussen switched on the lights, took a pair of dice from his pocket, and tossed them on the bed.

"Ever use 'em?" he demanded.

Harworth smiled and studied Magnussen.

"Now and then."

"No objections then?"

"No," said Harworth, "only do you think we ought to run out on the party like this?"

"What's the difference? They won't miss us."

"It's all right with me."

"Want to roll 'em on the bed?"

"The floor suits me better."

"You needn't be careful with me. I'm a novice. I shoot honest dice."

Harworth flushed.

"I didn't mean that, Mr. Magnussen. I just meant they rolled funny on a bed."

"Never mind," said Magnussen, then he took two pillows from the bed and gave Harworth one.

They knelt down and pitched a coin to see who'd handle the dice first. Magnussen won.

"What'll it be? Want to start light?"

"I'll start anyway," said Harworth. "Name it."

Magnussen glanced up at him.

"Well, this is just a friendly game. So I'll shoot ten."

Harworth took out his wallet and Magnussen saw that it was packed with big bills.

"You're faded," said Harworth.

Magnussen warmed the dice in his palms and threw a natural.

"Drag ten," he said.

"Don't mind me," said Harworth, tossing down another ten.

Magnussen shook the dice in his hand.

"This is real sport. I sized you up right. You like it, don't you?"

"Yes," said Harworth.

At one o'clock they were all crowded around Magnussen and Harworth. Magnussen was pretty drunk by this time and had his collar off. Harworth seemed very cool and self-contained. Magnussen had lost six thousand dollars and was trying to recoup. Jo was kneeling beside him, rooting.

Magnussen finally swore, then looked up and said:

"Pardon me, ladies. But really you shouldn't be here."

Then he laid down three fifty-dollar bills and without a word Harworth covered it.

But Magnussen hesitated and finally said:

"Harworth, I'm six thousand dollars out."

"That's right."

"I'll tell you what I'll do. I'll make a pass for all of it. If I fail I owe you six thousand more. If I make my point, or throw a natural, I'm even."

In a regular game Harworth would have laughed and said that he wasn't a sucker. But here it was different. He said:

"All right."

He kept his eyes on Magnussen, who rubbed his hand on Jo's bare shoulder and said:

"Give me luck, Jo."

Burne stood looking on with an expression of concentrated hatred. There they were tossing twelve thousand dollars around as if it were twelve cents, while he was forced to plead with his landlord and run a charge account at a restaurant.

Louise said:

"What a lot of money."

And Burne hissed:

"What fools!"

Larsen was sitting with his mouth slightly open, rubbing his hand over his face. Helen was bending above Harworth, wetting her lips.

Magnussen hesitated for a long time, then he warmed the dice in his palms, shook them and finally threw them out. One of them came six and the other, spinning on a corner and nearly coming five, came six also.

Jo burst out laughing.

"Good God!" cried Magnussen, "my usual luck."

"Too bad," said Harworth, getting to his feet and brushing off his knees. Magnussen got up and going to a mirror started to fasten his collar.

"A nice evening's work," said Burne.

"Well," said Harworth, "he suggested it."

"Of course," said Jo. "He always suggests it. He loves it."

"What are you going to do with all that money?" Helen demanded.

"Suggest something."

"Give it to me."

"All right."

Burne turned and walked out of the room. Louise said:

"You might at least divide it."

Everyone laughed but Helen.

"Seriously, I ought to charge rent for my bedroom."

"You'll have to talk to Harworth about that," said Magnussen, who had overcome his anger now and was smiling. "The winner always pays."

"Well," said Harworth, "I'll tell you. I'll give a party at my place if you'll all come."

"I accept," said Magnussen, "and I'm going to bring some crooked dice." Then he hesitated and said: "Have lunch with me tomorrow, Harworth.

I'll have a check ready for you then."

"Look here," said Harworth, "this was just a friendly little game. I'm satisfied with what I've got. We'll call the rest off."

Everybody stared at Harworth.

"No, no," said Magnussen, beaming. "When I lose I pay. But it's damn nice of you."

When Harworth got home he found Stein sitting in the library in his pajamas and a bathrobe. His bad leg was bothering him and he had neuritis in his shoulder.

"Hello, August," Harworth shouted. "I had a swell time and won twelve thousand dollars."

"Good God!"

"And that's not all. I'm going to lunch with Richard Magnussen tomorrow."

"Well, well," said August. Then he went on: "It's great to be young and have good legs and be able to sleep of nights. It's great to be happy and look forward to things. Frank, take a tip from me; shoot yourself on your fiftieth birthday."

SIX

Campi was lying on the lounge with his hands under his head, looking at the ceiling.

"And I called him and called him," Lily was saying, "but he's never home."

"Hrdlicka says he's flying high," said Campi. "Swell society people and that stuff. That guy was born lucky. He's nothing but a big tough and you know it."

"Yes," said Lily; "he's nothing but a roughneck. But he's sure got the dough."

Campi turned over with a groan and sat up.

"Well, if you let him run out on you, you're a lot dumber than I thought you was."

"Don't worry. I've got plenty on him."

"What?" Campi demanded eagerly.

"Never mind. But when the time comes you'll see."

"Yeah? Well, I've heard that kind of talk before. What you got on him?"

"I'll tell you some day."

"Say …!" Campi began, but there was a knock at the door and someone called: "Your number, Mr. Campi! Shake it up, please."

"All right," Campi shouted, then he got wearily to his feet. "What a life!

What a life!"

He went over to the dressing table, smoothed down his patent-leather hair, and put some powder on his face; then he brushed his coat and started for the door.

"See you after your last number," he said. "We'll go down to Cimini's for supper. Got any money?"

"Enough."

"All right."

He went out banging the door. Lily sat down at the dressing table and started to make up her face. Her last number was a gypsy dance and she wore a black wig and used brown powder. Once or twice she paused with the puff half way to her face and stared.

PART THREE

ONE

Magnussen leaned across the table.
"Do you really like dancing?"
"Certainly," said Harworth, smiling at Helen.
Jo said:
"Who doesn't! You're getting to be an old fogy, Dick. Good heavens! I don't know what I'd do without dancing."
"You could collect stamps," said Magnussen.
"Oh, don't be superior."
The orchestra started up. Jo dragged Magnussen to his feet, and shrugging, and winking at Harworth, he followed her to the dance floor.
"What a pair!" said Helen, laughing. "Dick has finally found his match. Jo says they're getting married."
Harworth looked at Helen gravely.
"Well, he has funny taste."
"You didn't have to say that," said Helen.
"I think it."
"No, you don't. You're just being nice. You're the nicest man I ever met."
"Oh, come off."
"That's right. The nicest, the most considerate, the politest, the most disinterested."
She laughed and looked away. The band was playing softly and the drummer was nasalizing in a high tenor about that "Precious Little Thing Called Love."
Harworth shifted uneasily; then to fill in the silence he motioned for the waiter.
"A couple more White Rock and three ginger ale."
Helen kept her face turned away. Under the brilliant lights of The Machine, he thought she looked rather old. There were wrinkles at the corners of her eyes and a few just under her chin. She must be thirty-one or -two!
The headwaiter came over and stopped, bowing. "Everything satisfactory, Mr. Harworth?"
"Fine," said Harworth, without looking up.
"Thank you," said the headwaiter.

Harworth wondered why Helen wouldn't look at him. Why was she sitting with her face turned away? And why had she said 'disinterested'? Was it because, fearing rebuffs, he had never yet had the courage to hold her hand, put his arm around her, kiss her? Women were funny!

Generally he was anything but timid with women; quite the opposite. But this was his first experience with a woman like Helen; he didn't know how to begin. He lacked enterprise; an unusual thing for him.

"Helen," he said, "want to dance?"

"No," she said, turning; "I'm tired."

He said nothing and she sat looking off across the dance-floor. Finally she said:

"Frank, I think I'll go up to Lake Winnebago next week. Dot Archer has a cottage up there. It's frightfully hot here."

"Yes; it's pretty hot."

She looked at him steadily for a moment, then she said impatiently: "Oh, let's dance."

Puzzled by her manner, Harworth got up and they walked to the dance floor in silence and began to dance. It was crowded and people kept bumping into them. Jo and Magnussen danced past and Magnussen said:

"Oh, for the peace and quiet of a bowling alley! What a nightmare this place is."

Jo slapped him lightly.

"You mustn't say that. This is Mr. Harworth's place."

"That's all right," said Harworth.

Two couples danced between them, separating them.

"Dick shouldn't talk like that," said Helen.

Harworth shrugged.

"He's right. That doesn't hurt my feelings any. This place is a nightmare."

Silently, as they danced, he looked about him at the architecture, the decorations, all rigid, angular, sharply defined, a sort of crazy geometry in black, white and silver. The orchestra on a huge triangular stage, was blasting away at its music, the trombones braying, the cornets giving off deafening peals, the drum rattling and thumping; no music, just monotonous, savage rhythm. He looked at the strained, or vacuous faces about him; at the carelessness, the indifference, the boredom.

"Yes," he said, half to himself, "it's a hell of a place. But it pays."

"That's what matters anyway, isn't it?" said Helen.

Harworth glanced at her, uncertainly, but she said: "I'm not trying to be sarcastic. I mean it."

"Well," said Harworth, "it matters a whole lot, yes."

When the music stopped, the four of them walked back to their table together.

"No fooling now," said Magnussen; "doesn't this place get on your nerves? It's so damned modernistic. Is that the word?"

"That's the word, I guess," said Harworth.

"I like it," Jo put in.

"You'd like collecting stamps just as well," said Magnussen. "It's a life work."

"Oh, silly!"

At eight o'clock the next morning the phone in the library rang insistently and Joseph hurried on tiptoe to answer it. But Harworth hadn't slept well and it wakened him. He heard Joseph say, "Sorry, madame; but Mr. Harworth never gets up before ten," then he shouted:

"Who is it?"

Joseph found out who it was then he opened the door of Harworth's bedroom and said:

"It's Mrs. Magnussen. What'll I say?"

"I'll answer it."

Without putting on a bathrobe he hurried to the phone.

"Hello," he said.

"Happy birthday," said Helen.

Harworth started, stammered, then said:

"Oh, you remembered. That's mighty nice of you!"

"I got you out of bed, didn't I?"

"Well, yes. But I was awake."

There was a short silence. Then Helen said:

"That's all I wanted to say, so I guess I'll ring off...."

"No, wait," said Harworth. He stammered, then said: "Look, you aren't really going away, are you? I mean, are you going up to Lake Winnebago?"

"Why not?"

"I just wondered."

"Any special reason for asking?"

"Well," said Harworth, hesitating, "we've had such a good time here."

"Have we?"

"I thought so. Go to dinner with me tonight?"

"Sorry. I'm busy."

"How about later?"

"I'll be busy."

Harworth was puzzled. He couldn't make her out at all. Here she was calling him up at eight in the morning, and now, when he had asked her to dinner, she seemed indifferent and her voice sounded cold and distant.

"Well, some other time."

"Just call me. Goodbye."

"Goodbye," said Harworth, holding the receiver poised and staring at the wall.

At nine o'clock he was sitting in a bathrobe eating his breakfast when Joseph came in with a package.

"Came by messenger."

"Open it."

Joseph tore off the wrappings and handed Harworth a book bound in leather and stamped in gold: a narrow, thin book with uncut pages. Harworth turned it over and over puzzled, then he opened it. On the front page there was some tall, erratic handwriting. It read:

"For Mr. Worldly Wiseman, from Helen."

He glanced at the title page and read the words slowly:

The Maxims of La Rochefoucauld

Translated by ...

Stein came in leaning on his cane and grinning.

"Well," he shouted, "what's the occasion! Hell, there must've been a fire in your bed, eh? I ain't seen you up this early for years."

Harworth handed Stein the book. Stein sat down opposite Harworth.

"From Helen," he read. "Who's Helen?"

"Helen Magnussen," said Harworth, proudly.

"Well, well. You sure are getting mighty high society, ain't you? It's all right; a man has got to pass his time some way."

Harworth was disappointed; he had hoped Stein would be more impressed.

"Joseph," said Stein, "what we got for breakfast?"

Joseph told him.

"Good," said Stein, tucking his napkin under his chin; "let's have it."

Harworth put the book beside him on the table and sat looking at it.

"Well," he said, after a minute or two, "you can laugh all you want to. But she's the only one that remembered me on my birthday."

"Oh, no she ain't," said Stein, and he took a little package from his pocket and tossed it across the table to Harworth.

Harworth picked it up and opened it. It was a small, silver cigar lighter with his monogram on the side.

"Much oblige, August. It was mighty nice of you."

"I'm working for you, ain't I? I got to keep in good with the boss."

"Sure," said Harworth, laughing.

"By the way," said Stein; "everything's signed up on that restaurant deal. I got half the money right over there in that safe, cold cash. It's off our hands now."

"What a break that was!"

"Yes; but you sure pulled a wise one when you wouldn't let Molina use your name. Molina's due for trouble. I get around. I hear things. He's too cocky."

"Well, that's his look-out."

Stein hesitated for a long time.

"Frank, Michaelson's got a syndicate behind him. He wants to buy The Burgoyne."

Harworth looked up.

"I won't sell. It's worth too much."

"Half cash."

"No."

"Look here, Frank; that place's going to cause you a lot of grief someday. Why not get out from under it while you can? Then you're straight. Legitimate business is enough, ain't it?"

"We're O.K. out there, aren't we?"

"Now, yes. But there's an election coming on."

"I'll take a chance."

"I'd advise you to take a reasonable offer."

Harworth didn't say anything for a long time, then he said:

"I've got to make more money, August. This is small stuff. I want to pile up a real, honest-to-God fortune."

Stein sat shaking his head.

"Frank, don't get swelled up. You've got a lot more money now than a man's entitled to."

"A man's entitled to all he can get!"

"All right. But where's the fun?"

"Well," said Harworth, stiffening, "I'm going to be a rich man, that's all."

"How about being a happy man? Good Lord, take it easy. Slow down a little and enjoy what you got."

Harworth got up and stood looking down at Stein.

"If I'd been satisfied with what I had I'd never put in with Otto Zimmerman; I'd never bought those restaurants; I'd never taken a chance on the Casa Alvarado or The Machine."

"All right. All right."

"Know anything about the stock market, August?" Harworth demanded.

"Yes," said Stein, "and here it is: 'lay off'!"

"When a man gets your age, August, that's his motto: lay off."

"Well, you can't lose anything that way."

"No; you just stand still."
Joseph came in with a tray.
"Ah, ha!" said August; "what a nice big orange!"
He began to eat with gusto, smacking his lips. Finally he said: "What put the stock market idea in your noodle?"
"I was talking to Mr. Magnussen...."
"Yeah? Well, listen here. Magnussen could put what you've got in his vest pocket and never know it. He can stand it."
"You're right," said Harworth. "That's just why I want to make more money. If they can make it, I can."
"Yeah; but 'they' didn't make it. Magnussen didn't, anyway. His old man did."
"Somebody did," said Harworth. "So can I."
Harworth picked up the book and went out. As soon as he had gone, Stein laid down his spoon and sat looking at the table. After a while he picked up his spoon and muttered:
"Well, nobody can live a guy's life for him."

TWO

"Hafey? I don't know anybody by that name."
Harworth turned to Stein. Stein said:
"Neither do I."
Joseph said:
"It's about some restaurants, I think."
"All right," said Harworth; "I'll see him."
Joseph showed Hafey in. He was a big man, over six feet tall, slightly stooped and with a paunch. His face was red, his eyes small and dark. When Harworth looked up he turned back the lapel of his coat, showing a badge. Harworth said:
"Sit down."
Hafey sat down and crossed his legs.
"You're Harworth, eh?"
Harworth nodded.
"I thought it was the other guy," said Hafey, jerking his thumb toward Stein. "You're pretty young, ain't you?"
"I don't know."
"Anyway," said Haley, "it's like this. You just sold a chain of restaurants recent, didn't you?"
"I did."
"Uh hunh."
"What about it?"

Stein began to whistle softly and tap with his cane.

"The deal's through, ain't it?"

"Yes."

"Money paid?"

Harworth studied Hafey for a moment.

"Wait a minute! Now let's get this straight. Why all these questions?"

"You'll find out."

"I'll find out before I answer 'em. This was a perfectly legitimate business deal."

"Well," said Hafey, glancing at Stein, then at Harworth, "if you want to get tough about it, here it is. I'm building a case against Joe Molina. I looked up your record and it's O.K., so I'm figuring you for straight till I hear different. All right. Joe Molina's away off on his income tax, see? That's the idea."

Hafey laughed.

"Course," he went on, "he's off on a lot of things, but it's tough to pin it on him. All I want to know is, what did you get for them restaurants?"

"That," said Harworth, "is my business. But I'll give you a tip. You got bad information. Molina didn't have anything to do with this deal. A man named Huntingdon bought my restaurants. Is that right, August?" Stein nodded. "Stein," said Harworth, "is my manager."

Hafey, who sat with his head lowered, glanced up at Harworth and smiled.

"Yeah," he said, "I know all about Huntingdon. He's Molina's ghost. That's Joe's way."

Harworth looked at Stein in mock surprise.

"What do you think of that, August? Do you know anything about this?"

"No," said Stein; "all I know is, I got the money from Huntingdon and he did all the signing."

Harworth turned to Hafey.

"See?"

Hafey grinned.

"Now you're going to tell me you don't even know Joe Molina, ain't you?"

"No," said Harworth, "why should I? I met him at a prizefight. He dropped down here to see me one day about buying my interest in Red Cannon, the middleweight."

"Oh," said Hafey, grinning, "is Red your boy? Damn good scrapper. I won fifty bucks on him the other night."

"He's a comer."

There was a short silence, then Stein said:

"Hafey, let me see that badge?"

Hafey started and got red in the face. Harworth looked at Stein in amazement.

"Hey," said Hafey, "are you trying to kid me?"

"No," said Stein. "Who do you work for anyway?"

"Why, the city."

"Well," said Stein, "what's the city got to do with Molina's income tax?"

"Never mind. Are you looking for a pinch?"

"Yes," said Stein, "pinch me."

There was another silence, then Harworth said: "All right, Hafey, say your piece."

Hafey got up.

"I'm on my way. You guys 'll hear from me later, see. Not a dick, ain't I? Just wait."

"I'd still like to take a look at that badge," said Stein.

"You'll get a good look at it in a couple of days." He went out, banging the door. Harworth sat staring at Stein.

Finally Stein said:

"Frank, we've made a bad move. We never ought to 've took Molina's money."

"Money is money."

"All right. But you see what's happening? That guy wasn't any more a dick than you are. I don't know what his game is, but I'm none too comfortable about it."

"You spotted him all right."

"Sure. I've seen too many dicks in my time. He wasn't right."

The phone rang and Harworth answered it. It was Canovi.

"Boss," he said, "did Tom Corson come in to see you?"

"Tom Corson? Never heard of him."

"Don't hold out on me. We tailed him to your place."

"Wait a minute. What does he look like?"

Canovi described him to his shoes and hat.

"Yes. He was here. Said his name was Hafey."

"Did he pose as a dick?"

"Yes."

"Did he get any information?"

"No. Stein had his number."

"Good. I'll call later."

"Wait a minute. What's his game?"

"Let it lay, boss, let it lay. You don't know a thing, see? It's healthier."

"All right."

Harworth hung up the receiver and sat looking at Stein.

"It was Canovi," he said finally. "He's on to Hafey."

Stein sat shaking his head and tapping with his cane.

"I don't like this a little bit. Not a little bit."

Harworth said nothing, but he began to feel very uneasy.

THREE

"This," said Magnussen, "is my last fifty. And I'll be damned if I'll write any more checks."

"Suits me," said Harworth; "you suggested it."

"I always do."

Jo was standing with her hand on Magnussen's shoulder; Louise and Helen were sitting on the bed, and Richman and Larsen were sitting on the floor with their drinks beside them.

"I'll pass the dice if you want to handle 'em," said Harworth.

"Thank you," said Magnussen, reaching for the dice. "I'll take advantage of your kindness once. People," he went on, looking up, "it's a pleasure to lose money to Harworth. He lets you shoot with your own dice. He never argues. I'll bet you he'd give me back what I've lost if I asked him, wouldn't you, Harworth?"

"Certainly."

"It's almost too good to be true," said Richman.

"No sarcasm, please," called Magnussen. "Put that stuff in your articles at so much a line."

"Don't be rude, Dick," Jo put in.

Magnussen looked up.

"Was I rude, Berg?"

"No," said Richman, "insulting."

"Well," said Magnussen, "that's all right then." He raised the dice over his head and began to shake them.

Harworth faded the fifty, and said:

"I'm pulling for you."

"Oh, dice! be good to me," cried Magnussen.

He rolled them; they came double four.

"That's a decent sort of point," said Magnussen. "If I can't make that, I'd better take up ping-pong."

Talking to the dice at every roll, he threw ten, five, six, five again, and finally, after a great deal of talking and coaxing: seven.

Harworth said:

"Too bad."

Magnussen nodded.

"Well, that's that."

Then he got to his feet and threw the dice into the waste basket. Harworth picked up the money.

"Now let's dance," said Jo.

They all went into the living room and Jo turned on the radio. Magnussen and Jo began to dance, then Richman and Helen. Louise went over to talk to Larsen. Harworth was left alone and sat in a corner watching the others.

He thought Louise looked ill. Her face was pale and drawn under her rouge. He could see that she was under some sort of tension; she couldn't sit still. She kept biting her lips and when she talked she would leave sentences unfinished and stare at nothing. He wanted to talk with her, ask her what was the matter, tell her that she could depend on him, but he didn't have the courage. She had been avoiding him; he could see that. She scarcely ever addressed a word to him, and when he talked, she listened but offered no comment. She had changed: at first she had seemed slightly insolent to him, sure of herself; superior. Now there was something apologetic about her attitude.

The phone rang and the maid came in and called Louise. Harworth thought she looked worried as she crossed the room.

In a moment she reappeared; her face was white.

"Helen," she called.

Helen turned, saw how pale she was, and hurried over to her. They left the room together.

Jo and Magnussen went on dancing. Richman went out to help the maid with the drinks. Larsen came over to Harworth.

"Poor girl," he said.

"What made her so pale?" asked Harworth.

"It's Arthur," said Larsen; then he bent down and said in a low voice. "He's a fool. He is so crazy about Louise he doesn't know what to do! She won't marry him. How can she? He can't get along as it is."

Harworth said:

"She's a wonderful girl."

Larsen looked at him.

"Are you telling me?"

Harworth felt a sudden wave of anger. He didn't like people to scowl at him.

"Yes," he said, looking hard at Larsen.

Larsen's face softened.

"You're right. Don't pay any attention to me. I'm upset. He won't give her a minute's peace. He was to come tonight. But he wouldn't. Now he calls up. What can she do?"

Harworth turned and saw Louise and Helen in the hall. Louise had her coat and hat on; she had been crying. He got up hastily and went out. Larsen followed.

"Can I do anything?" asked Harworth.

Louise kept her eyes lowered but said:

"Yes. May I use your car? I'll send it right back."

"Certainly."

"Louise," said Larsen, "let me go with you."

"Let me alone, Olaf," she said sharply. "You stay here."

"Will you be back?"

"No."

Louise turned and went out hastily, followed by Harworth. Helen shrugged and said to Larsen:

"She ought to tell him not to bother her. She takes things too seriously."

"She ought to, she ought to, yes. But she won't."

Harworth went down in the elevator with Louise and taking her arm guided her to his car. Sandy jumped out and touched his cap.

"Sandy," said Harworth, "take Miss Joyce wherever she wants to go and stay with her till she sends you back."

Louise took Harworth's hand, but kept her eyes lowered.

"Thanks," she said.

"It's all right," said Harworth, helping her into the car; then he hesitated for a moment as she sat down and finally said:

"If I can do anything for you, just let me know."

"No, you can't help me."

"I mean, any time."

Harworth thought he heard a sob and it made him very uncomfortable.

"You can't do anything," she said. "Everything's pretty hopeless."

"You shouldn't feel that way."

She said nothing. Harworth drew back, shutting the door. The limousine moved off.

Going up in the elevator he forgot, for once, to look into the mirror. He was thinking about Louise. He liked Helen; once he had liked Lily; but it wasn't the same. Lily had flattered him crudely, played up to him, told him he was so strong, so desirable; and he was very susceptible to flattery. But Lily was inferior to him in wealth, position and intelligence. Helen's flattery was more subtle and for that reason more effective. After all, she was condescending and Harworth knew it; at times she made him feel it by a sudden gesture, an indirect statement, a shrug, but never in words, never definitely, directly. She was very nice to him, deferred to him, even, at times, did things for him, gave him presents, but meanwhile, keeping herself more or less aloof, promising much by her attitude, but managing to leave a doubt in his mind.

But Louise was different. She promised nothing. At her friendliest, she was distant. But he could not get her out of his mind. Ever since that first evening at Joyce's he had carried about with him an image of her with her ash-blond hair shining under the lights, her throat curving. Or else he would see her sitting with her long, slender, silken legs crossed.

What could she see in Burne? He was all right, maybe; talented, of good family, but outside of that?

Harworth was puzzled and irritated. Unconsciously, he shook his head several times. Then he noticed that the elevator had stopped and that the boy was looking at him. He left the elevator hastily.

Helen met him in the hall.

"Too bad, isn't it?"

"I don't know anything about it."

"Arthur's acting up again. He told her he was going to kill himself. He's been drinking. Poor girl. She thinks he means it."

"Doesn't he?"

"Of course not. Want to dance?"

"Yes."

Jo had the radio going full blast. They danced in the hall. Harworth was abstracted, but became alert quickly when he realized that Helen was dancing much closer to him than usual. Her body touched his with an insistence that could not be accidental. He looked down at her. Her face was flushed and she avoided his eyes at first, then stared steadily. He hesitated, then put his cheek against hers. Her face was hot.

Magnussen called from the doorway:

"Helen, let's go take a ride or something. All of us, I mean."

"Shall we?" Helen demanded.

But Richman and Larsen came out into the hall.

"We're going," said Richman.

Larsen looked very glum.

The streets were empty. It was after three o'clock. Harworth had sent Sandy for the big roadster. The top was down and the night air was cold on their faces. Harworth was at the wheel and Helen sat beside him. Magnussen and Jo were in the rumble seat. From time to time Magnussen called:

"Say, is this a funeral procession?"

And when Harworth stepped on the accelerator and the roadster shot away, and the speedometer whirled from thirty-five to sixty, Jo stood up and yelled:

"Whoopee!"

They were going south on the Lake Drive. At their left was the lake, dark and silent; on their right twenty-story apartment houses, with a few lighted windows, towered above the trees of Lincoln Park. They passed a couple of taxis going north.

Helen said:

"What a lovely night!"

"Yes," said Harworth.

The wind was blowing her dress up and in the light of the dash he saw her legs far above her knees. Remembering how she had danced with him, he felt a sudden fierce desire for her. He took his right hand from the wheel and dropped it onto her thigh. She turned and looked at him. "Frank!" she said, sliding her hand under his. Smiling to himself, he withdrew his hand, but she leaned toward him and put her head on his shoulder.

Harworth took them to Stromberg's. The usual crowd was there and Magnussen said:

"Oh, what an education this is."

"I love it," said Jo.

Helen was holding Harworth's hand under the table and said nothing.

"It's pretty tough," said Harworth; "but the food's good."

He felt triumphant. He had lost his timidity with Helen; she was easy, easy. He turned. She was looking at him. He smiled and she lowered her eyes, then looked up quickly with an unambiguous glance. It said: Have patience; wait!

They ordered and Jo began to tell about a place in Berlin where the man with her had got so tight that he lay down on the floor and another man had put a bunch of celery in his hand.

Magnussen said:

"What nice times you've had, Jo."

"Oh," said Jo, "when you put on that expression, I know what you're thinking." She turned to Harworth. "He thinks I'm awful."

Harworth liked her but felt no desire for her. She seemed so simple, so childish. He laughed.

"I can't see anything wrong in getting tight," said Jo; "everybody does."

"Yes," said Magnussen, "it's the national pastime. I don't think you're awful, Jo. But you have the funniest sense of humor."

"Just because I don't laugh at your jokes," cried Jo, tossing her head.

Helen squeezed Harworth's hand then let go. The waiter was coming with the food.

They ate in silence for a moment then Helen said: "Jo, I don't think I'll go up to Lake Winnebago after all. Are you going?"

"If Dick can get away."

"Oh, don't mind me," said Magnussen.

"I do mind you," said Jo; "even if you criticize me all the time."

"Don't get maudlin."

Helen and Harworth were exchanging glances. Then he turned to watch Jo, who was playing with her food. Wouldn't she ever eat and hurry things along? Harworth bent over his plate and tried not to anticipate; but when Helen kept looking at him he flushed heavily and shifted his feet. Could she read his mind?

While they were finishing their coffee they heard a distant voice shouting down the street. They paid no attention until the voice came nearer then Magnussen said:

"It's an extra."

"I love extras," cried Jo. "They're exciting. I always buy an extra."

"You lovely child," said Magnussen.

A newsboy came in the door, shouting.

"Extra! Extra! Big gangster murder."

The cashier took him by the shoulder and pointed to the door, but men began to stand up at the tables, calling:

"Back here. Back here."

The boy had only a couple of papers left when he got to Harworth's table. Magnussen bought one and handed it to Jo.

"There," he said, "it's a nice murder. Enjoy yourself."

He took out a cigar and lit it. Harworth lifted his coffee cup, but his hand was shaking; he was stunned by a premonition.

"Listen," said Jo. "Monahan's lieutenant taken for a ride ... found riddled with bullets in abandoned car on North Side.... Tom Corson, labor racketeer and North Side gunman...."

Helen looked at Harworth. He was deathly pale.

"What's the matter, Frank?"

"I don't know," he said, avoiding her eyes. "I feel sick. It must be the lobster I just ate."

Jo went on reading and Magnussen puffed on his cigar, but glanced at Harworth from time to time when he was sure Harworth wasn't looking.

"Oh," said Jo, shuddering, "isn't that awful!" Then she turned to the waiter.

"A chocolate eclair, please."

"Where are you going?" asked Helen, when Harworth turned down her street.

"I'll take you home first," said Harworth, hastily. "It'll be more convenient."

"Suit yourself," said Helen.

Harworth hesitated for a long time, then he said: "I'll tell you the truth. I'm terribly sick."

"Oh," said Helen, putting her hand on his arm, "I'm sorry. Call me tomorrow. I'm not going up to Wisconsin."

"Fine," said Harworth with an effort.

Jo called:

"I won't sleep a wink tonight. Wasn't that the awfullest thing?"

Harworth sat in the library trying to compose his mind. Stein was in bed. The house was quiet.

Harworth had tried to sleep, but had tossed and sweated, and finally had given it up. As soon as he closed his eyes, he had seen Hafey sitting in the library, and then, in spite of the fact that he had tried to make himself think of other things, he had gone over and over his interview with Hafey: he'd see him shifting in his chair, a big, red-faced man with small hard eyes; he'd see him get up hastily and go out. Then he'd remember the words he had read in the paper: riddled with bullets! A conventional phrase which comfortable citizens would read with their morning coffee, read and forget, because they could not appreciate its reality. They wouldn't see a man dying alone in the darkness, shot down without a chance. They'd have no conception of his pain, his agony, his terror. They would say: "Well, they killed another gangster," and pass on to something else.

Harworth wanted so much to close his eyes and forget it; but the later it got, the further he was from tranquility and sleep. His nerves were so disturbed that he had vague pains all through him and his head ached so that he sat holding it rigid, not risking the pain of turning it.

It was a disagreeable morning and although it was five o'clock the windowpanes were but faintly gray. A hard, steady wind was blowing in from the lake.

Harworth finally got to his feet, selected a book, fixed a reading light above his chair and began to read. But he hadn't been reading fifteen minutes when he closed the book and sat looking off across the room. The book was a little life of Caesar which had been recommended to him by his bookseller, who knew what he liked. As a rule the reading of history eased him; the present, with its cares and burdens disappeared, and he'd be in the past, marching with Caesar's Legions, riding with Attila's Huns, or storming a difficult position with Napoleon's Grand Army. But tonight, war disgusted him; the role of conqueror seemed criminal. He wanted relief from the bitter lust of living; he wanted something beyond life, something he could hold at a distance and admire, something to gain strength from. He wanted to turn from success, from the lust and callousness and greed necessary for success in a harsh world, to something finer.

Getting up, he put the book back on its shelf and walked to the window. The sun was just coming up in a gray, cloudy sky. The lake was very dark, nearly black in the gray light, and covered with whitecaps. He saw a freighter toiling in past Navy Pier.

A few lines began to run through his head;

> "Wynken, Blynken and Nod one night
> Sailed off in a wooden shoe ..."

He walked hastily away from the window and stood looking at himself in a mirror. He saw a pale, determined face with a heavy jaw. What was wrong with him? Why had his mind veered suddenly from Caesar's career to nursery rhymes?

He was asleep in his chair, looking very pale and haggard when Joseph came in. Joseph glanced at him, then tiptoed about the room. But Stein, in a bathrobe, came in a moment later and seeing Harworth asleep in his chair, shook him gently. Harworth started, wide awake in an instant.

Joseph went out.

"Well," said Stein, "you must've had a night."

"I couldn't sleep," said Harworth.

"Tough on Hafey, wasn't it?"

Harworth winced slightly. "Yes."

"Well," said Stein, "if you take that kind of money you've got to expect some kind of trouble."

"Let's forget it."

"I'm willing."

Harworth's spirits revived while he was taking a shower. The lukewarm water eased his nerves and a glow spread through his body. It was good to be alive!

He went out to breakfast whistling and Stein, who was already seated, said:

"Well, well. Had a change of heart, eh?"

"The shower did it," said Harworth, smiling. "Water's a great thing."

"Externally," said Stein.

Harworth wanted to talk to Stein, to explain to him what had been running through his mind the night before, but he was afraid Stein would laugh. They ate in silence.

FOUR

Helen met him at the door.
"Hello, Frank," she said. "Over your illness?"
"Yes," said Harworth. "I brought the roadster. Want to take a ride?"
"Yes. It'll be fun." said Helen, but she didn't go for her coat; she stood looking at Harworth.
For a moment he was puzzled, then he suddenly reached out and put his arm around her.
"Frank," she said, "the maid!"
"Oh," he said, embarrassed, awkwardly releasing her.
"You clumsy!" she cried, laughing; then she went for her coat.
They went out to the car arm in arm and he helped her in. The sky had cleared; the night was cool and bright. Harworth drove north along the lake road. There was a strong wind blowing across the lake and big waves were running and breaking over the cement parapets.
"What a lovely night," said Helen, looking up at the stars. "I'm glad I didn't go away."
"So am I."
"You're not."
"Of course I am."
"Running away from me last night."
"I wasn't."
Laughing, Helen leaned against him and shouted: "You were. You were afraid."
Harworth turned and kissed her on the mouth. To do so he had taken his eyes off the road for a moment and as he was driving fast his car swerved. A man yelled at him:
"Hey, you bastard, want all the road?"
Harworth immediately jammed on his brakes and pulled over to the side of the road, but the man had gone on without looking back.
"Brave guy," he said.
Helen laughed.
"Like you," she said; "running away."
"Say," said Harworth, and turning he slid his hands inside Helen's coat and pulled her toward him. She turned her face away, laughing, then she kissed him repeatedly.
"Hey!" yelled somebody.
Harworth turned. It was a traffic policeman.
"You can't park here," said the cop. "Don't you know no better than that? If you want to neck, go out farther."

Helen burst out laughing.

"O.K.," said Harworth.

"You'll get your tail bumped necking on this road the way guys come flying out here."

Harworth drove off. Helen was still laughing.

"Oh, I love that," she said. "Were we necking, Frank?"

"We were."

He was driving fast now and the wind was whistling around them. Where had his doubts gone? He felt strong and young; it was good to be alive on a night like this, to feel the wind on his face, to have a powerful motor responding to a touch, to have a woman like Helen Magnussen beside him!

What good fortune!

He sat driving in silence. Helen slid down in her seat and put her head on his shoulder.

He remembered one winter night in Detroit when, broke, nearly frozen, he had found a pocketbook with a dollar and fifteen cents in it. He had been able to eat and get a bed for the night. The next day he met Joe Fry on the street and Joe lent him car fare back to Cleveland. It was luck; his luck. Things like that were always happening to him.

And now look!

Helen said:

"Why don't you say something?"

"All right," said Harworth. "I think you're about 'it.'"

Helen laughed.

"Is that the best you can do?"

"What's the matter with that?"

She pulled his ear.

"You're the most unromantic man I ever saw. You should hear some of them."

Harworth didn't like that. He said nothing.

"Yes," said Helen; "you should hear some of them."

"And they get the laugh for it."

"Certainly, but it sounds nice. We like to hear it."

"You'll never hear me."

"Don't be too sure."

Harworth suddenly lost his feeling of compliance, of good nature; she was taunting him. She was Helen Magnussen, yes; but a woman just the same. With a sudden twist of the wheel he turned down a side road and stopped.

"Why stop here?" Helen demanded. "It's dark as pitch."

Harworth said nothing. He slid his hands inside her coat and tried to kiss her. She turned her face away, catching his kisses on the cheek. She was not laughing now, nor playful. She sensed how serious Harworth was and she knew why: she had been teasing him and he had resented it. In a little while she began to return his kisses, lying up against him, but she held his hands which were restless.

After a long silence she cried:

"No! No, Frank!"

Harworth said nothing, but, after a momentary hesitation, let her go. There was a long, embarrassed pause, then Helen said:

"Well, Mr. Cave Man, that's a nice way to act!"

"What do you expect?"

"Nothing," said Helen. "I'd like to go home."

"All right."

He was hot with anger. So that was it! Playing around. He had seen a lot of women like that and he hated them without exception. All of them prettily lewd till you got serious. Hell!

He turned the car around and drove back along the lake road without speaking. Helen was sitting as far away from him as possible, but presently she began to look at him out of the corner of her eye.

Finally she said:

"What do you take me for, anyway?"

"Do we have to argue?" Harworth demanded. "Let's forget it."

There was a certain finality about this that chilled Helen.

But she said:

"Well, that's a nice way to act."

Harworth was gradually cooling off.

"Never mind. I got steamed up that was all."

"I should say you did!"

There was a protracted silence. He turned down her street and stopped in front of her apartment house; then he jumped out and opened the door for her. She got out and started to cross the sidewalk. He didn't move.

"Aren't you going to say good night?"

"Yes," said Harworth, then stammering he went on: "I'm sorry about ... I mean, well: I guess I wasn't exactly gentle."

She came back.

"You certainly weren't."

He said nothing. She put her hand on his arm.

"Don't you like me a little bit?"

"Yes."

"Just a little bit?"

"No; a whole lot."

She came closer.
"Frank, don't you love me?"
He hesitated for a long time, then said:
"Yes."
She took hold of his arm.
"Come in."

At eight o'clock the next morning, the phone in the library rang and Joseph hurried to answer it. He could hear Harworth snoring and didn't want to wake him. But it was Helen Magnussen and she insisted that he call Harworth. Hesitatingly, Joseph opened Harworth's door and called him. Harworth sat up and stared vaguely at Joseph; his hair was tousled and his face was swollen with sleep.
"What the hell!"
"It's Mrs. Magnussen."
"Good Lord!" said Harworth, jumping out of bed and pulling the bed clothes with him.
He ran to answer the phone, falling over an ottoman in his haste.
"It's Helen," said the voice. "I woke up thinking about you, darling. Did I get you out of bed?"
"Yes," said Harworth, "but I don't care. Have lunch with me?"
"Yes and dinner. When will you be over?"
"About one."
"Why so late?"
"I've got some business I've got to look after."
"Oh. Well, I'll see you at one. Goodbye, darling."
"Goodbye, babe."
He heard her laughing.
"What are you laughing at?"
"Nothing."
He became immediately suspicious.
"Yes, you were."
"Well," said Helen, "nobody ever called me 'babe' before."
"What's wrong with that?"
"Nothing. I love it."

FIVE

Lily was lying on the lounge looking at Harworth, who was standing with his hat in his hand. He had just given Lily a check and she was holding it up, looking at it.
"Well," said Harworth, "see you later."

Lily sat up.

"Frank," she said, "stick around a while."

"No; I'm busy."

"You're always busy."

"I can't help that."

"You used to could help it and how!"

Harworth said nothing.

"Yeah," said Lily; "I remember when you used to take that receiver off the hook so nobody could get you."

Harworth was exasperated, but said nothing. Helen was waiting for him and he didn't want to be late. What was Lily kicking about, anyway? He should have told her not to bother him anymore. As it was, he was just giving her money for nothing, but she had to start a row!

"Yeah," said Lily, "mighty funny you can't come around anymore, so we could have some fun like we used to."

Harworth stood looking at her, wondering why he had ever spent so much of his time with her. Her hair was dyed, she had her nails stained red, she wore big, long earrings; and you could smell the perfume she used across the room. He remembered Helen's creamy complexion, her delicate ways.

"Well," he said, "I'm going. I'll drop around to the Alvarado some night."

"Make it soon," said Lily; "or maybe you'll be sorry."

"What do you mean by that?"

"Oh, nothing. Only Hrdlicka says you're stepping around with a lot of high society folks. I guess I'm not good enough for you anymore."

"Oh, come off."

"All right. But you better be careful how you treat me."

Harworth was puzzled, then suddenly he thought of the silly letters he had written her. He started to ask her about them, but thought better of it and said:

"Tell Hrdlicka to mind his own business."

"Yeah," said Lily, "I know them society women. Campi dances with 'em once in a while. Ask him about 'em. They're red hot."

"All right," said Harworth. "You know."

He turned and started out. She called after him:

"You better listen to what I'm saying."

But Harworth shut the door.

Lily got up and stamped about the apartment in a fury, then she phoned Campi.

SIX

Harworth was slightly uncomfortable. It was the first time he had ever been near a college and the atmosphere seemed alien and unfriendly. Mechanically he reached for his monocle, which at one time had been his defense against embarrassment, but he had left it at home; Helen had laughed him out of it. She said it was silly. Harworth shifted, uncrossed and recrossed his legs and glanced out of the corner of his eye at Helen.

"I wish they'd start," said Helen, turning. "Poor Louise is so nervous."

Harworth did not like the way she said "poor Louise." He detected a latent enmity. He couldn't imagine why there should be ill-feeling; they were lifelong friends. At first he had thought that he was unduly suspicious, but now he was sure that Louise and Helen merely pretended to be friendly, that, underneath, they disliked each other intensely. And it seemed to him that Helen was the more aggressive in this enmity. Often he had the impression that Helen was envious of Louise. But why? Helen had everything; Louise nothing.

Harworth glanced about him. He and Helen were sitting in the rear of the big assembly hall which was empty except for the musicians on the stage, who were tuning up now, and a small group of students. Burne was sitting on a chair before the conductor's music stand, glancing vaguely out into the audience. Louise was in the first row.

"I hope it clicks," said Harworth. "I don't know anything about music, but Burne seems to me like a smart fellow. I hate to see a fellow like him getting the worst of it."

"Oh," said Helen, "he doesn't care."

"I think he does."

"Well," said Helen, shrugging, "what does it matter?"

"It doesn't matter, not to me. Only ..."

"There's an only, isn't there?"

Harworth looked at her in surprise. He thought she seemed very ill-tempered, but as he continued to stare, her expression changed; she put her arm through his and smiled.

"You like Louise, don't you?" she demanded.

"Certainly."

"Yes, I know you do."

He said nothing.

"Louise would give anything to get rid of Arthur."

Harworth said:

"Do you think so?"

Helen laughed.

"I know so. Arthur is impossible. Nobody could get along with him, and he hasn't a penny."

"They've been friends for a long time, haven't they?"

"Oh, yes," said Helen, laughing. "She nearly married him once."

"That so?"

"Yes; they had the license."

There was something in Helen's tone he didn't like. He glanced at her. She was sitting looking straight ahead; her jaw had an aggressive tilt.

"Why didn't they use it?"

"Louise decided it would be more sensible not to. Why marry a man without a cent and no prospects!"

"She doesn't seem like that to me."

"Of course not."

Harworth turned and said:

"Here come the rest."

Larsen, Richman and Magnussen had just come in and were standing in the doorway. Louise saw them and hurried back. Harworth watched her as she stood talking with them. She looked very tired. Helen called to her and she came over to them, bringing the others. Harworth got hastily to his feet.

"I hope everything goes off all right," he said.

"So do I," said Louise. "Arthur's half crazy. This is the final rehearsal, you know. If it doesn't go well tonight, Arthur's going to withdraw it from the programme."

"Maybe he's too particular," said Helen.

"I don't think so."

Magnussen said:

"Tell him not to worry. We'll all be here the night of the concert. Tell him he'll have his own claque."

Richman said:

"Harworth, may I see you a minute?"

"Sure," said Harworth, excusing himself.

Larsen stood without saying a word, staring at Louise.

Richman led Harworth back to a huge embrasure in the rear of the hall.

"Well?" said Harworth, slightly puzzled; Richman had never been very friendly.

"It's like this," said Richman, "I'm working on a novel."

He hesitated and Harworth said:

"Yeah?"

"Yes. You see, it's a satirical novel about a big city; Chicago, to be specific, and I'm using you as the chief character."

Harworth, puzzled but flattered, stood staring.

"You haven't any objections, have you?"

"Why, no."

"Good! I've already had an advance on it from the people who published my last book; so you see, it's not just one of those ideas writers have; it's going through."

"Well," said Harworth, expansive, "that's mighty interesting. When'll it be out?"

"It's scheduled for November. I've got to hurry with it."

"Well," said Harworth, smiling, "don't call me any names in it."

"Of course not. Only you must realize that it's a satirical novel. Funny, understand? Not real. I'm just using you and your peculiarities as a starting point."

"My peculiarities!" exclaimed Harworth, flattered that anyone had taken the trouble to notice them.

"Yes. The monocle, you see. Stuff like that. Surface peculiarities."

The musicians were tuning up loudly now, and turning, Harworth saw Burne rise and take his position before the music stand.

"It's starting, I guess," he said.

"Thanks, Mr. Harworth."

"That's all right."

Harworth hurried back to his chair in time to hear what Louise was saying; she was talking to Magnussen.

"That's all he talks about. It gives me the creeps. I try to help him get it off his mind, but it's no use."

"What's that?" Harworth asked.

Magnussen looked at him. But Louise said:

"Death. It's all he talks about."

Harworth felt a sudden twinge and the blood rushed to his face: Hafey was lying in a dark alleyway riddled with bullets.

But he said:

"That's queer."

Helen said:

"Sit down, Frank."

The musicians ceased tuning-up; Burne raised his baton. Louise turned and hurried to her seat in the first row.

Helen put her arm through Harworth's, and when the lights were dimmed she pressed her knee against his. Richman and Larsen stood in the back of the hall leaning against the wall. Magnussen sat down beside Harworth.

The music began: the English horn played a slow, sad, high-pitched melody against a background of dissonance from the stringed choir, muted.

Harworth felt a shiver go down his spine. He thought about Hafey, about his own father who had died of a stroke, about the man he had seen killed in a gunfight in Saint Louis. He turned and whispered to Helen.

"What does he call it?"

"'Lament For The Living.' Silly title."

Harworth sat listening intently. He knew nothing at all about music, except popular stuff. He had been a baritone once in a barbershop quartet; he was used to trite little tunes, to hackneyed harmony. This music was too much for him and gradually his attention wandered. He saw Burne bent over his score, beating time; he watched the rhythmic rise and fall of the violin bows. Helen squeezed his hand and after a moment he returned the pressure. But he felt uneasy; the music vaguely disturbed him. It went on and on, softly, the voice of the woodwind rising and falling; the strings muted. Once there was a sudden fortissimo and the piccolo shrilled above the others; Harworth winced slightly, the note was so piercing.

Before he realized it, the music had stopped with a roll of the kettle drums. The lights came on.

There was a burst of applause. Helen said:

"That's certainly peculiar music."

"It sure is," said Harworth.

He turned. Richman was still applauding; there was a queer expression on his face.

Magnussen said:

"Arthur's a real composer. If he wasn't so impossible he'd get some place."

"What do you know about it, Dick?" Helen demanded.

"Nothing, nothing."

Burne was in the middle of a group of students, who were congratulating him. Louise came back to join the rest of the party. Richman came over to her.

"That's great music. Great music."

Louise smiled.

"I wouldn't know," she said. "But it went off well."

Helen whispered to Harworth.

"Frank, let's go, before someone suggests a party."

They got up. Louise turned, saw that they were going and nodded to Helen, then offered her hand to Harworth.

"Thanks for coming."

Harworth pressed her hand, then Helen took his arm and they went out.

"See you tomorrow, Harworth," called Magnussen.

"All right."

When they had gone Richman said:

"Helen fell hard, didn't she?"

"Oh, I don't know," said Magnussen; "she never falls very hard. But she falls frequently."

They all knew about Magnussen's troubles with Helen; none of them laughed.

At two o'clock the phone rang and Helen answered it. Harworth had just shut the door behind him and was waiting for the elevator. She said "hold the line" and running from the room she flung open the door and called to Harworth. He came back.

"Phone," she said.

Harworth took up the receiver. It was Stein. He was excited. The Burgoyne had been raided and wrecked.

Helen, who was watching Harworth, saw his face turn red then livid. She started back in alarm.

"God damn!" shouted Harworth; then: "I'll be home in a minute."

"Wait," said Stein. "Molina's coming right over. He phoned."

"Yeah," said Harworth: "A fine lot of protection he gave me."

He banged up the receiver. Then he got up and stood staring across the room. Helen didn't know him; she felt a little frightened.

"Call you tomorrow," he said, coming to himself and going out into the hall.

"Kiss me, Frank."

He kissed her, a brief peck.

"What's the matter, darling?"

"Nothing; only this evening cost me a hundred thousand dollars."

"Good heavens!"

Harworth went out slamming the door. Helen walked up and down for a moment, then she sat down and tried to read a magazine. But it was no use. She couldn't get Harworth out of her mind. What kind of man was he after all?

"Snap it up, Sandy," Harworth shouted.

Sandy nodded.

Harworth sat shifting about nervously and cursing himself. Why, goddam it, he was getting as squeamish as an old woman! Yeah; imagine getting all excited about somebody bumping off a guy that needed bumping. Imagine wasting pity on a bird like Arthur Burne who had had it soft all his life, had a good education, and then couldn't make his way in the world. What was wrong with him? It was Helen; it was Magnussen. They didn't think as he did; they were making a sap out of him. Sure, it was wonderful when Papa left you a few millions to play around with; wonderful! and you could afford to cultivate your sensibilities; you could afford pity and other expensive virtues! But what about it when you had to make your own way in the world and snatch your dollars from a pack of wolves?

The limousine stopped and Sandy opened the door. "Through with me, boss?"

"Yes," said Harworth, starting across the sidewalk.

Sandy took him by the arm.

"Boss, could I use the roadster for a little while?"

"What for?"

"Well," said Sandy, "I got a little blond kid over here on Oak Street ..."

"This time of night?"

Sandy grinned.

"Yeah. You see the mister works at night on a newspaper."

Harworth shrugged.

"All right," he said. "But how about that Ford you was driving?"

"I sold it."

"What for?"

"I needed the money."

Harworth shook his head several times.

"What a guy won't do for a blond!"

"But, boss," said Sandy, "you ought to see her!"

"Different, eh?"

Harworth laughed shortly and went into the lobby and took the elevator.

Stein let him in when he rang the bell.

"Heard from Michaelson?"

"No," said Stein.

Harworth took off his hat and went into the library. Stein followed him, limping and leaning heavily on his cane. Harworth sat down and said nothing. Stein said:

"Frank, my leg sure is cutting up right now. I think I'll go to bed and ease it."

"All right. When'll Molina be here?"

"Ought to be here now. Frank, be careful. Molina's sore as the devil and he's going to cause somebody a lot of trouble."

"Suits me," said Harworth. "I been going around feeling sorry for people for the last week or two. That's a laugh."

Stein looked at Harworth for a long time, then he sat down.

"I think I better sit in on this conference," he said. "Molina's killing mad and you don't seem much better."

"What about Michaelson?"

"You know what I think. I always told you he was a crook."

"Think he engineered this?"

"Sure," said Stein, "and I think Bourke's behind him. That's the syndicate. You was making too much dough and when you wouldn't sell out they fixed you."

"Bourke, eh? I guess you're right. Well, Molina's got a fine drag, hasn't he? He can fix everything. What a laugh!"

"What's on your mind, Frank?"

"I don't know yet."

Stein said:

"Frank, listen to me once. Take your loss and say nothing. I never did want you in that business and now you're out of it. You got your two big night clubs left and they're coining money."

Harworth said nothing. It might seem like big money to Stein, but not to him. Since he had been associating with Magnussen his ideas had changed; Magnussen lost more money than he made. He was just piking along.

"I'll make a million before I'm through and then some," he said.

Stein looked at Harworth and sat tapping his cane on the floor.

"Frank," he said, "be sensible. You've got more money now than you need."

The doorbell rang and Harworth went to answer it. Molina and Frankie Dean came in.

"Well," said Molina, pushing back his hat, "nice little mess, ain't it?"

"Yeah," said Harworth. "Come on in."

They followed him into the library and Harworth introduced them to Stein.

"He's all right, is he?" Molina demanded.

"Sure; he's my manager."

They sat down. Molina said:

"Well, Michaelson don't care what happens to him, does he?"

"He ain't got no sense," said Frankie. "Never had."

"We'll learn him some sense," said Molina.

"How?" asked Stein.

Molina turned his eyes slowly in Stein's direction.

"Oh, we'll just reason with him."

Frankie laughed curtly.

"Wait a minute," said Stein; "I'm going to say my piece first, then you do as you please. The job's done; the place is smashed and nobody'll ever have the nerve to open it again. We might just as well take the loss and shut up about it."

Molina laughed.

"I was protecting that place," he said; "and they can't get away with that stuff with me."

"Well," said Stein, "Frank, here, lost about a hundred thousand dollars on that deal, and he's the one that's got the biggest kick coming. It didn't cost you a cent, Molina."

Molina jerked his thumb toward Harworth. "He's a friend of mine, ain't he?"

"Is he?"

Molina looked at Stein with narrowed eyes for a long time.

"Ain't doubting my word any, are you?"

"Well, I'd like to hear your story first."

"Say …!" said Frankie.

But Molina laughed.

"All right, Pop. I guess you're on the up and up."

Harworth sat listening. He was pale and kept wetting his lips.

Frankie said:

"See how it is? This is all over town. Joe, here, can't stand for that."

"No," said Molina, "I ain't standing for it. Michaelson's number's up. He'll leave town tonight."

"He's small fry, see?" said Frankie, explaining the lenience.

"And Bourke," said Molina; then he hesitated and laughed; "Bourke's in a tough spot."

Frankie threw back his head and laughed.

"And him a reform candidate," he said.

Stein got to his feet.

"Frank, take my advice. Keep out of this. I'm going to bed. I don't know a thing."

"Smart guy," said Molina.

Frankie said:

"You let Harworth alone, Pop. He knows his business."

Stein walked toward the door.

"Frank," he said, "take your loss and forget it. That's the best you can do."

"I'm running this," said Harworth.

Stein went out. Molina said:

"Nice old guy, but timid."

"Don't need to worry about him," said Harworth, "he's all right."

When Stein had shut the door, Molina leaned forward.
"Now we can get down to business."
"All right."
Frankie got up and began to pace the floor. He had his hat pushed back and he was picking his teeth with a match.
"I'll take the loss," said Molina.
Harworth sat up.
"What do you mean?"
"Listen," said Molina, "I like you. You're a young guy and you got the stuff. I'll put you in on my racket for what you lost. See?"
Harworth said nothing.
"When I give a guy protection, I give him protection. Hell, my word's good."
"Good as bond," said Frankie.
"And listen," said Molina, "it'll mean plenty to you, see? You get a cut and I'll see that you get a square one. We'll team up, only you don't need to do nothing. Just set back and make money. Got it?"
Harworth thought for a long time.
"All right."
He wanted money; he wanted lots of money. He was tired of feeling like a poor relation around Magnussen.
Molina sat with his big head on one side and his plump hands on his knees, looking at Harworth. Frankie walked around the room picking his teeth and looking at the pictures.
"Say," said Molina, "why don't you come out to my house and have dinner with me and the missus some night?"
Harworth didn't know what to say. He had no desire to go. What was Molina after all but a gangster? But he didn't want to offend him.
"I think we can arrange it."
"Fine," said Molina, "make it Friday night. We can talk things over."
Harworth was trapped. He shifted in his chair but finally said:
"All right."
Molina got to his feet and held out his hand. Harworth took it; it was soft and fat and sweaty.
"Easy on them fingers," said Molina, grinning; "you nearly busted my hand that night at the fights."
Harworth smiled.
"Listen," said Molina; "you don't know a thing, see? But Bourke 'll never be an alderman."
"Ain't that too bad," said Frankie.
Harworth felt suddenly uneasy. He had cooled off somewhat by now, but what could he say? He said nothing. Let other people look out for

themselves. It wasn't any of his business.

"So long," said Molina, at the door. "See you Friday. Six o'clock."

"So long," said Frankie.

When they had got out into the hall, Molina said to Frankie.

"Great guy, ain't he? I'll have to put on a swell feed for that bird. He's society; goes around with all the swells."

SEVEN

Mrs. Molina was very nice. Harworth liked her. She was a plump Italian woman of about thirty with pretty, dark eyes. She sat looking at her plate, eating with restraint, and from time to time glancing up at the maid, to see that she was serving things properly. Once Harworth was surprised to see her eyes flash suddenly as she looked up at the maid, who had put his salad on the wrong side of his plate.

Molina was beaming and expansive, making jokes about everything, and insisting that Harworth take more of this, more of that. Molina was well-dressed but he was wearing several big diamond rings and a diamond stick pin, and from time to time Harworth caught the sweetish odor of hair tonic.

Junior, in a sailor-suit with brass buttons, sat without speaking, staring at Harworth when he thought he wasn't observed. Occasionally his father would say:

"Junior, sit up straight now," or, "Junior, what did papa tell you about your fork?"

Harworth felt very much at home, very comfortable. He liked the atmosphere of Molina's home. He had never had any real family life. His mother had died when he was very small; his father had lived haphazard, paying little attention to him, but remembering to cuff him occasionally so he wouldn't be spoiled.

When it was time for the coffee he was full and happy.

Mrs. Molina said:

"I'm afraid you ain't had enough to eat, Mr. Harworth."

"I'm stuffed," he said. "I never had a better meal in my life."

Molina grinned.

"We set a pretty good table here, don't we Marie? Come often."

"You shouldn't brag, Joe."

Junior said:

"Well, I'm still hungry. Can I have another piece of cake?"

"Be quiet, Junior," said Molina.

"Well, I'm still hungry."

"You know you never get two pieces of cake, Junior," said Mrs. Molina.

Junior sulked, then he said:
"Sometimes I do. When we ain't got company."
Mrs. Molina flushed. Molina said:
"Junior, I'll put you to bed if you don't look out."
Junior sulked.
Harworth said:
"When I was a kid I never could get enough to eat."
Molina laughed.
"Me, too! Look at this bay window." He patted his stomach.
"Joe!" said Mrs. Molina.
When they had finished their coffee Molina took Harworth into the big living room. Mrs. Molina called after him:
"It's seven-thirty, Joe. I better put Junior to bed, I guess."
"Let him stay up a while."
Junior jumped down from his chair and capered, then he came up behind Harworth suddenly and took hold of his hand. Harworth was startled at the feel of the small cool hand.
"Say," said Junior, "want to see my animal book?"
Molina was going to protest, but Harworth said:
"Sure."
Molina said:
"What a boy! All he thinks about is animals. Tigers, lions, elephants. He draws pictures of 'em."
"I like 'em myself," said Harworth. "Ever go to the Lincoln Park Zoo?"
Molina laughed. He thought Harworth was kidding.
"Hell, no!"
Junior came back dragging a big picture book. He pointed to a chair and said to Harworth:
"You sit there."
Harworth smiled and sat down. Molina stood watching, smoking a big, black cigar. Junior started to climb up in Harworth's lap, but Molina said:
"Hey! Get down. You'll take all the crease out of his pants."
"It's all right," said Harworth.
Junior sat sideways on Harworth's lap and began to show Harworth the pictures in the book, and although he could only read the simplest words, like cat and dog, he knew all the animals at sight and named them triumphantly.
Molina sat down and watched them, smiling. When Mrs. Molina came in he winked and jerked his thumb at Harworth.
"Oh, Junior," said Mrs. Molina, pleased, "you'll muss Mr. Harworth all up."

"It's all right," said Harworth.

After Junior had gone through the book once he asked Harworth to read to him. Each picture had a short paragraph describing the animal it portrayed and telling about its habits. Molina and his wife sat in silence smiling at each other, while Harworth read to Junior. There was the aardvark, which ate ants, and the antelope, which could run so fast, and the armadillo, which rolled itself up in an armored ball. Harworth read on, feeling very self-conscious; his voice sounding loud to him in the quiet room. After a while Junior began to nod and finally fell asleep.

"Look," said Molina, "he's asleep. Ain't that cute?"

Mrs. Molina came over and took Junior in her arms and carried him out of the room.

"He's a nice little kid," said Harworth.

And he meant it. He had never paid much attention to children; he was hardly aware of their existence. But he felt queer and happy holding Molina's little boy on his lap. It wouldn't be so bad to have one of his own!

"He's a dandy. He was kind of shy and backward tonight," said Molina; "on account of you being here, see? But you ought to see him sometimes when there's just the three of us. Wow, what a kid! He nearly drives me nuts!"

Molina laughed. Harworth studied him. Sitting comfortably in his own house he didn't seem like the same person; didn't seem like the successful and ruthless Molina, who was probably the most dangerous man in the city.

Mrs. Molina came back. Harworth got hastily to his feet. Molina looked at him in surprise, then got half off his chair waiting for his wife to sit down.

She sat down and said:

"Maybe Mr. Harworth would like to hear some music."

Molina turned to Harworth.

"Yeah? Would you?"

But the phone rang and Molina went out in the hall to answer it.

"Always business," said Mrs. Molina. "That's the way we live." She shrugged and went on: "Joe never has a minute. Always somebody calling up, calling up. I say to him, Joe, let's go away. And he says, next year, next year. Always next year."

Harworth studied this handsome Italian woman, wondering how much she knew about her husband's business.

She said:

"Joe could make good money other ways. He's smart. But he won't listen."

Molina came back; he was scowling and looked determined.

"Ain't it hell!" he said. "I got to go."
"Oh, Joe," said Mrs. Molina, "can't you put it off one night?"
"No," said Molina; "I got to go."
Harworth got up.
"I'll go too."
Mrs. Molina said:
"I thought we could take in a movie."
"You go," said Molina. "Let Mr. Harworth drop you off."
"No; I won't go by myself. I'll stay home."
Molina shrugged. Harworth wanted to offer to take her, but didn't know whether Molina would like the suggestion or not. He said nothing.
Mrs. Molina got up and held out her hand to Harworth.
"Come again some time," she said, trying to smile.
"Thanks. I will. That was a wonderful dinner."
Molina kissed his wife and he and Harworth went out together. Frankie Dean and another man were waiting in the hallway. Molina paid no attention to them. They waited till Molina and Harworth had got past them, then they followed.
Molina stopped in the doorway and offered his hand to Harworth.
"Goodbye. Mighty glad you came."
"Thanks."
Molina thought for a moment, then he said:
"What a life! It's tough, brother, tough. Plenty of grief all the time. I wish I was peddling bananas."
Harworth said nothing.
"Yeah," said Molina. "And look at Marie. As swell a wife as you'd want. What a hell of a lot of fun she has, I guess not! She's sore at me half the time. She don't know what I'm up against. She knows I'm selling booze and making plenty of dough but she thinks it's easy. Hell!"
Harworth said:
"I guess you have your troubles."
"Plenty! Everybody says, look at that big stiff; got all the dough in the world. Easy money, easy money. They don't know."
They shook hands again and Molina climbed into his Pierce Arrow limousine, followed by Frankie who said: "Hello, Mr. Harworth." The other man got into the driver's seat.
"So long," said Molina, waving.

EIGHT

It was two o'clock in the morning and Harworth was sitting alone in the library figuring his accounts. Things weren't going so well and from time to time he swore out loud; and ran his hands through his hair. His gambling house was a total loss and the business at The Machine was gradually falling off. As his overhead there was very high this worried him. The Casa Alvarado was doing capacity business but Con Weiss was getting ready to open a big night club directly across the street. Harworth knew that he was slipping and it infuriated him. Things had been going too well the last few years; he had been very lucky. Real adversity was something he had nearly forgotten.

He closed his account book with a bang and got up.

"Well," he told himself, "I got to take a chance. Maybe Magnussen can put me on to something."

He got out his bank books, savings and checking accounts, and figured up his ready cash; then he made a memorandum and put it in the top drawer of his desk.

He walked over to a mirror and looked into it. He thought that his face looked sort of slack.

"Hell!" he said and going into his bathroom he weighed himself on the scales he kept there.

He discovered that he had lost about eight pounds in the last two weeks.

"Say!" he said, worried.

He'd been neglecting himself lately. He'd have to watch what he ate, and cut down on his cigarettes and get more sleep, and forget about Helen for a while.

"You can take the count mighty easy from a widow," he thought, then he laughed harshly, and sat down.

He felt stale and dissatisfied. Everything seemed pretty monotonous. There was a certain sameness about living that disgusted him. He did nothing but repeat himself in circumstances which varied but little. Lily and Helen; the difference was slight. Lily was more vulgar, more honest in her desires and less squeamish; Helen was exasperatingly timid till aroused and then Lily was outdone. But essentially they were the same.

He sat staring at the floor and after a time he began to nod. But a knock at the hall door brought him up with a start, broad awake. Who could that be?

He went to the door and called:

"Who's there?"

"Canovi."

He opened the door. Canovi was leaning against the wall, grinning.

"What do you want?" Harworth demanded.

"I got to see you," said Canovi. "Important."

"Well, you picked a nice time of night."

Canovi came in and took off his hat.

"I'm being tailed," he said, grinning; "so I go to bed and stay a while then I slip out the back way."

"Who's tailing you?"

"Some of Bourke's special investigators, I guess."

They went into the library and sat down. Canovi said:

"Listen; Windy and me ... Windy's one of Molina's boys, see ... we got some mighty fine information. I'm going to report to Joe tomorrow and he'll get the laugh of his life."

Harworth sat uneasily playing with a book of matches.

"Michaelson beat it," said Canovi. "He took a plane to Detroit. Was he scared! Wow! He's nothing but a dumb kike. Bourke and Monahan talked him into double-crossing you."

"He fixed The Burgoyne, all right."

"Sure; but wait! Bourke threw Joe over and teamed up with Monahan. He thinks Monahan's on the inside track. Ain't that a laugh!"

Canovi took out a little book.

"Boss," he said, "Joe's got you down for five grand."

"What for?"

"Don't ask questions."

Harworth laughed shortly.

"No? Well, don't expect me to hand out five thousand bucks for fun."

Canovi leaned forward.

"Boss, hell's going to hit this town in short order. If you don't know nothing, you don't know nothing! See? It's healthier."

Harworth stared at the carpet.

"Here's a tip," said Canovi, grinning: "Joe's going to put on a sideshow for the town. They been pushing him too hard. You're down for five grand and I'm collecting."

"I still don't get you."

Canovi's grin faded and he scowled at Harworth. "Come on. Put up. I ain't got all night."

"Don't get tough."

They sat staring at each other for a moment then Canovi looked away and said:

"All the big shots are putting in, boss. It's defense money, see; defense money. Got it?"

Harworth knew what Canovi meant now and a chill went through him. But he was in too far to back up; he had to put in with the rest and like it. Without a word he got up, went to the wall safe and counted out the money. Canovi took it with a grin.

"That's the way to talk, boss. I'll be seeing you." He started out.

"Wait a minute," said Harworth. "How did you get past the desk downstairs?"

Canovi shrugged.

"I didn't. I came up just like I'm going down: the fire escape!"

He laughed and went out.

Harworth stood in the middle of the room, staring. Why, a man wasn't safe in his own house!

PART FOUR

ONE

Magnussen shrugged.

"Southern Copper is already up ten points. It looks like a killing."

Harworth smiled and sipped his coffee. Magnussen went on reading the financial page, occasionally marking an item with his pencil. Finally he passed the paper to Harworth.

"The market's wild right now," said Magnussen. "All we have to do is keep away from the ticker and sit tight. Maynard says there's no top to it. Personally I don't know a damn thing about it. I play the market like I shoot crap: on the outside of the game. But it looks like we've picked winners."

Harworth laid down the paper and offered Magnussen a cigar, which he accepted.

"You did the picking," said Harworth; "I don't know straight up."

"Thank Maynard," said Magnussen. "He's made and lost half a dozen fortunes at this game. Yesterday he told me he'd never seen anything like this. It may be too good to be true."

"We can always sell."

"Yes; but Maynard said we'd better sit tight for a while. He thinks there are millions to be made."

"I hope so."

The waiter came and Magnussen signed the check, then they went into the library to finish their cigars. Harworth sank back comfortably into a big leather armchair, crossed his legs, and sat looking about the room. He was glowing with satisfaction. One after another his ambitions were being realized. Here he was sitting in the Lake Michigan Club, hobnobbing with Richard Magnussen, one of the richest men in the city.

One fall night, ten years ago, he had stood in front of this very club waiting for a bus to take him north. He had seen the doorman helping prosperous-looking men out of their limousines. Turning, he had watched these men as they entered the entryway and at last disappeared through a mysterious big door. Once he had caught a glimpse of a huge dimly lighted room and an attendant in livery. Standing there in the bitter wind from the lake, possessing nothing but the clothes on his back and about four dollars, he had wondered what went on behind that big door!

"How's the night club business?" asked Magnussen finally.

"Fair," said Harworth. "Competition is getting very stiff. I'd like to get out of it if I could sell at a profit."

"I understand you sold your chain of restaurants."

"Yes; for a good price. They made me some money, but they were a lot of bother. I don't think I managed them right. The responsibility was divided too much. I was always having trouble with my individual managers."

"Honest men are hard to find."

"Exactly."

Magnussen crossed his legs and stared at the lighted end of his cigar.

"Well," he said, "it's no wonder. There's no respect for law anymore. Get what you can and get it quick. That's the way it's done now. Nobody cares much how you get it as long as you've got it."

Harworth stirred uncomfortably, puffed on his cigar, but said nothing.

"Personally," said Magnussen, "I never cared much about money. I've always had it and I've always spent it as fast as I could. I'd probably be better off if I didn't have a cent."

"Don't be too sure about that."

Queer how rich men thought it would be fun to go hungry. He had heard Robert Joyce make the same statement once. At such times Harworth felt very superior to them. They didn't know what it was all about.

Magnussen looked up quickly and smiled.

"That's romanticism, isn't it?"

"Yes," said Harworth; "it doesn't work. You get too many protests from your stomach."

Magnussen laughed.

"That's putting it briefly. I'll remember that."

Harworth was pleased. Magnussen hesitated for a little while, then he said:

"But it seems to me you're suffering from a form of romanticism also. We're getting a bit philosophical, I think; but never mind."

Harworth looked surprised.

"How do you mean?"

"I may be wrong, but I'd say that your idea was, that the more money you get the more fun you have."

Harworth thought for a moment.

"That's right I guess."

"Well," said Magnussen, laughing, "speaking from experience I'd say you were equally wrong. But I'm not sure where the protests would come from. Not from the stomach. From the spirit, I imagine."

Harworth didn't follow him and said nothing. Magnussen sighed and stared at his cigar. There was a long silence. Finally Magnussen said:

"You and Helen are getting along nicely I hear."

Harworth glanced at Magnussen, who was sitting with his legs crossed, looking mildly off across the room. But something in his attitude warned Harworth to be on his guard; Magnussen was trying to pump him.

"Yes," he said. "I like her very much."

"She's very likeable when she wants to be. We were married nearly five years. We didn't hit it off."

"She speaks very well of you."

"Does she? That's nice of her."

Harworth thought that Magnussen looked very glum. He had often wondered about them. Richman had told him once that it was a love match and that Helen had tired first. There had been a scandal in Paris.

"Do you mind if I ask you a question?" said Magnussen.

Harworth lowered his eyes.

"Of course not."

"Is she very fond of you?"

Harworth smiled.

"No. I don't think so. We're good friends."

Magnussen glanced up and Harworth saw that his face was flushed and that he was making an effort of some kind.

"What do you think of a man who would ask a question like that?" he demanded.

Harworth lowered his eyes in embarrassment. Magnussen had always seemed so cold and calm, so careless to him; he had envied him. Now he saw that he was none of these things; that, in spite of his money, his position, his apparent indifference, he suffered as other men suffer.

"I don't see anything wrong with that question," said Harworth.

"Don't you?"

There was a long silence. Finally Harworth inquired:

"Hasn't Miss Paul come back yet? I haven't seen her lately."

"No," said Magnussen. Then he laughed. "What a girl!" he went on. "She's better than liquor or gambling. She takes me clear out of myself. I feel positively paternal with her. What a rattlehead; and one of the nicest girls I ever knew."

"I like her," said Harworth. "But I see what you mean. She ought to be playing with dolls or riding on the merry-go-round."

Magnussen laughed.

"That's it. That's what she's always doing: riding on a merry-go-round and getting brass rings. She has a wonderful time no matter where she goes. It's a gift."

Harworth smiled but said nothing.

"Jo's perfect," Magnussen went on, smiling; "nothing is ever commonplace to her. I don't think she was ever bored in her life. Quite a contrast to that bunch she goes around with. Helen gets so bored sometimes that she talks about suicide. Talks about it, you understand. But even that's something. Bob Joyce was born bored. Look at Richman! He's so bored he takes it out on other people and calls it satire. Louise is in a perpetual state of boredom, but she has some excuse, poor girl."

"By the way," said Harworth, "how did Burne's concert come off?"

"Fine. Arthur has lots of talent, but he's ineffectual. I mean he's somewhat lacking in character. Did you see the papers? Berg gave him a fine write-up. Louise told me that Stock was considering some of Arthur's music, so I put my uncle to work on him. My uncle's a queer old duck. He was educated in Vienna and wanted to be a concert pianist, but the soap business got him. Still plays and goes to Vienna once a year; to hear real music, he says. He likes to play the martyr but I think he's really more at home in the soap business."

Magnussen laughed. It made Harworth feel queer to hear old Henry Magnussen discussed in this fashion. He had seen him once at a theatre: a tall, thin, crabbed old man with aquiline features. He was rated the richest man in Illinois.

"Arthur's impossible," said Magnussen. "I'm surprised that Louise puts up with him."

"They've known each other a long time, haven't they?"

"Too long."

There was a short silence, then Magnussen glanced at his watch.

"Good Lord! It's after two. I've got to be going."

They got up. At the door they shook hands.

"See you at Helen's Saturday," said Magnussen.

"I'll be there."

When Harworth came in Joseph said:

"Mr. Stein wants to see you. He's very sick. The doctor just left."

"August, sick! Why, he told me he was feeling pretty good this morning."

"He was walking through the library about twelve o'clock and fell."

Harworth was stunned. He never gave much thought to Stein; he seemed permanent; someone he could always depend on. He stood staring at the carpet.

"And Mrs. Magnussen called," said Joseph. "You're to call her at seven."

Harworth nodded and went into Stein's bedroom. Stein was propped up in bed reading a newspaper and smoking a cigar.

"Hello, Frank," he called.

Harworth sighed with relief. He had pictured Stein lying pale and silent.

"Hello, August, you old devil. From what Joseph said I thought you were dying."

"Oh," said Stein; "that's Joseph's way. He's had a face a yard long ever since I took my tumble. I got dizzy and fell on my head, Frank."

"Why don't you quit drinking?" Harworth demanded, laughing.

"Say, I haven't had a drink today. I'm just getting old; ready for the boneyard. And my rheumatism's giving me hell. My knee's all swelled up. The Doc's a cheerful guy. He says it's only the beginning."

"Beginning of what?"

"Why, beginning of the end."

"Oh, cut it out. You'd think you were sick!"

"Well," said Stein, "if it's the beginning of inflammatory rheumatism, I'll be pretty hard to get along with from now on."

"It's probably gonorrheal rheumatism!"

Stein laughed.

"You flatter me."

Harworth lit a cigarette. There was a long silence and Stein went back to his paper. Harworth had kept his speculations from Stein for over a week; but he had begun to feel uneasy about it. Stein always knew all about his business; he had for years. Finally he said:

"August, listen. I put all that restaurant money into stocks."

Stein flung down his paper.

"So you're going to finish in the poorhouse after all. Speculating, eh?"

"Yes. Southern Copper's already up ten points. The others are up a little."

Stein said nothing for a moment, then he shifted about in bed trying to get his leg in a more comfortable position and swearing.

"Frank," he said: "give me a list of what you've got and I'll keep my eyes open. It'll give me something to do while I'm on my back. You ain't no good on earth, chasing after them swells. It's a good thing you've already made a pile."

"Just wait. I'll show you a pile. Magnussen and I are in on the same stocks."

"Yes," said Stein, "but he can afford to lose."

"So can I."

"Well, from all I can hear, and mind you, I don't know nothing about that racket; you got in at the right time. A fool for luck."

Harworth laughed.

"Yes, sir," said Stein, "but don't get swellheaded about it and hold on if she keeps going up. What goes up must come down. If I was you I'd sell that copper out now, if it's up ten points."

"She's going up farther. Magnussen's got a friend in the know."

Stein snorted.

"In the know! Jees, what a sap you are. Haven't you played in the horses long enough to know that that kind of information is worse than no good. You might just as well toss up. I'd like to have the dough I've lost on feedbox information. Yeah. I wish I had a dollar for every time some jockey or swipe has said to me, August, bet on this or that plug; he's as good as in; it's fixed."

"I can't imagine you plunging," said Harworth, laughing.

"No," said Stein, "I'm fifty some now and I've learned a lesson. But when I was twenty-odd I didn't have any more sense than you've got. I believed in Santa Claus."

Harworth laughed and got up.

"Going to get up for dinner?"

"Get up for dinner! I can't get out of bed even."

"You mean it?"

"Of course I mean it."

The smile faded from Harworth's face. He stood looking at Stein.

"Well," he said, "I'm going out tonight. But Joseph'll stay with you."

"Don't worry about me. Give me that list I was asking you about and I'll try to keep you out of the pokey."

Harworth took a pencil from his pocket and marked the stocks on the financial page.

"Put down what you bought 'em at," said Stein.

At dinner Harworth was lonesome without Stein. The big dining room was very still and Joseph walked about on tiptoes. It was early fall and the windows were already dark; one of the glass panels was open and there was a smell of fall in the wind. Harworth ate fast, taking no pleasure in it.

TWO

They came in late. The semi-windup was nearly over, and the fighters, an Italian and a negro, were clinching and hanging on, both of them tired. They had seats in the first row ringside and had to climb across the knees of half a dozen men, all of whom grumbled but stared at Helen.

"Oh," said Helen, looking up, "I never sat this close before. You might as well be in the ring."

"Personally I like the balcony better," said Harworth. "But you have to sit with a bunch of mugs and sometimes there're fights."

The bell rang for the end of the round and the fighters went to their corners. The negro was staggering; his handlers grabbed him and began to work over him furiously. The Italian sat on his stool gasping for breath and looking vaguely off across the stadium.

Someone leaned forward and put his hand on Harworth's shoulder. "Hello, Harworth. How do you rate seats like that?"

It was Molina. Harworth said:

"Hello, Joe. I'm just lucky, I guess."

Molina laughed and drew back. Helen turned to look at him.

The bell rang for the final round and the Italian came out throwing both fists. The negro was groggy and perplexed, and Harworth felt sorry for him. The crowd began to rave; it sensed a knockout.

Molina shouted:

"Go to it, Giovanni. Kill that nigger."

The Italian was leaping at the negro, trying to finish him. The negro, nearly out on his feet, shuffled about trying to protect himself. Harworth saw his head go back from an uppercut, saw him fall into the ropes and hang there, helpless. But the Italian was merciless; he pounded the negro about the body and then sent a terrific hook to his jaw. The negro groaned and fell forward on his face. The crowd howled while the referee counted him out.

"Good boy! Good boy!" cried Molina.

Helen grasped Harworth's arm and squeezed hard. He turned to look at her. Her face was flushed, she was gritting her teeth, and there was a cruel expression about her mouth. "Oh, wasn't that wonderful!" she cried. He was slightly disgusted and looked away.

The Italian had his bathrobe around him now and was dancing about the ring, mitting the roaring crowd. In the far corner the negro's handlers were trying to revive him. He sat with his eyes shut, his arms dangling, but gasped and jerked his head wildly when they put the ammonia to his nose.

The main-go was tame. Red Cannon, Harworth's boy, a boring-in fighter with a wallop, was too slow for his opponent, Mike Cerda, who ran from him for nine rounds, counterpunching all the time. In the fifth round the crowd began to boo Cerda and tell him what they thought of him. Once Molina leaned forward and said:

"He'd kill that hunky if he could get near enough."

Harworth nodded.

In the tenth round Cerda, exasperated by the crowd, tried to outslug Cannon, took a couple to the head and one to the short ribs which nearly doubled him over, then he began to run again. Cannon was given the decision and looked down at Harworth and grinned. The decision was a poor one but the crowd cheered and went home happy.

On the way to Stromberg's from the fight Helen sat silent. She was wondering who the big Italian that had sat behind them could be. She was positive she had seen his picture some place.

As Harworth helped her out of the limousine, she said:
"Frank, I'm not generally so inquisitive, but who was the man that sat behind us?"
Harworth hesitated.
"Why, that's Joe Molina."
They began to cross the sidewalk.
"Joe Molina!" exclaimed Helen, turning to look at Harworth. "*The* Joe Molina?"
"Yes."
"The man who always has his name in the paper?"
"Certainly."
"What a thrill!"
The headwaiter met them at the door and bowed.
"Evening, Mr. Harworth. Want a booth?"
Harworth nodded.
When they had ordered Helen said:
"My goodness; it's like looking at the Prince of Wales. And you actually know him?"
"Well," said Harworth, "yes, in a way. He wanted to buy my interest in Red Cannon and came to see me about it."
He always told the same story regarding Molina. It generally saved him further questioning.
"Do you like him?"
"Yes. He's all right. I think a lot of that newspaper stuff is exaggerated. Every time something happens in Chicago they blame him."
"He looks rather harmless."
The waiter came with their orders and for a while they ate in silence.
"Have you heard the latest about Arthur?" asked Helen, finally.
"No," said Harworth, "what now?"
"He hasn't been sober for over a week. I haven't seen Louise for ages."
"She certainly seems to have one hell of a nice time!" exclaimed Harworth, suddenly indignant.
"Now, now," said Helen, putting her hand on his arm.

But Harworth sat thinking about Louise. The last time he had seen her she had pressed his hand and smiled, rather timidly he thought. Why should a girl like that waste her life over a fellow like Arthur Burne! She shouldn't be standing between him and the world, trying to make things easy for him, trying to protect him. She should be protected herself. He shifted in his seat and stopped eating.

"I'd like to have a chance to do something for her," he was thinking. "Why, I'd marry her in a minute if she'd let me, and then she'd never have to worry again."

Helen touched his arm.

"Take those wrinkles out of your forehead," she said, "and stop staring. You've hardly eaten anything."

"I've had enough."

Helen went on eating for a moment, then, glancing up to watch the effect of her words, she said:

"Dick says Louise is going to marry Arthur."

Harworth said nothing.

"Doesn't that interest you?"

"Why should it?"

Helen laughed.

"Dear boy," she said, "that poker face doesn't fool me in the least. You think Louise is wonderful!"

"Maybe."

"And he tells me to my face!" said Helen, laughing. "I'm insulted."

She began to sip her coffee.

Harworth thought for a while, then he said: "I wish I had a sister like her."

Helen set down her cup and laughed, putting her handkerchief to her mouth. Harworth sat flushing and cursing himself for saying such a thing. He knew that he didn't mean it; but it was the closest he could come to saying what he did mean.

"Oh, Frank!" said Helen, still laughing.

"What's so funny about that?"

"You've been going to the movies."

Harworth felt a sudden wave of anger.

"Why do you hate Louise?" he demanded.

Helen stopped laughing to stare at him.

"Hate her! Why she's my best friend."

Harworth laughed but said nothing.

"What made you say such a thing?"

"It's the way you act."

"Oh," said Helen, smiling, "I see. Because I always laugh at you about her. Silly!"

Harworth didn't pursue the point. But he was sure that he was right. He had watched Helen too many times when Louise was present. He sat thinking.

In a moment Helen pressed his foot under the table, and when he glanced up she said:

"Look!"

He turned and saw Jo Paul and a tall young man coming into the restaurant.

The headwaiter guided them past Harworth's booth. Harworth got to his feet.

"Hello."

"Hello, Mr. Harworth," said Jo.

The tall young man bowed vaguely. Helen glanced up and barely nodded to Jo, who, without smiling, said:

"Hello, Helen."

They went on and were seated by the headwaiter. Harworth looked his surprise. Helen tossed her head.

"Jo thinks I slighted her. Isn't it queer? I thought she wasn't going to speak for a moment."

"You didn't encourage her any."

Helen smiled at him.

"Bright boy! You notice everything, don't you?"

Harworth said:

"I thought she was marrying Magnussen."

Helen laughed.

"Dick! Marry her!"

"He told me the other day that she was the nicest girl he'd ever known."

Helen said nothing. Harworth sat staring off across the restaurant, then he said:

"Shall we go?"

"I'm ready."

They were silent all the way home. As Harworth was helping her out of the limousine, Helen said: "Don't come in tonight, Frank. I'm terribly tired."

"All right."

"When shall I see you again?"

"I'll call."

He walked into the lobby with her. The clerk said:

"Message for you, Mrs. Magnussen."

Helen took the message and holding it in her left hand offered her right to Harworth.

"Good night, Frank. Thanks for the evening."

"Good night."

THREE

Harworth was sitting in his bathrobe reading when the phone rang. Stein was sleeping and the house was quiet. Joseph came in to answer the phone, but Harworth waved him away. It was Hrdlicka.

"Well?" said Harworth.

"I want to see you, Mr. Harworth."

"What's the matter?"

"Is it all right to talk over the phone?"

"Why not?"

"It's about Lily."

"Talk. Go ahead."

"Well," said Hrdlicka, "I can't handle her anymore. She and Campi think they own this place. Their act isn't going over like it used to, so tonight I told them they'd have to behave or hunt a new place. Is that all right?"

"Yes, don't take anything from them."

"All right, Mr. Harworth. But Lily said I'd better call you up."

"What else did she say?"

"Well," said Hrdlicka, hesitating, "she said she had something on you. That's exactly what she said. And that I better be careful how I talked to her."

"Put her on the wire."

"She's just ready to go on."

"Put Campi on ahead. Get her on the wire."

Harworth sat tapping with a pencil. Wouldn't things ever settle down so he could have a minute's peace?

"Hello, darling."

Lily's voice seemed strident after Helen's.

"Hello."

"Want me?"

"You know damn well I want you. Hrdlicka's been complaining about you. What's up?"

"Oh," said Lily, "he's a big stiff and needs a punch in the jaw. Just because I was late twice he gets all up in the air. Another thing. He expects us to panic that bunch of drunks every time we go on. Half the time they can't see … and …"

"Wait a minute. Did you tell Hrdlicka you had something on me?"

"Why, that liar. Of course not."

"I'm going to come down and settle this tomorrow."

"Come tonight."

"Lily," said Harworth, "I believe what Hrdlicka tells me. If you don't straighten yourself out you're going to be looking for a new job."

"Maybe."

"What do you mean 'maybe?'"

"Oh, nothing."

She sounded very sure of herself. Harworth hesitated.

"Well, if you've got anything on your mind, you'd better spill it."

There was a long silence, then Lily said:

"You don't treat me right, Frank. That's what I've got on my mind. You never come to see me anymore and you know how that makes me feel. I get all upset and then I have a row with Hrdlicka."

"Don't kid me. If you've got anything on me, say so; and we'll see what can be done about it."

Lily's voice sounded very innocent.

"You know I haven't got anything on you, Frank. I've only got those letters you wrote me a long time ago."

Harworth swore under his breath.

"I thought I told you to burn 'em."

"I couldn't. They were so cute."

He knew she was laughing at him. He said nothing.

"Coming round tonight, Frank?"

"No," said Harworth, "put Hrdlicka back on the wire."

"But Frank ..."

"I'll see you later, Lily."

"Well," said Lily, "that's a nice way to act."

In a moment Hrdlicka said:

"Yes?"

"Anton; put up with Lily and Campi till you hear from me. Try to make them behave, understand, but don't fire them or anything like that."

"Yes sir."

"This is between us."

"Certainly."

Harworth hung up and began to pace the floor. He wanted to wake Stein up and ask his advice; but poor Stein was pretty sick and needed all the rest he could get.

Harworth sent for Canovi, who came almost immediately.

"Hello, Mr. Harworth," he said, sitting down. "Didn't I tell you once that I'd come in mighty handy some day?"

Harworth ignored this and explained the situation.

"What's the price?" demanded Canovi.

"What do you think?"

"Well," said Canovi, pulling at his thick underlip, "beings it's you, five hundred."

"All right; but no rough work, understand?"

"Leave it to me."

They got up. Canovi said:

"Boss, you don't know nothing, see? But, listen; there's going to be all kind of fun in this man's town before long. Wait!"

When Canovi had gone Harworth sat staring off across the room. He was very uneasy and was rather sorry that he had acted on snap judgment. But right now a breach of promise suit might ruin him entirely and the alternative, blackmail, was even less to be desired.

He picked up his book and began to read.

"Oh, well," he said.

He was reading how Caesar had tricked his enemies; had made a place for himself in the world by violence and fraud. It reassured him and he laughed to himself, thinking of all the solemn nonsense written about Caesar in textbooks. A great man, he told himself, is one who succeeds.

FOUR

"Sure," Stein was saying, "but this is an inflated market, Frank. It can't keep on going up, anybody knows that. Some of these days the bottom'll drop out of it; then where'll you be. Sell!"

Stein was worse; he couldn't sit propped up now without suffering from nausea. He lay with only one pillow under his head looking up at Harworth.

"August," said Harworth, "I could sell now and make a nice bunch of money. But if I hold on I've got a chance to make a fortune. Magnussen just laughed when I asked him if he was going to sell now."

"It's your money, but you've worked darned hard to get it together."

"It won't break me if I lose it."

"No; but it'll bend you some."

There was a long silence then Stein said:

"Turn out that light, Frank. I feel rotten. I'm going to try to get some sleep."

"How're the legs, August?"

"Take a look."

Painfully he sat up, turned back the covers and pulled up the legs of his pajama pants. Both knees were inflamed and so swollen that the skin looked tight and shiny.

"What a pair of pins," said Stein.

"It's tough, August." Harworth was secretly appalled. Stein was failing; it was very evident. His cheeks were sunken; his hands trembled.

Stein rearranged the bedclothes and Harworth turned out the light.

"Going out tonight, Frank?"

"Don't think so. I'll be in the library. If you want me, send Joseph."

Harworth went into the library and sat down with a book. He read for nearly an hour, then he got up and began walking around the room aimlessly, staring at the pictures, and looking out the window. He had lost the habit of staying home, of reading for hours. Before he had known Helen and her friends he often stayed home of an evening and read; sometimes he even played pinochle with Stein to pass the time. When he went out at all, it was with Lily. Now he was scarcely ever home after eight o'clock.

Helen had been acting queerly the last few days; she had little to say; and avoided being alone with him. He didn't mind so much; only it aroused his curiosity. Helen was very cunning and always went roundabout to get her way. She was no one to face things and have it out. He wondered if she was tired of him. It was possible as he had noticed her yawning in his company more than once lately. At first she was all attention. She was very fickle; he knew that. Richman told him that she was noted for crushes.

He sat down and stared at the carpet. She had called him at seven o'clock to tell him that she couldn't keep her engagement, as she was not feeling well; thought she was catching cold. He knew that she was lying, but said nothing. Suddenly he thought about Jo Paul; her coolness; the tall young man. Could it be that Helen and Magnussen had made it up?

Harworth laughed and picked up his book.

"Well," he thought, "it wouldn't surprise me any, the way he was acting at the club. Trying to pump me." Then he turned to his page. "Well, he can have her. There isn't much to her after you know her a while."

Then of a sudden it occurred to him that she was a millionaire's daughter and the ex-wife of another millionaire. He lowered his book and smiled to himself, feeling very proud. Sometimes things like that, things he had temporarily taken for granted, were revealed to him from another viewpoint; the viewpoint of a tough, penniless young man with vague but powerful ambitions.

He sat thinking. He saw Lake Erie and a waterfront saloon. His father, a burly Irishman, was standing with his hands on his hips looking at him.

"Frank," he was saying, "if you don't mend your ways you'll end in the pen. I'm telling you!"

Harworth smiled and thought about all the money he had, all he might have in the future.

He remembered one time in Cincinnati. It was Hallowe'en and the streets were crowded with masqueraders. He was broke, flat broke. He hadn't shaved for two days and he looked tough. Someone accidentally tripped him and he bumped into a pretty girl in a clown suit. The man with her said: "What the hell you trying to do, you dirty bum!" He knocked the man down and ran. Several of the man's friends chased him, but he got away.

Harworth smiled with satisfaction.

"Dirty bum, eh?"

He glanced round him at the tier after tier of books; at the pictures on the wall; at the faintly glimmering mirrors.

Then he let his mind wander. He was in New Orleans, Pittsburgh, Detroit, Philadelphia, Mexico City, Los Angeles, Seattle: a tough young man with no money but plenty of brass.

Gradually he fell asleep.

He glanced up. Joseph was shaking him.

"Well?"

"Phone, sir."

"Who is it?"

"I don't know, sir. A woman. She didn't give her name."

"Find out. If it's Mrs. Magnussen I'm home. If it's Miss Devereaux I'm out; you don't know when I'll be back."

Joseph went out, but in a moment returned.

"It's neither of them, Mr. Harworth. It's a Miss Joyce."

Harworth stared at Joseph, then sprang out of his chair, upsetting an ash stand, and made his desk in two jumps.

"Hang up in the hall, Joseph," he said. "Leave that ash stand alone."

Joseph went out, shaking his head. Harworth took down the receiver and when he heard the receiver in the hall click, he said:

"Hello, Miss Joyce."

As soon as she started to speak he knew there was something wrong. Her voice sounded muffled and as if she was crying.

"Could you come over right away, my apartment."

"Of course."

He wanted to sing, to shout. But Louise began to sob and that sobered him.

"What's wrong?"

"Something terrible has happened. Arthur shot himself. Oh, please hurry over. I don't know what to do."

"Shot himself? Good Lord!"

"In the arm. It was an accident."

"I'll be right over."

Harworth didn't stop to get a coat. He put on the first hat he could find and ran out slamming the door.

Joseph called:

"Mr. Harworth ... where'll you be ...?"

But Harworth didn't hear him. Luckily he caught an elevator on its way down and in a few minutes he was in the garage at the back of the apartment hotel. Sandy was sitting in the office talking to the nightman. When he saw Harworth he got hastily to his feet.

"Get the limousine. Snap it up."

"This is a rush order sure enough," said the night-man, grinning; but Harworth paid no attention to him.

Sandy spun the big car around in the middle of the garage and Harworth shouted the address at him as he leaped in.

It was a cold night. A strong, chill wind was blowing in from the lake and it was snowing sparsely, the flakes melting as they struck the pavement.

When the limousine drew up at the curb outside the apartment building, Harworth leaped out and said: "Wait!"

Sandy nodded and switching on the light above him, took a detective-story magazine out of his pocket.

Louise let Harworth in. Her face was pale and drawn, and her eyes were red from crying.

"Where is he?" Harworth asked.

Louise pointed, then covered her face with her handkerchief and began to sob.

"Never mind now," said Harworth, "We'll get everything fixed up O.K."

"I didn't know who else to call," said Louise. "One time you said ..."

"Sure, sure," said Harworth, simulating a confidence he was far from feeling: "I'm glad you called me."

He patted Louise on the shoulder and then turned and went into her bedroom. Burne was lying stretched out across the bed. His face was chalk-white and he was groaning. He had his coat and vest off and his right shirt sleeve was ripped from wrist to shoulder. Louise had tried to bandage his arm with a face towel which was soaked with blood.

Louise came in behind Harworth and said:

"It's terrible. He's lost so much blood."

"What about a doctor?"

There was a short silence, then Burne moved his head slowly and looked at Harworth.

"We couldn't call one. Can't you get me out of this mess?"

Harworth turned to look at Louise. He thought she was going to faint.

"You see," said Burne, "it'd be an awful scandal. It'd get in the papers." Then groaning he burst out: "For God's sake, Harworth, can't you do something?"

Harworth took in the situation.

"Yes, I'll have you fixed up in no time. Phone in the hall?"

"Yes," said Louise.

"We don't want a doctor," said Burne.

"Leave it to me," said Harworth.

He went out and called Molina.

While he was gone Louise said:

"Don't worry, Arthur; he'll get everything straightened out."

"And I never was even decent to him."

"Never mind," said Louise. Then: "Does your arm still hurt?"

"It hurts like the devil."

Harworth came back and said:

"Everything's O.K. I've got a doctor who'll take care of this for you and not make any report. Do you think you can get an overcoat on over that arm so you can go in my car?"

"I'll try," said Burne, sitting up slowly and gritting his teeth to keep from crying.

Louise ran and got his overcoat and together they got him into it. Once he had to lie back and rest for a moment as the room swam before his eyes. Harworth put Burne's hat on him, then he said:

"Now we'll take it easy. You'll make it all right. If anybody sees you they'll think you're drunk."

"Especially if they know me," said Burne with a sickly smile.

Harworth turned to look at Louise; her face was so white that he was scared.

"Are you all right?" he demanded.

She cried out suddenly:

"The maid. She heard it. Do you suppose … I forgot all about her."

"Where is she?" asked Harworth.

"In the kitchen, I think," said Louise; "if she hasn't gone for the police."

Harworth left the room. Burne lay back with a groan and Louise sat down beside him and tried to soothe him. Harworth found the maid sitting in the kitchen. As soon as he came in she sprang to her feet and cried:

"I didn't have nothing to do with it, boss. She shot him. Miss Joyce shot him. I seen her with the gun in her hand."

She was confused and terrified, and thought that Harworth was a detective.

"You didn't see anything," said Harworth, harshly; "you don't know anything at all. If this gets out I'll know where it came from, so don't open your mouth."

The maid put her hands over her face and began to sob.

"I don't know nothing. I didn't see nothing," she said.

Harworth took a ten-dollar bill from his fold and put it in her hand.

"You stay here till you hear from Miss Joyce. Don't say a word to anybody."

"Yessuh. Nossuh," said the maid, looking at the money.

Harworth scowled at her.

"I'll put you in jail the rest of your life if you ever say a word."

"I won't say nothing. Not me. I'm mum."

When Harworth came in Burne was lying on the bed with his eyes closed. Louise was sitting beside him but got up immediately.

"Let's go," said Harworth.

"He's asleep or something," said Louise.

Harworth saw that she was on the verge of panic.

"Burne!" he called, sharply.

Burne opened his eyes and stared at them vaguely.

"Oh," he said; "I thought we'd gone."

Burne was only half-conscious and, afraid that he would get delirious and be too difficult for Louise and himself to manage, Harworth went down after Sandy.

"Sandy," he said, "this is between us. You don't know a thing."

Sandy nodded, and put up his magazine.

Doctor Cvengros was a small, dark man of uncertain nationality. He was as bald as a billiard ball and he wore thick-lensed glasses, through which he peered vaguely. There was something furtive about him. Harworth did not like his looks.

Cvengros nodded when Harworth told him he had been recommended by Molina.

"Ja!" said Cvengros. "He caldt!"

"Everything's all right then?"

"Ja!"

Harworth and Cvengros carried Burne, who had fainted, into the operating room. Louise sat down in the waiting room and tried to look at the pictures in a magazine.

Cvengros gave Harworth a gentle shove.

"You go. Vait. I fix."

But Burne opened his eyes, saw Harworth, and said:

"Everything all right, Harworth? Damn nice of you, putting yourself out. Keep an eye on Louise, won't you?"

"Sure," said Harworth; "don't you worry."

Burne closed his eyes and began to groan.

Cvengros pointed to the door.

"Go! Go! Vait. I fix."

Harworth went out. Louise was sitting with her head bent, staring at a magazine. Without a word Harworth sat down beside her. She seemed so frail, so helpless! He wanted to put his arm around her, but did not.

In a moment Cvengros came back smiling.

"All right. I fix. No danger."

Then he came over to Louise and held out his hand. She looked up in surprise. He was offering her two capsules.

"You take. I know."

Harworth glanced up at him. With a dazed look, Louise took the capsules and Cvengros got her a glass of water.

"You feel better," he said, smiling. "Nerves. I know."

Louise swallowed the capsules and drank the water.

"Now," said Cvengros, "I tell you. I keep him here, three, four days. After that he is well. I fix."

"You're sure he'll be all right?" said Harworth.

"Of course. Good as new."

Cvengros laughed. Louise said:

"I'll go see Arthur."

"No," said Cvengros, "he's asleep." Then he turned and motioned for Harworth to follow him, saying to Louise: "Vait!"

Harworth followed him into a little room at the side of the office. Cvengros shut the door.

"You see I take chances. This vill cost one thousand dollars. Now."

Harworth sat down and wrote a check for five hundred and handed it to the doctor, who began to shake his head.

"You get the rest when he's well," said Harworth. "Molina knows me. I'm good for it."

Cvengros shrugged and pocketed the check. "It's awful, eh? They get jealous. They shoot."

"Say," said Harworth, "you got this all wrong. It was an accident."

"Sure," said Cvengros, winking. "His wife?"

"The less you talk about this, the better."

Cvengros shrugged and opened the door. Harworth went out. Louise was standing, waiting.

"Three, four days," said Cvengros, smiling. "Good as new."

They went out. When the door was shut Louise said:

"What a horrible man!"

"Sure," said Harworth; "but what could we do?"

Louise put her hand on his arm.

"I'd 've been crazy if you hadn't come. I didn't know what to do."

She began to cry. Harworth helped her into the limousine.

"Where to?" asked Sandy.

Harworth looked at Louise, who said:

"No place. I want to ride for a while. Do you mind?"

"Of course not," said Harworth.

They rode. It was late now and The Loop was nearly deserted. A cold, strong wind was blowing in from the lake and big snowflakes were dancing down past the street lights. Sandy turned north at Randolph and started out Michigan Boulevard. The big skyscrapers stood dark and solitary; the town was quiet under the falling snow. They crossed the bridge beyond Wacker Drive. Below them a freighter was moored; there was a lone light in the cabin, whose roof was covered with snow. When they got beyond the Drake Hotel they felt the force of the wind blowing in from the open lake; it whistled round the windows of the limousine. Ahead of them the snowflakes eddied and whirled in the beams from the headlights.

Louise said:

"I can't thank you enough. What could we have done?"

She seemed calmer now. He felt her presence more strongly. He remembered the night at Robert Joyce's when she had agreed to go to the fights with him; it seemed very long ago. He had nearly given up hope of ever being friendly with her. But now here she was riding with him, depending on him. Funny!

"Glad I could help you," he said.

"It was terrible. Poor Arthur. He seemed so helpless. I felt so sorry for him."

Harworth said nothing.

"What time is it?" asked Louise.

Harworth looked at his watch.

"Ten after one."

"Is that all? What a long evening!"

She began to shiver.

"Cold?" he inquired.

"Yes, a little. I'd like to go home."

Harworth reached for the speaking tube, but she stopped him.

"No," she said; "I can't go home. I wouldn't sleep a wink. Take me to Helen's. I hate to run in on her at this hour, but she won't mind. Anyway, I've got to tell her about Arthur some time."

Harworth spoke through the tube to Sandy.

The clerk was sitting behind the desk, nodding over a magazine, but seeing them, he got up immediately.

"Good evening, Mr. Harworth."

"Good evening. Will you call Mrs. Magnussen's apartment, please?"

"Mrs. Magnussen does not wish to be disturbed."

"This is urgent."

"Well, that's the orders I've got. But I guess it's all right."

Louise stood leaning on the desk looking at Harworth out of the corner of her eye. She liked his assurance; he had a way of doing things. Could he be so awful as she had once imagined? She felt comfortable with him; he was a bulwark against the world. But imagine Helen running after him; it was a regular scandal; everybody was talking about it!

"She'll speak to you," said the clerk.

Harworth picked up the receiver.

"Hello, Frank. What a time of night to come here. I'm sorry I can't see you."

He was ready to reply when he heard a man's voice; he heard it vaguely, but he knew it was coming from Helen's apartment. It said:

"Well, I should hope not!"

Helen said:

"Just a minute, Frank."

He smiled. She had her hand over the transmitter no doubt and was squelching the owner of the voice.

"Hello," she said in a moment; "I couldn't find anything to sit on. Have you anything startling to say?"

"Well," said Harworth, "Louise is down here with me...."

"Louise ... with you!"

"Yes. She wants to stay with you tonight. She's very nervous. She'll explain everything to you."

"But Frank!"

He said nothing. Helen hesitated for a long time then she said:

"Tell her to come up. I'm ready for bed Frank; or I'd ask you up too."

"Don't bother about me."

The vague masculine voice cut in again faintly; he recognized it and smiled when he heard Helen saying "Shhh!"

"Send Louise up, Frank."

Harworth hesitated, but he couldn't resist the temptation, and before Helen could hang up, he said:

"You might tell Magnussen I'd like to see him. I'd like to have him drop around."

There was a pause, then Helen said:

"What are you talking about?"

"Nothing," said Harworth, hanging up.

The mystery was explained: now he understood Jo's coolness at Stromberg's; Helen's evasiveness. She and Magnussen had made it up.

"You had quite a conversation," said Louise. "Doesn't she want me?"

"Of course."

He walked with her to the elevator and offered his hand. She took it and pressed it.

"I feel ever so much better," she said. "I thought I was going to faint at the doctor's office. But now since I know Arthur's all right …"

She shrugged and smiled.

Harworth said nothing. He was hurt, though he would scarcely admit it to himself. Helen had lied to him, deliberately lied. He was of no account; just a part-time cavalier, a sort of boudoir mountebank, who helped pass the hours for a willful, lewd and fickle woman.

"I thought of you first," said Louise; "I knew I could depend on you."

"Of course," said Harworth. "Good night." He bowed slightly and walked away.

Louise stood looking after him, puzzled. Generally he was so polite, so considerate. What had made him so abrupt of a sudden?

Going up in the elevator she glanced in the mirror and started at the sight of her pale face. She hastily got out her rouge and lipstick. Helen was always so critical!

"I like him," she thought, gazing at her reflection. "I like him a lot."

Helen let her in.

"My dear!" she said, "what ever has happened?"

Magnussen looked into the hallway.

"Hello, Louise," he called, smiling.

"Well!" she said.

Helen laughed.

"Are you surprised? Dick wants me to marry him again. What would you do?"

Magnussen said:

"I'm a little tight. Maybe that accounts for it."

"Don't apologize," said Helen; her face was flushed and she was in a

very good humor.
Louise looked at them and said:
"It's about Arthur. Let's sit down. I may as well tell you."
They went into the living room and sat down. Louise refused a drink. Magnussen asked:
"Are you going to take Harworth up where Helen left off?"
"Hardly!"
Helen looked at her sharply, but said nothing.
"You could do much worse," said Magnussen. "Helen has seldom shown better judgment. In Paris it was a cheap actor."
Louise sat silent, looking at them.

FIVE

Harworth was very much depressed. Stein was worse and the doctor had been forced to give him a hypodermic to ease his pain. Stein was sleeping now, breathing heavily. Joseph went about on tiptoes, looking very grave. The house was quiet.

Harworth got a book, fixed his reading light, put his feet on an ottoman and tried to relax. He read for half an hour or so, shifting about in his chair, smoking one cigarette after another, and running his hand through his hair. Finally he noticed how still the room was. The silence was heavy; it pressed against his eardrums. In the room beyond the library he heard the big clock ticking the hours away.

He put down his book and sat thinking. His mind was clearer than usual; not cluttered up with plans for the present or immediate future. It was temporarily empty of plans; a very strange thing for Harworth, who, as a rule, spent most of his waking hours devising ways to further his career, add to his fortune, multiply his pleasures. He was in no sense a meditative man. His intelligence was perfectly suited to his station in life; it was a utilitarian instrument. He had no superfluity of brains; and this, together with phenomenal luck, was the reason for his success. He had a minimum of doubts regarding himself.

But tonight his thoughts moved on a different plane. Losing Helen, he had temporarily lost his grip on a definite scheme of life. He was floundering and he sat staring off across the room, thinking of the past. Before his fortuitous meeting with Robert Joyce he had been living in a world of his own manufacture: people, things, circumstances had been merely background for the meteoric Mr. Francis Cecil Harworth (born Frank Keogh), who dressed quietly and expensively, carried a cane, bowed stiffly from the waist, clicking his heels, was difficult of approach, seldom merry, a solitary figure wearing a monocle. An unnaturally superior figure, ignoring life.

His contact with Helen and her circle had modified his conceptions. Now he was more natural, normal. He had discarded the monocle, the unapproachable air, the Prussian bow, much of the gravity; his actions were more spontaneous, his attitude less difficult and artificial. He had begun to accept life as it is, without knowing it.

But neither of these attitudes was reasoned. Harworth had, strictly speaking, no general ideas at all, no philosophy. The meteoric figure, the monocled and correct Francis Cecil Harworth, was pure fiction and sprang from his unadmitted desire "to be a gentleman." The second figure, the natural, somewhat likeable, even affable, young man who associated on seemingly equal terms with the "best society" was the result of influence. The essential Frank Keogh was neither of these, though he approached the second more nearly than the first, and Helen's break with him, severing him from her unacknowledged but powerful influence, left him floundering.

Now, since his contact with Helen was at an end, he admitted to himself that he had never really been "one of them." He was merely a playmate; they associated with him as they would have associated with a famous movie actor, or an educated boxer. He was an outsider and would remain so to the end of his life.

They invited him to call on them, yes. They were seen with him in public places and treated him with civility, but, as far as actual society was concerned he was beyond the pale. Often, with a sinking feeling, he had read in the society columns where Mrs. Helen Magnussen, Mr. Robert Joyce, Mr. Arthur Burne, and Miss Louise Joyce had been present at a party Mr. So-and-So had given at his Lake Forest home. Or they were present at a luncheon at the Drake given by Miss Blank. None of them ever referred to these in his hearing.

Harworth was aware that his success with these people, such as it was, was due to one of Helen's many whims. He was "different" from the men she knew, perhaps even a little "dangerous," and this interested and amused her. They had had a pretty good time together, but now it was over. Of course if he had wanted to he could have caused her quite a lot of unpleasantness. But he had too much pride for that. He had caught her lying to him; she had broken an engagement. That settled it.

He had never cared particularly for Helen beyond the fact that she was a good-looking, well-dressed, and willing woman. In dropping her, he was doing himself no violence as far as affection was concerned; but that was the least of it. In reality he was cutting himself off from a class of people whose position he had aspired to all his life. He was thrown back on his own resources.

He tried not to think of Louise.

Harworth had always been a lonely man. He was not a joiner; he saw no virtue or pleasure in running with the pack. In the first place, he was too ambitious for that; in the second place, he had too much vanity.

Before he had known Helen and her friends he had had but two refuges against utter loneliness: Lily and Stein, and neither of them satisfied him except superficially. Lily was of the opposite sex, necessary but hardly exciting. Stein, more complex, more dependable, had taken the place of his real father, scolded him, advised him, steadied him and looked after his interests, but he was no companion.

Now, since his break with Helen, he had no refuge at all. Lily was making herself obnoxious and threatening to sue him for breach of promise. Stein was lying in his bedroom, just beyond, his strength gone, his faculties beginning to fail, a weak old man.

He was alone.

He sat looking down at the carpet, the book dangling from his hand. The house was profoundly still and in the silence he heard again the big clock in the room beyond the library ticking off the hours.

In a flash there came to him a realization of the impermanence of things. Ordinarily he moved in a solid world, a world with definite outlines, but now, due to the stillness and his depression, he sensed the fluidity of life, the mystery of living. Why, he was no more than a ridiculous mite, puffing himself up against eternity; a microscopic, posturing figure in a hostile, confused and ceaselessly changing universe.

He felt slightly dizzy and sat for a long time without moving, awed by his thoughts.

SIX

Canovi took off his cap, lit a cigarette, then handed Harworth a paper. "On the second page," he said, grinning.

Harworth turned to the second page and read an account of the robbery of Lily Devereaux's apartment. It was headed: Dancer's Apartment Looted.

"Well?"

Canovi put down his cigarette, took a big wallet from an inside pocket and tossed it to Harworth, who went through it, finding the letters.

"Good," he said; then: "What else did you take?"

"I took about fifty bucks in dough, just to make it look good."

Harworth nodded, read the letters over, flushing slightly, then he burned each one carefully and threw the ashes in the wastebasket.

"Well," said Canovi, "that's that."

Harworth nodded and, getting up, went to the wall safe, counted out five hundred dollars and gave it to Canovi, who said:

"It's all here, boss. The fifty's velvet, eh?"

"Yeah."

"Much obliged."

Harworth said nothing. Canovi was repulsive to him and he could scarcely look at him.

"Well," said Canovi, "all set for the election? It's going to be a dandy. A peach. Oh, boy!"

Harworth said nothing.

"Yeah," said Canovi. "Joe's tired of getting the run around. Just wait. We'll own the town pretty soon."

"If you're lucky."

Canovi cocked his head on one side.

"Don't say 'you,' boss. Say 'we.' You're in heavy with Joe Molina; don't forget that. What a break!"

There was a long silence. Harworth was fidgety, but Canovi sat contentedly smoking. Finally he said:

"Boss, know anything about a guy named Campi?"

Harworth looked up.

"Yes. He's Lily's dancing partner."

"He's thick with her, ain't he?"

"I wouldn't be surprised."

"Well, he is, all right. And you can bet your shirt he's in with her on this letter business."

"Probably."

"All right. He's got a cousin working for Monahan. It's a tip, boss. Monahan's had his eyes on you ever since you peddled them restaurants to Joe. Watch your step, that's all. Just watch your step. Monahan wanted them restaurants himself, and may do you dirt just for meanness."

There was a short silence and the phone rang. Harworth answered it. It was a man; he refused to give his name. Harworth told him he wouldn't talk to him, but the man said: "Wait! Wait! Have you seen the *Tribune?*"

"Yes," said Harworth.

"All right. We know who stole them letters and we're figuring on getting him."

Harworth glanced at Canovi.

"Here's how it is," said the man; "mail them letters back and no questions asked. If you don't, kiss a certain wop goodbye. That's all."

The man hung up. Harworth turned, hesitated for a long time, then told Canovi what the man had said. Canovi grinned.

"I had it right, didn't I? Only I'm the goat, which ain't right." Harworth was pale and silent but Canovi laughed. "Well, I'm on my way," he went on, getting up; "they tailed me here, I guess. But I know a way out. Hell, them guys are dumber than the bulls."

"What had I better do?" asked Harworth.

"Sit tight," said Canovi. "You ain't in any danger. I'll take this up with Joe. He's about tired of holding off of Monahan's mob. We'll fix it."

When Canovi had gone Harworth got up and began to pace the floor. He felt trapped and began to curse himself for ever having taken up with Canovi or Molina. It meant trouble, trouble, nothing but trouble!

But in the afternoon mail he got a check from Molina. It was for fifty thousand dollars and there was a note with it. It read:

> Dear Frank:
> Here is the cut I was telling you about. When I give a guy protection I give him protection. You have got more coming and if you want to turn this check back to me I'll give you a part interest in my business. Let me hear from you.
> I am writing this at home and Junior asked me what I was doing. I says I am writing a letter to Mr. Harworth and he says to tell you he has got him a new animal book you ought to see it.
>
> Yours respectfully,
> Joe Molina.

About four o'clock the phone rang and Harworth answered it. It was Campi. Harworth could tell that he was agitated. He apologized profusely for calling, then he went into a long, involved explanation regarding the robbery of Lily's apartment. Harworth could make nothing of what he was saying and told him so. Campi burst out:

"For God's sake, Mr. Harworth; I didn't have nothing to do with none of this. But they're after me. I got to leave town."

"Who's after you?"

"Everybody! Everybody!"

Campi was half crying and he was talking so loudly that Harworth took the receiver from his ear.

"Wait a minute," he said. "Get a cab and come right over."

There was a long silence then Campi said:

"Is this straight?"

"Certainly."

Was Campi actually afraid of him?

"Give me your word of honor this is on the square?"

"Of course," said Harworth, impatiently.

"All right. I'm trusting you, see? I'll be there in half an hour."

Harworth hung up, and stood staring. Things were moving too fast for him. Maybe it wouldn't be such a bad idea for him to leave town himself!

When Joseph showed Campi in, Harworth was sitting with his feet on his desk, reading a newspaper. Joseph went out. Harworth looked up. Campi was as sleek as ever; his clothes were immaculate, but showy; his hair shown like patent leather. But under the sleekness Harworth sensed fear. Campi's eyes were dull, where they had once been brilliant, and his face was grayish. He sat down.

Harworth said:

"Well? What's all the trouble?"

Campi wet his lips and kept his eyes lowered.

"It's an awful mess, Mr. Harworth," he said. "I can't make heads nor tails of it. But get this: I'm on the square."

"What about Lily?"

There was a long silence, then Campi sighed profoundly.

"Mr. Harworth, I'm going to take a chance on you. I'm going to tell you the truth. I knew about them letters, and since you give Lily the go-by, I was figuring you ought to pay for it. I'm giving it to you straight, see? But somebody staged a robbery and copped the letters so I said, 'Oh, what the hell; that's that,' and forgot all about it."

He hesitated and looked up at Harworth to see what effect his words had had, but Harworth was impassive.

"Well," he went on, "I got a cousin in the North Side mob. He's a tough mug and I never had nothing to do with him. But here he comes buzzing me. He wants to know a lot of things I couldn't tell him, then he tells me they're going to get a guy named Canovi. He copped the letters, they said. They been tailing him, see?"

Harworth nodded.

"All right. I told my cousin, 'I ain't got nothing at all to do with this. I'm out.' 'Out, hell'; he says. 'You're in.' Canovi works for Joe Molina, I guess; and they're fixing to cause him trouble. All right." Campi lowered his eyes and began to turn his hat in his hands. "But that's only the beginning. This afternoon along comes this here Canovi, and tells me I got twenty-four hours to live if I don't call off my cousin. Jees, what a spot! Here I am, gone either way you look at it. And I ain't got a thing to do with it. Two mobs trying to cut each other's throats and I have to get mixed up in it."

Harworth sat swearing to himself. If he had only listened to Stein he'd never have turned those collections over to Michaelson, never have known Canovi and Molina. As it was he was caught, caught like a fish in a net. His hands were cold as ice, but he was sweating.

Campi said:

"Give me a break, Mr. Harworth. I don't know what to do."

Harworth came to a sudden decision.

"All right," he said; then he took a roll of money out of his pocket and gave it to Campi. "Get Lily out of town. And then both of you stay out. If you hadn't tried to make me for dough, you'd never got yourself in this mess."

Campi was half crying, half laughing. He took the money and stuffed it into his pocket.

"You're O.K., Mr. Harworth," he said.

"Listen," said Harworth, "don't waste any time. Just you get Lily out of town. I'll fix things with Hrdlicka."

Campi thanked Harworth profusely. When he had gone, Harworth sighed with relief and mopped his forehead.

After a good dinner, Harworth felt better. He sat in the library smoking a cigar and listening to a broadcast from the Casa Alvarado. Hrdlicka, competing against Con Weiss's new place, The Shack, had hired a nationally known jazz band. Since the arrival of this band Hrdlicka had been turning people away; the Casa Alvarado had become, overnight, the most popular club in Chicago.

About nine o'clock Joseph came in and told Harworth that Stein had wakened up feeling much better and that he wanted a night edition to read.

"Feeling better, is he?" said Harworth. "Fine."

Things would work out. Stein would recover. What was the use of worrying?

"Shall I send down for a paper?" asked Joseph.

"No," said Harworth, getting up, "I'll go down and get one myself. I want to stretch my legs, anyway."

When Harworth stepped into the elevator, the elevator boy said:

"Evening, Mr. Harworth. Don't know where I could get a couple tickets for the game, do you?"

"What game?"

"Illinois-Northwestern game. I got a friend coming in from Rock Island. I hear it's a sellout."

"I don't pay much attention to football," said Harworth, "but you might drop around and see Joe Madox and tell him I sent you."

"Say! Thanks."

"Maybe he can't do you any good, but it's worth trying. Tell him the tickets are for me."

The boy grinned.

"Say!" he said; "thanks."

Harworth liked to do things for people. First, because he was naturally obliging where there was nothing at stake; second, because it gave him a feeling of power.

When he came up to the desk the clerk said:

"Evening, Mr. Harworth. Been out yet?"

"No."

"It's cold as the devil. That lake wind cuts like a knife."

"I think I'll stay in. I want a night edition."

"They're all gone," said the clerk; "but you can have mine. I'm done with it."

"Fine," said Harworth; "thanks."

The clerk handed him the paper with a smile.

"Well," he said, "I see where they killed another gangster. This sure is some town. Got a casualty list like the World War."

Harworth said nothing, but took the paper and glancing at the item the clerk was referring to; it read:

"North Side Gangster Found Dead. Agostino Campi ..."

Harworth's face began to twitch. It was Campi's cousin. He glanced up, saw that the clerk was looking at him, and ducked his head. He felt guilty. Why was the clerk staring at him like that?

"Yep," said the clerk; "they sure don't last long here. And it's a good thing. If they didn't thin each other out, this would be some place."

Harworth swallowed.

"That's right," he said; then he turned away abruptly and called over his shoulder: "Good night."

On the way up in the elevator, he stood pretending to read the sports page, but the print swam before his eyes and his hands shook so that the paper crackled. Stein was sitting propped up in bed smoking a cigar when Harworth came in.

"Hello, Frank," he said. "How's things? I'm feeling a little better tonight. I guess the old carcass ain't ready for the boneyard yet."

Harworth handed him the paper.

"Thanks. Joseph said you went down after it yourself."

"I did. I wanted to stretch my legs."

Stein turned to the financial page and began to read. Finally he said:

"Frank, all your stocks are up. The market's gone nuts. Oh, what a beating somebody's going to take before we're through. Why don't you get out from under?"

"What?" demanded Harworth, absently.

Stein looked at him.

"Say," he said, "ain't you a little pale tonight?"

"Maybe," said Harworth, edging toward the door to escape Stein's steady gaze. "I think I've got a cold."

"Well, stay on your feet. We can't both be down."

"I was never sick in bed in my life."

"Don't brag about it," said Stein; "knock wood. Wait a minute! Hand me that pad and pencil over there. While I'm feeling decent for a change I'm going to do some figuring!"

Harworth obeyed, then he said:

"I think I'll go take in a movie. I feel stale."

When he had gone Stein sat shaking his head, then he muttered:

"Something's wrong with that boy. He's got something on his mind."

SEVEN

When Louise opened the door Harworth, feeling very self-conscious, awkwardly took off his hat and smiled.

"Come in," said Louise.

He thought she looked frail and lovely. She had on a plain dark blue suit, which fitted her snugly, and her ash-blond hair was parted in the middle and combed very simply. She seemed thinner, paler.

"Just put your hat down any place. I haven't any maid now."

Harworth put his hat on a chair and followed Louise into the living room. They sat down. Louise hesitated, then she said:

"Were you surprised when I asked you to come over?"

"Well, in a way," said Harworth, keeping his eyes lowered. "You see, I've been intending to call you up. About Burne, I mean. How is he?"

"He's gone. He's gone to California."

"Gone ...!" said Harworth, staring blankly.

Louise took a note from her coat pocket and handed it to Harworth. It read:

> Dear Louise:
> I've decided to do what I should have done two years ago. I know you'll be happier and I can't be any more miserable than I am. It's really awful to fall back on my parents but mother has been very sick and so I've got a good excuse to go home. My doctor bill, I understand, has been settled, thanks to

Harworth. Please ask him the amount and I'll send it on to him (papa's money). I'm very grateful to him. Please give him this score. I haven't anything else to give him.

Goodbye, Louise. Write me care of the family at Pasadena, if you care to write. If not I'll think about you anyway and maybe that will help me over the rough spots I see ahead of me.

Yours,

Arthur.

There was a long silence. Then Louise handed Harworth an orchestral score. It was called: *The Dead*. Under the title Burne had written:

For Mr. F. Harworth,
With sincere regards.

Harworth sat holding the score and looking at the carpet. He was touched. He didn't know what to say, and kept wetting his lips and clearing his throat.

Finally he said:

"I ... I sure do appreciate this. I always thought Burne didn't like me. He always acted so funny."

"He didn't like you until he found out how nice you were."

Harworth blushed and sat looking at the score. The sight of the ruled lines filled with black notes dismayed him and he felt very ignorant and wished that he was educated so he could really appreciate things.

Louise sat looking at this big young man with the broad shoulders and the heavy jaw. She noted the careful crease in his trousers, the well-combed dark hair, the pale, determined face. Then she looked at his hands. They were pale too, but strong and hairy with a broad palm and short, blunt fingers. When she was a little girl her father's Italian gardener had had hands just like that.

"Poor Arthur," said Louise. "He's really very nice. But you never could depend on him."

"Gone away for good, is he?"

"Yes."

There was a protracted silence, then Louise said:

"I want to talk to you."

"All right," said Harworth, smiling slightly; "I'll listen."

"I suppose you know I haven't any friends."

Harworth smiled.

"What about Larsen and Richman and all the rest?"

"Oh, I'm serious. They aren't friends. They're just people I know."

Harworth thought about Helen, wondering, for an instant, what she was doing, but he said nothing.

"I've had a terrible time," said Louise; "I've been half out of my mind."

Harworth shifted uneasily.

"Why?"

Louise lowered her eyes. He felt a sudden impulse to get up and cry: "Marry me! I've got plenty of money. I'll look after you. You'll never have to worry again!" Instead, he sat very uncomfortable, shifting his feet.

"Oh, everything's gone wrong," said Louise. "It was Arthur mostly. He was always so depressed and when he was drinking, he'd always talk about what a failure he was. Then he'd say he was going to kill himself. I had that hanging over me all the time."

Harworth said nothing.

"Besides," said Louise, "father died bankrupt, you know. He didn't leave me a penny. If it hadn't been for Robert's father, I don't know what I'd 've done."

"It's awful to be without money."

"Yes," said Louise, looking up at him; "it's terrible. But you've made your own money. You don't know how it is to have everything and then have it taken away from you. People say money doesn't count." She laughed shortly and looked away. "I used to have more friends than I could count. Now I haven't any."

"You've got one at least."

Louise looked up at him.

"I believe I have."

"You have."

Neither of them spoke. There were hundreds of things Harworth wanted to say, but he couldn't bring himself to speak. He was in awe of Louise. He lost all his self-assurance when he was with her.

Louise said:

"I didn't intend to tell you all these things. There was something else I wanted to tell you."

"Tell me anything you want to. It'll never get any farther."

"I know that."

Harworth offered her a cigarette, which she accepted, then he took one and they lit up. Louise smoked in silence for a moment, then she said:

"Didn't Arthur's accident seem a little peculiar to you?"

Harworth hesitated.

"It wasn't any of my business."

"I'll tell you the truth. I've had it on my mind for a long time and it's been a terrible burden. I shot Arthur."

Harworth started and dropped his cigarette. Then he bent over, very red in the face, and picked it up. "I'm afraid I burned your carpet."

Louise ignored this and said:

"It was the most horrible thing that ever happened to me."

Harworth began to watch Louise and finally he came to understand that her calmness was a pose, a mask. Underneath she was near the breaking point. Her face was pale and drawn beneath the make-up. Her eyes were a little too bright.

"Well," said Harworth, trying to be matter-of-fact, though he was appalled, "things like that happen. It's dangerous to have a gun around. I keep mine locked up."

"But," said Louise, the corner of her mouth twitching slightly, "I'm not sure it was an accident."

Harworth cleared his throat and glanced off across the room.

"We'd been drinking," said Louise, "and Arthur had one of his spells. I tried to quiet him and reason with him. But it wasn't any use. Then I put him in my room and told him to go to sleep. I'd stood so much from him; he never gave me any peace."

Harworth glanced up at her, then looked away swiftly. Her face was twitching, and he could see that she was making a great effort to keep calm.

"I came in here, in this room, and tried to quiet my nerves, but I was furious. Arthur called to me and I went back to the bedroom. He had a revolver in his hand and said he was going to kill himself. Well, I didn't know what to do. I tried to talk to him, but he kept saying it wasn't any use living. So I took the gun away from him. Then he began to swear at me and call me names. He didn't mean it. He was drunk, but I had been drinking, too. Suddenly the gun went off and Arthur fell."

Harworth glanced at her. Her face was ghastly.

"He looked at me," she said. "It was the strangest look I ever saw. Then he said: 'Why did you do that, Louise?'"

"But," said Harworth, "it wasn't your fault. It was an accident."

"I don't know if it was. I don't think it was."

Before Harworth could say anything she put her hands over her face and burst into tears. She cried violently and hoarsely, the tears running through her fingers.

Harworth, appalled, went over to her.

"You mustn't feel this way. It was just an accident. You've got to forget all about it."

"Yes," said Louise, sobbing, "I've got to."

Harworth lifted her from the chair, then sat down holding her on his lap. She said nothing; she didn't even look at him, but sat with her head on his shoulder and her hands over her face.

Harworth sat in a daze, holding her carefully. He felt absolutely no desire for her; he wanted to protect her, he wanted to make the world easy for her, she was so frail. He thought about Molina's little boy and how tranquil it had made him feel to hold him on his lap. With Louise it was the same.

The room was very still; he heard the clock ticking in the hall. Gradually the sobs subsided and presently Louise took her hands from her face and looked at him. Her face was red; she was blushing.

"This is awful," she said. Then she smiled slightly. "You must think I'm a terrible fool. But I couldn't stand it any longer. I had it on my mind from morning till night."

"Feel better?"

"Yes," said Louise, then she got up quickly and left the room.

Harworth got up and walked about the room. He was still a little bit dazed. Had this really happened? Had he sat in that rather ordinary-looking chair holding Louise Joyce on his lap? He remembered when he had first seen her at Robert Joyce's and how she had looked at him and how he had wanted to pull her toward him!

"She's the most wonderful woman in the world," he said, glowing. He recalled how close her face had been to his; how delicate her complexion was; how her breasts had moved under her blouse.

Suddenly he felt a violent desire for her and began to walk up and down cursing. He didn't want to feel that way. She was something beyond this ordinary lust. Helen, Lily? It wasn't the same. He wouldn't let himself believe it was the same.

In a moment Louise came back. She had combed her hair and powdered her face. She smiled rather shyly, Harwood thought. His mind was in confusion, there was a buzzing in his ears; he took one step toward her, threateningly, then shouted:

"Why don't you marry me?"

Louise started back, astonished by Harworth's violence, dismayed by his contorted face.

They stood looking at each other. Harworth grew pale. He'd thrown it away. He'd thrown his chance away by his lack of self-control. But Louise said:

"Why not?"

Harworth stared for a long time. Then the color began to come back into his cheeks, his face lit up; and suddenly, to the astonishment of Louise, he jumped up into the air and waved his arms.

"Hurray!" he shouted.

This was too much for Louise. In a flash she saw Harworth as she had first seen him: with a monocle in his eye, bowing like a Prussian officer; a very cold, too correct, distant young man.

She smiled, then she laughed; in a moment she fell into a chair gasping, laughing and crying at the same time.

Harworth stood looking at her with his mouth open.

"If you could have seen yourself," said Louise.

Harworth stared, then his face fell.

"You were joking."

Louise was suddenly serious.

"I wasn't joking," she said.

Harworth came across the room and bent over her chair. Louise kissed him.

EIGHT

Harworth was pacing up and down the room pulling at his hair and Stein was sitting up in bed shouting at him.

"Call your broker! Tell him to sell! The market's gone crazy. Don't be a fool!"

"August," cried Harworth, "I can make a million dollars if I sit tight. That copper stock may go sky high."

"Damn you! Do what I tell you. You stand to make five hundred thousand dollars! Have you ever seen that much money! Have you ever heard of that much money!"

Harworth stared at Stein, who was pale and trembling; his grizzled hair was standing up all over his big head.

"You're getting married, ain't you? You want to buy a big house, don't you? Sell! Sell!"

Stein fell back with a groan. Harworth said nothing.

"I give up," said Stein.

Suddenly Harworth turned and went out the door, shouting over his shoulder:

"I'll call Magnussen."

Stein groaned.

Harworth called half a dozen places before he found Magnussen, who seemed to be drunk and insisted on being facetious. He told Harworth that he and Helen had decided to get married again, that they were sailing for Europe soon, and that the reason they were getting married again was because they wanted to comfort each other in their old age. Then he laughed and congratulated Harworth on his engagement to Louise. "I always knew Louise would make good," he said, then he laughed.

Harworth gritted his teeth and asked Magnussen what he was going to do about his holdings.

"Why," said Magnussen, "I'm going to hold on. I've made a fortune already and so have you, I think."

"On paper."

"Well," said Magnussen, "that's where most fortunes are. On paper. I'm going to hold on tight. Maynard says the market hasn't any top to it, and he knows. He's in heavily himself, anyway!"

"You think it's safe to hold on?"

"Nothing's safe in this world."

Then Magnussen invited Harworth and Louise to see them off on *The Century* and Harworth accepted and hung up.

He didn't know what to do. He sat at his desk running his fingers through his hair and biting a pencil. Maybe it would be best to play safe, now that he was getting married. On the other hand Maynard, who was supposed to know, was hanging on, gambling on another big rise. Harworth knew that if he sold now and there was another big rise, he'd regret it till he died. There was a great difference between five hundred thousand dollars, a definite figure, and the vague, limitless figure he might make.

He got up and walked around the room for a while, then he said: "Here goes!"

He took a silver dollar from his pocket. He had made up his mind to let the coin decide: heads, he'd sell; tails, he'd hold on. He smiled at the idea. When he was a young fellow he used to make every decision this way. He had a firm belief in luck; he had very early observed the tremendous part played by chance in all successful undertakings. His reasoning was simple: some men were lucky, some were not. He was one of the lucky ones.

He tossed the coin. It came heads. Without giving himself time to think he hurried to the phone, called his broker and told him to sell everything he had.

Then he rushed in and shouted to Stein:

"I've sold."

Stein sat up and said:

"Thank God. Now I have an easy mind. Give me my medicine and get the hell out of here."

Two days later the bottom fell out of the market. Stocks tumbled to nothing; there was an orgy of frenzied selling and many suicides.

Harworth read the extras with a feeling of satisfaction. He had won; he was rich!

The day of the big crash he called Louise:

"Darling," he said, "did you see the papers?"

"Yes," she said; "Bob lost thousands of dollars. He's half crazy."

"Magnussen lost a fortune."

"What about you darling?"

"I lost every cent I've got."

He heard Louise laughing.

"Don't you believe me?"

"Of course not."

"I made half a million. I'm going to buy you that house in Lake Forest, and a Rolls Royce limousine and all the diamonds you can wear."

"Darling. Buy my dinner tonight."

"O.K."

"Don't say O.K. Say something nicer."

"What?"

"Do I have to tell you?"

PART FIVE

ONE

A Red Cap took Magnussen's baggage.
"Where you located?"
Magnussen took his tickets from his pocket.
"Car 175; Drawing-room A."
"That'll be in the third section," said the Red Cap; then he picked up the bags and went through a door into the train shed.

Harworth was standing looking at Louise, who was talking to Helen. He was astounded by the change in Louise. She looked ten years younger; she had lost her air of uncertainty, of timidity. Helen looked a little faded in comparison.

Robert Joyce stood tapping the floor with his cane and from time to time pulling at his small, blond mustache.

Magnussen turned.

"Well, here we go," he said.

"What a relief," said Helen.

"We won't be far behind you," said Louise, smiling. "We're going to Europe in January, aren't we Frank?"

"Yes."

Magnussen put his hand on Harworth's shoulder.

"Lucky man! What's your formula? Do you carry a rabbit's foot?" He turned to Joyce. "Bob; Harworth and I bought the same stocks. He makes Lord knows how much and I lose more than I can afford to lose."

"What about me?" demanded Joyce, smiling slightly.

"Well," said Harworth, "I haven't got any formula. But I'll tell you something. I tossed up to see whether I'd sell or hold on."

Magnussen laughed and Joyce stared at Harworth.

"I'll remember that," said Magnussen; "that's the best way after all."

Two reporters had been standing at a little distance looking at Magnussen; now one of them came over.

"Excuse me," he said; "but aren't you Mr. Richard Magnussen?"

"Yes."

"Well; I'm from the *Examiner*. Will you confirm a rumor for us?"

"Maybe," said Magnussen, smiling.

"All right. Did you and Mrs. Magnussen get married again?"

"We did."

"Thanks. Now how about a picture?"

Magnussen turned to Helen, who said:

"Let's!"

The other man came over with his camera and while he was trying to get the correct slant, the first man talked to Harworth, Louise and Joyce, getting their names. There was a blinding flash and people in the station turned to stare.

Magnussen said:

"We're famous, Helen. We've got our pictures in the paper." Then turning, he touched Helen's arm. "Look!"

Harworth was standing with the reporter carefully spelling out his name for him. Louise had turned away and was looking uncomfortably off over the station. Joyce was smiling.

"Oh, well," said Helen, "there are some things Louise will have to put up with. But," she went on, laughing, "isn't Bob getting on the bandwagon in nice shape."

Magnussen laughed.

"Don't be too critical, Helen."

"After all," said Helen, "she's mighty lucky. Frank Harworth is far from a fool."

When the newspaper men had gone, Joyce said:

"Look here! I nearly forgot." Then he took a book from his overcoat pocket and handed it to Magnussen. "It's an advance copy."

"Thanks," said Magnussen. Then: "Oh, Berg's book."

Helen read the title aloud:

"'The Prince! The Prince!' What a silly name for a book."

"I don't think so," said Joyce. "It's a satirical novel and a very good one. Berg's much more amusing when he writes. He's a good deal of a bore in person. All authors are."

Magnussen turned to the title page. Opposite it there was an excellent caricature of Harworth: immaculate clothes, monocle, broad shoulders and all. Magnussen turned.

"Look! Harworth to the life."

They all crowded around. Harworth smiled.

"Yes. Richman told me he was using me as the principal figure."

"What an honor," said Helen.

Harworth looked at her, but could tell nothing from her smile. She seemed like a stranger to him; the past had vanished.

"Why, Frank," said Louise, "you never told me."

"I forgot."

"Forgot! Haven't you any vanity?"

"Plenty."

There was a short silence, then Magnussen said: "Well, we may as well get aboard. We've only got five minutes."

They shook hands all around and Magnussen hit Harworth on the back.

"All the luck in the world. Not that you need it."

Helen held out her hand to Louise.

"Goodbye, dear. See you in Europe perhaps."

"Goodbye," said Louise.

Standing close together they looked at each other for a long time; then they kissed briefly. Harworth saw that Helen was looking at him. He said:

"Goodbye, Helen."

"Goodbye," said Helen. "Look us up in Paris."

"Yes do," said Magnussen, but he shot a glance at Helen, who lowered her eyes.

The porter helped them aboard.

"Hope you enjoy the book," called Joyce. "It's with Berg's compliments."

On the way back Joyce went ahead of them to buy some cigarettes. Louise said:

"Dick's jealous already. What a nice time they'll have. Did you see the way he looked at her? He's jealous of you."

"Well, he shouldn't be."

"Well, he should be," said Louise, mocking him.

Joyce hurried back to them, showing them a paper.

A headline read:

REFORM CANDIDATES LEADING

"Look at that," said Joyce, smiling. "Isn't it disgusting?"

Louise said nothing. Harworth said:

"Well, the town's due for a turnover. It's been coming."

"Of course," said Joyce. "But it doesn't mean anything. The price of liquor will go up, that's all; and the quality will go down."

They all got into Harworth's limousine. Louise said:

"Take me home, Frank. I need a nap."

Harworth spoke through the tube. Joyce said:

"Queer the Magnussens getting married again. It won't last."

"Of course not," said Louise. "Helen likes men too well."

Harworth turned to glance at her. There was a determined look on her delicate face. Sensing his scrutiny, she slipped her arm through his.

"Happy?" he asked.

"Yes."

Joyce sat looking out the window, smoking and humming to himself.

TWO

They went out to smoke during the intermission and Harworth got a paper, which he stuffed hurriedly into his pocket after he had read the headlines and a few snatches of the articles dealing with the election. The reform candidates were leading in every ward except three; the three worst wards in the city. Armed hoodlums were threatening voters at the polls. A committee of business men were demanding "drastic measures." On the South Side an election judge had been badly beaten and was not expected to live. Open gun battle with three wounded in a near West Side ward.

When they got back the orchestra was already tuning up. They sat down. Louise said:

"It's too bad Arthur isn't here. Mr. Stock is simply wild over his music."

Harworth said nothing, but glanced about him at the huge hall which was gradually filling up again. He turned back to Louise who began talking to him about the Tchaikovsky Symphony the orchestra had played before the intermission. It had bored Harworth so that he had a headache. He had made the mistake of saying so. Louise said she wanted to convert him "to good music." She was very nice about it, but laughed at him a little.

But he didn't mind. What Louise said was right. He had surrendered his will to her. Whatever she wanted him to like, he would like. Whatever she wanted him to be, he would be. He sat there in the big noisy hall touching shoulders with Louise, perfectly contented. From time to time he glanced at her out of the corner of his eye. She was perfect, perfect.

Once an ugly thought had crossed his mind, making him wince. She was marrying him for his money; she was tired of struggling against the world and had taken the easiest way. Helen thought so, he could tell from her attitude. Stein thought so, though he did not say it outright. Magnussen, everybody thought so. But after all, what did it matter? Being rich made him powerful; his brains had made him rich. If he had failed, if he had gone down in the struggle, he wouldn't have deserved her, anyway. To the strong the spoils.

Success was everything.

Louise touched his arm.

"What are you thinking about? Smooth out your forehead and look pleasant."

Harworth smiled.

"I was thinking about you."

"Were you? What?"

"Tell you later."

Stock came out onto the stage and there was a roar of applause. The lights were dimmed and Louise slipped her arm through Harworth's and held his hand. He had never been so happy in his life. He wanted to tell Louise so, to give her some idea of how much she meant to him, but he could find no words and pressed her hand instead. He was glowing with tenderness and goodwill; he wanted to do things for people, to make them happy.

Stock raised his baton and the music commenced. It was soft, remote, sensuous music and Harworth enjoyed it. No crashing chords, loud blasts on the trumpets, resounding climaxes. He turned to Louise.

"What is this?"

"*L'Après-Midi d'un Faune*. Afternoon of a Faun. You mustn't talk."

Harworth sat with his eyes lowered while the music rolled over him in long, quiet, voluptuous waves. He didn't know what a Faun was. And he thought it was mighty queer for a man to try to give an idea of anybody's afternoon in music. It didn't mean anything. All the same he enjoyed it.

When it was over, there was prolonged applause and Stock bowed repeatedly and finally brought the orchestra to its feet with a gesture.

"Arthur hates Debussy," said Louise. "Why, I don't know."

Harworth said nothing. But he did not like to hear her mention Burne's name. He didn't want her to think of anybody else even. She was his!

The hall quieted down and Stock raised his baton for the final number. Louise said:

"I've never heard this played, you know. Arthur kept it hidden for a long time."

She handed Harworth the program and pointed. He read: "THE DEAD, a symphonic poem by a young Chicago composer, Arthur Burne." There was a long explanation of the composer's aims and a brief biography. Then there was a poem which, the program said, had been the composer's "inspiration."

Louise said:

"Arthur says the poem isn't much good. He always has the queerest notions. I like it."

Harworth nodded and absentmindedly put the program into his pocket.

The music began. After a moment, Harworth turned to look at Louise.

She sat listening with lowered eyes. What was she thinking?

The music went on and on; it made Harworth uneasy. It was low-pitched and monotonous, full of dissonance. Suddenly he wondered how far Burne had gone with Louise. Quickly something within him answered: all the way. He flushed and shifted about in his seat. Helen had often intimated as much. Well, it was none of his business.

But while the music went on and on, low-pitched, monotonous, Harworth's imagination got to work. In sudden flashes he'd see Louise and Burne in lewd attitudes. He'd see Burne begging, coaxing; he'd see Louise flushed and panting. Of a sudden he pressed her hand so hard that she turned to look at him in bewilderment. She seemed so frail and lovely and there was an innocent look of surprise on her face.

Harworth blushed heavily and said:

"It's good. The music, I mean."

"Yes," said Louise.

Harworth was suffering. He shifted his feet and tried to concentrate on the music. Vaguely he began to wonder if there was peace anywhere. He wanted happiness; ease from the bitter struggle of living. But it was nowhere to be found; it seemed as far off as ever now. He had Louise; he was rich and young. Yet he was no happier than he had ever been.

For a moment, a wave of anger swept over him, and his success seemed trivial, all out of proportion to his anticipatory thoughts regarding it. Why should he feel so strong, so all-conquering? Here he was ready to devote himself to Burne's mistress, who was marrying him for his money. Was this a triumph?

But Louise pressed his hand. The music had stopped; the lights came on. Louise said:

"It was good, very good."

They sat listening to the applause. Then they got up. Harworth helped her into her wrap. He looked down at her slender figure, her fine blonde hair, noticed the delicate perfume arising from her clothing. What was wrong with him?

Louise said:

"We'll go right home. I've already fixed a little lunch."

"That was mighty nice of you."

"I thought it would be fun."

"It will be."

Harworth wanted to apologize for his thoughts.

When they came out, the doorman was calling out the car numbers and blowing his whistle. There was a hubbub in the foyer. Newsboys were running about with the latest extras. Suddenly Harworth stopped and listened. A boy was shouting:

"Big North Side murder. Alderman-elect Bourke shot down."
Harworth bought a paper, glanced at the scareheads, then stuffed it hastily into his pocket. Their car was ready. He helped Louise through the crowd and into the car. Sandy whispered:
"Hell's sure popping, boss. They shot Bourke."
"I know," said Harworth.

When they had eaten, they went into the living room. Harworth seemed preoccupied and from time to time Louise glanced at him, wondering. At times she was very much puzzled by him. He'd sit pale and thoughtful, with his forehead wrinkled; and she never had the vaguest notion what he was thinking about. Often she'd study him when he wasn't looking. At certain angles there was a brutal look to his head and jaw. Yet he was very considerate and capable of real tenderness.
"Frank," she said, finally, "you look tired. Are you?"
"Sort of," said Harworth. "When I hear a lot of music like that all at once it wears me out."
Louise smiled.
"You admit things, don't you?"
"Sure."
"I used to think you were very pretentious."
"Did you?"
"Yes. When you were wearing a monocle and always bowing."
Harworth shrugged.
"Why did you?"
"Oh," said Harworth, "I don't know. It was just an idea I had."
Louise laughed, but she was puzzled.
"You see, I've had a pretty rough life. I've associated with all kinds of people: bums and gamblers and yeggs. I guess I was trying to get as far away from them as possible. You know. I wanted to be somebody."
"Well, you are. Aren't you?"
"Am I?"
"Frank, don't be silly. I think you've done wonderfully well."
"Well, I've got you."
"Oh, I'm not so much."
Harworth looked at her for a long time, then he came over and stood beside her chair. Sometimes he had moments of unbelief. In a flash he'd see Louise as he had seen her that first night: elegant, slightly insolent, inaccessible. Was she really his?
He bent over her and she took his face between her hands and kissed him.
"Darling," she said, "hadn't you better go?"

"Yes."

He backed away from her chair and she got up. Harworth tried to turn away and go out in the hall for his hat; instead he took a step toward Louise and put his arms around her. She put her arms around him. They kissed.

Harworth said:

"Listen; some time I'd like to tell you how much you mean to me. I never can seem to get it out."

"Don't tell me."

With their arms around each other they walked over to the window and stood looking out. Below them was a deserted, windswept street. It was a cold, clear night and the street lights shone brightly. Overhead the sky was vast and faraway and the stars had a frosty look.

"It must be very cold," said Louise, looking down into the street and shivering slightly.

"Round zero."

They stood looking out, silently. Finally Harworth said:

"I'm going. Get a good night's sleep. I'll call you around noon."

"Oh, I'll be up before that."

"I'll call at ten."

Louise laughed.

"Call at ten-thirty. You never get up any earlier yourself."

They laughed. Louise walked out into the hall with Harworth and helped him into his big ulster, then she kissed him. Harworth didn't want to go. He wanted to stay forever. Time lagged when he wasn't with Louise.

"Well," he said, "good night."

"Good night."

He started out, but turned to look at her. She was standing in the doorway, leaning against the jamb. When he turned she waved and said:

"Goodbye, Frank."

"Goodbye," said Harworth.

He started toward the elevator. He heard Louise shut her door. He felt sad. He had left all his happiness in that little apartment.

Sandy was sitting in the lobby reading a paper. When he saw Harworth, he got up, handed the paper to him without a word, and went out. Harworth put the paper into his pocket and followed.

Sandy was holding the limousine door open for him.

He said:

"This man's town is sure in hellish shape."

"She'll quiet down."

Sandy got in and they drove off. Harworth switched on the lights and took out his paper. The police were hunting Joe Molina, who was wanted for questioning in regard to the election day riot and the killing of Alderman-elect Bourke. The executives of the business men's committee were demanding the removal of the mayor and the chief of police; they wanted martial law declared. Two more killings on the West Side. A bombing on the South Side.

"Well," said Harworth, trying to laugh, "Joe certainly put on his circus all right."

Stein said:
"Help me back in bed, Frank."
Stein was better. His hands were steadier and there was some color in his face. He had been sitting up in an armchair reading and newspapers were scattered all over the room.
Harworth helped Stein back into bed.
"Well, Frank, I guess I'll live after all. Yep. I got a year or two in me if nothing happens."
Harworth laughed.
"You'll probably outlive me."
Stein sat shaking a forefinger at Harworth.
"Frank," he said, "for once you backed the wrong horse."
"How's that?"
"Molina bit off more than he could chew. It'll be tough for him from now on. This Old Burg'll just stand so much!"
"Oh," said Harworth, "it'll quiet down. It always does."
"Maybe. Maybe."
There was a short silence then Stein said:
"Well, good night. Turn out my lights, will you? I want to get a good night's sleep and maybe I'll be pretty fit tomorrow. The reports'll be coming round. I'm sick of being a dead weight."
"Don't let it worry you," said Harworth, turning out the lights.

He stood looking down into the windswept street. The city seemed desolate in the cold November night. He saw the beacon at the end of some far-off pier winking, alternately red and white. He saw the lake drive curving northward with its parallel row of boulevard lights. He sensed the lake beyond; it was rough tonight, probably, and big black waves, laced with foam, were pounding at the wharves and beaches.

He thought of Louise, of the house he was going to buy her in Lake Forest; a house larger and more magnificent than Magnussen's. He thought of their trip to Europe, of all the good times they would have. Momentarily he saw her as he had last seen her, waving to him.

But his mind veered. He saw Hafey lying in an alley riddled with bullets. He thought of Agostino Campi, of Bourke. It was horrible!

He sank into a chair and picked up a magazine, but he didn't read it, or even look at the pictures; he sat holding it on his knee looking off across the room. The house was very still. He felt oppressed by the stillness. Mechanically he reached for a cigarette, but instead, he pulled out a folded pamphlet, which he stared at in surprise. It was the Chicago Symphony concert program. He turned it idly in his fingers, then he began to read it with half his mind, the other half occupied with what he dreaded so much, with what he hated to hear mentioned: Death.

It was the end of everything. A man had no defense against it. He remembered his father; a big, robust Irishman with muscles like iron. He drank too much, ate too much. One day when he was walking across the saloon he made a grab for a table, missed and fell sprawling. All the men laughed. They thought he was drunk. He was dead.

Harworth read:

"The composer of this work, Achille Claude Debussy, was born at St. Germain-en-Laye (Seine-et-Oise), France, August 22, 1862 ..."

What was death? Once he had taken gas in order to have an infected tooth extracted. He lay back, trying to relax, while the nurse held the cone of the gas tube over his nose. At first he felt drowsy, then he felt himself flying away. He felt Frank Harworth flying away. He tried to restrain himself from leaping up, from crying out: "No! No! I won't!" The nurse said: "Relax, please. Don't fight it." He obeyed with a feeling of despair. Suddenly there was blackness; he was gone. Then he was in the midst of fantastic dreams. A little man was laughing at him, saying: "Ah ha! you took gas and now you are dead!" He pursued the little man through long, grotesque corridors trying to kill him. But presently the nurse was saying: "Now there you are. It's all over." And opening his eyes he saw the doctor in his white coat smiling at him. It was summer; the window was open letting in a cool breeze; and there was sunlight in the streets. He was sick but happy.

That was like death. Only you didn't wake up. You pursued the little man farther and farther until there was nothing, only darkness, eternal darkness. That was the end. There was no sympathetic nurse, no smiling doctor, no sunlight in the streets, no streets!

He read:

"As a child any musical aptitude he may have had was not noticed until his tenth year, when his talent was observed by Mme. Manet, the mother-in-law of Verlaine, the poet ..."

Harworth shifted about in his chair, sweating; then he began to turn the pages of the program. Absently he read about Burne ... "born in Chicago, Illinois, September 25th, 1898 ... educated at the University of Illinois and the Sorbonne, Paris. Studied under D'Indy ... his music has great power ... is serious, not frivolous like so much modern music...."

He read on and finally came to the poem Louise had spoken about. He read it.

"When I am dead,
The birds will sing of a morning
And at evening,
And the sun will glide through the heavens,
Westward.
The moon will rise,
And there'll be sweet days
And bitter days;
And the slow, unvarying procession
Of the seasons.

When I am dead,
The flowers will blossom, fade and die,
But bloom again.
And men will struggle bitterly
And cry with pain and happiness.
And there'll be pleasant friendships,
Love and hate,
When I am dead.

When I am dead....
But words are meaningless!
It is the lot of mortal man,
Who is no more than a little flame:
A quick and solitary flare
Between one great darkness
And another."

Harworth threw the program on the floor. He felt panicky and began to swear. Why write a poem about such a thing as that? Forget it! Forget it! We were all in the same boat; why talk about it! One time he had read in the paper an interview with a condemned man. He was cheerful. He told the reporter he was forty-five years old and in poor health. In a month he would be dead and out of his misery. Anyway, he said, why should he get excited. There was little difference between him and the reporter. He knew when he was to die; the reporter didn't. Everybody is condemned, he said.

Harworth got up and paced the floor. He wanted to forget about such things. He wanted to think about Louise and how much fun they were going to have. Why they were young!

He turned on the radio. An announcer was saying:

"... Joe Harley and his Southern Serenaders broadcasting from the Night Hawk Café. The next number is that hot little number: 'When I'm walking with my Sweetie ...'"

The band began to play. Harworth walked up and down, trying to listen. After a moment, he shut it off and went to his desk. The world had faded temporarily: the world with its hate and love and happiness and music. He saw himself stretched out in a coffin. People would come to look at him and murmur polite condolences, but he wouldn't know it; he wouldn't know anything ever again.

He picked up a pen and wrote hurriedly on a piece of writing paper:

For August Stein:
If anything should happen to me, if I should meet with an accident, my estate is to be divided equally between you (August Stein) and Miss Louise Joyce. I mean this. This goes!

Then he signed his name, put the note in an envelope and locked it in the wall safe.

"Jees," he said, running his hand over his face, "I must be getting nutty. I better try to get some sleep."

THREE

Harworth undressed and put on his pajamas, then he went over to his night table to look for mail. When he was away from home during the day Joseph usually left it there. He found six letters and a package, and sat down on the bed to look through them. Most of the letters were bills; one of them was a stock list from a brokerage house. But there was one letter in a dirty envelope addressed in large, childish hand-writing. He opened it. It was from Larsen.

Dear Mr. Harworth:
I have not seen you for many days so I would like to congratulate you by letter. Louise is the most wonderful girl that I ever knew and you are a very lucky man. I want to make you a present of the portrait. It is all I have to give for the wedding. Please do not offer me any money for it as that would offend me very much. The portrait is at present on view at the Chicago Art Museum and has been praised. It is my best work. I am glad Louise is marrying you. You will make life easy for her.

Yours truly,
Olaf Larsen.

Harworth, calmer now, sat holding the letter in his hand.
"A good guy," he said, half-aloud.
Then he opened the package. It was Berg Richman's novel and there was an inscription in the front and also a note. The inscription read:

For Mr. Francis Harworth, with sincere best wishes (offered with some temerity).

The note read:

Sorry I'll be unable to see you before going to New York. Congratulations and best wishes. Will you please invite a poor struggling author to visit you some time? I hope you like the book! The publishers are bugs about it and they think it will sell. I hope they're right. Goodbye.

Harworth fixed his pillows and lay down to read. First he read the blurb on the jacket, discovering that:

"'The Prince! The Prince!' is the Chicago novel we have all been waiting for ... ten laughs to a page ... you will follow the rocket-like career of a self-possessed, broad-shouldered young ruffian who elbows his way to the top ... a ruthless figure, part tough, part charlatan, part man of genius...."

Harworth's feelings were mixed. At first he felt a great glow of satisfaction. Here was a whole book written about him; he was but thinly disguised as Frank Harcourt, and his eccentricities were hit off to the life. He read how he swaggered when he walked, how he deftly handled a monocle, and how he was always ready to use his fists if insulted.... Still, as he read on, the figure of Harcourt grew monstrous and slightly ridiculous; he was involved in all sorts of swindles, which he carried off with an air, but he was abject where women were concerned and was pictured as being led around by the nose by a slight, laughing little blonde.

Harworth put down the book and lay thinking. It was good, good, but insulting. He remembered Richman's sharp tongue, his elliptical speech, his shrewd eyes.

"Damn smart guy, all right," said Harworth, "but he needs a punch in the nose. Yeah; I'll invite him, all right."

But after a time his vanity overcame him and he lay looking at the caricature of himself opposite the title page. It was good! It was fine!

He read on and gradually there emerged from the pages that strange figure he had manufactured for himself, that pure fiction, Francis Cecil Harworth; that mannikin without feeling which at one time he had held between himself and the world. Harworth felt very queer. He was unable to understand how Richman, with very little opportunity, had observed him so perfectly. The essential Frank Harworth, Frank Keogh, was not there, but the surface was uncannily true.

The book was a very short one, hardly more than a novelette, and he read it through. Then he put it down and lay thinking. In the concluding pages Harcourt had married an heiress with millions, had saved her father from bankruptcy by his adroit evasions of the law, and ended by becoming elected to the board of directors of a bank, which, because of its immense wealth, controlled the business destinies of Chicago.

The final picture was a good one. Harcourt, young, healthy, alert, unscrupulous, was sitting with the board, the members of which were all old, fat, puffing, conservative, ridiculous. While they argued Harcourt sat polishing his monocle and occasionally yawning behind his hand. One of the directors arises to speak:

"The burden of protecting this great community is on our shoulders...."
The book ends there.

Harworth was fascinated by the calm, all-conquering figure. Did he seem like that to Richman? Was his mask so perfect that Richman never guessed his doubts, his fears, his embarrassments, his sudden smothered rages, his essential impotence: all, in other words, which distinguishes a man from a fictional figure?

It was all very mysterious.

Harworth woke with a start. He had gone to sleep with the light on and three pillows behind his head. His neck was stiff.

What had wakened him? He looked about the room. The windows were still dark. He glanced at his watch. Four-twenty. Then he heard a slight noise and after listening for a moment, he jumped out of bed. The door knob was turning slowly from side to side. He went quickly to the bureau, took a bunch of keys from a box on it, and unlocked the third drawer where he kept his gun. But when he pulled the drawer open it stuck and made a loud screeching noise. Harworth started back, cursing.

A voice from beyond the door called:

"Harworth! Harworth! That you?"

It was Canovi.

"Yes," said Harworth. "What do you want?"

"Let me in. I got to see you, boss. Hell, don't waste no time."

Harworth took the gun from the drawer and holding it in his left hand, unlocked the door. Canovi came in and said:

"Get your clothes on quick and order both cars."

"What's the idea?"

"Don't argue boss, for God's sake. Let's get going."

"How did you get in here?"

"Up the fire escape. You better get some good locks for your doors. That front one's a pipe."

Canovi grinned, but he was pale. Harworth said:

"Say, what's the idea breaking in here?"

Canovi glanced up at Harworth's determined face and then down at the gun in his hand.

"Hold on, boss," he said. "Don't get me wrong. This is square. Joe wants you. He wants you right away."

"What for?"

"You got to help him. They're after him hot and heavy. He thinks he can trust you. They'll bump him sure if they get a chance. Monahan's on the warpath, since I ... since somebody bumped Bourke."

"Say, this isn't my fight. Where do I come off?"

"Ain't your fight, eh? Say, brother, you're up to your neck. You're on the list, see, on the list. Don't you think Monahan knows you're in with Joe? Don't you think he knows all about that letter deal? Say, Agostino Campi was one of the best guns he had."

Harworth felt panicky. He didn't know what to do. He looked about him trying to realize that he was in his own room, that things were pretty much the same as usual. He had a sudden feeling of hopelessness. What could he do?

Without speaking he hurriedly stripped off his pajamas, threw on his clothes and pulled a big white, turtle-neck sweater over his head. While he was lacing his shoes Canovi said:

"Joe wants to get his wife and kid out of town, boss. Monahan's crazy and Joe ain't taking no chances. See! This'll put you way up with the boss. When the town quiets down you'll own it. We'll all own it."

Harworth went on lacing his shoes, trying not to think.

"Listen," said Canovi, "I don't want to scare you none, but you're in a bad spot. Just like me and Joe and Frankie. Your number's up with Monahan. Joe says he ain't never got over that restaurant deal yet. He just went batty, blew his top, when Bourke got bumped. Monahan's poison when he gets going and he don't care no more for what might happen to him than a horse."

Harworth said nothing. He was debating whether he should wake Stein or not. He wanted to talk to him, ask his advice. But what could Stein do?

Canovi said:

"Joe thinks you better go along with him. As far as Milwaukee, anyway. Take it serious, boss, take it serious. This town's in awful shape."

Harworth was on the verge of panic. Suddenly he thought of Louise. He could wire her. She could come to Milwaukee. They might get married there and go west till things quieted down. He could call her now and make arrangements. But no, it would scare her and make her suspicious if he called her at this hour. He stood up.

Canovi said:

"Get both cars. You're the only guy Joe trusts 'cepting me and Frankie. Say, you ought to be glad Joe thought about you. You might never et no breakfast tomorrow morning, nor no other morning."

Harworth said:

"What's the dope?"

"Well," said Canovi, "you drive the limousine. Let Sandy take the roadster and follow. Joe's hiding out on the South Side at Tony Gozzi's dump. He's got the missus and the kid with him. Sandy takes the two of them to Detroit. You drive the boss as far as Milwaukee and he'll go on to Canada. He's got a plant in Milwaukee."

"All right."

He went to the phone and called Sandy, who didn't answer for a long time.

"Hello."

"Sandy. Come right over. This is Harworth. Get both cars ready."

"Both cars.... Say, boss; have a heart. I got a swell little lay here with me."

"Well, leave her there. Snap it up. Come right away. This is serious."

Sandy said wearily:

"O.K."

Harworth took his big ulster out of the closet, slipped his gun into the pocket, and stood waiting.

Canovi said:

"Let's go out easy, boss. We don't want to wake nobody. We'll go down the fire escape."

Harworth put on his ulster, then he hesitated. Something impelled him to look about the room. He saw his rumpled bed, the reading lamp casting a sharp light onto the piled-up pillows, his book on the floor, letters scattered about. When would he see it again?

It was bitterly cold and the wind from the lake was cutting. Canovi led the way down the fire escape and into the alley. Then they went into the garage through the alley gateway. The nightman started up when he saw them, but sank back and said:

"Hello, Mr. Harworth. Mighty early for you to be up. Or ain't you been to bed yet?"

Harworth said:

"Hello."

Canovi turned to Harworth.

"He's the kind of bright boy that gets himself in trouble asking questions."

The nightman looked at Canovi for a moment, then he went back to his magazine.

Sandy came in the front door and hurried over to Harworth.

"Say, boss, what's the dope?"

Trying to keep calm, making a great effort to appear matter-of-fact, he explained things to Sandy, who said nothing but stood with his eyes lowered. When Harworth was through he said:

"Yeah? I'll do it. I knew there was going to be hell to pay. Well, my old lady could use some insurance, anyway."

He shrugged and glanced at Harworth, whose face was pale.

"It's tough, boss, tough."

The nightman opened the alley gate wide for them, staring at them curiously, but saying nothing. Harworth drove the big limousine out first and Canovi hopped in; Sandy followed in the roadster.

Tony Gozzi let them in at the side door. He was a stocky little Italian with a dark, scarred face. He said nothing, but pointed upstairs. Canovi went first then Harworth and Sandy. It was very cold; Harworth was shivering.

When Canovi opened the door Harworth saw Mrs. Molina. She was sitting in a big chair pulled up beside a coal stove, which was red hot in places. Her face was pale and he could see that she had been crying. Molina in his shirt sleeves was standing in the middle of the room bouncing a ball, and Junior was capering around him, shouting.

Harworth said nothing. Frankie Dean got up off a lounge and came over to him.

"We're all in to our necks, Mr. Harworth. Ain't it Hell? Joe wants to get the missus and the kid started first. O.K.?"

"Yes," said Harworth, nodding. "Sandy's ready. It'll be a cold trip in that roadster."

"That's all right," said Frankie; "they'll get there sure. We need the limousine."

Junior said:

"Hello, Mr. Harworth. Hold out your hand."

Harworth glanced at Molina, who nodded. Molina looked sick. His face was pale and puffy. Harworth held out his hand and Junior threw the ball to him.

"Bounce it," said Junior. Harworth bounced it and Junior caught it.

Of a sudden Junior paused in his play and looked from Harworth to Molina.

"Where we all going?" he inquired. "This is like a party."

"You and mama's going to take a long trip," said Molina.

"Goody," said Junior, jumping up and down, but presently he went over and put his arms around his mother and said: "I'm sleepy."

His mother looked down at him, hugging him. Gozzi said:

"Joe it ain't far from sunrise."

Molina nodded. Then he came over to Harworth. "Brother," he said, "if you get the missus and the kid out of here you're fixed for life."

Harworth said nothing. Molina took a bill out of his pocket and handed it to Sandy. It was a thousand-dollar bill. Sandy gulped, but said nothing.

"There you are, kid," he said; "there's more where that come from and you got a friend for life."

Sandy nodded. Molina turned.

"All right, Marie."

Mrs. Molina got up and put Junior's coat on him. He had little mittens on strings and it took him a long time to get his hands into them. Gozzi said:

"Down the backstairs. You," he turned to Sandy, "get the roadster around in the alley and hit east. It's blind the other way."

Sandy nodded and went over to Harworth who shook hands with him.

"Get back as soon as you can," said Harworth.

Sandy nodded and went out. Gozzi opened the door to the backstairs.

Molina put his arms around his wife and kissed her several times; then he kissed Junior.

"Goodbye! Goodbye!" said Molina; then impatiently: "Go on. Go on." Mrs. Molina began to cry. Junior turned to look at her, then he said: "Ain't papa coming?"

"Sure. Sure," said Molina.

The door closed behind them.

Canovi said:

"Don't worry, Joe. They'll be O.K."

Molina burst out:

"Shut up! I ain't worrying."

Nobody said anything. They all sat listening. It was very still. Presently they heard the roadster pull away, heard Sandy shifting gears; then there was a long silence.

"That's that," said Molina.

Harworth was staring out the window. There was a faint streak of gray over the housetops. Frankie said:

"Well, boss?"

Gozzi came back.

"O.K.," he said. "I don't see nobody no place. But it's near sunrise, boss."

Harworth said:

"I'd like to make a phone call."

"Don't do it," said Molina. "This line may be tapped. Who knows?"

"Hell," said Gozzi, "it ain't tapped. What would they be tapping my line for? If they knew you was here they'd come after you."

Molina didn't say anything. Harworth noticed that his hands were shaking. This helped to calm Harworth. If Molina had the jumps, a guy like him, why, it wasn't any disgrace.

"Better put that call off, anyway," said Canovi. "Call long distance from Milwaukee. You'll be there in a couple of hours."

Harworth nodded. He felt trapped. He had acted hastily and now he repented it. Why hadn't he told Canovi to go about his business and taken a chance? He looked at Molina, who was putting on his overcoat; Molina's face was grayish.

The window panes began to get blue. Presently a band of yellow appeared in the east; smoke rising from the neighborhood chimneys was black against it. Harworth stood looking out at the dingy houses covered with snow, at the bleak, desolate, poverty-stricken streets.

"Let's go," said Molina. "Milwaukee next stop, eh?"

He tried to laugh, but the laugh was flat. Harworth put his hat on and buttoned his coat. Gozzi went to a clothes press and got out a Thompson gun.

"I'll be at the window, boss, just in case."

"O.K.," said Molina.

"Goodbye, Chicago," said Frankie, trying to grin.

Canovi went first, followed by Harworth. Molina let them get started, then he said to Frankie:

"See? What did I tell you? Harworth's a great guy, a great guy. I can pick 'em."

"Yes," said Frankie, "he is."

"Just wait," said Molina. "When she quiets down and we get square with Monahan and the bulls, I'll show you something. Me and Harworth'll run this town. He's got connections, boy, connections!"

Frankie said:

"Boss, we ought to 've gone the alley way."

"Nix," said Molina, "she's blind at one end. Not so good. We might want to turn around."

Canovi turned.

"All set?"

"All set," called Molina.

Harworth stood waiting, buttoning his coat collar up around his neck. He was calmer now. What was there to be excited about? Just four men getting ready to ride eighty miles in an automobile. His despair left him; also the feeling of unreality which had plagued him ever since he woke with a start and saw the doorknob turning, turning.

Molina slapped his hands together and said:

"Well, boys. I guess we're too smart for 'em!"

But overhead a window was raised and Gozzi cried: "Jesus! Look out!"

They all whirled suddenly. A big touring car turned the corner near them and bore down on them. Molina said:

"Oh, my God!" and made a dash for the door.

Overhead the Thompson gun began to bark. Harworth stood frozen with horror! The touring car was coming toward them slowly; he saw four men. Before he could run, guns blazed and he heard the sour whine of bullets. He saw Canovi fall forward on his face. Frankie yelled:

"For Christ's sake, duck!"

Then he ran a few steps and fell headlong, his hat rolling out into the street.

Something stung Harworth and he clapped his hands to his side. There was a sudden blackness and he seemed to be falling down an elevator shaft. Excruciating tongues of pain shot all through his body.

He began to crawl on his hands and knees. Molina was down now lying on his back. His hat had fallen over his face. He was screaming.

Overhead the Thompson gun continued to bark. Harworth, through a queer fog, saw the touring car veer, careen, then jump a curb and smash into a light post. Two men jumped out and ran.

Suddenly he saw Louise. She was standing in the doorway. There was a burst of light behind her. He tried to walk toward her but couldn't move. She glided away from him little by little until the burst of light was no more than a speck.

He opened his eyes. Two policemen were looking at him.

One of them said:

"They sure punctured that bird plenty."

He tried to shout but his words came out in long, muttering gasps.

"They shot me. A big touring car. Four men. Name's Harworth. Take me home, I'm dying."

"Four out of four," said the policeman. "That's a pretty good batting average."

One of them turned and called:

"Molina dead yet?"

"Yeah. Dead as yesterday's newspaper."

THE END

W. R. BURNETT BIBLIOGRAPHY
(1899-1982)

NOVELS
Little Caesar (Dial, 1929)
Iron Man (Dial, 1930)
Saint Johnson (Dial, 1930)
The Silver Eagle (Dial, 1931)
The Giant Swing (Harper, 1932)
Dark Hazard (Harper, 1933)
Goodbye to the Past (Harper, 1934)
The Goodhues of Sinking Creek
   (Raven's Head, 1934)
King Cole (Harper, 1936)
The Dark Command (Knopf, 1938)
High Sierra (Knopf, 1940)
The Quick Brown Fox (Knopf, 1942)
Nobody Lives Forever (Knopf, 1943)
Tomorrow's Another Day (Knopf,
   1945)
Romelle (Knopf, 1946)
The Asphalt Jungle (Knopf, 1949)
Stretch Dawson (Gold Medal, 1950)
Little Men, Big World (Knopf, 1951)
Vanity Row (Knopf, 1952)
Adobe Walls (Knopf, 1953)
Big Stan (as by John Monahan; Gold
   Medal, 1953)
Captain Lightfoot (Knopf, 1954)
It's Always Four O'Clock (as by
   James Updyke; Random, 1956)
Pale Moon (Knopf, 1956)
Underdog (Knopf, 1957)
Bitter Ground (Knopf, 1958)
Mi Amigo (Knopf, 1959)
Conant (Popular Library, 1961)
Round the Clock at Volari's (Gold
   Medal, 1961)
Sergeants 3 (Pocket, 1962)
The Goldseekers (Doubleday, 1962)
The Widow Barony (UK only;
   Macdonald, 1962)
The Abilene Samson (Pocket, 1963)

The Winning of Mickey Free
   (Bantam, 1965)
The Cool Man (Gold Medal, 1968)
Good-bye Chicago (St. Martin's,
   1981)

SHORT STORIES
Across the Aisle (*Collier's*, Apr 4,
   1936)
Between Rounds (*Collier's*, Aug 30,
   1930)
Captain Lightfoot (*Argosy*, UK, Nov,
   Dec 1954, Jan 1955)
Dr. Socrates (*Collier's*, Mar 23, 1935)
Dressing-Up (*Harper's*, Nov 1929;
   Ellery Queen's Mystery Magazine,
   June 1947)
First Blood (*Collier's*, Apr 23 1938)
Girl in a Million (*Redbook*, Jan 1938)
Head Waiter (*Cosmopolitan*, Sept
   1931)
High Sierra (*Five Star Western
   Stories*, July 1941)
The Hunted (*Liberty*, June 28 1930)
I Love Everybody (*Argosy*, UK, July
   1943)
Jail Breaker (*Collier's*, July 7, July
   14, July 21, Aug 4 1934)
Little David (*The Saturday Evening
   Post*, Feb 15 1947)
Mr. Litvinoff (*Collier's*, July 18 1931)
Nobody Lives Forever (*Collier's*, Oct
   9, Oct 16, Oct 23, Oct 30 1943)
Nobody's All Bad [Billy the Kid]
   (*Collier's*, Jun 7 1930; *Ellery
   Queen's Mystery Magazine*, Dec
   1953)
Protection (*Collier's*, May 9, May 23
   1931)
Racket Alley (*Collier's*, Dec 16 1950,
   Jan 6 1951)

Round Trip (*Harper's*, Aug 1929;
Ellery Queen's Mystery Magazine,
Dec 1950)
Suspect (*Collier's*, July 4 1936)
Throw Him Off the Track (*Argosy*,
Dec 1952)
Traveling Light (*Collier's*, Dec 7
1935; *Ellery Queen's Mystery
Magazine*, Sep 1951)
Vanishing Act (*Manhunt*, Nov 1955;
Mike Shayne Mystery Magazine,
Aug 1964)
War Party (*Lilliput*, May 1954)
Youth Is Not Forever (*Redbook*, Feb
1939)

ESSAYS
Whatever Happened to Baseball?
(*Rogue*, June 1963, article)
The Roar of the Crowd (Potter, 1964)

SCREENPLAY CONTRIBUTIONS
The Finger Points (1931)
Beast of the City (1932)
Scarface: The Shame of a Nation
(1932)
High Sierra (1941)
The Get-Away (1941)
This Gun for Hire (1942)
Wake Island (1942)

Crash Dive (1943)
Action in the North Atlantic (1943)
Background to Danger (1943)
San Antonio (1945)
Nobody Lives Forever (1946)
Belle Starr's Daughter (1949)
Vendetta (1950)
The Racket (1951)
Dangerous Mission (1954)
I Died a Thousand Times (1955)
Captain Lightfoot (1955)
Illegal (1955)
Short Cut to Hell (1957)
September Storm (1960)
Sergeants Three (1962)
The Great Escape (1963)

UNCREDITED SCREEN
CONTRIBUTIONS
Law and Order (1932)
The Whole Town's Talking (1935)
The Westerner (1940)
The Man I Love (1946)
The Walls of Jericho (1948)
The Asphalt Jungle (1950)
Night People (1954)
The Hangman (1959)
Four for Texas (1963)
Ice Station Zebra (1968)
Stiletto (1969)

"One of the most important American fiction writers of the twentieth century." –H.R.F. Keating

W. R. Burnett

It's Always Four O'Clock / Iron Man
978-1-933586-24-3 $19.95

"Burnett's experimental jazz novel, *It's Always Four O'Clock*... is prime Burnett, a character study of [a] fragile but brilliant pianist."
—Robin H. Smiley, *Firsts*.
"Should be read by any fan of the darker recesses of noir."
—Bruce Grossman, *Bookgasm*

Little Men, Big World / Vanity Row
978-1-933586-67-0 $20.95

"A practiced, precise dossier, shaded by humor and human vulnerability."
—*Kirkus Reviews*.
"Roy Hargis is undeniably one of Burnett's best creations, and the dark, mid-west city in *Vanity Row* is set is redolent of that atmosphere peculiar to Burnett's work."—David Wingrove, "A Good Man is Hard to Find."

The Goldseekers
978-1-944520-29-8 $15.95

"The prose tight and action bumpy, the scenery wide-as-all-out-doors, the characters brawling and bawdy by turns."—*Kirkus Reviews*.
"Reminiscent of B. Traven's *The Treasure of Sierra Madre*."
—Robin H. Smiley, *Firsts*.

High Sierra / The Asphalt Jungle
978-1-951473-73-0 $20.95

"Most noir fans will remember the film versions of these two vintage thrillers... but the experience of reading the familiar stories should open many eyes to the formidable talent of W. R. Burnett.
—Bill Ott, *Booklist*

In trade paperback from:

Stark House Press

1315 H Street, Eureka, CA 95501
griffinskye3@sbcglobal.net / www.StarkHousePress.com
Available from your local bookstore, or order direct from our website.

www.ingramcontent.com/pod-product-compliance
Lightning Source LLC
LaVergne TN
LVHW021234080526
838199LV00088B/4342